D0169487

AN EXAGGERATED MURDER

AN
EXAGGERATED
MURDER

A NOVEL

 **JOSH COOK**

🏠 MELVILLE HOUSE
BROOKLYN • LONDON

AN EXAGGERATED MURDER

Copyright © 2015 by Josh Cook

First Melville House printing: March 2015

Melville House Publishing   8 Blackstock Mews
    145 Plymouth Street   and   Islington
    Brooklyn, NY 11201   London N4 2BT

mhpbooks.com   facebook.com/mhpbooks   @melvillehouse

ISBN: 978-1-61219-427-1

Library of Congress
Cataloging-in-Publication Data

Cook, Josh D., 1980–
    An exaggerated murder : a novel / Josh Cook.
      p.   cm
    ISBN 978-1-61219-427-1 (pbk.) -- ISBN 978-1-61219-428-8
(ebook)
    1. Private investigators—Fiction.   2. Murder—Investigation—
Fiction.   3. Experimental fiction.   4. Postmodernism.   I. Title.
    PS3603.O5717E93 2015
    813'.6—dc23
                                                2014035357

Designed by Christopher King

Printed in the United States of America
    1 3 5 7 9 10 8 6 4 2

THE FIRST ONE IS FOR BETH AND RAY.

THE REST ARE FOR 'RISSA.

Excellent people, no doubt, but distressingly short sighted in some matters.

Sumptuous and stagnant exaggeration of murder.

—James Joyce

AN EXAGGERATED MURDER

ALL ORDINARY NOOKS OF CONCEALMENT

A daredevil's thrill surged up his spine as the blood approached the toes of his shoes; an inspiring and destroying thrill for criminals, detectives, and other artists of existence. If the observed pattern held, his adversary, Trike Augustine, would be awake, despite the lateness of the hour, wallowing through one of the labyrinthine fugues that plagued the young detective's many sleepless nights.

He checked his watch again. As planned, traffic had ceased on the adjacent road fifty-four minutes ago. There was no point in lingering in the study with the blood, but he found himself in an unforeseen grotto of calm. With the vibrant intensity of the preceding years vanished by the completion of the task and the subsequent actions awaiting The Butler's discovery of the crime in roughly four hours, it felt as though he encountered a new color, one only visible from a perspective of stillness. He looked at the fake books on the top shelves of the bookcase, at the lamps in need of new bulbs, at the antique furniture, and out the picture window. However one once classified these objects, now they were evidence.

He imagined how the young detective spent this last evening before everything in his career and perhaps his life changed. He pictured Trike obsessing over a cold case, cramming information into that brain by watching CNN while reading newspapers, churning through some esoteric conversation with Max, and sitting at the kitchen table drinking until whatever drives the motion of his brain slowed down enough for him to reach temporary unconsciousness. All nearly equal parts struggle and success.

With the blood seeping into the carpet, his theories about the response of criminals and artists to the misery of existence looked affected, like half-believed theories of *Hamlet* spouted on the way to the bar, or the pantomime of lethargy by an energetic French minister, or the promises quitting smokers make to themselves and the world, but, he thought as he inched his left foot back, crime and art are pied; colored simultaneously with their creation and their destruction.

He checked his watch again. Power does not come from the ability to seduce, but from the ability to resist seduction, so he ignored the thrill of the advancing blood, rejected the luxury of the calm moment, ceased imagining the activities of his adversary, and fled the crime scene.

FORGET ABOUT IT, JAKE

[Author's note: This chapter contains a spoiler for the movie Chinatown.*]*

Smoking six cigarettes in twenty-seven minutes and three seconds, with a nicotine patch on each arm, made Trike suspect he could smell time, yet he still held the miasma in his lungs as long as possible. This was his last cigarette. His real, true, actual, definite, genuine, indisputable, ultimate, last cigarette. Distinct from his three previous real, true, actual, definite, genuine, indisputable, ultimate, last cigarettes because Lola finally spotted him from her apartment.

He remembered The Case of the Commotion Outside the Hotel. He remembered Neill Broadbent. He remembered Marc Lacenaire and August Franzen. He remembered The Case of the Strong Tea, The Case of the Cracked Mirror, The Case of the Left-over Shaving Lather. He remembered every case. All those cases. All those criminals. All those cigarettes. He crushed the attenuating flame from the singed filter of the last cigarette on his heel and threw it and his real, true, actual, definite, genuine, indisputable, ultimate, last pack in the garbage bin at the corner. He had already kept Lola waiting, most likely with *Chinatown* cued up, for too long. Trike made two decisions walking back to Lola's door: ask her to replace the cigarettes in his house and office with nicotine patches and smoking-cessation gum, and break the bad news about the reward money for the kidnapping case tomorrow.

Lola saw *Chinatown* two weeks ago. Tuesday night. No money, of course. Sitting around watching the cable Trike arranged for her to get for free, and *Chinatown* was just on AMC. You catch up on a lot classic movies when you're not a sports fan, you've got no money, and your cable is somehow free. She waited as long as she could. But Trike was 11–1 or maybe 12–0, and this was a movie that could do it. And, even though it was a setup, even though it was only partially about spending time with Trike and even though he knew that, Lola knew when she said, "Hey, Trike, want to watch a movie tonight?" he'd watch that movie. No matter what.

Lola popped the popcorn. Trike brought the beer. And drank it. They watched the movie. Lola waited for the moment.

"Who is she? And don't give me that crap about your sister, because you don't have a sister."

"Here it comes," Trike said, through a mouthful of popcorn.

Lola paused the movie. Disappointed, even though she was prepared to be disappointed. "Here what comes?"

"One of the answers. A big revelation. The shock."

"Which you assume you've figured out."

"Ahh," Trike said, taking a dramatic sip of beer, "I see."

"You see what?"

"*Chinatown* is just the latest installment in your ongoing quest to find a mystery movie I can't solve."

"Maybe."

"Maybe? Ninety-three percent of the time you ask me to watch a mystery movie, it's in the hopes of stumping me. *Chinatown* was on AMC two Tuesdays ago, when you were bitching about not having enough money to go out. Every time you've tried to stump me, and I'm twelve–and-oh, by the way, you've used the phrase 'I just think it's a good movie, and you'd like it,' which you said today, and, just to apply the coup de grace, you've been giving me the eye the whole time we've been watching this."

"You're eleven-and-one."

"That's total bullshit. I figured out *Clue* would have multiple endings and I figured out, with eighty-seven-percent accuracy, two of the three endings. We just happened to see the other one on TV."

"So because you were wrong in the moment, you did a bunch of research to make sure it wasn't the case?"

"I did a bunch of research because what I saw didn't make sense. And, frankly, my third option was way better. Secret Nazis are cinema gold."

"Fine, we'll call *Clue* a draw. I didn't know there were multiple endings until you told me, and yes, I looked it up. And yes, secret Nazis are cinema gold. And we'll see how things go with *Chinatown*. It comes out of nowhere."

"Nothing comes out of nowhere."

"All right, I'll just leave it paused—"

"While I tell you the girl is Evelyn's daughter by incest with Evelyn's father, Noah Cross."

Lola was trained not to show emotion in conflict. Emotion tells your opponent about the effects of their actions, and above all else, in conflict, effects must be concealed. Her shoulders did not sag. Her eyes did not glare. Her breathing did not change. But she had to know.

"All right, I have to know. How did you figure it out?"

"First, the actress cast to play the girl bears a familial resemblance to Faye Dunaway. She actually looks like she could be Dunaway's sister or daughter. Why cast that actress unless she were a family member in the story? Second, Noah Cross's villainy would be too abstract for us to feel an emotional reaction to his deeds. Without the incest, his crimes are all politics and the economics of irrigation in Los Angeles. Heinous crimes, for sure, but not something we get angry about."

Trike took a dramatic swig of beer, "How much better would the world be if we could? So, in order for us to feel his villainy the way movies are supposed to make us feel villainy, we needed a crime with emotional content.

"As a corollary to this idea, there would no emotive sympathy for the murder victim, Hollis Mulvray. To the viewer, he is just a grumpy bureaucrat who gets upstaged by a flock of sheep and wanders around looking at culverts. Eventually we get a sense of his professional decency, but that's not emotionally heroic. Marrying a woman who had a child by her own father and then caring for that child, however, certainly is. And this is a Roman Polanski film."

"But none of your evidence actually comes from the movie," Lola argued.

"Where else would it come from?"

"No, I mean it didn't come from the world of the movie. Gittes wouldn't have used it to draw his own conclusion."

"It doesn't make my conclusion wrong," Trike persisted. "And it did come from the movie, just not from the story. It's evidence within the evidence."

"It's still cheating, because the information is totally out of context."

"The only context information can be taken in is the truth—I am totally going to say that to Horn-Rims someday—but if you want contextual evidence, here you go.

"Why would Hollis Mulvray be seen in public with a young, blond, pretty girl, and dozens of people see them in the boat on the pond, if he didn't have a legitimate reason to be with her, or at the very least, a reason his wife understood? This is the Thirties. Married men didn't just hang out in public with pretty young girls. And Evelyn didn't hire Gittes, because she knew why Hollis was out with the girl. Cross used an imposter to make a scandal of it and discredit Mulvray.

"Then the long pause after Evelyn says 'Father' at one-eleven left implies a relationship where that term is inappropriate. It's like she was looking for the right title to use for her relationship with Cross, or she knows 'father' is wrong, but must hide that wrongness.

"Next, Noah Cross offers an exorbitant sum of money to find a person he should have absolutely no connection to, meaning he has a connection to her. When Gittes presses him on it, Cross's response is 'Just find the girl.' That was at one-oh-six. Then there's the embarrassed posture Evelyn strikes after she and Gittes have sex, when the topic of her father comes up. She sits up, then covers herself with her arms. Bringing up dad after doing it is always awkward, I assume, but there is real shame in her movements. They practically tell you at thirty-eight minutes when Evelyn gives the girl a pill to calm her down after she finds out Hollis is dead, but it is not the fact of the pill, or that Evelyn was able to prevent the girl from seeing the newspaper, but the manner in which the pill was given. Motherly, not sisterly.

"And if that wasn't enough, when Evelyn tells Gittes the girl is her sister, he says, 'Take it easy. So, she's your sister, she's your sister, why all the secrecy?' to which Evelyn doesn't really give a response. Gittes himself offers the explanation, based on the girl's supposed relationship with Hollis. He should have listened to his own question, or at the very least, paid more attention to how she responded to it.

"We have a matrix of atypical behavior. I imagined different situations that would explain the matrix. Daughter by way of incest is the one that works with all the other information in the story."

"Okay, all of that makes sense, but what I don't get is that your conclusion is based on a thorough understanding of the subtleties of human emotions," Lola said.

"Yeah?" Trike said.

Lola just gave him a questioning look. Then she raised her eyebrows and tossed up questioning hands.

"Oh," Trike said, "right, I could see how you might be a little surprised by my thorough understanding of the subtleties of human emotions. I have two responses. The first, I know how to fake it, I just don't always have the energy, mental resources, or inclination to fake it. The second, I read books, you know."

"All right, all right. Does anything in the movie surprise you?"

"I'm shocked it's so hard to find a good secretary in the Thirties

9

in L.A. You'd think the place would've been crawling with 'em. The one at the Water Department couldn't deflect Gittes for two minutes."

Lola sighed. "So should I turn it off, since you already figured it out?"

"No, not at all. If surprise is the only thing a mystery has got going for it, it's got nothing going for it. And this," Trike pointed at the screen, "this has a lot going for it."

"That's true."

"And besides, if I walked out of every movie I figured out, I'd walk out of every movie."

"Yes. Of course. How could I assume otherwise?"

Lola hit PLAY. They watched the rest of *Chinatown*.

After the movie, and after Lola had swapped all the cigarettes in his place with nicotine patches and smoking-cessation gum while he stayed in her apartment in the dark remembering the blackened lungs and excavated esophagi of smoking-prevention education, and after he made a terrible, just terrible joke about culverts intended, somehow, to induce Lola to invite him to sleep on her couch, standing too far away and at too sharp an angle to see with any detail or be seen at all, Trike watched the rest of Lola's night through the pattern of her apartment's lights. Living-room light. Kitchen light. Bathroom light. Bedroom light. A ballet choreographed by our limited resources. And then the bedroom light was off and Lola was in bed.

Trike waited another twenty-seven minutes and fifty-five seconds, in case the soft refracted glow of lamplight told him she couldn't fall asleep and would knit while listening to talk radio until she could.

When the time passed, Trike walked back to the garbage bin and extracted from the crumpled pack his real, true, actual, definitive, genuine, indisputable, ultimate, last cigarette, to smoke while he drove home.

RECLUSIVE BILLIONAIRE VANISHES IN THE MIDDLE OF THE NIGHT, BAFFLING THE POLICE?

Columns of concrete interrupted by squared glass. Towers of glass squares ribbed by steel. Lines into triangles of wood. Bricks. Fiberglass. Plastic. Compounds of material science. A harmonic sound metallic and thin. Different from the vibration of interior activity. Sharp. Disrupting. The city's lights all turned on.

A tinny version of "Maxwell's Silver Hammer" trinkled from the only cell phone Trike would answer before one p.m. Only Max had the number, and he only called it when a crime scene was eroding.

Trike flopped his hand off the bed, excavating the surrounding detritus. Underwear. Soda cans. Beer cans. Cassettes. Spritzer bottle of vodka. Socks. *National Geographics*. Candy wrappers. The phone was found and answered.

"Maximus, tell me it's lucrative."

"Not . . . lucrative," Max said, pausing to find the most accurate word, "but . . . guaranteed."

"Just a sec."

Trike coughed violently for fifteen seconds; coughs like mountaintop-removal mining.

"Sorry," he said after catching his breath, "lungs still adjusting to life without tar. Anyway, seems a good time to tell you the reward money for the last case fell through."

"The money ... you're kidding."

"You think coughing like that left me enough energy to kid?"

"How can they do that?"

Trike shrugged. "Apparently they sneaked some unwritten must-find-her-alive clause into the contract."

"All about closure until it's time to sign a check."

"Nah, Maxilicious. They're just rich fucks and this is how you get to be and get to remain a rich fuck."

"Lawyer provide ... advice?"

"Lawyer provided this exact advice: 'Though you find yourself in a very actionable position, there is no guarantee you would win the case, and should you lose, you would not only be out the reward money, you'd most likely have to cover their expenses and court fees as well, and—this is where it really gets bad—would very likely be subject to a counter-suit.'"

"So if we were rich enough ... we could afford to recover the money we earned."

"Looks that way."

Max grunted. "You gotta go to the Joyce House—"

"Reclusive billionaire vanishes in the middle of the night, baffling the police?"

"Did I hear ... a question mark?" Max asked.

"Trying to be humble. Did it work?"

"No. Butler found a bloodstain in the study ... Yeah, Joyce is gone. Police want you to investigate."

"Must be a Harlem sunset with a Harrod accent to get me called in morning of."

"Yeah, they implied ... that."

"Standard consulting contract?"

"Standard consulting contract."

"Well, then M—" Another coughing fit cut Trike off. He spit five-sevenths of a teaspoon of lung butter into the wastebasket.

"And this is for your health."

"If we are to trust the Surgeon General of these United States of America—and if we have reached a point in our lives when we can no longer trust the Surgeon General of these United States of America then greater tragedies are building their own catastrophic momentum—then for the last eight years I have filled my body with toxins, and thus it is only expected and logical for my body to go through a violent purging process."

"Sure. The Man with the Facts said it was urgent."

"Well, Max, it looks like we'll be eating this week."

"You've been known to drink the checks."

"Fear not, Max. Two grateful clients have recently expressed their gratitude with booze."

"Not fearing. Anyway, the address—"

"Was mentioned in a fluff newspaper piece on restoring Victorian houses, three years, two months, three weeks, and four days ago. I'll meet you at the office when I'm done at the scene."

"See you then, boss."

Trike hung up and tossed the phone onto the nightstand. While there, his hand opened the drawer and rummaged for cigarettes. It emerged clutching nicotine patches.

A portion of his brain imagined how wonderful and perfect and awesome a cigarette would be, how thoroughly it would rouse his sluggish brain from the warm folds of sleep to the urgent intellectual challenges facing him this morn, how definitively it would drive away the clinging specters of dreams and sleep without dreams, allowing the tasks and responsibilities of waking life to stand at attention before him, how completely it would propel his motion from the bedroom to the kitchen for coffee to the bathroom to shower away the stubborn stuck-on bits of sleepish muss—

"No!"

Trike slammed his fist on the nightstand.

"If I can tell a Russian mobster sticking a gun in my face his mother's morning-after borscht was bland, I can not smoke a fucking cigarette."

He snatched open a patch and slapped it on his bicep.

He dragged his ass out of bed as if the daylight fit him for a Chicago overcoat. He rooted around for clothes that didn't smell too bad and found a pair of gray slacks, a black button-up cotton shirt, and the quiet red tie he believed matched everything. He spread the outfit on the bed and gave it a quick vodka spritz. Then he got socks, underwear, and an undershirt from the bureau.

He staggered to the kitchen and took a pitcher of coffee out of the fridge and with him to the bathroom. He showered, leaning out to guzzle from the pitcher. After the shower—and twenty-five ounces of coffee—he brushed his teeth, dressed, and returned the pitcher to the kitchen.

On his way out, he slipped into a pair of army surplus boots and put on his trench coat. He set a gray fedora on his head, as if vodka-spritzed clothes were a "look" that sustained a "finishing touch."

"Missing billionaire," he mused as he closed the door, "just might make some bills go away."

THE CONCEALED DUMBWAITER

Depending on the absorbency of the carpet, the bloodstain in the study required between 1.9 and 2.3 pints of blood, a range not insignificant to the blood's original owner. The picture window looking onto the back lawn was nailed shut and had been nailed shut since renovation created it. The circumnavigating bookshelves were floor-to-ceiling; however, the books on the top two shelves, each bearing a single letter on its spine, as if the letter were its title, were fake, which became reasonable when no ladder, step-stool, or other top-two-shelves-accessing apparatus was observed. In the last three days, the real mahogany executive desk had been moved three inches to the northwest, which just had to be way more effort than it was worth. The two-pen stand on the desk and its pens were decorative. The energy-saver lightbulb in the banker's lamp on the desk was out, pairing the also-out energy-saver lightbulb in the art noveau floor lamp next to the Queen Anne wing chair. And you'd think with that chair and that lamp, the matching ottoman would have shown more wear. Trike walked slowly and precisely around the room, gathered 327 more distinct observations in his sixty-three-second circuit, and concluded that the utilizer of this study knew the space was ideal for real work, even if she was not entirely sure what real work should be done.

The lead detective was shouting in Trike's ear as he walked.

"Listen, Mr. Augustine, I don't know who decided it was

shit-in-my-cereal day at the office and called you here, but let me be as clear as a fucking bell banging against your shit head—"

Trike noticed what little weight Horn-Rims had managed to lose in his face had ended up in his gut.

"This is my fucking case—"

Horn-Rims's maroon tie was new.

"So as long as it's my fucking case, I tell you where you go—"

A desperate gift from a family member who knew the only thing Horn-Rims really ever asked for was a little justice in this sick world.

"I tell you who you get to talk to—"

A previous gift, maybe last year, should have been perfect, but somehow it didn't work out. And Horn-Rims don't do entertainment. Unless you call rooting for the Mets entertainment.

"And what you get to see—"

"Do me three favors," Trike interrupted, "shut up so I can detect, re-gift that treadmill your sons got you last year to your brother, because you're never going to use it and he could stand to shed a few pounds, and send The Man with the Facts over so I can move this tea party past the crumpets course."

Horn-Rims took a deep breath through his nose. You could hear his ulcer pulsing.

He said, "Look, if you were half as smart as you think you are, you'd know there's some fucked-up shit going on to get you called in on the first day of an investigation, and just walk your freakish brain and your arrogant asshole right out of here and leave this to the people who don't get to choose which cases they solve." He looked about to say more, but instead, nodded The Man with the Facts over and left.

A small part of Trike's brain wondered if Horn-Rims spent any of his early career yelling at The Old-Timer. He caught his hands digging for cigarettes in his trench-coat pocket.

The Man with the Facts appeared at Trike's left shoulder and recited into his ear: "Joyce was reported missing this morning at seven forty-two a.m. The Butler entered the study to bring Joyce breakfast. The Butler lives off-premises, address available upon request pending approval from the supervising detective. According to The Butler, it was not unusual for Joyce to sleep in his study, and if so, The Butler would bring breakfast to Joyce there. The Butler knew Joyce had slept in the study the preceding night because on those nights Joyce does not wake up in time to get the newspaper from the mailbox before The Butler does and on the morning in question The Butler found the newspaper in the mailbox. The Butler saw the bloodstain immediately upon entering, set the breakfast tray down, and called the police from the phone in the adjacent hallway. No signs of forced entry or struggle. No forensic evidence besides the blood has been found yet, though we are waiting for the results of initial fingerprinting. The house is faced by only one neighboring domicile, a little white house across the street that has been abandoned for eight years. None of the nearest neighbors reported any kind of disturbance in the night or early morning. Interviews are being conducted. Family, friends, acquaintances, and business partners are being questioned, though we could not locate a single friend who'd had any meaningful contact with Joyce in the last five years. Witness are being sought. The house is being thoroughly investigated."

The Man with the Facts started to leave. Trike stopped him with a hand on his shoulder.

"Do me a favor before you go," Trike said. "Pass this on to your supervising officer."

Trike stepped over the bloodstain to the desk and nudged one of the pens in the decorative stand down. A section of the bookcase on the western wall swung open, revealing a steel door with six key and two combination locks. The cops groaned, cursed, shook their heads.

"You guys open that and get back to me," Trike said as he left the room. "I'll be setting an educational example by walking around with my eyes open." Trike's hand jumped toward his pocket

again. The exact moment he would have lit up under the NO SMOK-
ING sign.

In the hallway, he observed the portrait of Joyce, depicting Joyce wearing a Latin Quarter hat and holding an ashplant.

Trike started with all the purposeful rooms—kitchen, bed-room, living room, bathrooms—but a mansion that big with one resident is going to have a lot of rooms without inherent pur-pose. Having the right number of knives said something impor-tant about you, but so did filling a space that didn't dictate its own use. And Joyce was saying something with all those other rooms. Something in the voice of a museum curator. Or a lunatic. Or a lunatic curator.

They were organized around a precise decorative system. Ev-ery room had a central table with an archaeological magazine fea-turing a cover story about Troy on display. Every room had some kind of nautical picture on the wall, including a cruise brochure, a magazine illustration, several hotel art watercolors, and a dis-concertingly accurate copy of the stolen Rembrandt. Every room had an image of a three-masted ship. Every room had a minotaur figurine.

There were also objects idiosyncratic to their room: a tray of Stuart coins, a cracked looking glass, a faded 1860 print of Heenan boxing Sayers, a heavily annotated paperback edition of *Hamlet*, an ashtray with "THE SENSE OF BEAUTY LED ME HERE" written on it, a hard plastic name tag with a pin-style clasp for "The Name Achilles Bore Among the Women," and a pocket map of Dublin.

Those, plus thousands more observations stored in case subse-quent information engendered relevance, led Trike to hypothesize an explanation for the rooms: "Might just take the whole Joyce thing a little too seriously." Trike found his hands again doing things done when hands held cigarettes.

Three cops were sounding a hallway wall outside the last sit-ting room Trike had inspected. He paused. His right hand covered his mouth. He remembered all the distinct faces he'd seen at the house. Twenty-five. Way more cops than he'd seen at any other crime scene.

"Excuse me, fellas," Trike said. "Can I bend your ear for a sec?"

The oldest one barely gave Trike a look. "HR said we don't have to put up with any of your shit, so if you don't mind—"

"Yes, you're sounding the wall for passages and hiding spots, the gaps, crevices, and hollow spaces that catch the silt of order and law eroding into chaos and crime; those repositories of guilt-ridden secrets in potential in every three-dimensional structure; the flaws in every surface that give to life both its endless procession of problems and sorrows and everything that makes those problems and sorrows worth dealing with; and why, why would you be searching for secrets in a hallway wall two stories from the study? Well, if you asked, me I'd say it's because none of you has any fucking clue what's going on, which is doubly, nay, triply tragic because you've already missed the concealed dumbwaiter, but, despite your aggressive absence of cooperation, I'm just going to ask my question anyway. Why are so many of you here?"

"We're being thorough," one of them offered.

Trike walked to the wall they had just finished sounding and pressed a concealed button. A panel slid down revealing a dumbwaiter.

"Well, that's one answer," Trike said. "I'd leave you with a 'let me know if you find anything, I'll be investigating the attic,' but that would be embarrassing for all of us."

He pulled down the attic stairs.

"Attic's empty," one of the cops said.

"Dumbwaiter," Trike said, ascending.

The attic was empty.

It was the size of the entire footprint of the house and it was empty. Except for the paths shuffled by preceding investigators, the layer of dust on the floor was uniform. It made you whisper.

"Too uniform," Trike whispered.

He followed the tracks of the cops and sure enough, except for where they walked, the dust was uniform within millimeters. Decades of dust spread evenly.

"That's impossible," Trike thought.

He stopped and watched the dust slowly float in the light of the one window. He focused on one square foot of light and counted out a minute. Then he extrapolated the amount of dust movement that could reasonably occur in a minute and concluded that there was no less than three days and no more than nine days of redistribution present in the dust as he saw it. His hands were tapping together like a cigarette were there.

There was no point to an empty attic.

Trike said out loud to himself, "The intended effects of this arranged situation are threefold. First fold, some doniker-driver of a cop walks up here, says to himself, 'Why the fuck have an empty attic?' and leaves. Second fold, a cop with some blood in his brain says, 'This is some weird shit, keeping an attic empty for decades.' In fold three, we find a cop who actually uses the blood in his brain and he or she says, 'Hey, Mac or Marcy, take a good look at the dust. This place was designed to look empty.' And in the unconsidered fourth fold, I arrive, observe, and say this to court: 'Dust never settles evenly, nothing that settles settles evenly, so if someone wanted to make this look like it hadn't been used in decades it would have been more convincing and required less effort to just throw dust around and open the window for a day. Instead, the action of spreading, and thus of construction, is revealed by its own precision. May it please the court, Your Honor, whoever did this wanted it to look synthetic.' The astute judge would then ask, 'But why the fuck would someone want to make the attic obviously, synthetically empty?'"

Trike inspected the single latticed octagonal window that looked onto the front lawn, the street, and the abandoned little white house across the street. He noticed nothing of note about it. He walked back to the stairs, stepping in his footprints. At the top of the stairs he looked back. "Maybe it fits with the *Ulysses* stuff in all the rooms," he thought, "but I don't see the reference."

On his way down, he made sure the right amount of space was between the attic floor and the ceiling below. There was. But with the right tools you could hide a body anywhere.

Trike went to the study to check on the door. Instead of a locksmith, a battering ram, and an opening, there were three FBI agents. Horn-Rims stormed out. The Man with the Facts appeared at Trike's shoulder.

He whispered into Trike's ear, "FBI agents appeared exactly thirty-seven-point-two minutes after the call to the locksmith was placed and one-point-four minutes after the locksmith had started on the door, and instructed us that whatever may or may not be on the other side of the door was beyond our jurisdiction and we were to cease all further investigation into the door and what may or may not lie on the other side of it. Horn-Rims also instructed me to tell you, quote, 'That asshole deserves whatever the fuck this is. Let him talk to whoever he wants and see whatever he wants. He can name an ulcer after me,' end quote."

Trike's right hand covered his mouth while he imagined what could be on the other side of the aforementioned door. Secret passage. Reclusive billionaire. Federal agents. Barely enough data to suspect.

He said to The Man with the Facts, "Give me The Butler's address, I'd like to talk to him myself. Then send me the full report."

"The report, as it stands, will arrive via bike messenger between three p.m. and five p.m. today. Here is The Butler's address." The Man with the Facts handed Trike a piece of paper. "I am requesting," The Man with the Facts continued, "that you pass along an informal greeting from me to Max when you next encounter him."

"Will do, my man, will do," Trike said.

THE FUCKING NEWS TRUCKS

As Trike headed down the walkway, he partitioned just enough consciousness to exterior awareness to keep from walking into the street. The rest was organizing the Joyce House data into his detecting structure. That part of his brain was a sorting conveyor belt shaking bits of data into their appropriate memory boxes; direct evidence, one remove, tangential, milieu, and the surrounding area of the crime, because one could never be sure what subsequent revelations might create a need for.

It was a big, noisy, chaotic crime scene, so the conveyor belt slowly impinged on the portion of his brain paying attention to where he was going. He didn't notice Lola until she was right in front of him.

Lola stood on the sidewalk by Trike's car. She wore sneakers, shorts, and a long-sleeved running shirt. Her hair was in a ponytail and she wore a white headband. She was an inch and a half taller than Trike, with yellow-gray eyes. You could tell by the way she stood, by her muscles, and by her breathing that she was a runner.

But if she were standing there in scrubs you assumed she was a doctor. And if you saw her in an evening gown on her way to a wedding reception, you'd wonder if you saw her in that new movie or maybe in a magazine ad. Pick your outfit and she looked like a natural whatever it was. And this is all before she did anything. Trike never had a chance.

"Lola? What the fuck are you doing here?"

"Well, I—quit moving your hands around like that."

"Sorry." Trike stuffed his hands into his pockets. "They think they're holding a cigarette."

"And now you're digging around in your pockets."

"Sorry, there are a lot of unconscious drives going on here. Probably would've smoked half a pack without noticing if someone hadn't broken into my house and replaced all my cigarettes with nicotine patches."

"You asked me to."

"The original question. Let's not get sidetracked by the state of my addiction. What the fuck are you doing here?"

"I called Max to check in this morning and he said he was just about to call you with a case. Then I heard on the radio that this Joyce character had gone missing and figured I'd jog by here to touch base with you."

Trike scrunched his eyes in concern.

"You heard it on the news," he said. "When did you hear it on the news?"

"The nine-thirty news bulletin on the radio. Didn't say anything else, except that Joyce had been reported missing."

"Okay, teaching moment," he said, "and this one doesn't involve an almost inhuman ability to observe and remember."

"Well, that's a comfort."

"Based on the information you just gave me, what is the best question to ask?"

Lola looked toward the house.

"Don't look at the house."

Lola looked around, up and down the street, over at the little white house, at the garage.

"You should have seen it already."

"How did the news get out so quickly?"

"You approach, but have not arrived."

Lola folded her arms across her chest and tapped her left sneaker on the sidewalk.

"Where are the news trucks?" she asked.

"Where the fuck are the fucking news trucks?" Trike shouted. "Eccentric billionaire vanishes leaving behind only a pool of blood to mark his previous presence, baffling the proper authorities so catastrophically that they immediately turn to the brilliant but abrasively arrogant internationally renowned private detective Trike Augustine for help, and there are no news trucks, news crews, crime journalists, or cub reporters scratching out notes to this building sensation. Not even a fucking intern from the free weekly. It's one thing if the cops hadn't leaked the story yet, but if it's been on the morning news, it's leaked, so . . ."

"Where are the news trucks?"

"Exactly."

"That's really weird."

"The reward money for the last case fell through."

Lola's arms fell to her sides. Her jaw dropped. Perfect again.

"What do you mean the reward money fell through?" She flailed her arms to the cadence of her anger. "We were hired to find the kid and we found the kid."

"Parents have refused to pay."

"Trike, they can't do that. They signed a fucking contract. We can sue them."

"Already talked to the lawyer. We could sue them, and probably win, but we'd be out way more than we can afford if we lose."

"Trike. This is a fucking problem. I need that money for rent."

"Like I'm independently wealthy. This Joyce Case is a police department thing, so we'll start getting our stipend on Thursday."

"You know that's not enough. Trike, what the fuck am I going to do?"

"I don't know. Finish that Waterhouse copy. Grab a weekend shift at the Utrecht store, or that bookstore downtown where that guy is always giving you the eye. Start teaching self-defense classes at the Y again, accept one of those junk credit-card offers, or, I don't know, marry a hedge fund manager and kill him in his sleep. That one's a win-win for society."

"Trike, that's not funny."

"Frankly, Lola, it's still two hours before I usually wake up, these fucking patches are giving me fucked-up dreams, and I can't seem to control my hands. I'm not even sure I was telling a joke . . . though past evidence would imply it was half a joke at best."

"Trike, what the fuck am I going to do? I'm not going to make rent. Again."

"I don't know, pay what you've got now and ask for an extension. If need be, we'll send Max over. Max'll convince your landlord of, you know, whatever. And I've got practically an entire floor open in my house if you need it. We'll work something out."

"Yeah, well, even if I lived on the second floor of your place, I'd still have to risk my health and well-being walking through the first, and yes, an outdoor ladder is out of the question."

"Batpole?"

"What do we do now?" she said with the malevolent cool of a sniper.

"I'm going to head back to the office, where Max'll make sure I don't smoke, and wrap my brain around the crime scene. Then I'm going to talk to The Butler."

"There's a butler?"

"Welcome to lives of the rich and rich. You go ahead and finish your jog. It'll be at least an hour before we get in touch with you. And keep the weirdness of the news trucks in your head."

"Okay. Talk to you then." Lola took off jogging.

Trike started toward his car but stopped after a step to turn and watch Lola jog away. He saw her for 2.7 seconds before the curve of the road took her out of sight.

Trike walked around to the passenger side of his beige 1993 Nissan Stanza. He leaned all his weight on the joint of the front passenger door, lifted the handle, and tried to pull the door open. The physics of the ordeal required a precise balance. Twice the forces diverged with such vigor that Trike almost toppled to the ground. Eventually he got the door open, but only wide enough for him to reach his arm to the inside handle on the back passenger door. He popped that door open, crawled through it to the front seat, slammed both passenger side doors closed, started the car, and drove to the office.

ROOM IN BROOKLYN AT NOON

Lola jogged home from the Joyce House. Showered. Dressed. Ate breakfast. She planned to spend the time between her jog and meeting Max for coffee and a shake working at the cafe, on the sweater she promised Janice for her birthday. But with no reward money, she couldn't spare the eight to twelve dollars for tea and baked goods. Lola thought in blocks of time the way Trike thought in step-by-step plans. A disrupted block unsettled her. Here was a three-hour disrupted block.

She also had three unfinished paintings to work on: a Waterhouse copy her boss at the art supply store she stopped working for when reward money was coming through assured her would sell for four hundred dollars at least; an experiment attempting to merge Rothko's pulse with Mondrian's line into a singular expression of the sexual tension between reason and intuition; and another exploration through combination, combining the color palette of Van Gogh with the composition style of Hopper.

A small table came into the painting from the bottom left edge. A woman in a chair faced away from the viewer. Her right hand rested on the table. Her left hand was in front of her face. There was a solid sink in the background to the right side of the table and an undefined rectangle in the background above the woman; could be a cupboard, could be a window. The rest of the canvas was empty but for indications of erased charcoal lines.

Lola started it in a fury, consumed by an image raging through her consciousness like a neglected tengu. As it careened through the contents of her mind it picked up yokai of Hopper's *Room in Brooklyn* and Van Gogh's *Noon: Rest from Work (After Millet)*. By two a.m. the canvas was blocked. She was up at nine the next morning, and by the time she was completely exhausted at six, she had the table, the figure, and the sink.

And then a case came up. The Case of the Usher's Abode or Mr. Allen's Estate Wine or some other long case. For six months, she could only chip away.

After the case, stuff came up, though she couldn't say with any certainty exactly what composed said stuff. Ephemeral traces of the tengu haunted her thoughts, but never when she sat around at home with nothing to do. And then the painting was two years old.

Now, Lola sat at home with nothing to do, and, of the three painting possibilities for her disrupted block of time, it was the only one she could imagine working on. She set it up on the easel and thought about it.

Lola didn't use words to think about a painting. She saw options and their assessments in unified images. She saw the range of blues integrated with their emotions, implications, and references, and she saw the paths of possible lines with their emotions, implications, and references, and she saw the depths of texture with their emotions, implications, and references, all in a warped-geometry stop-motion film.

She considered the space that could be a cupboard or a window. A cupboard would allow her to use one color, something that could interact directly and boldly with the figure, especially if she went back to the figure and complicated its range of shades and hues. She could also reference the sky in *Noon*, or invert the reference top-to-bottom and use the shade of *Noon*'s hay. The Van Gogh blue was not far from the sky in *Room in Brooklyn* and there was something to the idea of encasing the sky in a kitchen cupboard. It could balance out the sink and create compositional permission to be bolder with form and color.

A window could give her the same color, just with a different frame. She could even use Van Gogh's brushstrokes there to contrast the Hopper of the rest of the painting. The question was whether she wanted the world of the painting to have an outside.

She also had the space on the right above the sink. It could hold a slice of window, perhaps with the sky the color of the hay, if she made the cupboard blue. Or she could reverse the colors, since the painting, as yet, had no visual precedent for unexpected coloration. But choosing typical coloration would limit the impact of an already constrained composition. Was there something important about a scene of sitting and looking that excluded the exterior?

If Lola shrank the length of the cupboard by a couple of inches, she could add a window frame with a small slice of atypically colored sky to the other side, making the exterior just a slice of color; the red of the outside buildings from *Room* or the bright yellow from *Noon*.

The image satisfied Lola enough that she noted her decisions in charcoal on the canvas. If nothing else it was a starting point for the next phase of the work. She squared off the cupboard and wrote, "Cupboard, VG Blue," in its middle. Then she ruled in the window frame. In the 1½ inches of the canvas enframed, she wrote vertically, "H. Building Red/VG Bright Hay Yellow."

The next step was creating the right blue. From *Noon*, she had a sense of it. As mixing went, it wouldn't take long. She checked the time. She had less than two hours before coffee and a shake. It would be tight. Even if she nailed the color in her first few combinations, she never once opened a tube of paint without eventually needing a sponge and a shower. The painting had waited this long. She put it away.

She turned on the radio and sat down on the couch with Janice's sweater. She had time to make good progress on that. She made tea. Couldn't find a station. It had been her plan to knit anyway. Tea. She'd been best friends with Janice forever. Turned on her computer for its music. It was the perfect pattern. Speakers were somewhere. It would look fantastic on Janice. Shuffle sucked. Where was the pattern? The completely wrong ambient noise. Wrong gauge.

Sometimes. You just can't do what you ought to.

Lola put the sweater aside. She still had over an hour before coffee and a shake. She still needed to figure out the soldering iron before she could work on her sculpture made from old coat hangers, and figuring out a soldering iron was not something she wanted to tackle with a ticking clock. And she didn't want to tackle the bike-frame-and-typewriter sculpture when unable to devote a full day to it.

"The Joyce Case," Lola thought.

She got up from the couch and walked to the large full bookcase against the opposite wall, next to the small TV. She moved an old parking meter that she'd seen lying on the street and simply could not just have left there. Extracted *Ulysses* from the bottom of the pile next to the case.

"Might as well start this," she thought, bringing it back to the couch. "Trike's been bugging me about reading it since he lent it to me, let's say, two years, six months, three weeks, four days, seven hours, forty-two minutes, eighteen seconds, and thirteen nanoseconds ago. On a Tuesday. In the rain. And the Cubs won."

She sat down on the couch. "Said he just wants me to try it. 'Won't think any less of you if you don't like it,' he said, '*Ulysses* isn't for everybody.' Well, we'll see."

Lola opened the book, finding a piece of card stock with a message in Trike's barely legible scrawl. It said, she guessed, "This wasn't written to be understood in a single reading, but to slowly reveal itself over many readings, the way the core and substance of an individual is revealed over years of friendship, but after the first read, at the very least, you realize why reincarnation is believable."

"Okay," Lola muttered to the bookmark, "I'll keep that in mind."

JUST BE PATIENT

Trike's office was on the third floor of a building on the limn of the financial district and the upper-middle-class residential district. Once a newspaper's offices, it now housed lawyers, accountants, and consultants, as well as a violin repair shop, an online used bookseller, a Tarot card reader, and Trike's two-room office.

Max looked up from his desk in the anteroom when Trike walked in.

Max was broad-shouldered and barrel-chested. He had a square jaw and wide palms with short, thick fingers. Though his physique lacked the definition modern aesthetics preferred, any experienced brawler worth his weight in medical tape would know to keep an eye on Max if things got ugly. He wore a navy suit, a white shirt, and a gray tie.

"Hit me with the mail while I get my shit together, Max. We got a missing persons," Trike said.

As Max talked, Trike took off his hat and coat and hung them on the rack in his office.

Max said, "Eight pieces of junk mail, an invitation to the annual municipal city ball, three death threats ..." He took a good look at Trike slowly re-erecting himself from what might very well have been a toe-touch. "I'm going to tell them to just be ... patient."

"Haven't had enough coffee to deal with your lip. Dying for a cigarette," Trike said, punching in the passcode on the locked cabinet of documents he chose not to memorize.

Max continued, "Finally . . . a letter from the P. E. Allen O'Pine Memorial Conference on Detecting."

"I suppose I could be proud they spent the time and money to reject me twice, but I choose to be bitter and indignant," Trike said, unlocking all the drawers in his desk.

"This is an invitation—"

"To spend five hundred dollars to socialize with flaccid theorizers regurgitating cowardly clichés while drinking overpriced house martinis and—"

Max held up his hand. "To give your Purloined Letter presentation."

"No fuckin' way."

Max shrugged. "Quote: 'Due to an unforeseen cancellation, we humbly request your presence as a presenter at this year's conference.' End quote."

"Unforeseen cancellation? Max, nobody cancels on this conference. It is the most prestigious detecting conference in the country."

"Prestige is a . . . concern, now?" Max asked.

Trike held himself up on a bar in the door jamb, with his feet out straight in front of him, while he talked. "Seventy-one-point-four percent of presenters are instantly promoted, obviously not a relevant fact to us, but thirty-two percent subsequently secure publishing contracts and twenty-one percent of those who publish become international consultants, which, well, we'll revisit the issue of our relationship to prestige later, but, more urgently, one hundred percent of presenters are paid a ten-thousand-dollar honorarium. Either 'unforeseen circumstances' is a euphemism for 'some unlucky motherfucker up and died right before his decades of thankless toil were going to pay off' or something profoundly fucking weird is going on."

"Want me to decline?" Max asked.

Trike dropped from the bar. "Shit, no. Ten Gs is ten Gs. And the conference is in town this year, so it's not a potential detriment to our current case. Just make a mental note, that when something totally fucking weird happens, I totally called it," Trike said, going to the coffee maker.

"Noted," Max said. "Speaking of the case, boss. How's it look?"

At the coffee maker, Trike grabbed the three-quarters-full carafe and filled a plain black mug. "I opened a secret panel in the study revealing a locked door and the FBI showed up and forbade us from investigating it."

Max's face fell off a cliff.

"Yeah, that's what I thought. Anyway, I'm going to my desk to drink coffee, analyze the shit out of my current data, and try not to remember how crackerjack a cigarette would be. You start trying to figure out what the feds could possibly be hiding behind the aforementioned door. Looks like it's the kind of thing where you gotta know a guy, and you, Max, you know guys."

"You got it, boss."

"And you're scheduled to meet Lola for coffee and a shake soon?"

"I am."

"Keep that schedule," Trike said. "The diner is a more fuel-efficient place for a materials exchange, it'll save her cell-phone minutes, and I've got to find the hare before I release the dogs."

"Sure, boss."

"And keep an eye out for the police report when you get back. It'll be here via bike messenger between three p.m. and five p.m. today."

"That's unusually ... precise for this department."

"Well, Max, the victim is rich and white, so he's getting society's platinum service package, but enough idle banter. Max, phone and FBI," Trike said, pointing at Max and the phone, "Trike," he said, pointing at himself, "coffee and brain, directly after which I am going to have a word with The Butler."

Max picked up the phone. Trike carried the three-fifths-full carafe into his office and sat down at his desk. He leaned back, put his feet up, and sipped coffee.

For fifty-three minutes, he analyzed his investigation of the Joyce House. Continuing the processes begun while walking to his car from the house, Trike began to create a psychological profile of Joyce, building a visual list of potential escape routes, and reviewing his mental database of criminals to generate a pattern-of-behavior-crossed-with-known-ability list of potential suspects. For his efforts, along with being almost certain Joyce dropped out of law school, Trike knew where he needed to look next; he needed Joyce's dirty sheets from The Butler, and, since the FBI wouldn't let him into the basement, he needed the architecture of the house from Lola.

Trike picked his feet up off the desk, carried the empty carafe back to the coffee maker, and got on the outside of what was inside the plain black mug.

Max was on the phone. Trike gestured that he needed to speak with him. Max held up a one-moment finger.

In the moment, Trike projected all the weapons and wounds that could account for the blood on the carpet onto a massive screen in his brain, blanking out in a hiss of white noise the ones evidence proved impossible.

"Yeah . . . just a sec," Max said to the phone. "Boss?"

"Sic Lola on the architecture of the house. Blueprints. Records of renovations. Contractors' contracts. All that stuff. We need to know about all the possible egress from the study. Might give us an idea about what the FBI is up to, as well. And most buildings with a secret door have secret doors."

"Architecture . . . got it. I'll put a folder together."

"And Max?"

"Yes."

"I'm passing along an informal greeting to you from The Man with the Facts."

"Thanks, boss. Success with The Butler."

"And you with the Feds. Catch you later."

As he walked to the car, Trike muttered, "... whether through the ill-formed comments of armchair detectives flailing about the chaos of existence for convincing illusions of order, or the string of abductions perpetrated by the man living next to the playground."

The full ashtray in Trike's car was a talisman he was incapable of considering, let alone exorcising.

The Butler's house was covered with knitting. Quilts; some patterned in the mathematical abstractions of Mondrian, others more traditional, and one with hand-embroidered squares depicting the settling of the West by the white man. Lace on nearly every flat surface; Nanduti, Irish Crochet, Carrickmacross, Bretonne Needle-Run. There were porcelain dolls with knit dresses, throw-pillows with knit cases, kitchen towels, amigurumi animals. Small-gauge cabled toques. Mittens, gloves, scarves. Even a Mary Tudor in a frame on the wall.

"I'm sure they would have given me Ritalin or something if I'd grown up today," The Butler said as Trike's ass hit the seat. "I was all over the place as a child. Just an explosion running around on two little legs. Knitting was actually my father's idea. He figured it would be a way for me to use up some of my energy and sit still for more than a minute at a time. It's the only thing that really ever connected the two of us. You see, the thing about knitting—"

"What the fuck are you talking about?"

"Oh," The Butler chuckled smally, "sorry. People always ask me about my knitting so I figured—"

"I don't give a fuck about your double-loop toe-up feather-and-fan lace socks on your addi turbos."

"Oh," The Butler gasped. "So you're a knitter too."

"No. I'm a genius, I need a fucking cigarette, you never seem to be able to return your library books on time, and I'm here to talk about Joyce."

The Butler's eyes flashed a kind of panic as his brain tried to parse the information Trike fired at him. The library books were upstairs in the bedroom. He settled into a kind of acceptance.

"Yes," The Butler sighed. "Joyce then."

"I know the kind of stuff you told the cops, so you can skip the formal profile. I want to know what winds his clock. What kind of guy is he? Unusual habits? Tastes? Hobbies? Benign but weird activities domestics can't help but experience in the due diligent execution of their duties? That kind of stuff."

"Well, Mr. Augustine, I'm going to have to disappoint you."

"How?"

"I don't really know any of those things."

"What do you mean?"

"I mean, Mr. Augustine, that I don't really know any of those things. I'm not sure what else I could mean."

"But you would've spent your days with him. He doesn't have a job, so he would have been home most of the day. Even if you didn't wipe his ass, you shined his shoes. Responded to his requests, catered to his foibles, dusted in a Greek water closet. You can't hide much from the guy who washes your sheets, if you catch my listing. You'd be the first to know if he were a lorry paperhanger or the head agent of the alibi store."

It took The Butler a moment to sort through that too.

"Well, I certainly spent my days there, but I didn't wash his sheets, as you say, or whatever you said. Didn't do much at all. In fact, with the exception of the times I brought him breakfast in the study, I almost never saw him. If the newspaper was in the box at the foot of the driveway, I'd know I needed to make breakfast and bring it to the study. If not, sometimes there would be a note in the foyer if he had anything for me to do. Sometimes he'd have me clean a particular room in the house, but most of the time I just did a little light tidying and sat around until seven p.m. or so when it was time to go home."

"And that was all you saw of him?"

"Yes."

"Where was he during the day?"

"I would guess in the study, but since, as I said, I didn't see him, he could've been anywhere."

"Then why did he hire you at all?"

"Frankly, Mr. Augustine, I wasn't about to risk an easy paycheck asking why the check was being cut in the first place."

"What about when you were hired? Didn't he interview you?"

"No."

"Then how did you get the job?"

"My great-aunt made the connection. I don't know how she knew him or what she said, but one day she called me and told me to show up at the Joyce House, follow the instructions, and I'd have an easy job that paid well."

"I don't know about you, but that would make me feel like the cat didn't finish her dinner."

"What?"

"Fishy. It would smell fishy. Didn't you ask your aunt anything about it?"

"She's my ninety-year-old great-aunt. I'm not going to interrogate her. I needed a job, and frankly, I didn't particularly want to work. I figured the worst that could happen is I show up, don't like the vibe, and leave."

"What about the sitting rooms? A lot of pretty interesting setups. Do you know about them?"

"Nope. They were all like that when I started. I dusted and vacuumed sometimes, but Joyce never explained them to me and never asked me to change anything."

Trike leaned back in his chair. He looked around the house. At The Butler's fingers compulsively fluttering socks into being.

"Tell me about when you found the blood," Trike said.

"I thought we were going to skip the police stuff."

"Yeah, well, you lied about how you got the job."

"I beg your pardon. How dare you—"

"The police could not locate a single friend who'd had any meaningful contact with Joyce in the last five years, and if your great-aunt was close enough with him to secure your sinecure, I would assume they had a pretty close relationship. Now, at present, I don't give a fuck why you just lied to me, but I could be convinced to gift-wrap that fuck and send it to you for Ujamaa if you give me any more smarmy lip. Now, tell me about finding the blood."

The Butler's fingers paused in the process for the first time in the interview. They restarted.

"There wasn't much to it. I saw the blood. I set the breakfast tray down on the end table in the hallway and then called the police."

"What did you say to them?"

"Oh, something stupid and hysterical, that there was a big bloodstain on the carpet and that Joyce was missing."

"And what did they say?"

"They said they were on their way."

Trike cocked his head. Leaned forward. "In your stupid hysterics, did you happen to tell the police the address?"

"Well," The Butler paused. His hands stopped knitting again. "You know, at the time I didn't think about it, but now that you ask, I don't know." His hands restarted.

Trike stood up. "Thank you for your time." He went to the door.

Halfway out, Trike said over his shoulder, "You shoulda used markers on that one. It's gonna be a bitch finding that dropped stitch now."

He slammed the door closed behind him.

CUT TO THE TRIKE GRIPES

The diner had one row of red vinyl four-person booths and a ten-seat counter with matching red vinyl stools. It had a linoleum floor grayed in layers impenetrable to the mop and bucket. Every other customer-accessible horizontal surface was Formica that gleamed with a cleanliness only long, slow, overnight shifts can produce. During busy shifts, there was a waitress for the booths, a waitress for the counter and the cash register, and the cook. His name was Joe, but no one ever seemed to know how they knew that. Overnight, one waitress handled all who might stumble in, and the food they ordered came out, so somebody cooked. The coffee was bottomless and the manager knew how to create a get-your-ass-out-of-bed special if the week had been slow. The neon sign in the parking lot, on top of a twenty-five-foot pole, had been out for a decade.

Even though she knew they were on a kidnapping case, Lola was still disappointed to see that Max hadn't taken off his jacket. It had already been weeks since their last coffee and shake, and with the new case, it could be weeks before the next one.

Max sat in the booth nearest the door, with a messy pile of newspapers. Lola kept her coat on and sat down across from him.

"Sorry I'm late, Max. There was someone in a wheelchair on the bus."

Max shrugged. He folded a newspaper section onto the pile.

"Gave me a chance to read the paper . . . without Trike radiating the scores."

The waitress appeared. She put a to-go coffee in front of Max and a to-go shake in front of Lola.

"Ordered and paid," Max said, "to speed the process . . . apologies to feminism."

Lola took a sip of her shake. "Apology accepted. But I got my eye on you, mister. What's the assignment?"

Max took a manila folder out of a briefcase and slid it across the table to her.

"Architecture of the house," he said. "Blueprints, renovations, construction . . . the like. Folder has the basic info from the police report."

"Really?" Lola tossed the folder open dismissively. "That's it?"

She flipped through the first few pages of the file while sipping her shake. Address. Legal name of occupant. Other data.

Max held his hands up. Leaned back.

"All preliminary. We've got an exit through a secret passage . . . basement, probably. This is just where we're starting."

"The police didn't search the basement?" Lola asked.

Max explained about The FBI and The Door Behind the Bookcase.

"If that's what Trike wants," Lola shrugged. "Only take a couple of hours though. What are you going to be up to?"

"Asking more guys I know about the door."

"Is it just me or does this seem weird already?"

Max nodded. "Weird."

Four young men in their late twenties burst into the diner, one in a jacket and tie whose cuts and colors proved he didn't wear jackets and ties very often. They sauntered to the corner and yawped orders for pie. The three others slapped Jacket and Tie on the back repeatedly, with the vigor of earnest congratulations. The key words sprayed from their banter told Max and Lola that they were grad students at the university in the English department, or perhaps Communications, or maybe even Media Studies. They were at the old-fashioned diner celebrating the successful defense of a thesis on "The New Information Being," and Jacket and Tie was going to celebrate it with pie whether he liked it or not.

"You headed home?" Max asked.

"Yeah. Should be able to get most of this done on the Internet."

"Want a ride?"

Lola checked her watch. The next bus was a half-hour away, if it was on time. "Yeah, I better. Clock is ticking."

"Always does," Max said.

As they made their way out of the diner to Max's car, Lola asked, "So, how was your date, Max?"

"Date? Long time since the last coffee and shake."

"Yep. My mom was in town last week, we had The Case of the Fuckers Who Won't Pay Us the week before that, and then you had something the week before that."

"Godson's wedding," Max said, starting the car. "Date went okay."

"Just okay? Isn't she the top match?"

Max pulled out of the parking lot. "She is."

"Haven't you been trying to set this up for like, three months?" Lola asked.

"Three months."

"And it just went okay? I thought you were going to spend all night talking about Charlie Parker, vintage cars, and, wait, there was one more."

"*Twin Peaks.*"

"Right. Charlie Parker, vintage cars, and *Twin Peaks*. What happened?"

Max shrugged. "We talked. Had a good time."

"But?"

Max rubbed his chin. "Perhaps we were trying so hard to be the 'top match' we couldn't connect."

"So, it's still the whole dating-site thing?"

Max shrugged. Took the next left. "You can't fix your car . . . mechanic . . . dating site."

"But you never meet anybody, Max. That's the whole point. It's not that you can't get a date if you get the chance, it's that you never get the chance. You work constantly, and the few times you ever hang out with somebody other than me and Trike, they never have any single friends. Just wait until your divorced friends start getting remarried. You'll clean up at those receptions."

"Sounds . . . familiar."

"Because we had this exact conversation when you asked me if I thought you should sign up."

Max sighed. Took the next right. Turned on the windshield wipers again. "You're still right."

"So, are you going to go out with Jessie again?" Lola asked.

"We discussed it. She had a business trip last week . . . now we have a case. Could be a while."

"Well, if it doesn't work out for anything more, you should be able to have a good conversation every now and again. And maybe she has some single friends."

"True. What about you and that guy . . . with the two first names?"

"Tom Howard."

"Him . . . what happened?"

Lola shrugged. "Nothing really. Janice knows him. He was nice and all and I wouldn't mind hanging out with him or whatever, but I just didn't see myself making time for him, you know. Like, I just didn't see myself putting down my knitting or painting if he called."

"Many a young man has fallen to the needles and knives."

"What's that supposed to mean?"

Max shrugged. "Same thing you said. We're relationship perfectionists. We just . . . justify."

"It's not just that, Max. We also have someone in mind."

"Someone not coming back."

"That's the truth, Max."

They were stuck at a long light in the back of the line. The rain diminished, so Max turned off the wipers. Lola flipped through the manila folder again and began identifying keys to the research. Max drummed a short rhythm on the steering wheel. A man dressed in black as if coming from or going to a funeral walked by on the sidewalk. He was closing an umbrella, staring up at the sky, with a baffled expression on his face, as if confused by some puzzle posed by the rain itself.

"We should cut to the Trike Gripes," Lola said, "since who knows when we'll get a chance to do this again?"

"Mind if I . . . initiate?" Max asked.

"Go right ahead."

"There is one thing I hate about debates with Trike."

"That he can have a fully functioning intellectual debate while thinking about something else entirely?" Lola offered.

"No."

"That he passively absorbs complex information, meaning he can learn intellectually challenging material while washing dishes?"

"Nope. Trike washes dishes?"

"Benefit of the doubt."

"Right."

"That he is constantly referencing stuff, not because the reference is necessarily relevant, but just to keep himself entertained?" Lola persisted.

"Not that. All of that . . . I've gotten over." Max paused and used his right hand to bring down the point. "What if he's wrong?"

"But he's not."

"No. He remembers perfectly what he has observed." Max chopped through his statement with precise hand gestures. "What if he observed someone else's mistake, or . . . he read a book that said one thing . . . three years later another book proves the first wrong. Unless the correction is observed ... the mistake is preserved."

"And unless you've got that new book handy, you'll never convince him he's wrong."

"It is statistically ... improbable."

"Thanks, Max. Now I have another thing to be annoyed about when I have debates with Trike."

"I aim to please."

"Okay, my turn," Lola said. "I hate it when he quotes things directly. You know me, I love looking stuff up. So every now and again, when I don't have something else to do, I've tracked down some of his sources. And he doesn't just tell you what the point or the fact is, he actually completely quotes the source material. Word for word. And it's like, dude, just make your point. You don't need to remind us yet again, that your brain is a miracle of human biology."

"Never checked his sources," Max said, pulling up in front of Lola's apartment.

"You just believe him?"

Max shrugged. "Don't care enough— Speak of the devil."

Max put the car in park and pulled the vibrating phone out of his pocket and read the text.

"Huh," he said.

"What is it?" Lola asked, unbuckling her seat belt.

"A text from Trike."

"I know that. Jerk. What does it say?"

"'Someone might have called the police before The Butler. Going to investigate,'" Max read.

He put his phone away. Tapped nervously on the steering wheel. Leaned back in the seat.

"Weird," he said. "Too ... weird. We should get cracking."

"Right," Lola said, opening the door and getting out of the car. "Good luck, Max," she said with the door still open.

"And to you," he responded.

Lola closed the door and Max drove off. She slurped her shake finished and threw the cup in the garbage bin on the corner. There was something touching, sweet even, about the mangled pack of cigarettes still in the bin. She unlocked the door and opened it in one fluid motion, thinking to herself, "Now, to unlock the Joyce House."

THE SWEATY MESSENGER

The walls of the police station were smeared with spleen, streaked with pancreas, and dappled with gall bladder. Desktops cluttered with kidneys. In-boxes topped with livers. Tendons tangled on drawer handles.

Strips of intestines draped over filing cabinets. Muscle tissue decoupaged to white boards. Lung curtains spun on ceiling fans. Limbs scattered on the floor like toys at a preschool. That only included smears, streaks, and dapples reasonably identifiable. Every surface with a certain level of adhesion was an abstract expressionist canvas of human carnage.

At least that's how Trike pictured it. Otherwise, the frustration would have made his canthi bleed.

He had a simple question: Who first reported Joyce's disappearance? He'd been at the police station for four hours.

The cops could keep the answer from him if they wanted. Even if it wasn't The Butler, they could tell him it was and he'd have no logical reason to further investigate. They could tell him he needed a court order to see it. Or they could just tell him it was an anonymous call.

Instead, he was shuffled from desk to desk. Secretary to secretary. Officer to officer. Up some undefined labyrinthine ladder of rank and permission.

They showed him a call from the same date ten years ago. Claimed the record had been deleted. Claimed the dispatcher had been suspended for unprofessional conduct. Claimed the computer file had been corrupted. Showed him other calls on the right date. Threatened to arrest him without cause. Threatened to arrest him with reasonable cause; he did raise his voice. Asked him if the Irish had a chance on Saturday. Probably should have arrested him; his gestures got violent. Asked him how the fuck in the physics of Newton's gravity he got away from Gustav Mace's assassins. Offered him a stale Danish. Made him show his license.

Whatever they were doing, they weren't lying. And if they were trying to put up roadblocks, they were hand-baking the bricks out of imported clay instead of towing in Jersey barriers.

Four hours.

Trike was hunched over with both hands on the desk of some temp secretary. His head hung so his chin rested on his chest. He took a deep breath. Tried to forget how kickass a cigarette would be. A cigarette would kick ass.

A copy of *Garner's Modern Usage* poked out of the secretary's messenger bag.

Trike said, "Listen, I know you're a temp making ends meet before the copyediting for the summer season picks up, and I know you were just reading a script someone with a bad sense of prepositions and the power to fire you told you to read, and I've heard student loans are a real drag when you've got them, but there has got to be—"

Trike was interrupted by an overweight man in a gray sweatsuit with sweat stains walking up to the desk.

The Sweaty Messenger said, "Horn-Rims said just let him see it."

Trike straightened up. Looked the messenger in the eyes. Eight months, two weeks, and four days ago, Trike had overhead this cop say to another about his new heart medication, "Put my pistol in my pocket, if you know what I mean." He remembered from the obituary two years and three days ago that The Sweaty Messenger's father died of a heart attack. And The Sweaty Messenger was clearly not getting the doctor-recommended exercise.

Trike took The Sweaty Messenger's hands and held them for a second. He looked into The Sweaty Messenger's eyes and said, "Two years, three months, one week, and one day from today. Heart attack." Trike patted him jovially on the shoulder. "At least you'll dodge the Alzheimer's that runs in your family," he added.

The Sweaty Messenger stammered nothing for a second. Then he stammered, "The dispatch room—"

"I know where dispatch is," Trike snapped and stormed off.

And wouldn't you know it, the record made things worse.

There wasn't a real name in the caller field. Nor was there "anonymous." Nor was there a typical pseudonym. Nor was there a name of suspicious origin. "Kpmsyjsm Fpr." Two jumbles of random letters.

Trike divided his brain into two processes: verbal reasoning and cryptographic analysis.

Verbal reasoning thought, "There are many reasons why an individual or group of individuals would want to obscure their identity as they report a crime, many of which are legitimate. The concrete in justice's basement is partially composed of anonymous tips. However, in the legitimate cases, the caller would obviously use the legitimately accepted identity of 'anonymous,' and the anonymity is created or preserved. Given that, there is no need for someone with illegitimate reasons for hiding their identity to use any other technique besides the one inherently accepted by the legitimate powers. The path of least resistance makes sense to criminals as well. Unless, of course, the need to obscure the identity arose after the identity was provided in the initial call. In that case, perhaps the record was subsequently hacked and altered. But the moment of altering brings us back to the exact same problem. If you can change the record, you can change it to 'anonymous,' or one of the accepted permutations of 'anonymous,' or you can even just delete the record. Deletion would raise suspicions, but there would be less substance to be suspicious with. Really anything but random fucking let—" The cryptographic analysis discovered something.

Trike put his fingers on the keyboard in front of him. Moved his hands one key to the right of home row. The entry was "Jonathan Doe," with the typist's hands one letter to the right of home row.

"I'll take evil genius any day," Trike thought. "Stupidity is undetectable."

He just stopped himself from smashing the keyboard to powder with his face.

"Helluva week to quit smoking," Trike thought as he stormed out of the police station to go home and drink until he didn't want to smoke an entire pack of cigarettes at once.

NEVER OPEN WITH A REFERENCE
TO THE BLACK PANTHER

Trike woke up. Night spent more unconscious than asleep. His hand prospected the clutter around the bed for a cigarette. His brain, eventually, remembered he'd quit. Trike hoisted himself out of bed like the crane was looking forward to the holiday weekend. Another addiction moved the body to the kitchen.

Someone wanted to scare him. To shock him. To make him scream. To thrust before his bleary eyes the gruesome truth of bodily mortality. To shake his confidence in the ability of law and order to keep him safe from the horrors of unrestrained violence.

But Trike knew where bacon came from. And blood is water-soluble.

There was a dead pig on his kitchen floor. Bleeding. A scrap of heavy fabric, with an embroidered message, was stitched to its flesh.

Trike stepped over the ham-handed threat to the automatic coffee maker and poured a mug of automatic coffee. He leaned against the counter. Considered the pig.

Dlugaz was the only butcher in the area that sold whole pigs. The pig was still bleeding, so it hadn't been butchered. At least, not properly. It hadn't started to smell. The outer edge of the blood seepage was a mere three feet from the carcass. The pig had been dead for at least five hours. Dumped in the last two. The fabric most likely came from a futon cover. The stitching suggested inexperience in the medium augmented by substantial dexterity.

The note said, "You are the black panther. Next time I won't hit the pans. Get off The Joyce Case."

Trike winced.

"Hey, why is your door unlocked?" Lola shouted as she walked through the door.

"The caterers didn't lock it on their way out."

"Trike, the whole spy code thing was never funn—" Lola stopped short when she saw the pig. "What the hell is this?"

Trike took a long, loud, slow slurp of coffee. "This, Lola," he gestured with his mug as if someday this could all be yours, "is a dead pig with a lazy *Ulysses* reference."

"What does it mean?"

Another slurp. "It means our threateners haven't read the Hades episode yet."

"What?"

Slurp. "If they had, they would have threatened to show up at my funeral in a mackintosh."

"What are you going to do?"

Trike shrugged. Threw down the ninth-best slurp of his life. "Not much I can do. *Ulysses* isn't for everybody."

"Trike!"

"Mademoiselle?"

"There's a dead pig on your kitchen floor."

"Blood is water-soluble and I bought a wheelbarrow after the last one. The pig is not a problem."

"So, the threat is the problem."

"The threat is stupid. One simply cannot react to stupid threats. It only encourages them. Besides, if they wanted to kill me they would have killed me. If you can break into my house and drop a dead pig on my kitchen floor, you can walk into my bedroom and shoot me while I sleep."

Nothing Lola could say.

In a gunslinger's gasp, Trike chugged the rest of his coffee and slammed the mug down on the counter. He clapped his hands together once and held them out.

"What?" Lola said.

"Well. You're here. So. The blueprints. Records of renovations. Contractors' contracts. All the weird stuff about the structure of the house."

"I couldn't find anything."

"You couldn't find anything?"

"Nope."

"Lola, how could you have not found anything about the house? That shit should've been like slipping Poe a cognac-flavored mickey."

"Right. Sure. Well, you should've heard somebody break into your house carrying a dead pig."

"I was in a state of profound contemplation," Trike responded.

"You were sleeping off a bottle of cheap port."

"Nice try. Alas, the crust on the rim of the port bottle on the floor of the living room you observed required at least four days to solidify. I drank that last week. Seventy-three percent for fun. The observation is commendable, though incorrect."

"Thanks. I think. Anyway, according to everything I could find, all the various usual records and documents for the Joyce House don't seem to exist," Lola explained.

"Can't say I'm a fan of the verb 'to seem.' Are you telling me they don't exist?"

"No. I'm telling you they don't *seem* to exist. I found references to plans and contracts that could have been connected to the Joyce House, but not the plans or contracts themselves. And I found gaps in other records, like in the online archives of a non-profit organization called the Amateur Victorian Restorers of America Association, that *seem* like something about the Joyce House should be there, but I can't be sure. The only concrete fact I could find about the house was that the electrical bills are exorbitant. All the other data you'd expect to find about an old house has either been stolen or destroyed, or somehow it never existed in the first place."

The muscles in Trike's face relaxed. His mouth hung open enough to say, "Huh." His eyes drifted around like he was following a pattern in the wallpaper.

Lola called the look his data-face. She'd learned that Trike could focus so much of his brain on acts of computation, imagination, and analysis, that he lost control of the muscles in his face. Sometimes she imagined a massive library crossed with a vast biotech research complex specializing in abominations of science, and sometimes she assumed it had to be a bear on a tricycle wearing a fez, riding in tiny circles at the speed of light.

After 2.3 minutes he said, "The near-impossibility of finding actionable information about the structure of the Joyce House leads to two likely possible explanations for Joyce's disappearance: either the kidnappers and/or murderers arrived at a moment when the door was open, or Joyce faked his kidnapping."

"How do you get to Joyce faking his kidnapping?" Lola asked.

"Joyce himself has the easiest access to the missing information, and thus, the most ability to make it missing should he choose to, and given the other circumstances, we can only assume that he would choose to make the information disappear to facilitate his own faked kidnapping. As it stands now, we cannot in good conscience rule out the possibility that kidnappers attacked when the secret door just happened to be open, but, given the planted nature of the bloodstain . . ."

"Joyce most likely kidnapped himself," Lola finished.

Trike data-faced again. Lola gracefully stood.

"I need you to focus on Joyce himself," Trike snapped back. "I need everything you can find on him."

"Okay. And the pig?"

"Heavy-duty trash bag, wheelbarrow, car, city dump. Lift with the legs, not the back."

"And the blood?"

"Bucket of soapy water and a mild bleach solution. Nothing easier than cleaning pig's blood off linoleum."

OFFICE COFFEE

As it sloughed to a stop, the engine coughed like an asthmatic with a loose loogie lounging in the lower lungs. It took a minute of leaning on the door of his car to get the stubborn bastard to allow egress. The door popped open suddenly. Trike combat-rolled to keep his face from bouncing off the asphalt.

He fixed his trench coat. Looked both ways. Threw the door closed behind him. It bounced off its frame and swung open. He tried to throw it closed again, but it stuck on its hinge, throwing him into the road.

Trike held the handle up. Leaned his left shoulder on the window and walked the door to the frame. Still leaning into the frame he let the handle go. It clicked victory. "Questions are raised with tenuous answers. Structures are constructed of flimsy materials. Atypical phenomena are left unjustified," he muttered as he walked into the building.

"You're late," Max said when Trike walked in.

"I'm always late," Trike responded.

"Late . . . relative to you."

"Unforeseen errands, Max, and yes, several hours of unforeseen errands."

"And you need a new car," Max added.

"Car runs fine, Max," Trike said, hanging up his trench coat.

"Then get a new door."

"Door works fine, Max. It just has personality."

"Doors shouldn't have personality."

"Well, Max, there is just something about a door with personality in a world where doors shouldn't have personality."

"Which is?"

"Nobody's hired me to find out. Any messages?"

"Agent Munday called."

"For me or you?"

"You."

"Shit."

"There's good news," Max consoled.

"Agent Munday is gay and only asked to meet me for coffee last week because she assumed I was desperately lonely for any scrap of feminine company and thus there are no hard feelings over the blatant stand-up?"

"No. See Lola?"

"Yes. And no psychological detecting until I've had my coffee."

"You drink a pot at home before you get here."

"No psychological detecting at the office until I've had my office coffee. Ethically, it's a very simple rubric," Trike clarified.

"Entered into the manual. Want the message?"

"Did you have good news because the message is Joyce Case–related?" Trike asked.

"Yep."

Trike's right hand covered his mouth. His eyes drifted to the shelf of binders above Max's head. He came back forty-eight seconds later.

"We can't inspect the hidden door and the basement it leads to because that is one of the many places scattered about this nation in which the federal government is growing an imperial fuck-ton of weed."

Max raised an eyebrow at Trike. Cleared his throat.

"Oh, right," Trike said. "Federal agents didn't arrive at the scene until after I revealed the door in the study—which was totally awesome, by the way. I just learned from Lola that, quote,

'The only concrete fact I could find at all about the house was the electric bills were exorbitant,' unquote, which would be explained by the lights and other electricity-demanding equipment needed to grow weed in a basement. And finally, the keystone that bears the weight of this conclusion—"

"Agent Munday is a narc," Max concluded.

"Agent Munday is a narc," Trike said with a nod.

Max leaned back and rubbed his forehead. Tapped on his desk.

"Changes things a bit," Max said.

"It does, Max, it does."

"... Weirder?"

"I don't know yet, Max. Though now I am certain that Joyce faked his disappearance and left the house through the basement. But we can't find information about the structure of the basement."

"Lola couldn't ... dig it up?"

"No."

"Weird."

"Yep."

"Still working on it?"

"Sicced her on Joyce. The man himself."

"Poor fella."

"Not as long as he doesn't have any secrets."

"It's ... possible."

"Okay. Max, you get back on the horn with your bureau buddies and give them a polite what-the-fuck. You might be able to get a little further now that you've got some more information."

"You got it, boss."

"I'm going to read newspapers while I analyze possible scenarios that make this ridiculous situation realistic."

"If I find anything ... I'll knock," Max said.

"I'm not going to be tossing knuckle children into the trash can. You don't have to knock."

"Boss ... it's creepy when you read."

"Really?"

"You hold your hands like you've got a book or a paper. You even . . . jerk your hands like you're snapping the paper straight, but you don't have a paper. It looks like you're reading your hands . . . and like you're a lunatic."

Trike shrugged.

"It's just a neuro-mechanical recollection technique triggering clearer recall through approximate kinetic replication."

"Easy for you to say. You look insane."

"So I shouldn't read that way at the coffee shop?" Trike asked.

"No."

"Explains why the new baristas sometimes give me free coffee."

"Could."

"Okay. Max. Phone. Trike. Brain," Trike said, pointing at each item. "Get me if Lola calls."

"Plan."

"And no smoking in the office."

"Haven't forgotten."

"I've quit smoking."

"I know."

"So don't tempt me."

"Won't."

"Even with one sneaked cigarette—"

"Read your book and let me call the Bureau . . . crazy-pants."

Trike gave a thumbs-up and went to his office. Max picked up the phone.

THE SLEEVES DAMN NEAR ROLLED THEMSELVES

During the three hours he'd been on the phone, Max hung his jacket over the back of his chair, unbuttoned his vest, loosened his tie, and rolled his sleeves.

Everyone he talked to knew that the Feds kept weed around. It was just that kind of world. Scientific research. Dog training. Something to give to undercover agents. Other.

Max never expected a personal file mailed to the office. He wasn't surprised that no one could give him even a lazy charades-hint of a name. The jacket was hung because the accountant below turned the heat up. Heat was still behaving.

One of his contacts was sure she could slide him something. She'd put him on hold with lines like, "Just give me a sec and I'll find something for you," and return with "That's weird. Can't seem to find it now." For forty minutes. Max's vest got unbuttoned.

His contact kicked him over to a hacker they knew. The guy could squeeze binary code from cat piss and tell you what its owner thought about NAFTA. He told Max it would be a couple of quick click commands. There were many awkward pauses. He assured Max that much would be revealed after a few gibber-ishes were jabberwocked. Nothing was revealed. That loosened the tie.

Four more calls and two favors later, Max ended up talking to someone at the end of paper trails. Someone without plausible de-niability. If he said, "Max, I can't tell you anything about this Joyce character," Max would have thanked him very much and politely hung up.

Instead, the guy who knew all the code names said, "Joyce? That small-time shit doesn't even get to my secretary's desk." Sleeves damn near rolled themselves.

After that chat, Max sat still for a while. He had plenty of favors left in the clip, but you don't empty a clip at a small target. Especially if, as Trike suspected, Joyce was not actually in danger.

Lola strode through the door and placed two full accordion folders on the waiting-room chair.

"Looks successful," Max said.

"Successful!" Lola launched. "Successful. Do you know what these folders are full of?"

"Not anymore."

"Nothing. There is nothing in these folders. I could find nothing. After a day of finding nothing, I figured, hey, that's got to be something. Nothing doesn't just happen on its own. So I brought samples of all the records I should have found. Because there's nothing. And that's got to be something."

"Pattern?"

"Not that I can see. You guys turn up anything?"

"One thing," Max answered.

"What's that?"

"Joyce probably grows weed for the Feds."

"Oh," Lola said with an expectant inflection.

"Calling the Bureau revealed nothing."

"But? Your sleeves are rolled up."

"True. Similar experience. Where there should've been something . . . there was nothing."

"This is getting weird, Max."

"I agree."

"Trike in? I should show him this," Lola said, indicating the folders.

"Reading."

"Oh, I hate it when he does that. It's just so creepy."

"I told him to stop doing it at the coffee shop."

"He's been doing it at the coffee shop?" Lola gasped.

"I can hear you, you know," Trike shouted from his office. "Stop draining the water cooler and get in here, so we can figure out what to do next."

Lola picked up the folders. Max held the door for her and they entered Trike's office.

"So the accordion folders are filled with records showing where information should be, but isn't?" Trike asked.

"Exactly," Lola answered.

"Including?"

"Driver's license, tax records, medical records, education, insurance, bank stuff. He didn't even buy the house himself."

"Who did?"

"A corporation that appears to have been incorporated for the sole purpose of purchasing the house."

"Tax dodge?" Trike asked.

"Not that I can tell."

"Does the company pay the utility bills?"

"Maybe."

"Maybe? Must say I enjoy afternoons spent with 'maybe' as much as I like waking up with 'to seem.'"

"The bills are in Joyce's name, but, and I included copies of receipts I could dig up, they're paid in cash."

"In cash?" Trike disbelieved.

"In cash," Lola confirmed.

"I have never heard of utilities taking cash payment," Trike persisted.

"As a rule, they don't, but there were a handful of other accounts paid in cash."

"Huh. And Maxitaxus, I see the phone call reached rolled-sleeve proportions."

"Got even less."

"So I heard. Care to shovel a pile of less my way?"

"Talked to many people. All had an awareness of the . . . situation, but no knowledge. Eventually got to somebody whose name cannot be shared, who told me Joyce wasn't even worth his secretary's time."

"Below the secretary, eh?"

"Important context . . . this secretary is relatively important."

"Of course."

Trike grabbed his fedora from the hook that kept it off the ground. Put the hat on. He leaned back in his chair and set his feet on the desk. Then he tipped his hat brim down and laced his fingers over his stomach. A gunslinger feigning sleep. He was still for 136 seconds.

Still still, he said, "Where's the money?"

"What money, boss?" Max asked.

"Exactly, Max. What money? Disappeared billionaire with an unclear wealth-generation mechanism beyond growing weed for the Feds, who, to all appearances, went through quite a bit of trouble to very poorly fake his murder or kidnapping, in order to go into hiding to do, you know, something. There should be money here. There is always money. If the two Ps are not present—"

"The two Ps, boss?"

"Passion and psychosis. If they are absent from the crime scene, then the source of the crime is almost certainly money. All this other stuff," Trike waved a dismissive hand, "makes me suspect that this involves vast amounts of money, far vaster than anything we have considered. In such quantities, money can conceal itself, but every magician runs out of smoke eventually. Unless, of course, we are dealing with something too dark and terrifying to consider while sober."

Trike unlaced his hands, reached one under the desk, pulled out a tallboy, cracked it open, and took a swig.

"Trike?" Lola couldn't stop herself from asking.

"Lola."

"Did you put a mini-fridge under your desk?"

"That is what is implied by the visuals."

"But did you?"

"No. I did not, in fact, put a mini-fridge under my desk. That would be ridiculous. I simply extracted the beer from the office fridge—which we all hold near and dear to our hearts—and brought it together under the desk with the top-shelf-records stool to create the aforeobserved gag. How'd it go?"

Lola and Max looked at each other. Shrugged.

"More effective on those who don't know how much you drink," Max said.

"Unlike the last one, this actually felt like a gag. And your timing improved," Lola added.

"Got a strange way of . . . entertaining yourself, boss."

"Well, Maxify, I got a strange self."

Trike took another sip of beer. Rested the can on his stomach.

"All right," he continued, "here's the plan. Lola, get us a map of the sewers under the Joyce House. He escaped through the basement, and if he planned to go anywhere else unobserved it would be easiest to do so through a nearby connection to the city's sewer system and let's just spend a quantum instant with the wild and fleeting fancy that the connection to the sewers and/or the sewers themselves imply a likely trajectory."

"I'll see what I can find online, but the maps might need to wait till Monday, when the Hall of Records and the Water Department open."

"Understood. Max, we need a van."

"A van?"

"A van. There are unattributed noises in the eaves of that house, and I want to see the squirrels scurrying or catch the ghosts on film."

"A . . . stakeout?"

"My apologies to your lost leisure time."

"Right. Leisure time. So, boss, the actual task. Find a van and convert it into a surveillance van without any money because the reward for the last case fell through."

"You're the best, Max."

Max sighed. Rolled his sleeves down.

"And what'll you be up to?" Lola asked.

"I am going to finish this beer, slightly warmed for the sake of the gag, and most likely several of its cool brethren, listen to the radio, and process the information you two have just provided, with the express intention of deducing a brilliant conclusion sometime in the middle of the night. Lola?"

"Yeah?"

"How are the folders organized?"

"This one is chronological. The other is organized by the strangeness of the absence, so it is extremely strange that something is missing with the stuff at the front, less so with the stuff in the back."

"Excellent. Max?"

"Yes."

"Are you sure you can't tell me the name of the individual with the relatively important secretary?"

"There would be consequences."

"Ah yes, consequences. Well, I'll be here for the foreseeable future. Contact at home over the weekend when discoveries are made. Good luck."

Max and Lola said casual goodbyes and left. Trike watched Lola leave from beneath his hat brim. When they were gone, he turned on the radio.

"The Hustle." "Stayin' Alive." "I Will Survive." "Funkytown." "Shake Your Groove Thing." "Shadow Dancing." "In the Navy." "Celebration." Breaking news story.

"This just in," the DJ broke in. "Sources are now reporting that an anonymous reward has been posted for the safe return of Joyce and/or the capture and conviction of his kidnappers or kidnapper or murderers or murderer. The reward is five million dollars.

I repeat, five million dollars will be rewarded, anonymously, to whoever solves The Joyce Case. Important note, disco lovers, and I'm quoting here, folks, the reward will diminish by fifty thousand dollars every day Joyce is not found starting tomorrow. So get shaking, folks. And since you're shaking, this is WDSC, bringin' you the best disco of the seventies and eighties, so get on this case and get your tail feather shaking."

"No," Trike said. "That's the wrong money."

DEBT, DISAPPEARANCE, AND
THE ORGANIC WHOLE

Vanishedreclusivebillionaire1.9and2.3pintsofbloodTypeONegativeisthe
universaldonorfakebookswindownailedshutdeskmoved3"NWdeco
rativepenstandlampsswitchforsecretdoorlightbulbsoutQueenAnnc

It is not uncommon for wealthy people to use vast portions of that wealth to secure even vaster amounts of wealth, generally through a variety of legal, semilegal, not delineated, and illegal methods of hiding income from the institutions that would levy taxes upon it, but bodily disappearance is not one of the ways to hide income; bodily disappearance is one of the techniques used to shed inordinate amounts of debt, and if the disappearance is properly planned and executed, one is able to shed said debt while retaining a meaningful portion of whatever wealth was generated and was not leveraged in service to said debt, unless of course one is subsequently found, at which point the original mechanisms of debt collection will be supplemented by whatever law enforcement consequences are earned through the actions of disappearance, and, if debt is the issue, the anonymous reward money, at least in the purely theoretical sense, would have some explanation, but one would have to conclude that the debt owed to whoever posted the reward must be in grand excess of the $5 million posted, which calls into question

wingchairlittleusedottomanTristramShandyUnderSHinsteadofST
LaurenceSternebornNovember241713diedMarch181768reported
missing7:42AMbutlerabigknitterlives3blocksawaynotunusualfor

the entire idea of dodging debt, as it is very difficult to generate a debt proportionate to the reward with legitimate lending institutions; institutions which would, rather than adding an additional cost to the recovery process of an anonymous reward, leverage existing legal methods for recouping that debt; however, a loan shark or other illegal or semilegal lending institution or organization would use techniques appropriate to its nature to pursue the disappeared, through direct contracts either with private eyes, collection specialists, or thugs, and certainly would not want to risk drawing attention to itself by posting a $5-million reward, for such rewards are never completely anonymous, and this is before considering the FBI connection, because, of course, the FBI would have that kind of money lying around and would be able to post that kind of reward without fear of legal recrimination because they are the recriminators, and one could at the very least consider the possibility that Joyce has $5 million worth of secrets and information in his head, and the FBI would certainly also have motivation to obscure their involvement with Joyce by making the reward

66

smallwoodeddeciduousareainbackunlikelylawnwascrossedsitting
rooms:periodwallpapercentraltablesarchaeologicalmagazinesofTroy
rangeofnauticalimagesCroppyBoyplusdistinctionscopshiddendumb

anonymous if Joyce is involved in something particularly unsavory, which we can be almost certain almost certainly involves growing and perhaps selling weed, but they know I am on the case and would know of their involvement and would discern said unsavoriness, adding an additional and substantial risk, at which point one would have to ask why bother even offering the reward as, no matter the amount, they are not going to attract a more capable detective than the one already busting his brain over the problem, unless, of course, the reward is an attempt to either draw Joyce himself out of hiding, which would, of course, only work if he were more in need of the money than in need of the disappearance, and regardless of what money he is receiving for his services to them, unless there is the previously discredited issue of debt, it is unlikely that Joyce would need money more than disappearance, given just how much wealth is indicated by the house and especially the sitting rooms. Maybe the Rembrandt copy, though that was probably paid for in cash, with no reason for the gallery to keep track of anything about the purchase once it is finalized, but even if

waiterovertlyconstructedemptyatticdustspreadlessthanaweekpre
viousappropriatespacebetweenceilingandfloorFedsarrive8.7
minutesaftercalltolocksmithDisappearanceannouncedonmorning

Trike took his feet off the desk. Before he could stop them, his hands opened the drawer where cigarettes would have been if he hadn't quit smoking. His hands found a pack of completely inadequate nicotine gum. Since the pack was in hand he popped a piece into his mouth. He was mugged by a coughing fit that almost knocked him out of his chair. The gum was lost.

Since the drawer was open, he took out a notebook and put it on his desk. He kicked back into detecting posture. An unforeseen stiffness in his back rendered the position untenable. He snapped to standing and began circumnavigating the room.

Philosophically, Trike did not separate the brain from the body, seeing all differentiation as superficial misunderstandings of an organic whole. Though it is obvious to most that the functioning of the mind affects the actions of the body, it is not as clear or as certain that the actions of the body, besides obvious health issues and chemically induced states, have a direct effect on the functioning of the mind. However, Trike believed in the idea enough to incorporate it into his belief structure. In practical terms, this meant Trike believed different aspects, realms, avenues, and abilities of cogitation were available or unavailable depending on the actions being concurrently taken by the body. Essentially, one thinks differently while one is pacing than one does while sitting. Furthermore, one thinks differently at all different levels of intoxication and all different levels of recovery from intoxication, as well as at all different states of exhaustion and alertness, starvation and satisfaction, pain and comfort, etc. So Trike would sit, pace, walk, drink, sleep, eat, and, for so very long, smoke, smoke, smoke, during a case, all with the express purpose of providing different perspectives from which to consider the problem.

Many, in the course of their lives, will wish for new eyes from which to view what barriers stand before them. They believe that difference is vital to solution. They are right. And the eyes are there. And they can be created if the effort is truly undertaken.

Trike sat down. The desk was still desk.

he'd paid in sweet sweet traceable credit, there is no hunchable
connection between this painting and Joyce's actual disappearance, and at this juncture it is only safe to assume that this
copy is, in fact, a copy, for if it were one of the most famous
thefted paintings in the world it verges on the impossible that
Lola would not find traces of the personal data that would have
been connected with a person capable of such an acquisition,
although it would not necessarily be entirely fruitless to assume new developments in disappearing personal information, developments that Lola has yet to catch up to, but the
innovation would have to be both thorough and devious, both
rigorous and creative. But the question of where Joyce is now
should not need a complete picture of who Joyce is to be answered, for, though the past is a strong indicator of present
and future action, unless the past reveals an event, fact, or trait
that definitively influences current action, it should only be
treated as components of character and not pieces of evidence,
which leaves us lurching back to the only thing that ever seems
to make any sense in cases like these: money, the absence of
money, the potential for money, the money hidden away in

creative locations, which, because this seems to be the buck of this bull, tangles back into the lack of personal information, because I still don't see how someone could be making money on all of this; though it would not be impossible for the reward to be a very elaborate tax dodge, whatever would be saved in taxes was spent several times over on the information wash, unless Joyce didn't pay for the information wash, which is possible if he were in the witness protection program, but if that were the case, Max should have at least found that fact even if he could find no more, and if that were the case, why didn't the FBI take over investigation, or why not open up the basement just to Max and me, since we already know it's there and already know what's being done in there, they could even clean out the weed if they wanted, and then we wouldn't have to extrapolate from sewer maps to see at least where he went last, or shit, why not just tell us what the exit possibilities are from the basement and let us go from there, if there even are exit possibilities from the basement, seems like Max should have been able to drag that tiny bit out of his contacts, though it could be that everyone at the FBI simply has better things to do with their time than fuck around with Joyce, but that fact itself raises its own maelstrom of problems, not the least of which is the idle speculation about just how much fucking weed a dude has got to grow to get on their radar, breaking in could make some very inconvenient enemies, which would not be worth it at least at this juncture of the investigation, especially since it is likely that nearly all evidence has since eroded from that space, if there were any evidence in that space to begin with, still... something tells me Joyce wouldn't go far, there is so much money involved and so much that needs to managed, but that isn't necessarily a meaningful limitation, especially if he has prepared properly and/or has a sophisticated and supple communication system, OK, different angle, who could have a stake in this that I haven't already considered, not a creditor but an ally of some kind, a business partner, a boss, or perhaps one more remove, someone who could benefit from his disappearance in an indirect but powerful way, someone who needs him to perform a task for them that can only be accomplished when he vanishes...

Trike stood up. Went to the window. Still window. Nothing he looked for was visible. Still, he looked with as much of his brain as he could spare. The free vodka was at home, and if he was going to have a good old-fashioned think-and-drink, it would behoove him to drink that instead of the client scotch and gin. He took a deep breath.

He gathered his things to brave the constant adventure that was his car.

On his way out, Trike tipped his hat back at his desk. He liked to imagine his father sitting there, wishing him luck.

A KEY IS JUST A SYMBOL OF PERMISSION

Max walked into the living room. He shoved a pile of magazines against the wall with his foot. He shuffled food wrappers and dirty dishes around to make an open spot on the floor. He put the pile of newspapers cluttering the couch there. He cleared a bunch of empty beer bottles off the coffee table. He sat down. Put his feet up. Turned on college football.

Max's relationship with college football was rationally engaged. He never went to a bowl game, bought a fancy cable package, or called a sports radio show. Except for that one time. If Auburn, Michigan, or Rutgers were on, he'd watch from pre- to post-game, getting supplies or going to the bathroom only during commercials. If they weren't, he'd mix in chores, reading, or a crossword puzzle.

They weren't. Max picked up the top paper. Scanned the headlines. At least the game gave him a chance to see a Heisman-hopeful quarterback. Max flipped to the world news section. Skimmed it during the first quarter.

"Max!" Trike shouted from the hallway that led to his bedroom.

"Afternoon, boss."

"What the fuck are you doing here?"

"Watching poor decision-making hurt Heisman chances."

"Why the fuck are you doing it here?"

"Cable's still out."

"So you break into my place to watch college football?"

"I have a key."

Trike fact-checked the assertion in his memory. He wore poorly fitting athletic shorts, calf-length distorted white tube socks, and a threadbare D.A.R.E. T-shirt that was more bare than thread. The fact of Max's assertion did not quite check out.

"I've changed the lock three times since I gave you that key."

"A key is a symbol of permission."

Trike didn't respond. He went to the kitchen. Came back with a carafe of coffee in one hand and a mug and six-pack in the other. He put it all on the coffee table. He found a hot plate in the debris around the couch. He set that on the table and the carafe on it. Then he plugged it into an extension cord that poked from the edge of the rug. He poured a mug full of coffee and sat down next to Max.

"Is he really hurting his Heisman chances?" Trike asked.

Max shrugged. "Affecting draft position."

"What's your feeling about some afternoon drinking and relaxed theorizing about the case?"

"Knew watching here had . . . risks."

"Think of it as an in-kind donation for the cable you're stealing."

"You're stealing this cable."

"There's a famous amendment to the Constitution that handles awkward questions like the one implied by your wild speculation. Besides, it'd be like burning fifty grand if we do nothing about the case today."

Max held out his hand. Trike filled it with a beer can. Trike opened his own and leaned back into the couch.

"So what do you think, Max?"

"Anything in particular?"

"General sense of the case. Nature. Essence. Soul of the problem. The nougat center."

Max took a healthy swig of beer.

"I never realized eccentric billionaires were real. I've met billionaires who were eccentric. But they had a normal core . . . recognizable through the wealth."

"And Joyce is an eccentric billionaire?"

"Sitting rooms. Secret passage. Mysterious money. Self-kidnapping. I don't know. I don't like it one bit."

"Once we figure out where he's gone and why, it will all become clear."

Max rubbed his forehead.

"This is different," he said. "Different in a different way."

Max sipped and continued. "Working undercover in narcotics, I met some wealthy insane people. Pet kangaroos. Mansions with waterfalls. Cars with espresso machines. But there was a recognizable . . . core beneath the opulence. The process from poor farmer's son to kingpin was . . . apparent. They could be killed any day. Their volume was off—"

Max interrupted himself to point at the screen. "See. Didn't read the zone coverage. Guy underneath was wide open."

"What about the defensive end in the lane?"

"Tackle was on him. Never get his hands up in time."

"Little hard on the guy, don't you think? Safety stepped forward like it was man on the snap," Trike argued.

"That is what separates Heisman hopefuls from Heisman winners."

"All right, I accept your argument," Trike conceded.

They watched the next few plays without talking. Trike poured himself a second mug of coffee.

"So, Joyce doesn't seem like a narco kingpin?"

"No."

"So that makes him an eccentric billionaire?"

"It makes him . . . unusual."

"*Unusual* is the word, Max."

They watched the rest of the first half without speaking. Even with a miscue or two, the quarterback and his team were coasting to victory. Trike finished the coffee and unplugged the hot plate. They each finished their first beer and got a second. When the teams ran to the locker rooms for halftime, only the fundamental doubt of existence remained.

"You must have some ... thoughts," Max said as commercials rolled.

Trike sighed. Took a big swig of beer. Looked at the ceiling, over at the front door, into the kitchen, down at the coffee table, back to the television. Left himself dehydrated something fierce. He took another big swig.

"I do not have some thoughts about this, Max. I have thousands of thoughts knitting themselves into a sweat-and-vomit-soaked blanket of intellectual frustration. A bog of possibilities. A swamp of equally irrational solutions. An algae slick of suspicions hiding a tangled, rotting, neutrally buoyant morass of mundane detritus, solidified toxins, dead sea life, and wild speculation drawn from the fuzzy satellite photographs of the investigation. I'm standing on a Victorian-era Central European train station, Sofia perhaps, poorly attired for the weather, on the busiest day of the century, clutching a ticket to Vienna that must be given to the worthiest traveler and every person who passes me explains why they deserve the ticket without telling me what they plan to do once they arrive, while hovering above, in the invisible gap between up and down spins, a time-traveling super alien magic cat judges me based on criteria revealed to the Judeo-Christian god of salvation and damnation engendered from myth for the sole purpose of ferrying me to my deserved final destination, and in the balance, one knows not what is at stake. On top of it all, my brain threads the thin trails of spider silk of my efforts across the problem that never build into patterns, never remain long enough to be progress, never stabilize enough to be mistaken for temporary paths through the dark-and-noise-ridden fairy-tale forest of this mystery, whose roots tangled into cells imprisoning enchanted looms weaving divergent puzzles into being that mix opposed languages into offensive pigments sprayed into impenetrable overlays over my most cherished childhood memories, all so an accountant in New Jersey, who doesn't even pretend to love his wife anymore, can calculate the fates of the would-be great leaders of the next generation, assigning life and death by carelessly filling out ten-ninety tax forms, and tell his snooty professor cousin that getting the references never made anybody a million dollars and a million dollars will keep mattering more than the references that make having language more than just an elaborate excuse for semaphore."

"Jesus Christ, boss. Warn a man next time."

"Sorry. I got caught up in the moment."

"Moment? Watching college football?"

"There's a lot going on under the hood," Trike said, tapping his forehead.

"Amounting to?"

"I don't know what the fuck is going on."

"Welcome to a crowded boat," Max said.

"I've never been in this boat."

Max shrugged. "Buffet's bad ... music's all right."

Trike stood up. Took a quick lap around the living room while guzzling beer. He emptied the can and dropped it. He grabbed another, then sat back down next to Max.

"Here's the plan."

"You and your plans."

"We're going to spend the afternoon focused on football. We still haven't settled our differences on zone blitzes in the college game. Then we'll part ways for the rest of the weekend to intensely ruminate on the evidence as it stands now, both feeling free to augment those ruminations with any research we feel is required to feed further rumination."

"And get a van," Max added.

"And get a van. On Monday, assuming Lola, as she suspected, has had to wait until then to acquire useful sewer maps, we will formally continue the investigation, incorporating insights we are sure to have over the course of the weekend, and then come up with our next steps. How's that sound?"

"No Notre Dame."

"Deal. Heartbroken, but deal."

"I'm in. Pass me another beer.

"You got it, Max."

THE OLD-TIMER HAS HIS FIRST SAY

Trike slammed the door of his car. The window slid down with a plastic clunk and locked the door. Even with the window open, even in the bad part of town, Trike wasn't worried about his car being stolen. The starter was uniquely degraded and the wiring was faulty. He needed to turn the key, press up on the steering column with his knee, and step on the gas to get it started. No one would put that much effort into stealing a nice car.

Trike sat on the trunk with his feet on the bumper. He put the key in the lock, took a deep breath, popped half a foot off the trunk, turned the key, slammed his weight down, bounced off, spun in the air with his hand still on the key, and tried to throw open the trunk. Got it on the third try. He took out two bags of groceries. Left the trunk open. Closing it was another production.

The apartment building looked like a wino drunk on canned heat slouching next to the gutter; a hiccup away from collapsing. Most of the windows were broken. The front door was so dilapidated, Trike pushed through it with his arms full. He didn't even look at the elevator. The concrete stairwell smelled like urine, vomit, bug bombs, and three other things too faint for Trike to identify. The Old-Timer had lived in this Section 8 apartment since his third wife divorced him and kept the house.

Trike kicked The Old-Timer's door as a knock.

"Go fuck yourself," The Old-Timer shouted.

"It's Trike."

"I know. Any booze in those grocery bags?" The Old-Timer shouted, no closer to the door.

"I've got a fifth and an afternoon."

The Old-Timer let Trike in, then sat down in an ancient recliner. Trike put the groceries away. Poured two fingers of whiskey apiece into two glasses and brought them to the living room. He handed The Old-Timer a glass and sat down in an old director's chair.

They finished their first whiskeys over three minutes of silence. Trike refilled their glasses. Then the tire fire started burning.

"The worst thing about the batshit-crazy cases, is how much you come to need them. After a few years of walking into a scene where a guy's brains are all over the living room and knowing before you take your hat off, his wife told him to fuck himself with a shotgun, you start looking forward to the cases you get to scratch your head about. Don't ever underestimate your ability to be bored. I knew it was time to hang 'em up when I found myself picking the starting quarterback on my fantasy team while some mob thug taught me how to smell the back of my neck. I don't care how hot your wife is, you pound her pussy long enough, she'll end up looking like an overweight high school gym teacher to you. Near the end I busted open this huge case, dogfighting, puppy mill, money-laundering thing. The organization was all over the place and I brought those bastards down pretty much all on my lonesome. And do you know what it felt like when I saw the cops cuff the ringleader? Entering focus group results into an advertising database. And I just saved puppies. Hundreds of fucking puppies. Even when I saw the feel-good report on the local news of those puppies getting adopted by loving families. Not a fucking thing. Just another fucking day draining the fucking water cooler at the fucking office. And it gets worse. The better you are, the faster boredom gets to you and the harder it hits when it does. And then the boring shit needs to be even more boring for court, so when that door finally gets the battering ram and the fucker you've chased halfway around the world finally gets his face slammed on the coke-bought mahogany desk, you don't think about the thrill of the chase, or the justice, or the reward; you think about convincing a bunch of dangling dingleberry jurors that you're an expert witness while smelling like whiskey in a suit that hasn't been cleaned in a year. You don't even give a shit about the truth anymore because it's just too damn easy. It don't matter how great her tits are if you can see 'em whenever you want. Fuck it. See if you can con yourself into disability payments. That's where it's at, I'm told."

Trike refilled both glasses.

"You ever have a case misbehave?" he asked.

The Old-Timer smirked. He slammed his whiskey and wiggled his glass at Trike for a refill. Trike refilled it.

"Yeah, I had a couple misbehave. Cops in Baltimore called me in on a serial killer case, and you could just hear it in their voices that it was a shit-blower stuck in reverse. This fucker had an agenda, but he was smart enough to cut up a random corpse every now and again to throw us off-track. And he'd cool it right after some arrest made the papers, give the DA a chance to believe they had something on somebody already in custody, and then, bam, another body with too wide a smile. Another was this kidnapping, and let me tell you, when they call with a kidnapping, they want a janitor, not a detective, because they've already given up on whoever the fuck went wherever the fuck. Everything was wrong. The scene. The parents. The kid. Whole fucking thing. Turned out the kid fell down the stairs roughhousing with his older brother, high school, good grades, baseball scholarship, just horsing around with his kid brother, and the parents figured, spitting this one into the maw of American Justice ain't gonna bring baby boy back, so let's cover it up and move on. Losing one son or maybe losing two sons. Let me tell you this, you arrogant twat-dripping, justice is a transvestite, so never pay full price up front. But you didn't say 'Hey old man, this shit happen to you?' just to stroll down memory lane in my skid row, you want to know what old fuckers like me and your pops did when cases misbehaved. You treat a misbehaving case like you treat a misbehaving child: smack it across the face just hard enough to get it to stop. If it keeps up with the bullshit, smack it a little harder. With the serial killer, I followed a prime suspect day and night until he pulled a blade. Then I did what the cops had practically begged me to do: shot the bastard through his sick-ass heart and planted a gun on him. The papers pinned the murders on him better than any court could. The kidnapping. Well. The real ball-render with misbehaving cases is it's real easy to knock the brat's teeth out. And if you're angry when you swing. Fuck. You can take the poor kid's head off.

"The kidnapping. They hired me to find the kid. So, I found the kid. I convinced the husband the wife was going to pin it on him so she could divorce him, get away scot-free and keep the house. I wasn't there when he barged into the police station to tell everyone and their diddling uncle where the body was buried. Yeah. The truth was a good lay back then. Now, I'd'a helped them build a concrete patio over the body. What am I telling you? You get what you get. Now get the fuck out with your fucking fuck, so I can make myself dinner and watch the game without you mumbling statistics in my ear. You'd be the worst coach on the planet. Always knowing which play had the highest statistical likelihood of getting the first down."

"I could keep it to myself."

"Yeah. That'd make it better."

ATTACKER FAILS, KNIFE VIBRATES, AND LOLA DOES NOT DRAW A TREE

Sharp glare of early sun off moist asphalt. There was plenty of asphalt in the parking lot of the Breeckow Administrative Complex where the city's Hall of Records was located. Even on a Monday morning when the building was open. As Lola suspected, there were no pictures of the city's sewer maps online. She'd found references, descriptions, and files that had been removed, but nothing that would contribute to the investigation.

Which was fine by Lola. Opening an ancient ledger had emotional content that downloading a file did not. And Lola didn't care why.

"Good morning, Lola," the clerk at the Hall of Records droned. He didn't turn to greet her. It was 9:02 a.m.

"Good morning, Arthur. How did you know it was me?"

Arthur Neil sighed. Like he'd been exhausted forever.

"You're the only person who has ever, ever come here this early in the morning. In fact," Arthur sighed so hard that a thirteen-year-old in Omaha discovered The Smiths, "most of the time you're the only one who ever comes here. Usually to send me scampering around the entire hall." He put on a tight faux smile. "Now, what can I do for you?"

"I need current maps of the sewer systems."

"Yes. Of course," Arthur stopped completely. "You do."

"And if for some reason, a full map is unavailable, I could make do with a map of the sewers around this address."

Lola handed the clerk a slip of paper. He took it. Eventually. As if it were an asp.

"Ah, the Joyce House. I should have known. In my vocational capacity as gatekeeper of the city's records, it is my duty to ask you: Why would you come *here* for this information, when it would be readily available and far more complete at the Water Department?"

Trike drew conclusions like six-shooters. Took shots so precisely cruel that whoever stood in his way answered whatever he asked, just to make sure he never said anything about them again. But Trike would know something important and truthful about Arthur from the prescription and style of his glasses. Without that arsenal, Lola just told Arthur the truth.

"I can walk here. I have to drive to the Water Department."

"But you have a car, have gas or the ability to get it, and live in a nation devoted to the automobile. I must say, I fail to see why that is a *compelling* reason."

"And I fail to see why you're such a dick. You're a clerk at the hall of public records. It is your job to bring the public its records."

Arthur stormed off into the stacks.

"And that attitude is killing the planet," Lola shouted after him. "And I don't really have gas money," she thought.

Feet shuffled in the hallway, up to, but not past, the door to the Hall of Records office. Someone muffled a cough. There was a plastic pop. A cap coming off a bottle of mace. Someone lurked in the hallway.

Jumping her in a public place made no sense. But with the FBI connection and the missing information, it never hurt to have a strategy.

Step into the hallway crouching low with hands over face while stepping away from the attacker. Set weight, kick attacker's left knee. Come in low, wrap the attacker around the waist forcing weight on kicked knee. Hip toss and roll to land on top with knees on shoulders. Chop whichever wrist holds the mace. Have a very awkward conversation. Planning took two seconds.

Lola listened as the lurker shuffled and fidgeted, intending to alter her strategy in response to any change in location. Whoever it was didn't seem to have the sense to press him- or herself against the wall. Or stand far enough away from the opening door to ensure the efficacy of the mace.

Arthur stomped back to the counter and slammed a massive ledger on it. It boomed like a shotgun.

Whoever was in the hallway screamed. The scream was followed by a hissing sound. The hissing by a receding series of screams.

Lola relaxed. Whoever was in the hallway had somehow maced themself and run away. She reached for the ledger. Arthur pulled it away.

"Alas, this is not for you. The sewer maps are gone."

"Gone?"

"Yes. Gone."

"Were they checked out?"

"Lola, as I've told you, oh, let's say hundreds of times, this is the Hall of Records, not a lending library. Our materials are not 'checked out.'" The clerk added contemptuous air quotes.

"Then where are the sewer maps?"

"This may also come as a shock to you, but *I* am not a detective. I am a clerk in the Hall of Records. Perhaps you could hire an astonishingly arrogant, compulsively cruel, blond Satan to find them for you. Or are you so broke the one you work for won't even take the case for you?"

A knife suddenly stuck in the wall to Lola's right. It vibrated from the speed of its impact. Arthur jumped back at the sudden motion.

Lola said in a clear, quiet tone, "The knife is not a threat. Just a reminder. Something to think about. Life is strange. You assume you never need the help of someone who can draw a knife so quickly and throw it so accurately that it fixes a comma splice, and, in general, you would be right. But things happen. Coincidences. Mistaken identities. Wrong place at the wrong time. So, if you end up somehow, somewhere in your life needing someone who can draw a knife that quickly and throw it that accurately, you'll have to count me out of your pool of potential saviors."

Arthur blinked. The knife was out of the wall and Lola was stepping back to the counter. "Now," she said, "doesn't the absence of the maps concern you at all?"

Arthur cleared his throat. Regained his composure. "It concerns me greatly. But *I* am going to go through the *proper* authorities." He picked up the phone. "Right now." He dialed. While it rang he said, "Looks like you'll have to drive out to the Water Department anyway. Not so green after all, eh?" He turned his back on Lola and talked into the phone.

Still waiting for that Constitutional amendment about assholes.

Lola considered her options. She could walk home, pick up her car, and drive to the Water Department. And make Arthur right. A bus could get her a half-mile from the Water Department, but that route was two connections away. The department was a little less than five miles from her apartment. She could jog there without killing herself in about thirty-eight minutes, but she'd be a sweaty mess when she got there. It was only 9:12 a.m. She couldn't afford organic but she bought it anyway. This was not a time to give in. Jog.

Lola went home, put on jogging clothes, and packed her bag with a towel, deodorant, a more professional outfit, her phone, a sandwich of hummus and sprouts, a manila folder, and her small sketchbook. She jogged to the Water Department.

I'd give you a dollar for every head that didn't turn when Lola ran by. You'd owe me fifty cents.

Lola approached the receptionist at the department, dried, changed, and deodorized as much as possible in a public restroom. It was 11:45 a.m. The receptionist was putting out a sign with a clock indicating 1:00 p.m. and the phrase, "Gone Until."

"Sir, just one thing before—"

"I'm sorry, Miss," he said, "but I'm already late and this is an all-staff meeting, so there's no one else to help you."

"I know, but I just—"

"There's a nice little sandwich shop just around the corner if you want to grab some lunch. I'll be back at one to help. Sorry." He left through the back of the office.

Lola didn't have enough money for a sandwich or anything else from the nice little sandwich shop just around the corner. She didn't have enough money for an energy drink from the convenience store she'd jogged by. Since it was before seven p.m., she didn't have enough money to get the weekly call to her mom out of the way.

Lola strolled out to the front lawn. There was a bench facing the street. With limited options, Lola sat there. She took out her sketchbook. Scanned the world for something to draw while she killed an hour.

She saw a one-story battleship-gray building with two short wings. A rectangle with a side missing. Barely featured. An HVAC cylinder and an HVAC box on the roof. A driveway led visitors to a central glassed-in lobby. The sign above that entrance was too small for Lola to read. A line of hedges ran along the street the length of the outside wall.

The interposition of the driveway in the open square created by the wings enclosed two essentially useless spaces. To mitigate or obscure the company's unwillingness to pay for gardens to fill those spaces, two benches were installed. They were empty, though it was lunchtime.

The building could have housed a biotech, or a telemarketer, or a regional headquarters of a national retailer, or a credit-card company's call center, or any business that required little space per employee. It might have held interest to an architect or someone willing to provide the intensity of attention that always reveals substance, but Lola wasn't an architect and she didn't have the resources for that attention.

A lawn landscaped into monotony stretched along the street stage left. A monotony monotonously broken by a landscaped-into-the-scenery old leafless tree. A fine subject for a pencil or charcoal drawing. Its essence was expressible both in bold abstract strokes and through thousands of short, light, precise lines. Lola had drawn, sketched, and painted hundreds of trees. For as many reasons. Some of which art. She did not want to spend time on another.

Behind the tree, a hill dropped off. The horizon was drawn by the tops of deciduous trees. The corporate lawn stretched to the curve in the street that was the border of Lola's vision.

She closed her eyes, hoping to induce a sketchable image in her visual consciousness. Sometimes it was like fog receding from a landscape. Portions solidified. Vagueness dissipated. Certainty grew until she knew what she looked at.

Sometimes the fully formed image just popped into her mind. There would be when she could not see it and there would be when she could. A Planck-scale border of consciousness.

Sometimes it felt like an archaeological action sequence: solving puzzles, eluding traps, and braving dangers to arrive at something she knew existed, yet was unseen.

But none of those things happened. Just a sudden certainty that she would see nothing on the inside that needed to be brought outside. Her eyes snapped open.

"Think about the case, then."

Lola thought about a case in two different ways. The first was common: verbal reasoning in notes on paper.

She set the sketchbook down in her lap and let her eyes and mind wander over the few notes she'd made. Phrases seemed about to assemble only to unify first with their own impossibility. Three times Lola put her pencil on the page, but before depositing graphite, the fundamental flaw in whatever she intended to jot revealed itself.

The process halted.

"Wish the universe had told me about this hour of free time," she thought. "Would've shoved some other research in my bag."

Lola endeavored her other way of thinking about a case.

When a problem was particularly abstract, she created, in her mind, a visual equivalent for each component of the problem and assigned it a role in the process of painting. One component was the line, another the color, another the brushstrokes, another the blocking. If the resulting image made compositional sense, she assessed it to better understand the elements of the problem itself. If the first assignment of visual metaphors did not make compositional sense, she rearranged the assignments. The background color became the frame. The line became the color. Combination after combination until something made visual sense.

Though this process rarely produced a definitive answer—at least before Trike produced a definitive answer—it often produced productive questions. "Why would they use a hatchback instead of a small pickup truck?" "Why would she wear an old dress to an anniversary dinner with her husband?" "Why would they use Christmas wrapping paper?" "Why did they carry the suitcase, when they could have rolled it?"

Trike would pause when she asked the right question. His eyes flashed. Then he would rush off to whatever action the answer demanded. Occasionally, he bothered to thank her.

But The Joyce Case wouldn't paint.

Sitting on that bench, looking at a landscape built by humans with no evidence of humanity, Lola couldn't make an image of what she knew. Not the painting of a madman compelled by psychosis; a torture victim painting a lie as fast as possible just to make it all stop.

Lola ate half her sandwich slowly and deliberately to do something that didn't ache her brain.

It was ten to one.

Then a procession, from each direction, of evenly spaced cars. Five minutes of automobile flow. The range of sensible American vehicles. Lola guessed lunch breaks, but she had no idea what nearby entities could foster such an exchange.

It was five to one, with an empty road before a corporate landscape. Lola figured she might as well spend those five minutes waiting in the waiting room. Maybe the receptionist had come back early. She packed her sketchbook and returned to the Water Department.

Lola went straight up to the reception desk. No one was there. Lola sat in one of the waiting room chairs. She waited. 1:17. 1:31. 1:44. 1:50. 2:03.

Lola went to the desk looking for a bell or buzzer. Neither. She peered over the counter into the workspace. She saw a blotter, a computer monitor, phone with headset plugged in, notepad with a blank page, pencils, pens, and a stapler. Near the back wall by the door the receptionist had left through were three unlabeled filing cabinets. Next to them was a cork board with a half-dozen papers pinned to it. Legally required workplace posters filled the wall on the other side of the door. Back on the desk there was also a coffee mug with "I'M NOT EVEN SUPPOSED TO BE HERE TODAY" printed on it, and an iPod paused on "Rockaway Beach."

Lola sat down.

2:12. 2:18. Lola sketched a little more. 2:34. 2:41. 2:57. 3:12. Lola ate the rest of her sandwich.

At 3:39 the receptionist burst through the door behind his desk apologizing.

"I am so sorry to keep you waiting. You know how these meetings can be." He sat down. "Now," he bent down and turned his computer on, "how can I help you?"

"I would like to see the city's sewer maps."

"The city's sewer maps," the receptionist repeated, dropping his head and tone.

"If it's not possible to get maps for the entire city, I would like to see maps around this address." Lola handed the slip of paper with the Joyce House address toward the receptionist. He did not take it.

"I'm sorry, Miss. There's been some recent policy changes. I'll have to double-check with my supervisor just to be sure. Hold on just a second. I'll be back as soon as I can."

The receptionist stood up quickly and as quickly dashed back out the door.

"Why didn't he call?" Lola thought. "Weird to go in person." She wrote, "couldn't call superior, had to see in person," in her book.

3:47. 3:52. 4:09. 4:19. The sound of $50,000 evaporating and with it the colors of paint she needed to replace, the chance for quiet time at the cafe, new inserts for her running shoes—Lola arrested her frustration as well as she could. 4:27. The receptionist repeated his bursting and apologizing.

"I am terribly sorry for keeping you waiting again, Miss. It's funny that you would come in today, because that meeting was actually about our new policy on the sewer maps and I just wanted to double-check with my supervisor about it because, obviously, this is the first time I've had to apply the policy."

"You have a new policy about the sewer maps?"

"Among other city records, yes. Well. You see, in light of certain security concerns, the Water Department, in conjunction with The Mayor's office and the City Council, has decided to restrict access to certain city records and documents, including the sewer maps. I'm sure you can see why, in today's world, we would want to be careful about these things, which is a real shame if you asked me, but, well, nobody did, but if they had I would've said the best way to keep ourselves safe is to stop acting like arrogant douchebags, but what are you going to do. Anyway, the point is that we're going to have to run a background check on you before access to the maps is provided. And you won't be able to make any copies of them, of any kind."

"You're kidding."

"I wish I was, Miss. I really do. But if you give me your driver's license or other state-issued identification, I can get this taken care of as quickly as possible."

Someone had been waiting for her in the Hall of Records. After a suspicious delay, the receptionist was asking for ID. Lola assessed the security situation.

Both entrances were in full view. There was no one else in the waiting room. If someone came from the offices, they would have to get around the partition first. Whoever was in the Hall of Records would still be crying pepper-flavored tears. The assessment took one second. Lola handed over the license.

The receptionist took it and reenacted his dashing and bursting. "Back in just a sec."

4:38. 4:42. 4:49. 4:53. 5:08.

The receptionist returned without the burst. He sulked. Handed Lola her license and sat down.

"I'm really sorry about this, but while we were running your check, which totally checked out, we got word that we are not allowed to show the sewer maps to anyone under any circumstances."

Lola remembered the mug and the iPod. No tie. Goatee. She drew a conclusion.

"Sir." Lola dropped her voice, leaned closer, and told a kind of a lie. "I am investigating a kidnapping. A kidnapping that could become a murder at any moment. I know what your superiors told you, and I'm sure they have their reasons for such an authoritarian policy. But you have a chance to help save a life. Policy is policy. Life is life."

The receptionist sighed. "Under any circumstances, I was told. In this case, I'm sure you can get a court order."

"So I'm supposed to wade through a bunch of red tape to talk to some stuffed-shirt judge. It'd make more sense to start digging the grave."

"I'm sorry, Miss. Under any circumstances. Even if I wanted to help you, I couldn't get the maps without talking to my supervisor."

"Can I talk to your supervisor?"

The receptionist leaned back in his chair. His face had exhausted all of its apology muscles. It was the end of the day. He only had enough energy for a stony countenance.

"She's left for the day," he said.

"Of course."

"I can take your name and phone number and call you when the records are available again."

If she had Trike's six-shooter—Lola stopped the thought. It is irresponsible to speculate about weapons one could never employ.

"I'll just call ahead."

"Sorry, again, for everything."

"Don't apologize to me. Wait for the headline and then apologize to the family."

The receptionist tried to offer some final formality but Lola had already turned her back and was ducking into the bathroom. Wanted to go out on that one.

She changed back into her jogging clothes. Decided to head home. One level of Internet research had turned up nothing, but there were others. She didn't make eye contact with the receptionist. Ran through the door, down the walkway. She was at pace by the sidewalk.

WAS SEPPUKU INDUCED?

Trike committed the police report to memory Monday afternoon while vigorously circumnavigating his office. A page of data per circuit, set on the desk when completed.

Most of the data were the police version of what Trike had observed at the crime scene. The next significant percentage was the police version of what Lola and Max had discovered, a lesser approximation of meaningful nothing. The remaining data were a long, empirical elaboration of the statement, "Not a single extant individual gives two flying fucks in an artisan food truck about this rich fucking fucker."

With the report assessed, sorted, labeled, and correlated with the data they'd uncovered since the report was generated, Trike began his rigorous analysis. Discovered underlying investigative assumptions. He sat in a client chair. Discerned trajectories of future research. He stood by the window. He muttered, "What follows is perhaps one of the great moments of inexplicable, inexcusable, inhuman dickishness committed to literature." Constructed preliminary deductions. He lay down on the floor. It was definitive that the FBI weren't talking to the police, but that was pro forma. All else remained open to interpretation.

After three hours of applying typical tools, Trike opted for his intellectual dynamite.

Hung up his fedora. Cleared a spot on his desk. Sat down in his chair, put his feet up and his hands behind his head. Closed his eyes. He imagined possible explanations, instantaneously fact-checking them. Dynamite that sometimes reached deeper parts of his imagination; one discarded explanation involved disgruntled students from a bankrupt clown college. Dozens of stories a minute. Without moving. For another two hours.

As long as there is one more trial than error.

Max showed a young woman into Trike's office.

"Someone to see you, Mr. Augustine," Max said.

Trike didn't move. Kept his eyes closed. "Just doesn't make sense, Max."

"What, boss?"

"Crime entertainment tells many lies about crime to those who are entertained by it, but perhaps the most persistent and most damaging is the lie of the impersonal criminal. There are jewel thieves and gangsters and drug dealers, but most crime is personal. There is a preexisting relationship between the criminal and the victim. And yet, here we have what looks like a very personal crime and no evidence whatsoever, either from our research or whatever it is the police do, that Joyce had any personal relationships of any kind."

"Right. Someone to see you, boss."

"The influence of the FBI does raise certain impersonal possibilities, but given what you have discovered, not very satisfying possibilities. There is also the chance that the relationship is simply so distant, so tenuous, so concealed that no one investigating has yet discovered it. Then, of course, the whole issue of relationship might be irrelevant as there is convincing evidence that there is no other in this crime, and that includes the recently announced anonymous reward. Five million dollars is quite a lot of money, even as it diminishes, and the only person, thus far, definitively involved in the crime definitively able to part with such a sum, is Joyce the victim/criminal himself."

"Right. Someone to see you."

"Is it Joyce?"

"Not according to the portrait."

"Is my visitor about to confess to the kidnapping and/or murder of Joyce?"

"No."

"Take said visitor's information. I will continue imagining thousands of possible solutions to the mystery."

"I'd open your eyes."

Trike knew when to listen to Max. Opened his eyes.

He saw the second-most beautiful woman he'd ever seen in person. She was a little over five foot six, not counting heels. She had rich brown hair as thick as it was wavy, cut so it fell one and a half inches above her shoulders, a sprinkle of freckles across her pale nose, and large blue eyes. She had the physique of an action-movie star. Maybe a dancer. At least someone who taught fitness workshops at the Y on weekends. She wore a retro-style blue polka-dot dress with an open collar and a matching belt. Athleticism rippled the liquefaction of her clothes. Intelligence flashed in her eyes.

"Just let me pick up my jaw, sweetheart. Then we can get down to business."

"I'm just delivering a message. I wouldn't call this business."

Sometimes you say things you know you shouldn't say. "Then what are we going to mix our pleasure with?"

She sighed. Stood with poise waiting to see if Trike offered any additional folly. "If you don't mind, I get an extra five hundred dollars if I give you my message before seven."

Sometimes you do it again. "I'll give you an extra five hundred dollars to never leave."

An elfin incarnation of charmed blush whispered across her countenance.

"How about this," she said. "I will give this gentleman my card," she handed Max her card, "and then the legendary, and now that I see him, fairly attractive, in an indie-band-drummer kind of way, Trike Augustine can use the five hundred dollars to take me to the symphony and a very fancy dinner and we can interact without all the detective posturing. Now, I was given a thousand dollars to say, 'Unless you get off The Joyce Case, your life will be like a coffin that's fallen from its hearse and flopped its corpse into the street.'" She checked her watch. "Now, if you don't mind, I have student loans to pay."

Trike and Max watched her leave. A second after she was gone, they both shook their heads.

"Posturing?" Trike muttered.

"No . . . questions, boss?" Max asked.

Trike shrugged. "You heard the dame, got student loans to pay. Besides, whoever is behind all this is an autoclave artiste. She'd have a key to the Midway, if she had anything."

Max pursed his lips. Furrowed his brow. "Autoclave . . . sterilized information. Key to the Midway . . . football bat. Need a phrase book with you."

"Second edition is due in the spring."

"Thoughts on the threat?"

"If one does not have the balls to get to Nausicaa, one is not capable of meaningful threats."

Max pursed his lips. Furrowed his brow. "No idea."

"Threats drawn from Oxen in the Sun, however, are to be heeded."

"What?"

"Strange. One might think Joyce himself sent these messages, given their shared reference universe with the sitting rooms, but doing so makes as much sense as sassing soldiers outside brothels."

"What?"

"Forget it. Let's just get some Thai food."

"Sure thing, boss."

They went through the process of leaving the office.

"Will you call her?" Max asked.

"Like I need another seppuku-inducingly beautiful woman in my life."

"More than anything."

"Max, I don't pay you to be piercingly insightful about my emotional being."

"You pay me?"

"Not if you keep that up. But then again, you're the kinda guy who'd throw penny cakes to seagulls."

"What?"

"Forget about it. You get a van?" Trike transitioned.

"I got a van."

"I do not like that tone, Max."

"With no money ... you get what you get."

"I like that statement even less."

"It'll do the job."

"You are somehow making this worse, Max."

"You haven't seen it."

"I picked a hell of a week to quit smoking."

"Yep."

Max closed and locked the door behind him.

LIKE THE DARK WHEN YOU TURN ON THE LIGHT

Five masked robbers stormed into the city's largest bank. Firing guns into the ceiling. Shouting for everyone to get down on the ground. Shouting over the screaming and panicking that they were not playing around. Four of the robbers grabbed the four tellers. The fifth made the manager open the vault and head for the big bills.

For 180 seconds he pressed his gun right at the top of the manager's spine. Whispered about wife and kids. Encouraged the manager to stuff fistfuls of hundred-dollar bills into a bag. On second number 180, the robber coldcocked the manager. A fistful of bills still filling his fist.

Ten seconds later, the four tellers got the same good night.

With the employees napping, the five robbers stalked back into the lobby. They stomped around the people lying on the ground. Shouting about nobody moving and everybody behaving and let's not have any heroes and other robber nonsense.

Sirens approached.

One by one the robbers slunk to the back of the bank. When 210 seconds had elapsed, there was only one voice shouting. Tires screeched in the parking lot. The voice shouted, "You there, you get down, I said get down." Someone got down.

The cops bullhorned at the bank. About coming out with your hands up and surrendering peacefully and having the bank surrounded and other cop nonsense. No response. Nothing cops hate more than being ignored. They stormed in.

The robbers were gone. Like the dark when you turn on the light. The only people in the bank were unconscious or kissing carpet. A gun-drawn squadron of cops surrounded by silence is a Kraken of anxiety. The robbers vanished with $978,000.

The second-largest manhunt in the history of the state was launched. Three weeks later, two of the robbers were arrested at the state line. They had to tell somebody the setup. It was just so damn clever.

You see, it all came together when the oldest brother learned how to throw his voice. And boy, could he chuck that thing. You got him in a place that echoed, like a bank lobby, and it was like someone was shouting at you from across the room. The youngest's job as janitor of the bank became the best thing that ever happened to them.

They filled money bags on an exact schedule based on average police response time. When the bag-filling time was up, they walked quickly around the people lying down so no one could keep track of their feet. While the other four made their way to the back, the oldest kept up the shouting. When the others were gone, he threw his shout one more time and, mask and gun passed off, proned himself like everyone else. He walked right out the front door after the police secured the bank. Even gave a statement.

The other four went to the janitor's closet in back. It had a big drain for dumping out mopping water. They removed the grate.

Eighty years ago, the Jameson brothers had pulled off the biggest bank heist in city history by escaping through a janitor's drain into the sewers.

For hours, Lola only found places on the Internet where pictures of sewer maps should have been, but weren't. She drank three pots of tea. She ate four strips of fruit leather and a bag of trail mix. Three times she took quick jogs around the block. Twice she watched ten minutes of TV, just to look at a different screen. She took alarming comfort when Dig Safe matched what the Water Department had told her.

But data are the weeds of society. You can never kill all of them, and never everywhere.

On the fourteenth search return page of the sixth keyword permutation, Lola found The Jameson Brothers' Bank Heist.

There were dozens of websites devoted to the robbery and manhunt. None had pictures or descriptions of the sewers, concerning themselves with guns, acoustics, and speculations, but nearly all identified *Temporary Moles: The Jameson Brothers' Bank Heist* by Roger Casement as the definitive work. Written eight years after the heist, it included eyewitness testimony, police reports, and complete maps of the city's sewer system.

According to the library's online database, as of 11:57 p.m., two copies were available.

At 8:59 the next morning, Lola strode through the freshly unlocked door of the public library.

"He-hello," the librarian said, not making eye contact as she blazed past him.

"Hello, Mr. Seaman," she said, noticing his wilted posture. "Wonderful day," she offered as she climbed the stairs.

Lola double-checked the Dewey number she'd written down. Both copies of the book were exactly where they were supposed to be.

"Now, that is what I am talking about," Lola said, pulling a copy down.

She flipped right to the plates where the maps would be. They were blank. She flipped around the rest of the book. All the pages were blank. She set that copy down and grabbed the other one. It was blank.

"What the fuck," Lola muttered out loud.

Then she thought, "If I wanted to make sure nobody found the information in a particular book, I would just check it out. Or steal it. That would be even better. Or, actually, the best way to get rid of these would be to just shelve them in slightly the wrong spot. Put them in fiction, they might stick out, but just move them to a different history section, and they'd be impossible to find for anybody actively looking for them. But even if I couldn't find them, I could probably still find a used copy somewhere."

Lola held the blank book in one hand and put the other fist on her hip. "But I can still find a used copy somewhere," she continued thinking. "Checking out, stealing, re-shelving, or replacing with blanks all lead to the same subsequent action, so why go through the effort of making them, putting the Dewey sticker on them, and sneaking them in? A ton of extra effort for no tangible benefit. Really fucking weird. Should take a copy to show Trike."

Lola brought both books down to the desk. The librarian looked away as she approached.

"Mr. Seaman, these books are blank," she said.

Mr. Seaman looked at his hands. His fingers drummed on the desk. His feet fidgeted under it. "Were they in the right location?" he asked.

"Yes."

"Were the indicated number of copies there?"

"Yes."

He cleared his throat. "Then I have met my, um, uh, my, ah, the full requirements of my position."

"What?"

He focused on a point over Lola's shoulder. "As a librarian, a, um, systemic maintenance person, my responsibility is to ensure the proper functioning of the library system, which is composed, in its entirety, of the indicated number of copies of the book in the proper location."

"Why are you talking like that?"

"I cannot be held responsible for the, um, content of said books as such con-considerations fall outside the functioning of the system I oversee. Their content is only relevant in initially establishing their proper location."

"Aren't you concerned that someone was tampering with your books?"

"Yes. Um. Yes. This is clearly a sumptuous and stagnant, uh, exaggeration of murder, and steps will certainly be taken. Now, if you'll excuse me, I am locked in a death feud with entropy and cannot be further detained."

He turned his back on her. Frantically scanned in returned books.

Lola leaned forward and put her hands on the desk.

"I can see you're nervous, Mr. Seaman, that you have been asked to do something you are not comfortable doing," Lola said in a precise tone her father taught her. "I'm not going to pursue this matter, because I know that whatever bribe you received to look the other way while the books were switched, and to recite that script when the switch was discovered, was probably in the form of an anonymous donation to the library. It's hard for me to be mad about that. It's hard for me to be mad at a librarian at all."

She stood up. Slid one of the books across the desk. Mr. Seaman had not turned.

"But this could change," Lola continued, "and I might find myself required to get mad at a librarian. If I do, that donation will not remain anonymous and your involvement will not remain a secret. Now, I would like to check out this blank book."

Mr. Seaman slowly turned around. Started to say something. Stopped himself. Checked the book out to Lola.

THE HARE COURSES THE DOG

Trike felt as though he had fallen through a trapdoor, the ultimate absurdity; pantomimic, bathetic, grotesque. An alteration in strategy was required. Since the actions of the intellect are profoundly influenced by the state of the body, and the content and trajectory of thought is guided, if not determined, by the words that compose it, Trike, still in bed, resolved to change both his typical detecting bodily orientation and lexicon. He would lie in bed all day and channel his own synthetic Alan Grant.

His non-emergency-case-update phone beeped a text from Max. He prospected it from the layers on the floor. "Van ready," it read.

Trike texted back, "At home, channeling the force majeur in being. Consult."

"The problem," he spoke, dropping the phone, "is that The Joyce Case is a warped Centre Pompidou, in which all the context has been perverted. The museumgoer must seek meaning in opposition to the construction of the galleries themselves. What I need . . ." Trike paused while the appropriate reference arrived, "is something earnest and statistical. Tsetse flies, or calories, or sex behavior."

His front door opened. Someone strode resolutely through the house. The length and lightness of the stride told him a laden Lola lugged substantiated evidence toward his inspection.

"In the bedroom," he shouted, "being arch about vice."

Lola graced into the room. She unslung her backpack as an actress might gesture offstage.

"Ah," Trike said, gaze fixed on the ceiling, "at last, sewer maps. An avenue of further investigation will be opened or closed."

"Actually," Lola said, "the book is blank from cover to cover. There were two copies of this at the library and both were blank."

"Both books blank?"

"Yep."

"It's a technique from which some works of literature would greatly benefit. They would sit on shelves assuring everyone of the progress of literate society, while containing none of the twaddle that so easily dazzles contemporaries."

"Sure. Whatever. And Mr. Seaman was bribed to recite a script for when the books were discovered. Which is even weirder than I thought at first, because there was no reason to involve him at all."

"Mr. Seaman recited a script?" Trike asked.

"Better than you'd expect," Lola answered.

"So, at this point in the investigation into the sewers, either Arthur continues his aggressively passive-aggressive assault on your ability to succeed or steps were taken at the Hall of Records, you were followed by someone remarkably able to mace themselves, the Water Department is newly secretive, and now books purported to contain sewer maps have been replaced with blank replicas. I dare say, it is a slightly odd state of affairs."

"Trike," Lola said out of patience with the sober reception to her broadside, "this is a breakthrough. This tells us specifically that whoever did this doesn't want us to know about the sewers, which tells me, the sewers are exactly where we need to look."

Trike considered quietly for 223 seconds. There were no sparrows to talk today. Only the soft sound of rain against the window, again.

He said, "The sewers are of no consequence in this martial moment."

"So what is of consequence in this martial moment?" Lola asked. Each word a sharpened shiv.

In response, Trike delivered a soliloquy Lola knew was more productive than communicative, designed to impart energy to his intellect, rather than a message to his listener.

"Every human action, from the grandest to the most mundane, produces signal and noise, broadcasting both its intentions and unintentional, irrelevant, and random data. When you bring lilacs to a friend convalescing in the hospital, you express emotions of comfort and your opinions about the comforting properties of lilacs. Sometimes the signal-to-noise ratio of a specific action is of vital importance and sometimes it is just a fact of interaction, but there are two realms of human activity that have quite different relationships with their own signal and noise, both of which, you, Lola, have intimate knowledge of.

"Crime and art. Though art is not at issue here, it should be noted in this consideration that, unlike perhaps any other human action, in art, sometimes the noise is as important or even more important than the signal. It is not a specific idea or emotion or expression that gives a work of art its ability to endure across cultures and generations, but the meaning others find in the noise that co-exists with the signal. Artists, you might say, work in the signal, but live in the noise. In contrast, the fundamental goal of the criminal is to produce neither signal nor noise. A crime is perfect when no one knows it occurred. In general practice, this means doing as little as possible. If one lock could be picked instead of two, the criminal will choose the course of action in which only one lock is picked.

"And yet, here, with the sewers, the criminals are broadcasting. Of course, they would have wanted to obscure the fact that they used the sewers if they did, but this radical expression of data does nothing to any potential evidence surrounding that potential fact. If they acted on information, it would be on the information in the basement, which we are not allowed to see anyway."

Trike laced his fingers behind his head. "Fuck the sewers. Don't need them."

He finally looked at Lola. "Don't look so astonished," he said with a smirk, "it isn't tactful."

"I'm not really sure how I should look."

Trike turned back to the ceiling. "That is not my department at the Yard. However, my department at the Yard would like to know more about the real-estate angle."

"The real-estate angle?"

"If I know anything about real estate, and as with most things, I do, it's that real-estate transactions require the kind of attention to detail that often leads to believing that the CIA uses dust to record your dreams."

"You really know how to sell a project."

"Legitimate real-estate transactions are already vastly complex, and any way one might try to obscure such a transaction would only increase that complexity. With that increase in complexity comes an increase in the potential for a mistake."

"Should I look for a particular mistake?" Lola asked.

"No. Assume that everything about what you find will be utterly, profoundly, horrifyingly weird, but be aware of anything that is weird in a different way from the newly normalized weirdness of the entire endeavor."

"And if I don't see anything like that?"

"Then I look forward to one of your terrifying accordion folders of absence. You have a written report for the sewers?"

"A list of all the places that maps should have been but weren't. It's in the book."

"Excellent. Good luck on your newest quest," Trike said.

"What are you going to do?"

"Continue apace," Trike replied.

"You're going to lie in bed all day. While we lose another fifty thousand dollars." Poison-tipped shivs.

"That is an ocular-centric description of the observed

phenomena, but, in truth, I will be engaged in the most heroic of intellectual endeavors."

"And that would be?"

"Discovering what is known but not yet articulated in languaged thought."

"That's heroic?"

"It's got to be a real doozy to be unlanguaged in my brain."

Lola nodded at the point.

"Okay, then," she said, "I'll get in touch with you if I find anything urgent. Otherwise, I'll drop the feared folder at the office."

"Sounds like a plan. You are welcome to augment it with a preceding passage of prone-with-Trike time."

Lola slapped her forehead. Her transcendental poise. Like a queen. Like a nun. Like a head nurse. "With all the practice and that big fucking brain, you are still terrible at hitting on me."

"That is a defensible conclusion."

"Good luck with your heroic endeavors."

"And good luck to you, Lola."

Lola left. A lasting lacuna.

The substance of intuition is the unconscious, not the unconscious of drives, demons, hauntings, and past lives, but the utilitarian unconscious of data storage. "Stored" and "silent," however, are not equivalent. The stored data can whisper, imparting vague sense, atmosphere, and impression. The data give us, in the expressive parlance of American detective vernacular, a hunch. For Trike, however, most of that unconscious information was conscious, if sometimes tedious to retrieve. But most is not all. Hunches then, he still had, but drawn from such esoteric and obscure sources as to be violent affronts to the functions of reason.

In searching for his hunch, itself a paradox, Trike analyzed the character of Joyce's face. The face, when properly observed, is a font of intuitive data. What hunch lurked in Joyce's face?

The bench or the dock?

Neither. Joyce had the face of a middle manager with a good

sense of humor. A high school math teacher just this side of inspirational. An excellent customer-service rep.

Max showed up forty minutes later.

"Max," Trike said while Max walked through the hallway, "judging by Joyce's face, would you put him on the bench, or on the dock?"

"What are you talking about?"

"You've seen the portrait of Joyce or a representation thereof?"

"Yeah."

"If you knew he was involved in a trial and had to guess whether he was the judge or the defendant, would you put him on the bench or on the dock?"

"Ah. I would put him ... on a diet," Max replied.

"Yeah. That's pretty much what I came up with. Probably afraid of dogs. Which is something. I guess."

"Is this the ... consultation, boss?"

"As you well know, Max, detecting is a process of drama removal. One arrives at the drama of a blood-soaked carpet in the study and in the end it is all a matter of estate taxes. The story is only told in grand sweeps of notable action once journalists, novelists, and screenwriters claim it, for it actually resides in an advertisement in the paper, the sale of a house, and the price of a ring. The detective is distinguished by the ability to see past the drama to the grocery receipts and credit-card bills.

"However, up to this point, we have only found ghosts of those bills, receipts, and ads. We have been left with evidence of their creation, but not with the things themselves. We are finding as much drama in the banal as in the blood. The hare is coursing the dog. I have now cast some hope in Lola being able to find what we seek in the real-estate transaction of the house. But ... to reiterate, the real history is written in forms not meant as history."

"You're nervous about the case," Max said.

"What generates that conclusion?"

"You're ... referencing something."

"I don't think references work for me the same way they do for everyone else."

"I'll add that to the list."

"Pull my desk chair over, Max. Consult in comfort."

Max dragged the chair through Trike's domestic detritus. He sat down with the air of an Englishman sitting down to his port after the women have left the table.

"Lola take the maps?" Max asked, seeing no maps.

"Hall of Records didn't have them, Water Department wouldn't let her look at them, books purported to contain them were blank, and pictures of them have been removed from the Internet."

"Wow."

"Indeed."

"So they must have used the sewers."

"The sewers are a red herring."

The look on Max's face was audible in the next room.

Trike responded. "The initial hope was that an investigation of the sewers would reveal an extraordinary action, such as digging a tunnel, and though we did find an extraordinary action, it is in relation only to the information about the sewers. One would not be imprudent in concluding that the extraordinary action taken on the information implies extraordinary action taken in the sewers themselves, but that fact ensures that it does not do what it would not be imprudent to assume it does do. The very extraordinariness of the information efforts imply an act of misdirection.

"And once we factor in what a sewer investigation would consist of, it is almost certain they want us in the sewers. With no other data besides a strong suspicion that something happened, we would wander around for who knows how long, never certain whether or not we have found what we sought. Of course, one could begin the absurd process of reasoning sometimes thrust upon even and odd, and conclude that this direct implication was designed to keep us from inspecting the sewers by leading us to exactly what I have concluded, but it would have been much easier to do nothing to the information at all. No, Max, although you are more than welcome to spend whatever free time you possess scouring the sewers in the hopes of discovering evidence, I shall not endorse it as an official investigation strategy."

Max sighed. "What's next, boss?"

"In the distant future, even the particles of dust born from our decayed bodies will be dispersed into the essential nothing at the end of all things. In the immediate future, you're going to have to listen to me talk through some of what's going on in my head to ensure that it makes sense to someone who cannot concurrently process multiple systems of analysis."

"Cohesive narrative test. Ready."

"I wish it were the cohesive narrative test. This is more a realm-of-thought test."

"Realm-of-thought test. Ready," Max said.

"From Joyce's face, we both concluded he would be neither a destroyer of innocence and synonym for villainy, nor an upholder of justice with Agincourt for glory and the stake for zeal, and though, since most crime is committed by ordinary people stuck in situations they were not prepared to face, an absence of extreme character is usually no real limitation in an investigation, in this case, the extraordinariness of the crime strongly implies an extraordinary criminal. What is most troubling to me about the conjunction of this face and this crime is that, perhaps above all else, Joyce does not look like a person in charge, and whatever is happening, somebody needs to be in charge.

"Disappearing maps from the Hall of Records requires a certain kind of effort, one that is not necessarily difficult, but is distinctly different from the kind of effort required to bribe a librarian, write a script, and replace substantive books with blank books, an effort also distinct from the kind of tedious, technical, and time-consuming effort needed to cull images from the Internet. And if you have the appropriate surname or know someone who does, manipulating Water Department policy might be easy, but it does require a different set of resources from what we have previously considered. There is nothing particularly challenging about incorporating a business if one knows how to do it or can pay a lawyer who does, and once incorporated there are simply no meaningful barriers preventing it from purchasing property, but, again, we have traveled into a different realm of skills and resources. Add to that the ability to conceal facts of identity from Lola and you get evidence of a powerful, efficient, well-organized effort."

"But ... no mob," Max said.

"You, sir, are shoveling coal on my train of thought. We might still hold out hope that the effort in question is organized by the FBI, but everything you've discovered suggests the contrary. Another force is at work here."

"Big sum-up, boss?"

Trike was quiet for a second. He shot up to sitting and shouted, "But Thomas More was Henry the Eighth!"

Max waited for the translation to supply itself.

It took a minute.

"This is not an issue of an organizing entity, but an organizing principle," Trike translated.

"Need more, boss."

"The effort we have seen thus far has not been following a strict set of instructions laid out by a supreme executive, but an organizing principle. The underlings were not instructed to do specific things, but a specific type of thing."

"Which is?"

"Remove or obscure the world of information around Joyce, no matter the implication and whether it has a connection to the crime or not."

"Because?"

Trike slumped back to prone, like a thrown coat that caught the hook for a second.

"Given how pointless the effort is, I don't know."

"So?"

"So, we'll start the stakeout tonight."

"Okay."

Max pushed himself up from the chair and started to leave.

"Just keep one thing in mind, Max."

"What?"

"Taps on hospital doors are not apt to be tentative."

"What?"

"Joyce is a tragic figure, but not tragic in ways that popular belief understands tragedy. We'll have to listen for that tentative tap that should not be tentative."

"Okay, boss."

"I'll meet you at the office for the stakeout. We start at eight p.m."

"See you then, boss."

THE FONT OF INTUITION

One would not turn away from direct contact, certainly not with the nervousness that strong personalities will induce. Nor would one be compelled to maintain direct contact.

Though eyes cannot communicate genre of thought, they can imply the vigor of thought. The brain behind these eyes looks to be exerting itself to remember if there is a new episode or a rerun of its favorite show on tonight. Perhaps the difficult decision of whether to stop for gas now or later.

There is a relaxation of the muscles around a killer's eyes as though a moral freedom has led to a distribution of unconscious relaxation. Joyce does not have that relaxation.

Three-quarters open, looking slightly to the viewer's right, displaying relaxed passivity. Not uncommon in those who have made enough money to not give a leaking shit about anything or anyone else on the planet.

Fair guesses: Never pointed a gun at someone, never had a gun pointed at him, can ignore being looked down upon, enjoys charitable events where children open presents he paid for, assumes he is an outstanding parallel parker, chuckles with the phrase "big-boned," wears reading glasses, ruefully indulged his mother's whims, sweet tooth, never exercises, cares for but does not sculpt his eyebrows, tennis fan ...

Distortion of character caused by the isolation of consideration? Attention can both discover and generate data.

Unfair guesses: Never punched or been punched, frets over balancing his checkbook if he hasn't done it in a few days, only reads the stocks and the classifieds in his morning paper, orders the same thing every time at his favorite restaurants, obsesses over the thermostat, doesn't understand why people keep pets, is one of the thoughtless millions whose favorite book is *To Kill a Mockingbird* for the wrong reasons ...

Doesn't roll his eyes much. Only compliment in this consideration.

Not interested in the rewards that come from efforts demanding ample amounts of responsibility, as though he just wants to successfully follow directions and earn what he thinks is fair if he does so. Someone who wanted to get As in school, but didn't really care about learning.

Never thinks he can make the yellow light.

Dabbled in bird-watching to impress a foreign bachelor.

Probably afraid of dogs.

Might be an excellent liar. There are always ways to tell, but it appears as though he can control at least a fair amount of the outward signs of dishonesty; primarily, he might be able to keep his eyes steady.

Eyes about to say, "Oh well. Who wants to go to IHOP?"

Laugh lines like he often doesn't get the joke.

Eyes for Rembrandt or Freud, a fleshiness like they had their own stomachs.

•

"There is a road from the eye to the heart that does not go through the intellect."

"The eyes, like sentinels, occupy the highest place in the body."

 "The eyes indicate the antiquity of the soul."

"The eyes have one language everywhere."

"A wanton eye is a messenger of an unchaste heart."

"The eye sees only what the mind is prepared to comprehend."

"The eye speaks with an eloquence and truthfulness surpassing speech. It is the window out of which the winged thoughts often fly unwittingly. It is the tiny magic mirror on whose crystal surface the moods of feeling fitfully play, like the sunlight and shadow on a still stream."

"The eyes of the soul of the multitudes are unable to endure the vision of the divine."

"In a real estate man's eye, the most expensive part of the city is where he has a house to sell."

"It is the eyes of other people that ruin us. If I were blind I would want neither fine clothes, fine houses or fine furniture."

"Why has not man a microscopic eye? For the plain reason that man is not a fly."

"An animal will always look for a person's intentions by looking them right in the eyes."

"One's eyes are what one is, one's mouth is what one becomes."

"For as the eyes of bats are to the blaze of day, so is the reason in our soul to the things which are by nature most evident of all."

"Wicked thoughts and worthless efforts gradually set their mark on the face, especially the eyes."

"Anyone who has ever looked into the glazed eyes of a soldier dying on the battlefield will think hard before starting a war."

"Fear has many eyes and can see things underground."

Never been broken.

Wide nostrils plus some indication of internal swelling. Maybe indication of manageable allergies after all.

Background to the face unless you're really looking at it.

Obesity blends its slope into the cheeks.

Like a diagonal line used in the composition of a painting; nose moves the eye away from it to other parts of the face.

Seems like it would be a joy to punch. All that fat and cartilage. Like somebody stuffed a bunch of marshmallows into a little bag and taped it to his face. Enough give to keep your knuckles as safe as they can be while punching someone in the nose, but you'd still hear the satisfying sound of the break.

If he weren't so fat this nose would get him punched twice a year.

Reads with the book/magazine held close to his face.

•

"A large nose is in fact the sign of an affable man, good, courteous, witty, liberal, courageous, such as I am."

"A thousand woodpeckers flew in through the window and settled themselves on Pinocchio's nose."

"Ambition may be defined as the willingness to receive any number of hits on the nose."

"He that has a great nose, thinks everybody is speaking of it."

"If you had a face like mine, you'd punch me right on the nose, and I'm just the fella to do it."

"My nose itched, and I knew I should drink wine or kiss a fool."

Perceived kindliness comes directly from the chin. It is the shape of the chin that suggests joviality.

Gesture free; never stroked, scratched, or cupped in thought or agitation. To him, just that point in the middle of his jaw.

Chins only discussed when hyperbolic, and then almost always only in the context of the jaw in total, and then generally only when they complete a strong, square one.

One cannot consider a fat man's jaw. It is like thinking about a cow's thighs.

Fat since birth, a bodily state like the color of his eyes.

Like the nose, never been struck with real purpose or emotion.

Not Churchill. Not Taft either. Not even late Henry VIII. Almost George III if George were a little fatter and a little less inclined toward a beard. Functionary. It's the chin of a functionary. Perfect for cradling a phone while taking a message.

Will masquerade as Santa Claus before he dies, if he has not already and if nothing more dramatic gets in the way.

"A dimple on the chin, the devil within."

Perhaps the cheeks contain the ambiguity one feels in the total face. Two shiny baseballs just sitting there, gleaming in a frantic and desperate commitment to the principles of mediocrity, a passionate obsession without the violence of either emotion, with putting two cars in the garage and two kids through good colleges.

Tennis balls covered by slabs of bacon.

Know 74 people with comparable cheeks and don't give a fuck about a single one of them.

I see the fat monk of medieval satire, the well-fed joviality mixed with manageable guilt mixed with more than a pinch of just-don't-give-a-fuck. In a way, there was no greater villain, for the basics of villainy were coupled with a profound bastardizing of the fundamental moral system of the era.

Space holders of the face. Why there are so few quotes about them.

Cheeks like William Eustace, historian at the BM. Died of a heart attack, probably on his way home from a hard day's work to tell his wife how much he loved her.

A fat man married to a thin woman in a way that neither one noticed the disparity. If Joyce could ever marry.

They imply a man who detests action.

Smooth, wrinkle-free, implying a care for the skin and appearance that is diligent, but not indulgent. Unscented lotions only.

•

"Let age, not envy, draw wrinkles on thy cheeks."

"One bites into the brass mouthpiece of his wooden cudgel, and the other blows his cheeks out on a French horn. Do you call that Art?"

The first place one would look to avoid or break eye contact.

Dishonest indicator of age; Joyce has the forehead of a man seven years younger.

A life with eyebrows little raised and brow rarely furrowed. Little wonder, surprise, or consternation.

Disregard knowledge of phrenology.

Like so much the contours and visible textures imply an average life free of the problems that would keep a man awake for a week straight, but reasonably filled with the problems that would keep a man awake for a night. Rarely rubbed. Seldom slapped. Allowed to age lightly until it eventually dies.

Beware the face kept free from gestures of the hands, because the hands must be doing something else.

No breaking, plates, scars, or other evidence of urgent care.

Reverse Richard III? Face so ordinary he had to be extraordinary.

Of course, Richard III didn't have Richard III syndrome. Reverse Marty McSorley. Yeah.

Once spent the night resting on a slick yet sticky bar, in his youth, in New Orleans.

●

"High heels were invented by a woman who had been kissed on the forehead."

"If the best man's faults were written on the forehead, he would draw his hat over his eyes."

"The Creator has not thought it proper to mark those in the forehead who are of stuff to make good generals. We are first, therefore, to seek them blindfold, and then let them learn the trade at the expense of great losses."

HIS RIGHTEOUS SENTENCE

Lola and Max stood by an open manhole. They double-checked the batteries in their headlamps. Went over their hand signals. Secured weapons. Put on gloves.

Lola wore an old pair of wind pants over spandex, tucked into wellies, and an old long-sleeved T-shirt over a quick-dry running shirt. And her knife. Her hair was in a ponytail and her headlamp was on over a sweatband.

Max wore wickaway hiking pants tucked into a pair of hunter-green waders. The pants had the right pocket cut out, to allow access to his gun, which was in a holster under the pants. He wore an old long-sleeved T-shirt and an undershirt. As sweat started to drip down his forehead and collect along the edge of the headlamp's band, he wished he'd brought a sweatband as well. Max wondered if Lola learned the trick camping, or if it was just another one of those things she figured out, or somehow always knew.

Lola spotted the bead of sweat, ran back to the car, and returned with an extra band from her bag.

"Always prepared," Max said.

"Nah, just completely forgot I'd put one in when I packed last night. But if you ever go all Dr. Watson on us, make sure to write that I was prepared."

"Deal."

Lola descended first, landing lightly from the last rung of the ladder onto the moist masonry below. Max followed, folding his shoulders slightly to fit down the hole.

Max pulled a street map out of his pocket. Using the streets above, they highlighted in blue an approximate route to the Joyce House. It wouldn't be exact, but it would give them a sense of when to look for lefts and rights. Max took a yellow highlighter out of his pocket. Uncapped it and set it down on the map on their spot.

"Left," he said. "I'll keep track . . . to scale."

Lola nodded. "Okay. And we're looking for anything. Any suggestion Joyce went through here, or used the sewers at all. They're hiding something, Max. You don't make that much information go away for nothing."

Max nodded.

After a few turns they reached an intersection that should have been almost directly below the Joyce House. Five tunnels met in a large higher-ceilinged room. There were dry gullies running down the middle of each tunnel. Along one wall, a rusted metal ladder led to an exit that had been paved over. Other than that, a big, boring concrete room. Just like every room and every tunnel in just about every active sewer system in the world; boring but for the occasional rat larger than one thought evolution allowed or object one assumed to be unflushable. People tend to make things interesting to people and when sewage flows through sewers people spend very little time in them. But sometimes the sewage is stopped. Changes in demographics, topography, other construction projects. Sewers dry up into limited-access tunnels. People find them. They get interesting.

"We've already been a little lucky," Lola said as they entered the intersection.

"Why?"

"It doesn't look like the Water Department uses this section anymore."

"True," Max said.

Max confirmed on the map that they were as close to beneath the Joyce House as they could definitively get.

"Area sweep," Lola said.

They stood shoulder-to-shoulder, with their headlamps angled at the ground, then slowly moved their beams along the space in front of them and up the wall, all the way to the ceiling directly above them. Then Lola turned a degree to the right, Max to the left, and they repeated the gesture.

At 168 degrees, Max illuminated a fading red arrow pointing to what had become his right.

"Huh," he said.

Lola looked. "An arrow? Looks old."

"In this climate . . . age is difficult to determine," Max said.

"Seems a little, I don't know, silly to follow an arrow."

"In the sewers . . . you're against silly," Max said with a sly smile.

"Fair enough. You stay. I'll go."

"Maintain visual contact. Turns out we don't have sewer maps."

"I forgot how sarcastic you are in the field."

"Been a while . . . hasn't it?"

"We'll ask Trike. He'll tell us the day and the hour."

The last time they were in the field was two years, four months, three days, and one hour earlier. It was during The Case of the Riverside Gang, and Trike had sent them out to patrol one of the bridges while he followed a lead he correctly thought would connect the roving gang of muggers and assaulters with a local politician looking to use the crime spree as leverage in the upcoming mayoral and sheriff elections.

They'd been out for four hours and were discussing the implications of Trike's theory for the general political environment when they heard a woman scream. It was on the other side of the river and they were out of their hiding spots and running across the bridge before the screamer needed to catch her breath.

When you hear one woman scream you expect a range of scenarios. Mugging. Assault. Attempted rape. You expect a struggle with some version of violence between a woman and at least one man. A simple situation for two professionals to handle. Already halfway across the bridge, Max and Lola saw a very complex situation. Three men, two women, at least two guns, and a backpack in the middle, most likely containing either drugs or guns. Not a one-woman-one-scream situation, and not the kind of thing two professionals rushing in expect to handle. Unless they got creative.

"Follow my lead," Lola whispered at Max once the severity of the situation became clear.

She took off in front of him and began shouting for help. Max shouted, "Come back here, you bitch," once he figured out the strategy. Everyone in the group looked at the pursuit approaching them. They were confused. Unnerved. Assaults weren't supposed to run into drug deals. When Lola reached them, she transitioned her wild, shouting running into a series of rolls and throws that left both guns in her hands and everyone else on the ground. Max arrived and called the police while Lola covered the stunned group.

Lola followed the red arrow, moving one step at a time, swinging the beam of her headlamp in a full circle in front of her before taking the next step. She found a second arrow pointing in the same direction. After a shouted conversation, Max met her at the new arrow, highlighting the route on the map.

The subsequent arrow gave them a right turn.

"Lo," Max said at that arrow, "this might be what Trike warned us about."

"Following mysterious arrows?"

"No. He'd ... understand the arrows. It's all the time ... with no direction."

"We've been here less than an hour. Look, if you think we should conserve our time here, let's do this. We'll give the arrows another half an hour and if we don't find anything, we'll go back to the spot near the Joyce House, finish our full investigation of that, and call it."

"Agreed."

One arrow.

Two arrows.

Sometimes it's enough to know misdirection is possible. Once you think about the possible interpretations of a series of red arrows and how the action of interpretation of a series of red arrows can be incorporated in their intention, consideration quickly devolves into the pantomime of logic used in Rock, Paper, Scissors. The key is keeping problems from becoming a matter of concluding that your opponent is about to throw Rock.

Lola and Max found something after the third arrow.

It was a round wooden object, about two feet high and two feet in diameter, slightly tapered at the top with white lines in triangles centered by white stars. A headlamp sweep revealed three more identical objects. Then they found three yard-long, two-by-four blocks painted in the same color scheme. Lola took a picture of each with her phone, adding a caption describing the object's location.

"I feel like I've seen things like this before, Max. How about you?"

"Familiar? Yes. Relevant to escape? Not sure."

"But think about the sitting rooms. Joyce sculpts his environment. Even if these things aren't directly involved in the escape, they still could be part of one of his settings."

"That listens," Max said. "Let's see what else we can find."

They found a chest of brightly colored, badly decayed fabrics. Lola laid out and photographed each fragment. Individually considered, it was clear they were clothes or costumes before the decay. Max examined the chest itself and found nothing.

"Same as those other things," Lola said, replacing the fabrics.

"Familiar?"

"Yeah."

"From a case?"

"No, not from a case. From, I don't know, life."

They heard voices. A hushed conversation. A look and a hand

signal established their strategy. Lola took point, pressed against the wall with her headlamp turned off. Max was behind her, gun drawn, headlamp taken off but still lit and pointed straight down to provide necessary ambient light.

As a former FBI field and deep-cover agent, Max initially assumed he'd take point in all dangerous situations. After Trike dispatched Gustav Mace's hit squad, in thirty-four seconds, alone, hungover, Max figured he could do worse than cover the young buck.

Max learned that Lola took point in one of the most terrifying minutes of his life. He and Lola were out in the field for only their second time together, staking out a chop shop, looking for the remains of a car that was stolen with a very special suitcase in the trunk. Max quickly counted the armed guards. Eight. Way more than the place normally had. With hand signals he told Lola he was going to text Trike the info and they were going to bail. She nodded.

Max never really got a handle on the whole texting thing. Stubby fingers made his typing inaccurate. And then he'd get impatient, always hitting the number one time too many so he had to go all the way around again to get back to the right letter. And even then he had typos. And when you're sending code, typos are a real pain in the ass. Max finally sent the message out.

When he looked up there were only five guards in front of the chop shop. And they were all looking out his way. He'd lost track while he was texting. And three guards were about to flank them. He cursed under his breath and turned. Lola was nowhere to be seen. A bolt of terror shot through Max's being. He'd never lost anybody in the field before and here he was about to lose a kid on her second trip out because he couldn't get his fat fingers to text fast enough.

Max assessed the situation. He began his strategic fallback, hoping Lola had enough common sense to get out of Dodge. He didn't see Lola until he'd made it all the way back to their car, a mounting dread like he'd never felt before in every step he took. She was calmly waiting for him, the three guards unconscious and tied up just out of sight of the street. Then it all made sense.

Before she could offer an explanation, Max said, "Lola Lenore, as in Roderick Lenore?"

"Yep. He's my dad."

All the explanation Max needed. Lola took point from then on.

Perpendicular firelight revealed an upcoming intersection in the sewers. They heard a group of at least three men, fifty feet away, to the left. There was urgency in their voices. Anxiety. Fear.

Another exchange of hand signals. Lola crouched and slid along the wall closer to the voices. Max stayed put so they wouldn't see his light. After listening for a moment, Lola returned and waved them back to their previous location.

"Some homeless guys," she said when they arrived.

"Sounded ... agitated," Max said with concern.

Lola shrugged. "They were kicked out of an abandoned warehouse a couple of days ago. They're worried about getting kicked out of here too. One of them might have a warrant out on him, but I'm guessing they pretty much live their lives agitated."

"Question them ... with financial incentives?"

"They only got here two days ago."

Max nodded. "Back to the search, then."

"Yep."

Another arrow led them to a cluttered stretch of tunnel. There were three bureau-sized objects covered in mildewed sheets. Max pulled one sheet off in a dramatic gesture, imbuing the scene with more spores than gravitas. The object was a popcorn cart. The next, revealed with much less vigor, was labeled "PeaNuts." The third was a calliope.

"A circus," Lola said. "That's what this stuff is from. A circus."

Max nodded. "More stuff this way," he said.

The debris led them to a large, cluttered room. They found, in various stages of disintegration, disassembled trapezes, Indian clubs, longes and coils of rope, and a chambarrier, a Russian bar, and a unicycle, as well as stacks of wood and plywood, empty boxes, bolts of sturdy fabric, and jars of paint.

Four additional hallways radiated from the larger room. Max and Lola divided the hallways and investigated ten paces into each one before returning to the large room.

In her two hallways, Lola found a large metal makeup box, a podium, a whip, and a sturdy wooden chair. Five large metal hoops. Two padlocked steamer trunks. More clothes, ropes, and pieces of metal, wood, and masonry.

Finally, she found a clipboard. The metal clip was rusted. There was writing directly on the degrading board. Most of the letters had faded beyond definitive identification, but Lola was able to make out two words: "Bloom" and "Code."

Max found a top hat, a vintage bicycle, and a slapstick. Three pairs of old spectacles. The handsets of three very early telephones. A pair of clown shoes. A bullhorn. A long heavy metal chain. Strongman's weights. A wooden box with a slit in the top that might have been used to collect tickets. A whoopee cushion. The circus setting certainly gave the sewers a sculpted feel.

Max had seen sculpted environments before. Twice, deep cover brought him to drug-lord mansions. They were a cross between theme parks, strip clubs, and military bases. Radical expressions of lives lived at atypical volumes. Peg kangaroo. Interior waterfall. Masterpieces of art. Mechanical beds. Women arranged like furniture. Gold-plated video-game consoles. Halls of mirrors. The mansions were externalized ids; desperate expressions of life from men who knew they could be shot to death, not just any day, but any moment. A highly orchestrated series of *Ulysses* references was not an externalization of the id. Heaven help the PI, if a highly orchestrated series of *Ulysses* references was the externalization of an id.

"Max, I found something," Lola said when they reconvened.

"What?"

"Two steamer trunks in pretty decent condition, locked with padlocks, and this clipboard. It looks like it was labeled to hold the 'Bloom Code,'" she said, handing Max the clipboard.

Max took it and squinted at the letters. "Bloom Code?"

"Yeah. You can just see it there," Lola said, pointing, "Bloom is the main character in *Ulysses*."

"Looks old," Max said.

"Sure, but you said yourself that it's hard to determine the age of stuff down here because of the climate. Some of the circus stuff is definitely vintage, but who knows about everything else?"

"And two locked steamer trunks."

"Exactly. I don't think we've found anything indicating that Joyce escaped through here, but he was certainly arranging this stuff."

Max pondered the situation and its evidence, handing the clipboard back to Lola.

"Okay," he said, "You get pictures of the stuff in this room. I'll poke around the piles of material. After a break topside we'll return with bolt cutters and forensic equipment."

"Plan."

Lola went back through the room taking pictures of the various objects, the clipboard tucked under her arm, while Max poked around the piles of building material. He didn't see anything until he reached a stack of large plywood boards leaning against a wall.

"Huh," he said as he flipped through them. Before he could investigate what caught his eye, they heard voices again, this time coming from the direction of the Joyce House. They hid in one of the hallways, again with Lola at point, and Max a step behind, gun drawn, headlamp in hand pointed down.

Three men walked into the room with flashlights. They all wore the same kind of suit: a red one-piece jumpsuit made of a stiff plastic material that went over their shoes and zipped up the middle, with white stripes down the sides and arms, and cinched at the waist with white nylon belts.

They walked with the air of routine inspection, not reacting whatsoever to the objects around them. Their posture and uniforms said they were innocent sanitation inspectors. Their conversation said anything but.

"I don't get why we have to put on these getups every time we come down here."

"Come on, you know how the boss is. There's a system and goddammit he's going to follow that fucking system no matter what."

"Lay off with that already. It's his ass if we get seen down here without these outfits."

"How many times what we been down here and how many people we seen?"

"You never know. Jesus, the way you go on you'd think they sewed a spiked retysnitch in the crotch of yours."

"I just don't like doing things what I don't see the point for."

"You ain't been working your whole life?"

"Yeah, and I been asking questions about this shit the whole time."

"How did you end up in the sewers again?"

"Oh, that's real nice coming from a guy what spun back odometers for a living."

"Least I can keep my trap shut. You're worse than my wife after a spritzer."

"Oh, I'll give your—"

"Both of you can it. We're stuck down here until we get the shit done and your little slap fight ain't gettin' the shit done. You got it?"

"Got it."

"Got it."

"Jesus, I'm e-mailing that Dante guy. Tell him to add a few more circles on the outside for schmoes like me who bailed on library fines . . ." The group passed out of earshot.

Max and Lola waited a few moments to make sure they were gone. Then whispered out their next move.

"Looked suspicious, Max."

"Yep. Let me check one more thing. Then . . . topside."

"I'll keep a lookout."

"Plan."

Max and Lola quietly returned to the large room. Max went straight to the pile of plywood. Lola kept a lookout. After some frustrated finagling, Max pulled the board that caught his attention free from the others. He let out a low whistle. Turned around so Lola could see.

It was a red placard. Written, in fading white circus font, was the phrase, "His Righteous Sentence."

Lola let out a low whistle. "Looks like somebody's planning something, Max."

"It does."

Lola took a picture of the placard with her phone. They followed the arrows back to the intersection beneath the Joyce House and Max's highlighted route back to their manhole. When Max was halfway up the ladder his phone beeped a new voice mail.

"It's from Trike," he said as he finished ascending. Something heavy and shadowy fell to the pit of his stomach. He'd been working with Trike long enough to know that sometimes he called right after you got to the other side of the minefield to say thanks, but once he realized there were reading glasses in the glove compartment, the rest was elementary.

"From when?" Lola asked as she followed, already consoling herself that if Trike solved the case without input from their investigation of the sewer, at least there was a pot of anonymous reward gold at the end of that disappointment rainbow.

" 'Bout forty minutes ago."

They got back to the surface. Replaced the manhole cover. Packed up their lights and gloves and the clipboard. Lola checked her phone while Max listened to the message. She'd missed a call from Trike about the same time.

Max's face fell as a Mount Rushmore face would fall.

"What?" Lola said.

Max handed her the phone. "Press three to repeat."

Lola did.

Trike's voice mail said, "Maxish, just checking in. Nothing important. Though, I couldn't get Lola either, which is a bit strange. Makes me wonder ... Huh .... If for some reason you two, against my better judgment, decided to go tromping around the sewers, you might want to know there's some circus stuff down there left over from a failed movie studio. They were working on a kind of *Grapes of Wrath* set in the circus when they went out of business in 1952. The movie was called *His Righteous Sentence*, also taken from 'The Battle Hymn of the Republic' if you're keeping track, and it was directed by a man named Henry Bloomfeld. If you still feel like solving a mystery in the sewers, nobody seems to know how the circus stuff got there from where the studio was. The original theory was that the studio owner meant to hide the stuff from his creditors and then resell it on the sly, but who knows? A good place to start would be *The Daily Register* as they had someone looking into it a couple of years ago, but, since they never ran the story, I imagine they didn't come up with anything. The sanitation inspectors might have an idea about the logistics of the place. I know they still have to go through there even though it's only been used for emergency runoff since 1940, though I doubt they'd be in a good mood if you saw them; some kerfuffle over new sanitation suits or something. Anyway, give me a call and I'll catch you later. And remember to bring a sweatband to wear under your headlamp. Way more comfortable. See you tonight at the office for the stakeout. Trike signing out."

Lola deleted the message and handed the phone back to Max.

"I'm glad this was your phone, Max," she said in a tone that was dead inside.

"Why?"

"If it'd been my phone, I would have thrown it on the ground as hard as I could and I can't afford a new one."

"Passed it to you so the same impulse would ebb," Max said.

"You're a smart man, Max. A very smart man."

ON MARTY McSORLEY

When you have no money, you get what you get. It's worse when you're on a schedule. And it's not like there's a big two-ton windowless van market.

Max checked the classifieds. Went through Swap 'n' Sell. Searched the Internet. Made some calls. With no money, on a schedule, Max got a van.

A guy he knew told him about a heavy-metal band calling it quits. The bassist was looking to unload their tour van. He needed money for a sensible car and room in his garage. And his wife was getting on his case. It wasn't the easiest van to sell. Where would we be if these things never worked out?

So Trike and Max were parked two streets from the Joyce House, in a two-ton windowless van. Its base color was a vivid metallic blue. Painted on each side was a massive wizard, complete with a long white beard, flowing gray robes, crystal-ball-topped gnarled wooden staff, and tall pointy gray hat, bursting from a tsunami. Titling the scene, on each side, in lightning font, was the word "Thalassacreteo!" The exclamation point was, of course, a lightning bolt.

On a street where an idling UPS van would stand out, in a neighborhood that learned about windowless vans from *America's Most Wanted*, Trike and Max told themselves that a sorcerer-themed heavy-metal van was less suspicious than a plain one. Max let the police know they'd be there, just in case.

To set it up for the stakeout, Max removed the back set of seats. He bolted a set of modular bookshelves to the frame. Four scrounged TVs filled the shelves. Each one was connected by an adapter to a wireless remote-control camera covering one of the square house's sides. They bought the cameras years ago, with some of their small-business startup loan.

Trike and Max sat on sharp metal folding chairs that had been left in the office by the previous tenants. Empty espresso beverage cans and empty potato-stick tubes cluttered the floor around Trike's chair. Max's ring was composed of empty Frescas and beef jerky bags. Trike and Max had already dried out their eyes for twelve hours.

Hadn't worn out their jaws yet.

"That is my point," Max continued.

"That Marty McSorley is the professional-hockey manifestation of the Richard III effect, in that he was compelled by the peculiar gravity of Western culture to be as thuggish as his name sounds."

"No. What?"

Trike shrugged. "Idea appeared the instant you said his name. Figured I'd get it out. You know. Aneurism prevention."

"Because it'll be an aneurism."

"Better safe than keeling over while loosening bituminous sands into an over-capacity refinery."

"What?"

Trike popped a piece of nicotine gum in his mouth. "Never mind. Please continue. You were about to, against all odds, prove there is a logical reason for grown men to start punching each other in the face in the context of a professional sporting event."

"That's . . . an intentionally ridiculous phrase."

"I gotta say, Max, of the fifty-three phrases I considered, that one was the least inherently ridiculous. However, given your intellectual quality, I eagerly await your argument. If the edge of my seat weren't so sharp, I'd be right on it."

"Safety."

"Fuck you."

"Because of physics."

"Eat the spilled fuck of a wobbling donkey truck."

Max soldiered on. "Estimate how hard a strong man can punch another man. Factor in that they're on ice skates."

Trike looked away. Absentmindedly scratched a wide nostril. "All right."

"That should be the upper limit of things, given . . . equipment, defense, the like."

"Entered into the official record of this argument as the upper limit of things."

"Now, calculate how hard a player moving at roughly twenty miles per hour can hit another player with a shoulder or elbow."

"I did psi for punch."

"Do force . . . fewer variables."

"Right. Okay." Trike looked away again. Scratched the other nostril. Then he said, "Huh."

"See. The severe risk of injury—"

"You may continue if you are compelled, as I understand there is a level of satisfaction in sharing your own reformulations of existing knowledge, but I have discerned the entirety of your argument."

"Go ahead."

"To protect players from the catastrophic potential of certain kinds of hits, a defense mechanism evolved in which Marty McSorley—"

"There are other enforcers."

"He is the Yggdrasil from which they all sprang."

"Of course. He is . . . what you said."

Trike slapped a nicotine patch on his arm. "To continue, in order to discourage potentially catastrophic hits, Marty McSorley fought opponents he believed put his teammates in jeopardy through such hits."

"Well done. But there's more."

"Can't wait."

"The biggest reason for fighting in the last twenty years was . . . the holding penalty."

"The holding penalty?"

"The holding penalty," Max said.

"Now you're just fucking saying whatever."

"The logic is sound."

"I have to say, Max, that although I appreciate the sentiment, being a professional and dedicated practitioner for much of my life, I feel a moral obligation to state that sound logic is not always as sound as you would like it to be, but that is not at issue here. Please proceed."

"In the eighties and nineties the holding penalty was laxly enforced. As long as an arm wasn't wrapped completely around, players could get away with clutching and grabbing."

Trike popped a piece of nicotine gum into his mouth. "Seems to me, Max-O, that something fundamental was lost."

"Pretty much. Now—"

Max was cut off by the first activity they'd seen. The Butler was at the front gate.

He wore beige corduroys and a pale-blue button-down shirt with a gray cabled sweater. He carried a tote bag with a skein of yarn and two long metal knitting needles.

"Is this going to be the day?" Trike mumbled to himself. "Will this be it?"

"Will this be what?" Max mumbled back.

Trike zoomed in with the appropriate camera. The Butler took the newspaper out of the box. He looked at it in its plastic sleeve.

"It is," Trike whispered. "It is."

"It is what?" Max exasperated.

The Butler sighed. Stood next to the newspaper box. He tapped the box once with the paper, and then walked up the path to the house.

"Ha!" Trike exclaimed with a clap of his hands. "Today is the day."

"The day for what?" Max Max-level shouted.

"The day The Butler puts a hold on the newspaper subscription. You were prattling on about holding, Max."

Max rolled his eyes. "You drive a man to drink, boss."

"Just imagine what it's like on the inside of this," Trike said, tapping his forehead.

Max sighed. Figured he might as well continue. "Players could slow down goal-scorers. They could just ... grab Gretzky—"

"I can sum up this one too, if you like."

"Charming habit."

"To get opponents to stop not-quite-holding Gretzky, Marty McSorley punched them in the face."

"Correct."

Trike popped a piece of nicotine gum. "Is this a parable, Maxitus, something passed down from the wise old hat to the dashing young upstart?"

Max smirked. "I'll never tell."

For the rest of the day, they followed The Butler's movements through the house by the lights he turned on. He spent most of the day in the kitchen, most likely knitting. He went to the bathroom three times. Wandered into a couple of the sitting rooms. Watched TV for 3.7 hours.

Trike and Max each took a three-hour break. Got some air. Stretched their legs. Ate food that didn't come wrapped in sealed plastic.

When Max left, Trike moved his chair back against the opposite wall so he could see all four screens at once. He set his hat upturned on the floor in front of him. He adjusted its position several times, to ensure that it was in his field of vision. He took a pack of playing cards from his trench coat pocket. Threw them one by one into the hat, while he watched the screens.

The unspeakable things he would have done for a cigarette.

Trike divided his brain into three distinct functioning sections. The first consumed the information projected by the screens. The second backtracked from the tampered-with information to identify employees, associates, and other likely allies in the tampering effort. The third told stories about Joyce and money, eliminating those not possible given known information. He tossed cards to use up anything that remained, lest it occupy itself with visions of cigarettes and Lola.

And something watchful and silent remained. Without an image. Without a term. Assessing the assessing. Something that usually signaled when other processes were right, wrong, or the third thing.

When he finished the deck, he reached out with his foot and dragged his hat within reach. Collected the accurate cards. Left the inaccurates where they were. One character trait was confirmed in all the processes Trike ran. Drawn from the clothes in the closet, the displays in the sitting rooms, the general state of the interior and the upkeep of the exterior of the house, Trike knew Joyce was meticulous in what he presented to the world. A self-hiding meticulousness, which meant one always thought Joyce looked nice, but never remembered what he wore.

While Trike was gone, Max listened to Charlie Parker on his iPod. He had his notebook ready in case anything happened on his shift. Nothing happened on his shift.

Max had a professionally trained level of focus, but even that ran out after watching nothing happen in a big house. With the four screens and the Charlie Parker, Max inexorably wondered about the inside of Trike.

Trike described columns of text, tickers of information, topographical concept maps, and, of course, multiple screens. So Max had some metaphors but metaphors didn't solve the mystery he was curious about.

Max remembered what computers were like when he got started, knew what computers were like before that, and used the agency laptop. If physics allowed us to go from the computer of the '50s to the computer of now, biology should let us go from Max to Trike. So the scale wasn't the mystery.

With the Charlie Parker on and nothing happening in the house, Max tried to imagine what it felt like. As usual, he came up with a big, massive monolith of no idea.

Trike had Max search him for cigarettes when he got back. There were none. Trike also had Max give him a thorough smell-down to ensure any sneaked cigarettes would be detected and shamed. None detected. But Max was a smoker so his sense of smell wasn't definitive.

At six p.m., The Butler left. Two hours later, the stakeout hit the twenty-four-hour mark.

Trike sighed. "Let's pack up, Max."

Max gave a quick nod and started unplugging cords. Trike collected the trash in a garbage bag.

While Max coiled cords, he asked, "What were we looking for?"

"I was hoping for some kind of warrant-generating indication that Joyce was still in the house."

"Hidden in plain sight . . . 'Purloined Letter.'"

Trike popped a piece of nicotine gum into his mouth. "No, Max. Hiding in the basement. As I prove in my presentation, 'The Purloined Letter' is bullshit."

"I know you think that."

Trike shrugged. "At the risk of incurring the universe's harshest of punishments for hubris, there usually isn't a big difference between what I think and what is true."

Max shook his head. Started packing up that which was not bolted to shelving or frame. "Do you think Joyce is still in the house?"

Trike paused in the middle of knotting the garbage bag. Twenty-seven seconds later he said, "Much less likely but not impossible."

"Eating MREs in the basement?"

"Exactly. But if he is, he's not contacting the outside world."

"Anything else get more likely?"

Trike's hands went toward his pockets as if cigarettes were there. He found gum and patches. Looked Max right in the eye and said, "Not one fucking thing."

LOOK AT THIS FUCKING COLOR CHART

Buying a house is one of those convergences of brain-sploding complexity and eye-melting boredom uniquely able to break spirits. Even when it's just one person buying a house from another, there are pre-approvals, points, mortgage rates, closing costs, credit checks, realtor commissions, inspections, and more. You throw in a corporation looking to dodge taxes, claim losses, file income as capital investment, and the like, and a boring stupid tedious hedge maze is transported to a five-dimensional warped-gravity version of itself. That's still boring.

But the Joyce House Limited purchase of the Joyce House was the simplest real estate transaction Lola had ever seen. One cash payment for the undisclosed price of the house, including all the closing and inspection fees, to the estate of Miss Martha Clifford. One deed. One transfer. Since nothing in the case thus far had been simple, Lola dug deeper.

Joyce House Limited wasn't publicly traded, so Lola could only discover so much. She learned that Joyce was steward of the property, appointed by an unidentified "executive board." Lola couldn't find a revenue stream, what the company was incorporated to do, or even a phone number. Just a P.O. box and the statement of stewardship. She had seen a lot of shady businesses in her day and this was shaping up to be the shadiest. But from what she could tell, a company that did nothing and made no money was on the up and up. Something was wrong. Lola looked up, blinking from the collating, and realized that the innocence was the suspicion. And that was enough of that.

She turned her attention to the estate of Miss Martha Clifford. The house was the only property in the estate and the executor was not a member of the Clifford family, but a lawyer working for a small firm in Santa Fe. A firm that spent most of its time on cases involving trade between the United States and Mexico.

Lola had never been so happy to see crime. The Miss Martha Clifford estate was a front set up by Mina Kennedy. In the 1920s, Kennedy ran a brotheling and bootlegging empire in the Mid-Atlantic states, before developing an international smuggling operation once Prohibition had ended. Before she died, she set up the estate to leave the Joyce House to her daughter Lydia and allow Lydia to sell the house without the scrutiny of a dozen different law enforcement agencies in seven countries.

But Lola couldn't find any connection between the front estate and The Joyce Case. The evidence indicated that Joyce House Limited believed the estate was legitimate. So Lola turned her attention to the incorporation of Joyce House Limited itself. Perhaps crime loitered there.

What Lola found was horrifying. Insult to reason. Abomination of nature. Affront to god. But no crime.

There's nothing worse in detective stories than the breakthrough moment. The character stops what they're doing; mid-stride if walking, mid-word if talking, mid-fuck if fucking, and, if this is the moving pictures we're talking about, the actor has to make with the wide eyes and maybe open the mouth a little and maybe leak a few words like, "But Summer Street is one-way on that block," and then the dramatic rush off to somewhere leaving everybody hanging 'cause there's just no time to waste.

Lola didn't do the breakthrough, or rather, Lola had one breakthrough when she first started doing research for Trike and it's been a matter of form and time ever since. And it wasn't a breakthrough of finding two and two and making four. It was inventing the plus sign.

Research presents three distinct but not necessarily disconnected challenges: finding data, sifting data, and organizing data.

If the individual under investigation is Average Joe, the challenge is finding data. Most people don't leave much of a paper trail and most of that paper trail—credit-card receipts, bills, wills, and the like—taunted you from behind a barbed-wire fence made of you don't have a warrant yet. Sometimes you've got to bug, sometimes you've got to tail, and sometimes you've got to hack. Which was not as hard for Lola as it would be for you. She owned quiet shoes and kept her head down while walking in them, hacking is easy when you're only looking, and very few average Joes and Josephines could keep their traps shut when Lola asked questions.

For the average Joe, the data is hard to get but easy to sift. The important stuff stands right out. Booked a flight to Cancún. Stayed late on a Friday for the first time. Started paying for everything in cash.

Public figures presented the opposite problem. The public, for some reason, wanted to keep track of what their elected and appointed officials were doing with themselves, and so there was always plenty of reading materials on governors, senators, representatives, diplomats, and the like, even before revealing the information they tried to hide. Same thing for presidents and executives of corporations. Generally, the more people who thought you were important, the more you were supposed to keep track of yourself. So when millions of dollars are going back and forth, the trick is finding the $250,000 that went to Topeka instead of Ottawa. Which was not as hard for Lola as it would be for you. Lola inherited a monomaniacal focus she could turn on and the mental and physical stamina needed to use it for hours at a time. She could sit there and read three years' worth of transactions in one marathon session. Just happened to be part of the whole hand-she-was-dealt thing.

But data is nothing to a detective until it is turned into information through an organizational and analytical system. It's one thing to find out Billy Criminal went from Las Vegas to Sacramento to Seattle to Anchorage and another to see he rented a car from a different rental agency in each state and another to know he stopped using his credit card in Seattle and started writing checks in Anchorage, but another entirely to figure out what all that means.

Which was not as hard for Lola as it would be for you. Lola had a system.

Before embarking on a research assignment, Lola generated or received from Trike a list of keys: words, phrases, categories, terms, numbers. And she would associate each key with a color. Dollar green, for example, or blood red, or anything within the variation that someone who studied color theory in the course of formal artistic education could imagine.

If she encountered the key in a data stream, she saw the color. The colors could combine, compound, and grow so that at the end of a data stream, she would know its exact nature and value from its color swatch. A large magenta swatch told her exactly the types and amounts of keys that the data stream contained. The sifting, inherently, was the organizing and analyzing. The breakthrough was a matter of course. When it came time to put together an accordion folder for Trike, she just arranged the swatches and colors in whatever order she thought most productive and it was done.

In the early stages of this technique, Lola made color charts to keep it all straight. Later she supplemented her mental structure with color Post-it notes or marker lines. After a few years of practice, that too, became unnecessary.

Unless the case was like two data tornadoes fucking on top of an information hurricane. Then Lola made a color chart.

When Lola got to The Incorporation and the Lawyers she made a color chart. And wanted to shoot herself. And the nearest three innocent bystanders.

It wasn't translating the lawyerese that bothered her. Everybody who wanted to hide something but still had to write that something down somewhere knew that it's not enough to just lock up the file, you've got to lock up the meaning of the file in its own words. Through the years of practice, Lola was damn near close to fluent.

The complexity of the incorporation wasn't the problem, either. People have been hiding shit in complex documents ever since paper made complex documents cost-effective. If a few subclauses referencing appendices in previous addenda make your eyes cross, detecting is not your ideal profession. And Lola did have the colors and the color charts.

It wasn't even the cost of all those lawyers at all those hourly rates. The amount of money rich people were willing to spend to make and keep even more money infuriated Lola for a while, but she encountered it too damn often to stay furious.

It was the inefficiency.

If the goal was to obscure an incorporation, there were a hundred different ways to do it, most of them legal, and all of them at least as effective and a hundred times easier than whatever it was Lola now faced.

Even the color chart made Lola's eyes swim.

It was like the pointlessness itself was the point, which was all well and good for certain modes of human expression, but not for crime.

As Lola assembled the accordion folder for Trike, she thought, "Wish I'd known in college that I was this good at this stuff. Who knows where I might have ended up if I'd majored in a science and done art on the side?"

The thought stopped Lola mid-filing. Were all of those career opportunities gone forever?

Could she become a research apprentice? Sure, she's finding missing children and putting criminals in jail, but she could throw her brain at cancer. If she needed another degree for that, well, could getting it be harder than acquiring and making sense of Archibald Bodkin's research notes on Guam? And what would a few more student loans really mean if she could research for a steady paycheck instead of the occasional stipend and inconsistent reward money?

Regardless, the lawyers represented a potential avenue of research. Lola put together a spreadsheet of all the firms, their specialties, the particular lawyers who worked on the incorporation, and the estimated driving times to those nearby.

A day and a half of research and Lola wasn't sure what she'd found. Another $100,000 just about gone.

She texted Trike to see if he was still at the stakeout. He texted back that he was done with the stakeout and back at the office. She'd meet him there.

Lola organized everything she'd printed out and annotated into six accordion folders. One was for the purchase of the house. Three exposed the Miss Martha Clifford estate. Two recorded the odyssey of incorporation. She packed it all up and took a bus to the office.

When she got there, Trike was standing behind his desk, looking down at five notebooks.

"That's not good," Lola said. She thumped her backpack next to Trike's desk, then sat down in one of the client chairs.

Trike didn't look up. "That didn't sound good either."

"It's not," Lola said, unpacking the folders.

Trike glanced up. "If I'm not mistaken, and this is me we're talking about, I'd say you just dumped a truckload of bullshit on my floor."

"I did."

"That can't all be about the purchase of the house."

"It's not."

Trike looked at Lola, scrunched his eyes. "You know, I originally thought that response would be a relief, but now that I've heard it, I'm terrified."

"You should be. I can start with the good news if you like."

"Proceed."

Lola put the Miss Martha Clifford estate folders in a pile on one side of Trike's desk. "The purchase of the house was as simple as it could be, but it was purchased from a front estate set up by Mina Kennedy."

"Well, hello there, evidence of organized crime." Trike clapped his hands together and rubbed them in glee.

"Except there is no evidence that Joyce House Limited was in any way suspicious or aware of the estate. From what I could tell, the sale was completely and totally on the up-and-up."

"Coincidentally purchased from an international smuggling syndicate?"

"Looks that way."

Trike popped two pieces of nicotine gum into his mouth. Chewed furiously. "Coincidence is the void. Can't wait to see how you follow up that little emotional roller coaster."

"So I figured there might be something in Joyce House Limited itself, and initially, there really wasn't, so I looked into its incorporation."

Lola piled the incorporation folders on Trike's desk. "And discovered an incorporation spread out over sixteen different law firms, none of which usually does incorporation."

"Sixteen?"

"I mean, look at the fucking color chart I made." Lola waved a complexly colored piece of paper. "I haven't had to make one of these since The Case of the One-Armed Adulterer."

Trike sighed. He rubbed his eyes, pulled on his nose, and data-faced for 153 seconds. Then he threw the third notebook from the left out the window. He sat down and started to say something. But he stopped and threw the first notebook on the right out the window.

"You could have used those for something else, you know," Lola said.

"Lola, sometimes something has just got to go out the window."

"Stakeout didn't turn anything up?"

"Stakeout did not."

Trike folded his arms in front of him on the desk. Set his head down.

Lola waited for him to say something. His dramatic sulks were often moments of deep intellectual process before a major breakthrough. Other times, Trike was just someone who couldn't tell when a silence was awkward.

"What about the police?" she asked.

"They suck and I hate them."

"No, I mean, have you heard anything useful from them. Crybaby."

Trike picked his head up. "I have not heard anything from them."

He jumped up from his desk. Dashed to the office phone on Max's desk. There were eight messages. None from the police. He double-checked the mail. Nothing there. He sat back down at his desk.

"Lola, in my own quest for self-knowledge, it has come to my attention that I'm not terribly popular with our fair city's law-enforcement agency—"

"I've seen them burn you in effigy."

"Really?"

"Yep. It was at a Halloween party, so there was an atmosphere of mischief, but there wasn't much debate about who was getting the torch."

"Probably when things started going wrong with my car. Damn cop voodoo."

"The trunk and the doors were broken when you bought the ecru asphyxiator."

Trike popped a piece of nicotine gum into his mouth. "Is that what you're calling my car now?"

"It is."

"Automobiles and personalities aside, it is a waste of money to hire me and then cut me out of the investigation. They've held information from me three times—once for legal reasons, and twice in the foolish, almost charmingly misguided belief that in doing so they would discern the truth before I did—but even in those instances, they told me what they were doing. I mean, at the very least, they should have finished all the forensics. And they were still pursuing possible interviews."

"Maybe they're mailing the reports to you."

"Why would they do that?"

Lola shrugged. "Cheaper?"

"Ostensibly, someone's life is on the line, and though the police make the Joads look like spendthrifts, their miserliness is rarely fatal."

Trike leaned back in his chair. Interlaced his fingers across his stomach. Sighed.

"Okay. Go home for tonight. I'm going to have to sift through this pile here before I know what I'll need from you next. If you're bored, feel free to swing by the police department and see if you can find out what's up with the radio silence. But don't bother if you've got another lead you want to pursue, or really, if you want to do anything else at all. Read a book. Learn a trade. Take up Scotch. Whatever."

"I'll go say hi. They tend to be a little more polite to me."

"Can't blame 'em, really. Dame like you. And, of course, every now and again someone at the newspaper gets it in their head to print what I say about the cozzers."

"Yeah. Let's blame the newspaper."

"Will do. You want a ride home?"

"I thought you were going to stay here and sift through the folders."

"Might take them home with me."

"It's still not on the way."

"Might not be going home. Might just drive around. And when you're just driving around, everywhere is on the way."

Lola gave Trike a look. "What are you planning?"

Trike shrugged. "I may or may not have plans. You know how it can be."

"Sure. But no, I'll take the bus. Less chance of carbon monoxide poisoning."

"Well then, let me drop the folders off in my car and walk you to the bus stop."

"No. I'll help you bring the folders to your car and if you want to hang out while I wait for the bus, I would like that very much."

Trike slapped a nicotine patch onto his forearm. "Never an inch with dames like you."

"Not one single inch."

COCAINE, ASSAULT RIFLES, AND STOLEN ART

The whole case made Trike want to do something with his hands. Preferably something illegal. And there was this Amateur Victorian Restorers of America Association hanging around with the bad kids. Trike decided to see what that kid packed for lunch.

And he hadn't broken into a place in a while. In Trike's line of work, sometimes you've got to get through a locked door before somebody dies. So even if his investigation of AVRAA turned up nothing applicable, it still gave him a chance to keep his picking skills nimble.

The office of the Amateur Victorian Restorers of America Association was in a two-story neocolonial house with a long driveway, a four-car parking lot, and an acceptably maintained lawn. It had one full-time employee, the executive director; a website; and a library open to the public from two to five on Fridays. It published an annual guide to Victorian homes Restored by Amateurs in America. AVRAA looked like a hobby organization for the twelve wealthy individuals on the board of trustees.

Until Trike got to the front door.

Everybody locks their doors. Very few lock their doors with a high-security double-cylinder deadbolt, a Mortise Lock, and an Abloy Electromechanical Industrial lock. If someone were bleeding out, Trike would have gone through the window. Fifteen minutes later he was inside.

He went to the executive director's office first. Every drawer in the desk had an individual high-security lock. The cabinets had Abloy Exec high-security cylinder locks. One chest had a Brinks Shrouded Padlock.

He'd picked locks like those before. Cocaine, assault rifles, and stolen art were behind them.

Office supplies. Old budgets. Publicly available tax records. Files on homes restored were behind these. One part of Trike's brain ran screaming madly into the wild American night. It came back.

He spent two hours and eight minutes on the office and still had the library and storage closet to go. A question occurred to him.

"Why spend money on locks like these, but not on a security system? If you're spending seven thousand dollars on locks, whatever you're protecting is probably worth two hundred fifty a month to make sure the police know when somebody's picked them all. Besides, burglars don't pick locks. They smash shit. For someone with a little talent looking to be delicate, this is just a time dump—"

Trike's brain went three ways. The first got him out of the building without leaving a trace. The second prioritized the places someone might target: Lola's place, Max's place, his place, the office. The third ran probable setups that could have been set up while he was picking locks to nothing.

Trike decided to swing by Lola's first. Given AVRAA's location, of course. Even if he didn't get there in time to help, he'd get there in time to help clean up the mess she made of any intruders. Then he'd call Max and head over to the office. Then home for a polite conversation with any traps, ambushes, or other affronts to the sanctity of his domicile.

Trike checked his phone when he got back to the car. No messages. He started the car and pulled into the street. He talked through the logic of the situation while he drove, hands occasionally phantom-smoking.

"Over two hours and what I found wasn't worth an intern at the free weekly. Assuming there isn't a psychopath who's using the locks to make sure the Cubans don't steal vital restorative technology, there are two branches of possibility: the setup was specifically for me, and it was not. If it was for me, they'd have thrown it together in the small amount of time since The Joyce Case started. Not unrealistic for many of the locks, but the shit on the door had to be installed. Ordered on Thursday, installed yesterday. Not impossible, but I'd end up as one damn suspicious locksmith. Of course, they wouldn't know I'd come tonight. Just had to be ready when I did. Lookout at the corner back there for when I drive in and out. Mischief and mayhem in the middle.

"If it's not for me, it branches in some strange ways. Could've been set up for whoever ended up investigating The Joyce Case. Any shamus worth the slang would want to get on the other side of that door once they saw the locks on it. Not much of a problem to find out the important places to a hypothetical dick. Most probably wouldn't have gotten here as soon as I did. Some might not have bothered at all. Keep the receipts and return the locks when the show is over. Leave the fancy shit on the door, call it a capital investment.

"And then it goes to all the shit it could be that doesn't have anything to do with Joyce. No substantive reason this should be connected, no matter how amateurish the renovations to his Victorian house are. In America. Association."

Trike arrived at Lola's place. There was one light on in Lola's living room. That meant she was knitting to late-night AM radio. Her basic insomnia. Trike gave her a call just to be sure.

The phone rang. The light went out. They'd set a trap connected to her cell phone. And Trike tripped it.

"Lola!" Trike shouted when the phone was picked up on the third ring.

"LOLA!" he shouted again, rushing into action when there wasn't an instant answer.

"JESUS CHRIST, WHAT?" Lola shouted back.

"Are you okay?" Trike asked, half hanging out of the back passenger-seat window.

"Except for the burst eardrum, yeah, I'm fucking fine."

"Why are you out of breath?"

"I'm not out of breath."

"You're Lola-level out of breath."

Lola sighed. "Somehow you managed to reveal expert knowledge of my breathing patterns without being creepy or romantic."

"What about the light?" Trike asked, less frantically hanging half out the back passenger-seat window.

"What light?"

"It went off when your phone rang."

Lola sighed again. "It was a whole big thing, and I mean a Lola-level whole big thing, and I'll tell you the whole big thing at some point, but the executive summary is, I couldn't come up with something to use that old bike for, so I turned it into a pedal generator to charge my phone and laptop."

"And run that light," Trike said. Trike shifted from acting to observing and saw Lola's faint outline facing away from the window. From her height and angle on the bike, he knew she'd moved her coffee table to make room for the bike and whatever structure she added to ensure that the non-exercise bike was exercise-bike stable at Lola-level speeds. There was only one place a coffee table made from half a repurposed long board could fit in Lola's small apartment.

"The light tells me it's working," Lola said. "And why the fuck are you calling me from outside my apartment, anyway?"

"Just in case something unusual happened, I'm not going to tell you exactly what I've been up to this fine, though unseasonably damp, evening, to ensure that even under the strictest of definitions, you are not accessory to anything, but there is a chance I was intentionally occupied for a sufficient amount of time in order for harm to be done to me and/or the people with whom I work."

"I'd have rather served time than listened to that sentence," Lola said.

"What's done is done. Anything weird happen tonight?"

"No."

"Were you home all night?"

"Don't have the money to go anywhere else."

"Okay. Good. No. Never mind. I'm going to give Max a call, then swing by the office before heading home. You call me if anything weird happens."

"I'll summon my knight in shining armor, even though he's only up twelve to nine in sparring matches, to save me and my damselhood from marauders, evildoers, Republicans, highwaymen—"

"All right, I get it. And I'll call you if anything weird happens to me. Not one fucking inch."

"Thank you."

"Just one more thing, Lola, before I go."

"Jesus fucking Christ."

"What?"

"Your fucking *Columbo* thing," Lola cursed.

"It's not a thing. It's just, you know, it's just, as a detective, it is a satisfying way to end a conversation."

"Have you actually seen *Columbo*? Because I have, because you do this thing, and he convinces the criminals that he is stupid so they'll let down their guards and reveal something about the crime."

"I'm familiar with the source material. I just like to keep things straight—"

"Zip! Yeah, see, there you go, but you, you don't let anyone forget for a nanosecond that you're a genius, so with you, it's not even a reference."

"It's just about all those loose ends—" Trike persisted.

"You're just going to fucking do it anyway."

"Awfully hard to stop once it's started."

"Am I going to like your one more thing?"

"................ No."

Lola groaned. "Just tell me."

Trike took a deep breath to break out of the format. "The coffee table is against the Western baseboard."

"The coffee table ... ?" Lola started. Then a frustrated furious growl leaked from her throat as she realized she needed to unbolt and completely rearrange the pedal generator she just spent the entire fucking night arranging and bolting to make sure the coffee table didn't catch fire when the heat turned on.

"Good night, Trike," she grumbled and hung up before Trike could say anything else.

Trike sat in his car and had a slightly groggier version of the conversation he had with Lola with Max. Only without the whole damselhood business. He took the opportunity to warn Max about the e-mail he was going to receive soon with a list of lawyers to question and the context in which to question them. Max grumbled something about the end of his rest. Trike reminded him he was the best.

The office was undisturbed. Trike drank a tallboy, sent the e-mail, and then went home.

No tripwires. No bombs. No gases. No traps. Accounting for natural entropy, home was identical to how he left it.

He grabbed a tallboy from the fridge. Drank it over the sink.

"Something is very wrong," he said.

He finished his beer, crumpled the can, dropped it into the sink. Slapped on a patch and went to bed.

THE OLD-TIMER AIN'T HOME

Trike brought the bag of groceries to the car. Chips. Pasta. Spaghetti sauce. Canned peaches. Microwave dinners. Instant noodles. Instant coffee. Candy bars. Orange juice. *The Economist. The New Yorker. Guns and Ammo.*

Lola pulled in on the driver's-side back door so Trike could open the passenger's-side back door. He put the bag in the backseat to avoid the tragic opera of opening and closing the trunk, setting it next to a bag from the liquor store containing whiskey, vodka, beef jerky, and a two-liter bottle of cola.

When the second bag was settled, Lola let go of the door and shifted to push up on the ceiling with her back so Trike could shut his door. Got it in one try.

They got into their appropriate front seats. After buckling his seat belt, Trike took a pipe out of his pocket and put it in his mouth.

"So," Lola started.

"Yes."

"Then—"

"I read the warning label on a bag of cheap pipe tobacco three years, two months, two weeks, and two days ago, in a moment when I considered converting from cigarette smoking to pipe smoking in order to reduce my chances of dying a slow painful death of lung cancer, and learned that pipe tobacco is not a safe alternative to cigarette tobacco. However, I am not, currently, attempting to alter my smoking habits so as to subject a different portion of my person to increased cancer risks, but to end the habit entirely. In service to said goal, I purchased this very cheap pipe from the liquor store to use as a prop for the gestures in my life that have, up to this point, been satisfied with a cigarette, an action that should bring a sigh of relief from the innocent of the world as each day my idle hands have inched closer and closer to tearing out some stranger's larynx for deliberating an extra moment at the coffee shop."

"So—"

"I did not even buy tobacco with this purchase, which, I guess, would raise the question as to whether or not this is now, or ever was, a pipe."

"Right, but—"

"And it is true, like stone tablets found on Mount Sinai, the brandished but unsmoldering pipe is ridiculous and, when combined with my trench coat and profession, lilts gently into the realm of life as parody of parody of life, but, you, of all people, will understand why I have chosen this problem over the other; the problem of potentially looking like an explosive douche canoe, over the risk of rotting from the lungs out."

Lola sat quietly for a minute to make sure Trike was done.

"So, I was actually going to ask why you always go see this guy."

"It's not obvious?"

"Every time you see him, you end up drinking yourself to sleep, even when you get home at like two in the afternoon, and I don't see what the return is."

Trike started the car and pulled out of the lot. He was quiet as he drove.

At the first stoplight he said, "I'm afraid I'm going to say a bunch of stuff and then end up telling you, 'You just wouldn't understand.'"

"There's nothing wrong with that. The effort would be meaningful to me."

The light turned green.

"The Old-Timer gives me a perspective cultivated over years of getting punched in the face, tailing slippery characters, putting up with cranky cops, and sniffing truth out of the smoke screen of evidence that can be vital, if a bit indirect, to solving a case."

"Can't you get that perspective from Max?"

"I get one perspective from Max, but remember, Max has actually been a private eye less than I have. The bulk of his experience was with the Bureau. The official world. Badges, warrants, expense accounts, and the like. The Old-Timer was a PI from start to finish."

Lola gave Trike a doubtful look. "Does it have anything to do with your father?" she offered.

"Yes. Definitely. The Old-Timer lived pretty much the same life Octavian led, only a little more on the edge. So, you're right, I do get a surrogate connection with my dad on these visits."

"For someone so good at telling when other people are lying, you're a terrible liar."

"I don't practice much. Can generally find an effective truth. You believe any of it?"

"Knew you were lying from the first word."

"Right. Okay. This is probably a bit shallow, in a dance-monkey way, but he is one of the great characters in my life. I mean, you and Max are the most important non-Mom people in my life, but this guy is a character. To him swearing isn't poetry, it's a fucking ecosystem. Seriously, his cursing has a food chain. But he also has this persistent intensity you only really see in old cops and crooks. Talking with him is like watching a tire fire. And the perspective point wasn't a complete lie. He does give me different perspectives from which to view evidence."

"Okay, then," Lola said. "Particular worldview, surrogate connection, real character."

"Well, that was disingenuous."

"I just didn't want you to have to say I wouldn't understand."

"Well."

"Listen, I get those points, but they don't explain your reaction. They tell me something, but nothing about the drinking."

"I drink a lot in general."

"It's different."

Trike parked in front of The Old-Timer's building.

"It is," Trike said. "You want to come in or wait in the car?"

"Oh, choices, choices. I think I'll risk the interior. Since I have to help you open the door anyway."

They gathered the bags and entered the run-down rat-riven building.

"Listen, Trike, I've watched you drink plenty of times, but after you've seen this guy, it's different. There's almost, well, fear. Drinking to hide from something, rather than drinking for a different state of consciousness."

"And you want to know why?"

"I do."

"I assume, because you're a friend and you care about me."

"You assume correctly."

They got to The Old-Timer's apartment and knocked on the door. No answer. Trike waited seventy-two seconds and knocked again. Nothing. Lola gave him a nervous look. Trike knocked one more time. Nothing. He tried the door. It was locked. He breathed a sigh of relief.

"He's just out." Trike said. "He doesn't lock the door when he's home, unless he's in a bad mood, and then he shouts at me to pick the lock. And he promised that if he ever offed himself, he'd leave the door unlocked and do it in the bathtub."

"So what are we going to do with all of this stuff?" Lola asked.

"You are going to hold this," Trike handed her his bag, "while I pick the lock."

Trike picked the lock.

"Then, we'll drop this stuff off," he continued, "put the perishables in the fridge, and go."

They dropped the stuff off, put the perishables in the fridge, and went.

As they walked downstairs, Lola said, "You know, I'm not letting you off the hook on this one."

"I know."

"But if you don't want to keep talking about it now, we can talk about it later."

"Would you believe me if I said I don't know why I visit The Old-Timer?"

"Not when you say it like that."

They didn't bother with the decaying handrails on the stairs, even as they picked their way around rotten boards. You didn't notice the roaches in buildings like that. They got back to the car and went through the slapstick ballet needed to open and close both front doors.

When he was settled, Trike took a deep breath. He said, "I want to believe that someone would bring me groceries if I ever end up like that."

"Trike, you're not going to end up like that," Lola assured him.

"All three of his ex-wives told him the same thing."

COMMUNICATION AT ITS FINEST

The quiet tapping of Max typing the second part of the first half of lawyer interviews. Cars in the street. The mini-fridge humming. The bass notes from the accountant two floors down who blasted death metal once everyone else left the office. Water running in one of the bathrooms.

Trike leaned back in his chair. Tried to decide what to focus his mind on. Replay the contents of the AVRAA office in case he missed something. Analyze the first part of Max's lawyer report. Trawl for data about Lydia Kennedy he might have absorbed. View the Joyce House sitting rooms assuming they were created with a psychopath's compulsion to leave clues. Figure out why the cops weren't talking to them. He muttered, "We must think through several levels of implications. We must explore for what is not written. We must subject every assertion to an interrogation. We must move fact by fact, byte by byte, through the story as if an archaeological grid had been placed over it, and every square must be the focus of obsessive inspection. What arises through this critical inspection is a range of implausibilities and absurdities that we are—in the course of a typical reading—manipulated into accepting as truth."

He decided to correlate the lawyer stuff he had with whatever he could remember about Lydia Kennedy. Maybe she wasn't out of the family business. He split his brain. One part held the lawyer stuff. Part two searched for Lydia Kennedy.

An image of Trike descended a spiral staircase, past the floors that held frequently relevant information. Past the floors of data consciously remembered. Past the stuff everyone needed to keep in their heads. All the way down to the floor where the stuff that just stuck was collected.

On that floor, the image of Trike walked four years into the past. On this floor, dates were correlated with intentionally remembered events, events that acted as moorings for whatever else Trike observed. He went to "Lola and I try that new pizza place." Starting from that event, he reconstructed the rest of his day, sifting the effort to prioritize news media. Every day took him about thirty-one seconds to reconstruct. "Lola and I fight about Sherlock Holmes." "Flat tire outside the office." "First sparring match: Win." "Took Lola to the museum."

A brick smashed through the office window.

Trike spun out of his chair, dragged it into the middle of the room, and hurled it out the window. The chair landed on the roof of a car, shattering into clattering kindling and splinters. A string of scared curses was hurled back. Car doors slammed. Tires squealed. The brick throwers sped away.

Max poked his head into Trike's office. "Why is it always the chair?"

"Imagine, if you will, Max," Trike said, "what goes through their heads. Dusting off their hands, another brick well thrown, when suddenly they hear the sound of more glass breaking above them. The sound connects with their preconceived notions of projectiles and windows, and their minds see the brick coming back before their eyes can see the brick coming back. But it is not a brick. For an instant, gravity has been turned inside out. Everything they know about their world, everything they believe forms the base of their world dissolves. The turtle we rest on stirs. It breaks their brains, and then," Trike waved his hand as though he were coaxing the aroma of freshly baked apple pie to his nose, "the particular tenor of their curses." He sighed like the office was filled with fresh mountain air.

"That's worth the cost of a chair?" Max asked.

"Replacing the window is the expensive part. After that, ten bucks for a pawnshop chair is negligible."

Trike picked up the brick and extracted the affixed note.

"What's Joyce say?" Max asked.

"Huh," Trike said, after reading the note.

"I hate it when you say that."

"It's not from Joyce."

"It's not from Joyce?"

Trike popped a piece of nicotine gum. "Nope."

"What's it say?"

"Horatio Bottomley never forgets."

"Bottomley? Glad to see . . . he can afford bricks."

"See, this is what threats are supposed to be like. It's direct, simple, causes me consternation, imparts a clear message. The maximum effect for a minimum effort. A whole pig, still bleeding, with a hand-stitched note, is a lot of effort to convey a message.

"And unheeded threats are supposed to escalate. If you start with a pig, you follow up with a dog. Not a shoot-yourself-in-the-face-beautiful grad student. Of course, escalation can be replaced with persistence and achieve the same effect. A pig a day would be a real downer. And threats should be realistic."

"Like Bottomley's bricks."

"Exactly. Bottomley is rotting in prison and will be for at least five more years. Any threats of tangible action would be meaningless because that action is impossible. He's just staying in my consciousness until he can threaten action."

"Simple. Elegant. Expressive."

"This is communication at its finest," Trike said, waving the brick. "Joyce has created a system of information exchange that is the opposite of communication."

"All data . . . no meaning."

"Exactly. I mean, he's not even sending deviously coded taunts as a way to flaunt his superior yet villainous intellect. Even if he knows the capacity of my intellect, or perhaps, because he knows the capacity of my intellect, he should feel an inexorable drive to create hidden clues."

"He should."

"Makes me pine for a brick from Joyce. One wonders how one could induce such a throwing of masonry."

Trike tossed the brick to the floor by his desk. Went to the threats drawer in the filing cabinet and added the latest entry. "Care to join me on a trip to the pawnshop?" he said after the filing.

"In your affront to automotive engineering? I've got to finish the lawyers."

"Did you really need to insult my car?"

"It's that bad . . . I feel a duty to bring it up."

"Well, don't pull an all-nighter. You've got another round of interviews tomorrow, and, if the lawyers follow the same pattern as everything else, it'll be all canned heat and cackle bladders."

"Right."

"And once you're done with this particular avenue, I think it might be time for a home visit."

"A home visit?"

"Not sure what it will lead to," Trike said, putting on his trench coat, "but it might be worth our while to stir the ashes in Lydia Kennedy's fireplace."

Max gave a terse nod. "Good luck finding a chair, boss."

FIELD AND GRAY

The waiting room at Field and Gray was carpeted in burnt-umber shag. It had four lime-green plastic chairs and a matching small rectangular coffee table stacked with old magazines. Stained-wood walls. Framed images someone must have called art. The receptionist's desk was gray and metal. The kind assigned to football coaches at junior colleges. It created a narrow hallway between the room and the lawyers' offices. The room was so small Max could have slapped a person sitting across from him. If someone sat there. If they deserved it. A water cooler and a fake ficus added a final claustrophobic dose of client repellent.

Max sat with his hands folded in his lap. He wore his formal detecting outfit: gray slacks, white shirt, navy tie, gray tweed sport coat, and matching fedora. He'd been talking to lawyers for two days, in person and over the phone. Since he didn't have a subpoena or a bribe, the only thing he'd gotten for his troubles was a ruined shoeshine. He was looking forward to visiting Lydia Kennedy.

All the conversations started with the lawyers talking like they knew everything that had ever been torted. By three questions in, it was clear they knew even less about the incorporation than Max did. Edward Marshall Hall barely understood how an incorporation worked. Which wasn't his fault, since he specialized in litigating the importation of plants and animals. Marie Elmsely had a sense of corporate law, but she buttered her bread with professional athletic contracts. Bill Brown and Jim Jones were corporate lawyers, but they spent their time on intellectual property rights for advertising firms. Fifteen different lawyers and not one regularly did incorporation.

Max was about to the meet the sixteenth. Archibald Bodkin. A divorce lawyer specializing in child-custody disputes. He kept Max waiting for forty minutes. Max never touched waiting-room magazines.

"Mr. Bodkin will see you now," the receptionist said, like a three-day weekend was minutes away.

Max stood up and walked past the receptionist's desk to the indicated interior door. He looked at the calendar on the desk. The current date was empty under Bodkin's name.

Archibald Bodkin stood looking out the window behind his desk. A big barrel of a man in a navy pinstripe suit. Bodkin clasped thick hands at the small of his meaty back. He was built like a weightlifter and had a full set of salt-and-pepper hair. He stood with the relaxed air of someone who knew exactly what he was capable of.

"Please sit down," Bodkin said without turning around.

Max sat down.

After a pause, Bodkin turned around. He stopped short when he saw Max.

Max raised his eyebrows. Cocked his head. A whisper of a smirk bent his lips. "Sir William Gentle," he said. "Please have a seat."

Sir William Gentle descended. A condor landing. "So your real name is Max?" he said. "Or perhaps the early retirement is a cover."

"It's real."

"Yes. That would be the response."

Max leaned back. Crossed his arms at his chest. "I suspected you bought an island . . . to hide on."

"It is actually rather difficult to hide on a self-purchased island," Sir William Gentle responded, "and establishing a mi-cronation, or at least one that could truly repel the extradition attempts of members of the UN security council, is not as simple as one might assume, if you would further suspect the purchased island was a step toward sovereignty."

Max waved a dismissive hand. Idly slapped his knee. "This is a pickle," he said.

"What is?"

"I need information from Archibald Bodkin," Max explained, "middle of his graduating class from a technically accredited law school divorce lawyer. Now I can get that information from one of the great, though criminal, legal minds of our era."

"Ah yes, The Joyce Case does seem to require the deft intellec-tual manipulation of which very few are capable. A number that, of course, includes myself. How can I be of service?"

"That is the problem."

"I don't see how you could have a problem with my assistance."

"You are the Super Bowl ... Joyce is pickup football."

Sir William Gentle cleared his throat. "Personally, I could not help but notice the somewhat alarming level of coincidence pres-ent in this potential apprehension."

Max narrowed his eyes. "What are you implying?"

"A portion of my funds could be transferred to you. Once in custody, my financial records would be laid bare to the scrutiny of the state, and such a transfer could not escape notice. Many would raise questioning eyebrows when the bribe to the man who appre-hended me was discovered, but answers would be found.

"As you correctly said, I am one of the great legal minds of our era. It would not be unreasonable for me to defend myself in a court of law and, regardless of the ironclad evidence the state would assume it had, be found innocent of all the crimes of which I stood accused. And, as you well know, one cannot be tried for the same crime twice.

"Should this occur, people could not help but think back to

that strange transfer of funds and notice how convenient the entire situation was for me; how I was able to avoid capture until the exact moment when I had the resources to mount a successful defense.

"It is true, there might be one out there with the requisite imagination to wonder why, of all my transactions that were erased or cleansed, this particular one was preserved, but, well, you know how much power and influence is given to those with imaginations. And even should that avenue of understanding be pursued, and even if it is determined, in the legal sense, that I gave you money against your will, you will never free yourself of the cloud of suspicion the interaction generates."

"Anonymous tip."

"It is folly to bargain beyond one's control. If we came to an arrangement, you would give me your word that such a tip would not be made, and all evidence suggests you would keep that word, but it would be impossible for me to hold you to it. I didn't get where I am by trusting phenomena I cannot influence. Besides, would you really want to deny your partner the case of his life?"

"What do you mean?" Max said cautiously.

"Your presence has vouched for Mr. Augustine. I find it hard to believe a man of your stature would spend his time with an arrogant blowhard if there weren't some underlying quality. Unless, of course, there is an entirely different level to this relationship. Regardless, I think all of us would enjoy the chase, should there be one. Think of the newspaper sales."

"Someone would have to hire him."

Sir William Gentle chuckled. "Yes, well, I'm sure someone will get around to it."

Max breathed deeply through his nose. He knew three agents who'd cut off a nut to be sitting where he sat. "Okay. The Joyce Case."

Sir William Gentle dropped a shamefaced smirk. "And after all that, I know little of use. I was given very specific instructions, and paid very well, in one meeting with Joyce himself. Obviously, I was perplexed that someone would approach a divorce lawyer for help with an incorporation, but I was told my style was appreciated. I was then given a very specific assignment: to ensure that the incorporation, as completed by the others, could be recognized in Maryland, Virginia, Delaware, the American Virgin Islands, and Guam. I had no contact with any of the other lawyers involved, and none with Joyce, once my very small, very simple task was completed."

Max slumped in his chair. "Maybe Archibald Bodkin was hired because he's Sir William Gentle."

"Given my current legal standing, I am going to assume that is the case; however, there is no evidence to indicate that this is so."

Max rubbed his forehead. "You read about the case?"

"As the newspapers have reported it."

"As a professional . . . what's your take?"

Sir William Gentle chuckled. "It's a bit funny, you know. I have been thinking about it. With the disappearance and, of course, my very small personal involvement. It has not stolen sleep from me, but in idle moments I have done my share of speculation. It is just so curious. The money is in all the wrong places."

"What do you think we're looking at?"

"To be honest, Max, I have no idea. However, I am certain that, whatever it is, it looks nothing like crime."

CLASS WAR

Calling the bad part of town the underbelly suggests it's been fed. It ain't been fed. If some hack making a word count needs something from the body, liver would be better. But that's wrong too. Waste leaves the liver. Even the colon gets rid of what it doesn't want. What ends up in the bad part of town usually stays there. Colostomy bag is more like it.

Medical terms don't make good pulp.

Trike and Max drove through the bad part of town to visit Lydia Kennedy. They smelled a con. Her mother was a criminal, but she was good at it. If she could set up the Martha Clifford estate, she could make sure her daughter didn't end up in the bedpan of town. Even if Lydia only saw the Joyce House dough, that would be enough for a nice little place in the suburbs.

Trike had been phantom-smoking for a minute.

"Thoughts, boss?" Max said.

Trike snapped his fingers out of their gesture. He rubbed the bridge of his nose. "Well, Max, I've been thinking that Lydia Kennedy might not be out of the family business."

"It's possible."

"Seems like if that were the case, and she's half as savvy as her mom was, she'd stay light-years away from whatever Joyce is up to."

"Likely."

"And another thing troubles me."

"What's that?"

"These streets are never empty."

"Yeah," Max said with a lilt of concern.

The corners were vacant. No one was on any of the stoops. Windows closed. No kids on the sidewalk. Neither gang in its alley. No bums in the gutters. Empty streets. The bad part of town don't got much going for it, but it's never lonely.

Max unbuttoned his holster. Trike hopped into the backseat. A Dumpster rolled into the street in front of them. Max hit the brakes. Put the car in park. Another Dumpster rolled into the street behind them.

"This should be interesting," Trike said.

With a nod, they threw both driver's-side doors open. Then both passenger's-side doors. Trike rolled back into the front seat. They ducked out of the car, Trike covering the front, Max covering the back. Assailants spilled from the alleys ahead and behind. Trike and Max convinced them to retreat with a persuasive spray of gunfire.

It got quiet once the bullets stopped flying. You could've heard a page turn in a third-floor bathtub.

Trike stood up.

"Christ . . . a speech," Max said.

"Feel your pulse. Fill your lungs. Touch the pavement. Smell the filth. These are the components of life. They are yours to experience because my partner and I decided we'd rather converse with you . . ." A head poked out of an alley. Trike put a bullet nearby. The head dove back. ". . . than with coroners. I do not know who hired you for this folly. I do not know why he, she, it, or they are so careless with your lives. I do not know what you were told. I do not know the punch lines to the nervous jokes you shared before the ambush. But I do know that my partner and I have more pressing matters to attend to. So, unless you would like this little chat to turn fatal . . ."

Trike dramatically reloaded his gun. The old clip clattered to the ground. "I'd move your fucking Dumpsters."

They moved their fucking Dumpsters.

Trike picked up the dropped clip. Still had three bullets. Bullets aren't free. He and Max got back in the car and drove on.

"What the hell, boss?"

"Probably wasn't my best speech, but—"

"No ... the ambush."

Trike shrugged his shoulders. "You know, Maxataxus, the evidence suggests it was meant for somebody else."

"Where are they?"

Trike shrugged again. They took two more turns and pulled up in front of Lydia Kennedy's building. It looked barely erect.

"Notice anything weird about the building, Max?"

Max observed. "No."

Trike pointed up. "All the windows on the top floor are intact."

Max took a deep breath through his nose. "I do not like that."

"Me neither," Trike said, grabbing a can of spray paint from the backseat. "Let's see what tune this bird sings."

Kennedy's apartment was on the top floor. Everything looked like a half-struck set. Insects scuttled over whatever could be scuttled over. Rats scurried over everything else. There was a miasma of mold. It was somehow in worse shape than The Old-Timer's building.

Except for the top floor. The top floor was solid. The paint was fresh. It was clean. There was only one door. Steel with seven locks and a peephole.

"That's ... surprising," Max said.

"Bet there's a support structure from the top floor right to the ground, running through the rest of the building."

"Why would someone do this?"

"Well, Max, I'm sure there are lots of reasons, but I'd put my money on hiding highly remunerative illegal activities. Give 'em your FBI knock and I'll see what I can do with these locks."

Max knocked three times, quickly and heavily with the side of his fist. He projected, "Investigators on official business for Lydia Kennedy." He replicated the knock and waited.

Feet shuffled on the other side of the door. Someone said, "Who, who is it?"

"Investigators on official business," Max boomed.

"Jesus, you get a degree in that?" Trike muttered, already through four locks.

"Associates" Max muttered back. Then he boomed again, "Investigators. Official business to see Lydia Kennedy."

"I'm, I'm sorry, but I can't let you in. No, no, you simply can't come in—" a weak voice muttered.

Trike picked the last lock and pushed the door open. "Sorry, got bored," he explained.

A diminutive but dignified butler stammered in disbelief for a moment. Then he scurried off into the massive penthouse apartment.

Trike and Max both whistled. There was a hundred-gallon saltwater aquarium and a massive flat-screen television in front of three rows of stadium-arranged sofas. The kitchen looked like a showroom for a royal wedding registry. There was a glass-enclosed balcony at the back of the building. With a Jacuzzi.

Lydia Kennedy appeared from one of the rooms off the hallway with a fist on her hip. She wore a handmade authentic Japanese kimono. Her dyed blond hair was pulled back in a tight bun. She had dark eyebrows, high cheekbones, and a sharp nose. A real nasty sneer twisted her whole face and half her body.

"What are you doing here?" she demanded.

"Pardon our intrusion, Miss Kennedy. My name is Trike Augustine, and this is my partner Max. We're investigating the disappearance of Joyce and were hoping to ask you a few questions about the Joyce House."

"I see. Well, I don't know if I can be of service, but I will do my best. Would you two care for a drink?"

"No thanks, Miss Kennedy, we're driving."

"Mr. Augustine, you act like you don't trust me."

"You've kept one hand hidden."

"Yes, of course. I'm being observed by Trike Augustine, the genius."

"It doesn't take a genius to spot your pepper spray."

"In case you forgot the method of your entrance, you broke into my house. I should think it would be well within my rights to protect myself from whatever violence you might have intended."

"You are correct, Miss Kennedy. And you'd have to agree that we are well within our rights to stay out of range of your pepper spray on the off chance that this conversation leads to any misunderstandings."

Lydia Kennedy snapped her fingers. Two gigantic men in dark suits appeared at her side. The kind of guys someone in the family business would have at the snap of her fingers. "If at all possible, I would advise you to avoid misunderstanding. It would not turn out well for you."

Trike smirked. "I'll do my best, Miss. I'd hate to see your friend on the left tear that bum knee again. As you are clearly busy, I'd like to get started on my questions."

"Go right ahead."

"Just tell me what you remember about the Joyce House. We'd appreciate any information you have."

"I must say, I have to disappoint you."

"How so?"

"I've never set foot in the Joyce House," Lydia answered.

"But after it was scrubbed clean, it would have been one of your mother's safe houses," Trike argued.

"You are correct. After it had been scrubbed clean, it would have been one of my mother's safe houses, but not one I ever went to."

"What about when it was being sold through the Martha Clifford estate?" Trike asked.

"What about when it was being sold through the Martha Clifford estate?"

"Did you ever go to the house then?"

"I never set foot in the Joyce House. I've never been there. And before you bring up any other permutation of what you think is possible, I have never under any circumstances been to that building."

"Did your mother ever talk about it?" Trike continued.

"You'll be shocked to learn that she never discussed the architecture of any of her buildings with her young daughter."

"She never mentioned any secret passages?"

"I would include the mention of secret passages in discussion of architecture."

"Not even in the context of an exciting adventure story or something like that?" Trike persisted.

"Mr. Augustine, I know how easy it is to assume that one's own consciousness is representative of all consciousness, but it is ridiculous to believe that I would remember a stray comment or story my mother told about a place I'd never been. It is possible that she talked of nothing but the architecture of the Joyce House, but since it would have been meaningless to me, I don't remember it."

"You're not lying to us, are you, Miss Kennedy?"

"I thought the great Trike Augustine could always tell when someone was lying."

"I spread that rumor myself," Trike lied. "It encourages honesty."

"Since I am not lying and our discussion of the Joyce House is over, I believe your business here is concluded."

"You don't happen to know Joyce himself, do you?"

"No."

"Did you meet him during the sale of the house?"

"No. That was all handled by lawyers. Given the nature of the estate, you could not blame me for maintaining a certain distance from it."

"No. No. Of course not. So no dealings with Joyce at all?"

"Do you enjoy making me repeat myself, Mr. Augustine? I've never met Joyce. I've never corresponded with Joyce. And I know nothing of Joyce."

"I guess that's it, then."

"Then I believe it is time for you to go. Luckily, you are close enough to the door to see yourself out."

"It was excellent planning on our part, I think. Max?"

"Yeah, boss."

"Let's punish some pavement."

"Sure thing, boss."

Max opened the door and stepped into the hallway. Trike followed, but stopped and turned back, holding the door open.

"Just one more thing, Miss Kennedy, before I go."

"Christ," Max muttered.

"What is it, Mr. Augustine?"

"Just a little thing I'm confused about."

"Yes, Mr. Augustine," Kennedy said with diminishing patience.

"I just can't seem to get my mind around the property in Santa Fe."

"The property in Santa Fe?" Miss Kennedy looked startled.

"The one your mother transferred to you before she died, so it wouldn't be subject to an estate tax."

"What is confusing about that, Mr. Augustine?"

"Oh, that? Nothing's confusing about that. Rich assholes like you fucks find ways to skip out on society all the time. No, that part I get. I mean, you'll all burn in hell, but I get it. It's just, and this is for my own personal benefit, because, well, what I don't get is that it was built with a double-level basement."

"Yes. So?"

"Well. It's just that it was built right after a change in the zoning laws made basements like that legal. I'm sure a savvy property owner like you knows how crazy zoning laws in Santa Fe are."

"I am familiar with those ordinances. Get to the point, please, Mr. Augustine."

"It's just the weirdest thing. Because it was also built right before they started doing all those sweeps for illegal immigrants. I mean, you'd almost think somebody from immigration tipped off your mother and then she bribed the City Council to change the zoning laws to make it easier for her to keep smuggling in undocumented workers. Probably wouldn't be too shabby at processing cocaine either."

Lydia Kennedy pursed her lips. Glared at Trike.

"But I'm not working on that case. Probably just a coincidence anyway. You have a nice day, Miss Kennedy, and let me know if you suddenly remember anything about Joyce or his house."

Trike slammed the door behind him. Then spray-painted "CLASS WAR" on it.

"That's why you brought that," Max said.

"Always be prepared, Max. Always be prepared."

They walked down the stairs. Max tried to find the theorized support structure. Trike gave Lola a call and told her to train her X-ray specs of a brain on AVRAA.

"She lying, boss?" Max asked.

"Yes, she was, Max. Yes, she was."

"Sure?"

"I am."

"Why?"

"I have no fucking clue."

"Really?"

"I just don't see what she has to lose by telling the truth. If there was something involved with the house itself, it would have been a very small part of the whole Kennedy operation. And if Joyce were a big enough player for a Kennedy to feel the need to protect him, Lola would have found something."

"Maybe the connection is personal?"

"Like they're friends or something."

"Or more."

They got into the car. Max started it.

"It's not impossible, Max, but I get the sense she's playing a part. Obfuscating the information because the obfuscation is the point."

Trike slammed the door closed.

"Lot of that going around," Max said, pulling into the street.

"There certainly is, Max, there certainly is."

THE SURPRISE PARTY OR THE AMBUSH

If you believe in miracles, it was a miracle it took Trike so long to hit the whiskey. After getting back from the home visit, he went through the stuff Max had been able to drag out of the lawyers. There was something extra-weird about that Bodkin guy, but there wasn't enough data for a conclusion. That put whiskey in his mind.

Lola's visit to the police was more productive, but not by much. She didn't get to the bottom of the radio silence, but learned that Horn-Rims had been taken off the case. Which wouldn't be weird if they'd reclassified the case as a missing person. Which they didn't. That put whiskey in the glass.

Then he started going through Lola's AVRAA research.

If you believe in miracles, Jesus Christ himself would've clapped when Trike didn't rush out for cigarettes after wrestling with the AVRAA folder. Lola had discovered that AVRAA was a perfectly poised tax shelter. That no one was using.

Since there were guns in the house, Trike decided to take his whiskey buzz, flask of sustenance, nicotine withdrawal, and inferno of frustration for a walk.

The city was quiet. Everybody held their breath before the surprise party. Or the ambush.

Or it was two in the morning and the legitimate world slept.

It started to rain again. Trike took a sip from his flask at the corner. The coincident convergence of action and geography suggested a pacing strategy. Take a sip at each corner. Trike thought. Facts of the case. Logic that would fit them together. Something that would give it purpose. Before too much more of the reward vanished. Nothing.

Another corner, another slug of whiskey. He turned right. Left there was a bar with a cigarette vending machine. Straight ahead was a convenience store with the best cigarette selection in the county. Fucking cigarettes.

A large black sedan drove up on the sidewalk across the street and ahead of him. Trike sighed like your annoying cousin found a new TV show to enthuse about. The back driver's-side window rolled down. The snub of a small caliber handgun stuck out. It coughed a puff of smoke. A chunk of sidewalk ten feet from Trike jumped like a flea.

"Your persistence in the Joyce issue is becoming a nuisance. I would advise you to cease your investigations or I will singe the sweet tang of urine from your being," said a voice behind the gun.

"Well, I advise you to cease being a douchebag or I will tell everyone you still haven't read past Hades," Trike responded.

"You have quite a lot of confidence. For a man with a gun pointed at him."

"I never let anyone point a gun at me without pointing one back."

"You're not pointing a gun at me," the voice said nervously.

"That you can see."

The gun vanished from the window. Trike heard a hissed, "Drive! Drive!" The car sped off. At the stop sign, it came to a full. And complete. Stop. The driver looked both ways. Then sped off again, tires squealing on the moist asphalt.

Trike watched it go.

Man standing in a trench coat.

"That you can see?" he repeated himself. "Where the fuck would the gun even be? Trained squirrels? Mercenary pigeons? Damn whiskey," Trike took a huge slug of whiskey. "Damn rain. Damn case. Damn cigarettes. Messing with my retorts."

A memory floated to his consciousness. City hall. Parking lot. Reserved spot. "That was The Mayor's car," he said to himself. He took another long sip from his flask. "Why did he just show me The Mayor's car?" He emptied the flask with the next sip. "The Mayor's car? Definitely need more booze. Gotta go home. Only open place with booze present and cigarettes absent. Fucking cigarettes."

Trike walked home. Tried to keep his brain quiet. Let it slosh around in the whiskey. Just, you know, look at shit. Highlights of the dumbest things he'd said to Lola played in the idle space. Like he needed to feel worse. He brought up some Joyce matrices instead. Idleness was the ivory-billed woodpecker in his brain.

There was a thick manila envelope on Trike's doormat. It was addressed using his full name. The return address was fake. No such street in said city. The stamps were real. The postmark was not.

Trike stood a foot away, considering it. He paced up and down his walkway, talking out his points.

"Substantial effort has been made to present this envelope as though it were delivered in the standard manner, that is, by the United States Postal Service, and a lesser detective might be convinced such was the case. But not for long, for any research would reveal the fakeness of the return address. Of course, a fake return address does not an unmailed delivery make, but the fake postmark does. It is not categorically impossible that the mark was applied and then the envelope was sneaked into the delivery mechanisms of the aforementioned national service after such a mark would normally be applied, but that assumes an extraordinary effort, and extraordinary effort is never a safe assumption."

Trike bent at the waist and examined the envelope. It was bodily safe and bomb-free. "This fake would generally serve its purpose in initially convincing nearly everyone that it was delivered in the standard manner."

Trike started pacing again. "However, if the individual who directed the delivery of this envelope has any knowledge of me whatsoever, and it is safe to assume said individual does, then said individual should know enough about my abilities to know I would see through—"

"Knock it off already!" a husky woman's voice shouted from next door.

"Oh. Sorry, Mrs. Kuhne. I didn't realize I was talking out loud," Trike apologized to his neighbor.

"Yes, you did. You do it all the time, you inconsiderate prat. Just keep it down. It's three in the goddamn morning."

"I will. I'm sorry. Good night, Mrs. Kuhne."

She muttered something as she closed the window. Probably not "Good night."

Trike went to the sidewalk. Paced there. He recommenced at a lower volume, "... the ruse so quickly that it makes one wonder why the ruse was employed at all. Furthermore, and here we arrive at the true point of this discussion, why address an envelope, waste several perfectly good stamps, put a substantial amount of effort into creating a fake postmark, all with the apparent goal of convincing the receiver that said envelope was delivered by the United States Postal Service, and then drop it off at three in the fucking morning?"

Trike threw a barrage of furiously sloppy punches, while a low-register growl dribbled from his throat. He recovered from the eruption of frustration.

"When criminals interact with the law, they try to limit the number of questions the law asks about the crime; ideally, to the one question, 'Who did this?' It is through the other questions that arise from the evidence that the aforementioned fundamental question is answered. Those questions find the mistake. But whoever left this demanded that I ask additional questions. Everything about this case has demanded additional questions. Why use between one-point-nine and two-point-three pints of blood? Why mess with the nine-one-one call? Why drop the pig in the kitchen? Why replace books with blank copies? Why incorporate a business to buy a house? Why use sixteen lawyers to handle the incorporation? Why put those locks on AVRAA? And now, why put this effort into a fake envelope and then undo that effort by delivering it at three in the morning?

"One could suppose this is like a magician forcing a card: that the criminal intends to control the investigation by controlling the additional questions asked, but that would involve even more risk of detection than the traditional method of limiting the number of questions, as it would create data. Maybe they just assumed I was asleep and would not wake up until after standard delivery time. Though my mail comes around four, that strategy lives near reasonable."

The rain picked up again. Trike walked quickly, picked up the envelope, and went inside. He tossed his coat on the couch, kept his hat on, and set the envelope on the kitchen table. He got a glass, some ice, and brought them together with three fingers of vodka.

Then he opened the envelope.

The police reports. Forensics. Interview transcripts. Officer depositions. Everything. "Fucked up," he said. "Way too fucked up."

He made the vodka in his glass go away. Recorded the new data. Pushed the reports to the side of the table.

"Here's the plan," he muttered. "Step one: think about all of this shit for awhile, drinking as much vodka as is required. Step two: pass the fuck out here at the kitchen table, as befits the predicament. Step three: wake up, make myself pretty, give the reports to Lola and Max and enjoy the looks on their faces. Step four: pay a visit to The Mayor. Yeah. Good plan."

THE MAYOR'S CAR AND THE MATRICES

Butlerworebeigecorduroyspalebluepoloshirtgrayfleeceravelrytotebag
yarnneedlesbutlergetspaperdecidestocancelsubscriptionwentroomto
roommostlyinkitchenwatchedTVleftat6unlikelybutnotimpossibleJoyce

State of AVRAA   **Mayor's car**

AVRAA defrauds   Influence zoning to   Car bought/stolen
donors   encourage restoration   w/out his knowledge

                        Citywide Scam

AVRAA potential   Awareness of futur
tax haven/money   zoning changes
laundering

Kennedy in w/Feds   Kennedy/Joyce   Joyce not a person
                        connection

Lydia Kennedy   **Joyce House Ltd.**

isinthehousehidingJoyceHouseLmtdhelddeedJoycenamedsteward
boughtfromestateofMarthaCliffordManagedbysmallfirminSanteFe
MarthaCliffordcretedtoprotectpropertyasitactuallybelongedtoknown

criminalMinaKennedyLydiaKennedyabletosellJoyceHousethrough
MarthaCliffordincorporationinvolved16lawfirmsnoneofwhichdidcorpo
ratelawin6statestook3yearstocompleteeasierwaystohideeverything

State of AVRAA   **Mayor's car**

E.D. OCD   Car lent without knowledge
                                  of use

            AVRAA renovates buildings
            for criminal purposes

Kennedy restoring   Coming renovations   Mayor to buy JH Ltd.
as yet unknown   to JH to facilitate
buildings for   criminal activities
criminal activities

            Facilitate inheritance   Facilitate inheritance
            by Kennedy's and Joyce's   by illegitimate
            illegitimate child   child

Lydia Kennedy   **Joyce House Ltd.**

2hours8minstopicklocksperfectforatrapbutnotrapwassetKennedyin
badpartoftownonlytopfloorwindowsintactmassivepenthouseapart
mentrichlyfurnishedLKwearingvintagekimonodyedblondhairdarkeye

State of AVRAA   **Mayor's car**

Doubles as a locksmith   Mayor's getting rid of
training facility   evidence

Joyce & Kennedy
secretly on AVRAA Board

Kennedy owns a   Laundered money   Every company
Victorian house in   funds Mayor's   needs a car
restoration   campaign

Establishing drug
dealing connections

                                        Facilitate purchase of
General Family   property through
Business   purchase of business

Lydia Kennedy   **Joyce House Ltd.**

minutesaftercallVanishedreclusivebillionaire1.92.3pintsofblood
fakebookswindownailedshutdeskmoved3"NWdecorativepenstand
lampsswitchforsecretdoorlightbulbsoutQueenAnnewingchairlittle

State of AVRAA   **Mayor's car**

Course for a   An exact replica
lock-picking contest

Elaborate feint for
some greater attack

Theme park!

Santa Fe
properties

Beneficial status
for unusual
collection

Leftover of an
aborted business
plan

Lydia Kennedy   **Joyce House Ltd.**

usedottomanTristramShandyunderSHinsteadofSTreportedmissing
7:42ambutlerlives3blocksawaynotunusualforJoycetosleepinstudy
newspaperinboxifJoycehasButlersawnewspaperonmorningsaw

Trike snapped out of his matrices. He had two fresh detecting resources in front of him; the mysteriously delivered police reports and a bottle of vodka. He switched to his favorite fuck-my-life vodka cup.

He liked to save that cup for special cases, but he figured he'd earned its privilege by quitting smoking. Trike poured four fingers of vodka into his glass. At four matrices a second for forty minutes, Trike had discovered that not a fucking thing made a fucking bit of sense.

Trike could render explanations for why AVRAA was locked up like a coke king's mansion, or why someone shot at him from The Mayor's car, or why Lydia Kennedy lied to him, or why Joyce's house was owned by Joyce House Ltd. But nothing could get them all to stick together. And even if they did, it was only possible that such an explanation would indicate Joyce's present location.

Trike found a portion of his brain searching for the possibility of a cigarette somewhere in the house. Fallen from a pocket; shaken to the floor while being shaken from the pack; dropped from his mouth after he passed out drunk. None came to mind, which meant there were none.

It is possible that such a situation occurred while an intense amount of focus was on some other problem and thus was not recorded, but to confirm or deny such a scenario would require the kind of search where stethoscopes are pressed to walls, long needles are stuck through couch cushions, and gimlet holes are bored into furniture. There was too much vodka in the bottle in front of him and too much bullshit in the day behind him to mount such an effort. He could barely get through what he was being paid to do.

He turned to the police report. He worked through it page by page, committing every word to his easy-recall memory. Vodka sips paced by page turns. Halfway through the report he refilled his cup. Fuck his life. When he got to the end he consolidated the data, removed redundancies as well as he could, and drew an initial conclusion.

The report was bursting with depositions, forensic evidence, and official statements, all attesting to the irrevocable certainty that all involved and questioned didn't know shit about shit. Mere anarchy.

Through the window over his sink he saw the dim blue light in the dark that most likely came from Mrs. Kuhne's TV, as she watched *Animal Planet* to get back to sleep after being so rudely awakened. His glass was empty. Again. The bottle of vodka was at an alarming level.

"Step one completed to reasonable satisfaction," Trike said. "On to step two."

Trike folded his arms in front of him on the table, put his head on them, and passed the fuck out.

FIVE PERCENT OF
GOLD CUP CASINOS INCORPORATED

In the last four days, The Mayor moved his desk an inch to the left. He skipped breakfast. Bought an SUV. Read the sports and classifieds sections. His wife lost sleep to infomercials again. He planned to leave early to play raquetball. Time at the accounting firm was stressful but lucrative. His son would be visiting in a month. So would his mother-in-law. He was cutting down on caffeine. He didn't understand blind carbon copy. He did not know about the car.

Trike saw it all walking from the office door to the chair in front of the desk. To Trike, the world was a teleprompter of itself.

The Mayor stood up so fast that his Kennedy hair waved. He robustly thrust his arm for a handshake. "The great Trike Augustine graces my office," he said, in the tone of politico-enjoyment cultivated over decades of pretending to care about people.

Trike didn't shake. Sat down.

The Mayor shook his head, unthrust his arm and sat down. "Ah, yes, the quirks of genius," he said, as if remembering the quirks of genius he experimented with in college.

"Yes," Trike said, "how enlightened society is to allow those who demonstrate atypical abilities to eschew conventions of decorum, how indulgent it is of the differences between individuals, how accepting it can be when it knows there is a give-and-take between talent and manners. However, as you well know, this is not a true act of openness. At the core of this indulgence beats a weak and quivering heart of fear, a fear that if precautions are not taken, if foibles are not accepted, if the talented are asked to dance the same steps as the mediocre, they will turn their talent upon you, wreaking a cruel and terrible revenge.

"But that too is an inversion of the formula, for it is not society that indulges the genius; the genius indulges society. You think you show forgiveness by allowing me to not shake your hand, but rather it is a very grudgingly given permission on my part, to allow you to believe in the value of the shaken hand, to believe that something is accomplished when hands are shaken, to believe that it is something more stable than enlightened self-interest that keeps those of us with atypical abilities from tearing the reins of power from your weak little fingers and relegating you to tasks commensurate with your limited abilities.

"But I did not come here to tear comforting veils from your eyes and expose the core precariousness of your existence. No, I am here for much more immediate, much more tangible, perhaps even more mortal reasons.

"You see, Mr. Mayor. You sold your car."

The Mayor looked like his tonsils were pulled out and set in a commemorative cup on his desk.

"Yes. So? What does my car have to do with anything? I mean, I cleared my schedule for you. I assumed, given your prominence, that you had something important to discuss. Instead, you tell me I sold my car."

"You didn't ask how I knew you sold your car."

"You looked at my shoes. Who knows with you? Maybe there was something on my secretary's desk—ooh, or maybe you'd just pretend it was something like that, but really you just saw a different car in my parking spot, eh, was that it? That was it, wasn't it?" The Mayor pointed at Trike with a level of triumph.

"Somebody shot at me from the back window of your car last night."

The color spilled from The Mayor's face. Lungs, not tonsils.

"They—someone shot at you?"

Trike shrugged. "They weren't too interested in hitting me. Just made a vague threat about The Joyce Case."

"The Joyce Case?"

" 'Least your ears work. It was odd. Once the real estate world became involved, I figured a busybody like you with an inflated sense of self-importance had to be nosing around. But then I couldn't figure out how you'd make a profit on it. Busybodying is one thing, but you've got a lifestyle to maintain. And there's no way you've got the intelligence to be in charge, or the executive or administrative ability to be delegated even a supporting role. So, I guessed you'd have your ear to the ground, just in case something worth your while came up. But then someone goes and quite forcefully suggests your involvement. Why do you think they would do that?"

"I have no idea."

"It gets stranger. 'Cause it's your car, they might as well have left a trail of gold-plated bread crumbs to their identity."

"Trike, before you go on—"

"We're not on a first-name basis."

"Listen, I'm just going to be honest with you, since there is no point in hiding things from you—"

"You're lying."

"I just want to come clean with you—"

"Still lying."

"This is something I need to get off my chest—"

"Lying."

"Okay. Fine. When the next election cycle comes around—"

"Ohmygod, still lying. But trying harder."

"Damnit, Trike! What do you want me to tell you?"

"Where Joyce is."

"I don't know. I never met him. I knew some of the stuff about the property, like you said, but it was all so minor, I didn't pay much attention to it. To me, it actually looked aboveboard. Stupid but legal."

"Why did you sell him your car?"

The Mayor shrugged. "Legally, I didn't. I was offered twice the Blue Book value for it by a proxy whose name I'm sure you can determine, if you haven't already. I'd been looking to upgrade for a while, and I saw this as my chance. Obviously, I would have rethought my decision if I knew he was going to use it to send you here, but, as it stands, I haven't done anything, well, prosecutable. I'll even give you the name of the guy who bought it."

"When did you know the sale was connected to Joyce?"

The Mayor shrugged again. His casual shrug. "Well, I didn't *know* it was connected with The Joyce Case until just now. It was implied, but not with any kind of certainty."

"Implied how?"

"They told me that it was being purchased for someone maintaining a low profile who was willing to pay a little extra for discretion. As I'm sure you know, that is not a small group of potential buyers."

Trike looked over The Mayor's shoulder. It was dusted with dandruff from beneath his designer toupee. Trike sat there for ninety-eight seconds.

"That doesn't make sense. I can't think of a way for that to make sense. Even as a red herring, it's stupid."

"People do strange things sometimes, Trike."

"No. We replace lack of information with lack of sense. It makes sense to the psychopath. And we're still not on a first-name basis."

"Then I suppose there's nothing more I can do for you," The Mayor said, leaning back in his chair, as if he'd put a lot of effort into the conversation.

"I suppose not."

Trike stood up. He eschewed The Mayor's outstretched hand and went to the door. He opened it partway, stopped, and turned back to The Mayor.

"Well, Mr. Mayor, there is just one more thing."

"Oh, Christ."

"Just a little thing I can't keep track of in my head, totally for my own benefit, I just like to get all of these things straightened out."

"Mr. Augustine—"

"Finally, I'm Mr. Augustine."

"Mr. Augustine, that spiel only works for Columbo because he convinces the criminals that he isn't very smart so they fall into his traps. You, on the other hand, never let anybody forget that you're a genius."

"Oh, it's not that at all, Mr. Mayor. In fact, it's probably nothing at all, I just, these things, they just get caught in my head and bother me until I get them straightened out."

"You're still doing it."

"Oh no, no, not at all, I just have a thing about loose ends, you know, they keep me up at night, and I'm sure an important person like you knows all about being kept up at night."

The Mayor slapped his desk with a flat palm. "You're not going to stop. Because you're a fucking arrogant bastard who just does whatever the fuck he wants."

"It's just a little thing, I'm sure there's a perfectly logical explanation for it, that I just can't figure out myself—"

"Okay, fine. Fucking fine. I own five percent of Gold Cup Casinos Incorporated and that's why I funneled those campaign contributions to the referendum supporters in the next county. Okay. Just fucking stop that."

"I was just going to ask why you got anti-glare treatment on your windshield. Makes it practically impossible for the defroster to work in the winter. But I'll keep that other thing in mind, you know, in case something else comes up."

Trike clicked his tongue for goodbye and walked out. Left the door open.

THE TWENTY-TWO BROKEN BONES

The office walls radiated hatred. The desk seethed loathing. The carpet oozed disgust. His own eyes looked upon themselves with acidic disdain. After three hours, seventeen minutes, and forty-three seconds of recording, reviewing, analyzing, and imagining data, every facet of every surface Trike could see, feel, and smell had become a font of awful.

Max and Lola had left for the day. Another fifty grand essentially gone. If there was one bright spot, Trike did enjoy the looks on their faces when he gave them the police reports to investigate. Since then it'd been just the data grind.

Some of the work of private detecting made for good TV. The other 99 percent was as exciting as doing your taxes. And as a small-business owner and private consultant, a lot of it was actually doing his fucking taxes.

But he couldn't quit it. He didn't know the answer so he couldn't quit it. He just had to get out of the office. Before something unreasonable became reasonable. He packed up the ten notebooks he'd been using to quickly visualize different arrays of data and slammed the door on his way out. He muttered, "One could argue that the true point of 'The Purloined Letter' has nothing to do with detecting, but rather, is to provide a succinct and complete definition of . . . friendship," while he walked to the car.

The diner was one of Trike's places. They let him nurse

bottomless coffee. Order off-menu. Take up a booth. Smiled warmly when he called himself "The Baconator."

Trike waved for coffee as he sat down at his booth. Pushed a week's worth of newspapers to the side of the table. Took out his notebooks. Continued his work from the office.

Trike was looking for money. It was a crass oversimplification of the chaotic complexity of human experience, but it was a productive axiom. Usually the person who held the money held the gun. Trike could find no money in whatever Joyce was up to. The time at the office, plus the subsequent fifty-five minutes at the diner, plus the less-focused speculations that piled up over the course of the investigation, all pointed to the same conclusion. Joyce was up to something, but there was no money in it.

Mid-fifth sip of his third cup of coffee, Trike decided to ride another old gray mare of detection. Once you rule out money, you're left with love and revenge. So Trike shuffled the notebooks around in the hopes that a mosaic of revenge would emerge from their pattern.

Another forty-three minutes and no mosaic. But revenge felt plausible. The next logical option was to pick random actors in the case and run possible scenarios that matched with Joyce seeking revenge on them, eliminating those determined impossible. Thinking of the procedure gave Trike something like a headache. Something like a headache that swallowed an atom bomb and crop-dusted all over his waning hopes for happiness.

He packed away the notebooks and dragged the pile of newspapers in front of him. It was a mess of a week's worth of the city's two papers. Instinctively, Trike organized the pages into sections, and the sections into editions, separating those into two chronological piles.

The big story in both papers was the sexual assault and murder of a teenage girl at one of the city's nightclubs. The atrocity of the murder and the youth and beauty of the victim conspired to produce intense excitement.

She was found savagely beaten in the alley behind the club, in a position that suggested her murderer was attempting to dispose of her body in a Dumpster. All the evidence related in the papers suggested that this was an ordinary crime, atrociously committed. Probably a boy she'd gone to the club with. Got too close. Things got out of hand.

"Probably should just solve this," Trike mumbled to himself as he read.

"What was that, hon?" Matilda called from behind the counter.

"Oh, nothing, Matilda, just muttering to myself. But, actually, could you put in an order for some wheat toast?"

"Sure thing."

"Thanks. You're the best."

The Daily Standard took particular tabloid glee in listing the injuries. Trike had to assume the list was accurate, as a sensationalist newspaper would never dare such a catalog of wounding if it were not true. *The Register* was terser but no less effective at communicating the viciousness of the assault. It was a crime like thousands of other crimes, but for the twenty-two broken bones. "Mental illness in here somewhere. Or something else atypical," Trike theorized.

As time passed and no discovery ensued, a thousand contradictory rumors were circulated. Gangs were imagined. Drug dealers. Perverts. The almost-forgotten name of a never-caught serial killer. Somehow a theory about an escaped ape from the nearest zoo found its way into print.

But Trike could read, from the details the police provided, that they had a good idea of who the killer was. Something was preventing them from making the arrest. They had the truth but not the evidence. It is a fact of detecting life, that much of what is rejected by the court is the best evidence to the intellect. That's the other thing left out of the movies. The truth had to be subjected to a second process, after discovery, for it to become evidence in a court of law.

"Here's your toast, hon," Matilda said, dropping off the order.

"Thanks, Matilda."

"Let me know if you need anything else. Or just mutter under your breath."

"Thanks."

The more he read, the more he was convinced. And the more he knew about the killer. It was a minor, probably a kid from the high school. His family had money. And a lawyer who had specifically instructed him on what to say and what not to say. There was a piece missing. Some act of confirmation the police needed before they could get a warrant. If it hadn't been raining the night of the murder they would've wrapped this up the morning after. Now they had to hope the kid said something he'd been instructed not to say.

The door opened. Horn-Rims walked in like somebody broke the only bowling trophy he was proud of. Heaved himself onto a counter stool. Nodded for coffee. Being demoted didn't change the fact that Horn-Rims was the best homicide detective in the city. He had to be on the girl's case.

A terrifying idea flashed across Trike's mind. A horrifying idea. An embarrassing idea. An idea that made the very core of Trike's detecting identity shudder with disgust. Goddamn, he wanted a cigarette.

Trike heaved himself onto a stool next to Horn-Rims. Horn-Rims jumped when he noticed who sat next to him.

"What the fuck do you want?" he asked.

"Information exchange."

"I don't have time to mess around with your little game of tiddlywinks."

"I can put him at the scene of the crime."

Horn-Rims grunted.

"Since it's a kid at the high school," Trike continued, "I can put him at the scene of the crime on the night in question."

The coffee arrived.

"All right, hotshot, you can shit in my ear if it makes you feel better. But then buzz off. I've got lives on the line."

"That club is exclusive. Even on the all-ages dance nights, it's hard to get in. Low capacity. Dress code. Guest lists. That kind of thing. Kids at the high school keep their ticket stubs in their wallets as a status symbol. Whoever this kid is, he's not a professional. That ticket stub went right in his wallet the second he got it back from the doorman and it's still there. And it's dated. If his parents or their lawyers are stonewalling you, you can place him at the club on the night in question."

Horn-Rims took a deep breath. A long sip of coffee. A longer sip of coffee. He nodded for a refill. When Matilda came over, he ordered a Reuben.

"Someone has been systematically removing every honest cop from The Joyce Case," he said. "One demotion and a bunch of re-assignments. A lot of other paperwork isn't getting done. The case is getting pushed around and pushed around with nobody doing anything about it and without being closed. As of yesterday, pretty much all work on it has stopped."

"Why?"

Horn-Rims shrugged. "Don't know what the point is, but the result seems to be that you're the only one with any chance to solve the case."

Trike took a deep breath. He went back to his booth. He added the new information to one of his notebooks. He nibbled at his toast. He slapped on a nicotine patch.

He tore precise blank corners off notebook pages. Arranged them in three rows in front of him. Then, consigning one letter to each scrap, he wrote, "Why does it matter who solves the case?" He stared at the arrangement of information. It started misting outside, again.

He needed something else. He knew where to get it. It was time to see The Lady on the Corner.

He swept up the scraps of paper and stuffed them in his pocket.

It was 2:47 a.m. She'd be out by the time he could scrape together every last bit of cash he had access to. Finally, quitting smoking returned a tangible reward. He probably had an extra hundred bucks kicking around. And The Lady on the Corner's intel was expensive.

He called Max as he walked to his buff insult to the American automobile industry, to see if Max had any useful amount of cash handy. Max didn't. Even half-conscious, Max could tell from the question that Trike was heading to see The Lady.

"Reached that point," Max mumbled.

"We have," Trike confirmed.

Trike got into the car. He couldn't drive and talk at the same time, so he finished up his conversation with Max.

"Hoping for anything?" Max asked.

"I'm beginning to suspect that this is an act of revenge, Maxilicious. I'm hoping The Lady on the Corner will tell me the who and who of the relationship."

Max mumbled something that was probably an approximation of "Good luck."

"And good luck to you," Trike responded. "I'd wish you sweet dreams, but I'd much rather you dreamt about revenge."

Trike hung up.

The Lady on the Corner. Goddamn.

Trike popped a piece of nicotine gum. Then began the cabalistic ritual of starting his car.

THE VOID

Trike lurched into the office. The opening door smacked one of the filing cabinets stuffed into the small room. Max was arranging a stock of filled legal notepads on his desk.

"Anything, Max?" Trike asked as he hung up his coat.

Max gestured at the stack of notebooks as if revealing prizes on a game show. "Same old, same old," he said.

"Jesus. I can only imagine what Lola turned up with her half of the reports."

"No need," Max said.

He picked up an accordion folder from between his desk and the office fern and waggled it at Trike.

"What the fuck is going on here, Max?"

"You saw The Lady on the Corner. What'd she tell you?"

Trike leaned against the doorway to his office. He focused on a spot on the ceiling. Then started talking.

"The Old-Timer sent me to her. I trusted his opinion, but I didn't put much stock in it, if you know what I mean. And when I saw her for the first time, I didn't know what to expect. The corner. The costume of rags. The precise schedule. But when she told me that Frank Foer and Sons was a concealed subsidiary of Arthur Train International, I knew she was the real deal. It wouldn't have meant anything to anybody else, but to me, it meant the stolen Van Gogh was in a deposit box at John Lloyd Brokers and Hedge Fund Managers.

"The second time, she told me the *Sainted Moore* was scheduled to leave San Francisco on December 15, which sounded like a bad joke about spy code, but told me George Joseph Smith was actually the foreign-currency trader Adam Wirth, whose faked death was imminent. The third time, she just gave me the address of the U.S. embassy in Sofia. Anybody else would have thrown their cash on the ground and stormed off cursing her name, but it made me realize the money was being funneled into a spurious charter jet company so it could be recovered in bankruptcy insurance held by an investment bank.

"And this time. This time, Max," Trike popped a piece of nicotine gum, "she told me that Joyce is using this whole mess to get revenge on someone."

"You knew that," Max responded.

"And when I made that point she said, 'You suspected it. Very different. Now you know for sure and can act accordingly.' Which is true, but not actionable."

"Expensive?"

"She was icing three very-poor-decision-making thugs when I showed up, so she had me do a song-and-dance eyewitness number for the police, making a very long night a whole helluva lot longer and markedly more unpleasant."

Max shrugged. "Kept your money."

"There is that."

"So what's the plan, boss?"

Trike blew a concentrated stream of air out of his mouth. "You got more work to do on the reports?"

"I could."

"Keep going till you're exhausted. Or have some brilliant idea. What's Lola up to?"

"Internet . . . at home."

"She give you a summary of that particular monstrosity?" Trike gestured at the folder.

"No, but she said this. Hold on . . . wrote it down. She said,

'The person responsible for this should hang, either at The Hague or the Louvre."

Trike raised an eyebrow. Quickly slapped a nicotine patch on his arm. "Fantastic. Well, Max, keep on doing what you're doing. Lola will keep doing what she's doing. I'm going to listen to the radio while I figure this out. Wet my whistle with whichever of those notebooks you think is most useful."

Max handed him the one on top.

"Was it really the one on top?" Trike asked.

"Not sure any are useful. Figured I'd be . . . efficient."

Trike took the notebook and went into his office. Scanned his memory for reports of companies and/or individuals losing exorbitant sums of money in the weeks before the disappearance. He glanced at the notebook and then tossed it onto the desk. He sat down, leaned back in his chair, put his feet up, and reached back to turn the radio on.

The void.

Trike froze. He knew exactly where his radio was supposed to be. He knew where everything important in his life was supposed to be. He turned around slowly. With horror. Gone. His radio.

"Max!" he shouted.

"What?" Max shouted back.

"What the fuck?"

"What do you mean?"

"Where the fuck is my radio?"

"If you don't know, I don't know."

"Max?" Trike shouted, exasperation sneaking into his voice.

Max threw the door open. "What?"

"Who the fuck stole my radio?"

"I don't know. Is there a note?"

"A note. Yes. I'll see if there is a note."

"Ladies and gentlemen . . . the miraculous intellect of Trike Augustine."

Trike checked the spot where his radio should have been.

There was a note. He grabbed it and sat down. A violent perplexity contorted his face.

"It says, 'I've stolen your radio like I took the key to the tower. Get off The Joyce Case before it's too late.'"

"Gonna insult the reference?"

"No. I mean, references this bad are more perversions than references, but that's not the point."

"What is?"

"How did they know to steal my radio?"

Max shrugged. "Surveillance."

"But why?"

Max shrugged again. "I don't know ... You break into places for fun."

"Practice, Max. Practice."

Trike was quiet for a moment. "Have you heard of anybody else working on the case?"

Max shook his head. "Nope."

"You'd think with a reward that big, even as it shrinks, shamuses amateur and professional would be crawling on the case like ants in your nightmares."

"True."

"And Horn-Rims told me the police really aren't trying to solve it. In fact, 'someone has been systematically removing every honest cop from The Joyce Case,' so that, at least from the police perspective, no one but me has a chance to solve the case."

"Wait. You—talked—to Horn-Rims."

"Stay focused, Max. The Lady on the Corner told me Joyce is getting revenge on someone. Someone stole my radio. Which is annoying with remarkable precision."

"What are you getting at?" Max said suspiciously.

Trike took his feet off the desk. Leaned forward and put his head in his hands.

"What if Joyce is trying to get revenge on me?"

Max's jaw dropped. His eyes went wide. He slowly walked across the room and sat down in one of the client chairs.

"Max," Trike said. He reached under his desk and grabbed a tallboy from the mini-fridge. "I need a moment," he cracked the beer, "and then I need a plan."

THE PIPE WAS NECESSARY AND THE WEDNESDAY JOG

Trike's face rested on the kitchen table. He had the long-party hangover. Ache in the back. Dense fog in the brain. Disavowal of life. Pulsing absence of vitality. The structure of his thoughts disintegrating like books in the rain.

There are two solutions to the long-party hangover; pin your ears back, grab a glass, and get drunk again or pop a couple of low-octane painkillers and go to sleep. And Trike wasn't getting to sleep. Too much bullshit in his head. And getting drunk didn't appeal, either.

The reason was initially obscure. An iceberg in the distance. It took awhile for Trike to identify it. He had not considered the case from this state of mind. Perhaps it was the right one.

He was forced to grab the biggest objects bobbing in the sewage of his thoughts and pin them down with great acts of violence. Connect facts with dynamite. Argue points with sledgehammers. Remember events with steel chairs.

And the largest turd in the flow was the fact that Joyce was seeking revenge on Trike. If the goal of revenge was frustration, Trike had to admit, the technique was a runaway success. But what kind of revenge is frustration?

Trike picked his face off the kitchen table. In a second and distinct motion, he raised the rest of him up from the chair. He dragged himself to the living room, where he picked up his pipe off the coffee table. He didn't have the energy to keep his thoughts on the inside. He stalked about the house talking his brain out. The pipe was necessary.

"Perhaps there is no emotion in human experience more thoroughly understood than desire for revenge. Though its inherent escalation can lead to radically irrational-appearing action, the process is perfectly logical. No matter how distasteful the violence might be to our other sensibilities, we understand why someone murders an entire family to avenge the murder of a single brother. To deter potential future harmful actions, we demonstrate exponential retaliation to harmful actions.

"However, if frustration is the intended effect of the revenge, then, assuming the exponential response, calculating back to the original event, we find an offense that would not warrant revenge at all. But if frustration is not the point, what is?

"At its core, revenge is a message. A message to its target and to the wider world that might observe it. To the target, the message is essentially tautological, 'I am getting revenge for' the previous harm. To the wider world, the message is essentially prescriptive, 'This is what happens when someone harms me.'

"Joyce is sending me a message.

"About something I did.

"I have no idea what he is trying to tell me."

With the jolt of a somnambulist, Trike found himself on the near-empty second floor of his house in front of the bookcase holding eighty-four blank-on-the-inside notebooks. He believed that every case would be the one he finally wrote down and sold for the money Lola needed, but, after writing the title on the cover, barrenness swept over his brain like a breeze across the prairie. Facing the notebooks, Trike started remembering everyone who might want to get revenge on him, eliminating those who were definitely unable to act as Joyce had.

He stalked his way back to the sink.

Trike harmed criminals for a living. And could be a real ass-hole. There was no limit to potential revengers. The process seized.

"I need to induce direct communication. If he knows me well enough to steal my radio, then he must know the inherent risks of bodily attack, the small amount of value I place on most other objects in my life, and my ability to disassociate fear from my decision-making process. Why hasn't he gone after Lola?"

Trike's city ceased.

"He doesn't know I love Lola."

Trike put his hands on the sink. He imagined scenarios that would tell Joyce about Lola while giving him the opportunity to act on the new knowledge. Fifty-three seconds later, the invitation to the Annual Municipal Fancy-Dress Ball sitting in the office re-cycling bin occurred to him.

Followed by a hollow certainty.

"Mayor will blab my attendance to anyone who will listen. No security. Lots of exits. Two into back alleys. Opportunity for chaos, like pulling the fire alarm, to cover things. Dress up as EMTs or something. Even a shitty kidnapping could work. And should the kidnappers get nasty, Lola would get nasty right back at them. Once they take her, they'll have to send a message of some kind. Decode message. Collect remaining reward."

Trike clapped his hands together.

"A plan. A motherfucking plan. Just got to tell Lola without Joyce knowing it's a plan, which means I should probably stop talking out loud. But if the place is bugged, Joyce knows about Lola now, even if he also knows about the Ball Plan, and I'm too tired and, something else, to keep my mouth closed. So I've got to tell her the plan and convince her to agree to it," Trike checked his watch, "on her motherfucking morning jog."

He cursed at the sink.

And there was still no way he would get to sleep.

Trike sat on the couch and turned on CNN with picture-in-picture of the most reliable local news. There was a mound of local, regional, and national newspapers by the couch. He read them while absorbing the information on TV. An event in the world could always become the fact in a case.

In that way, Trike passed the time.

Then he changed into his jogging outfit. Maroon sweatpants tied up with shoelaces because the elastic was no longer elastic. A souvenir T-shirt from a Greenpeace fund-raiser that happened before he was born. A Chicago Bears Super Bowl Shuffle sweatshirt with the hood cut off.

He drove to Lola's place and sat down on the front steps. He muttered, "This means that entire ranges of divergent intelligences—the most brilliant to the most imbecilic—would share the same action, rendering the entire exercise of establishing the opponent's intelligence as a technique in discerning action completely and utterly pointless," while he waited for her. She bounded out the door three minutes and twenty seconds later. Stopped short when she saw him.

"Jesus Christ, Trike, you could fucking call first and let me know."

"Let you know what? That I wasn't going to skip our Wednesday jog again? I feel bad enough missing the last few weeks."

Trike stood up. Stretched and ran in place. Lola hopped down the stairs, shrugging.

"All right," she said, "let's go."

Lola started jogging. To most, Lola started running. Trike caught up. Their conversation was cadenced by Trike's breathlessness mixed with grunts of pain and ennui.

"I have a plan for The Joyce Case," Trike started.

"Are you sure we're under surveillance?"

"Because I'd put myself through this on a hunch."

"Okay, what's the plan?"

"I need you to go to the Ball with me and get kidnapped by Joyce."

Lola sped up.

"Fuck. God. Damn. Doughnuts. You. Gofaster."

"Is this a problem? Is it too fast for the great Trike Augustine?"

Trike caught his breath after the acceleration. "Joyce is trying to get revenge on me. I'm a hard guy to get revenge on. In terms of the surveillance we can safely assume has been conducted, I'm a high-functioning sociopath, an emotionless detecting machine, who assuages the endless agony of his irreparable disconnect from the emotions of human society through binge drinking and public displays of social disregard."

"Yeah, they're way off-base."

"You can jog. And be sarcastic?"

"You of all people should not be surprised by multitasking."

"Point taken." Trike secured enough oxygen for the next statement. "Through your attendance at the Ball as my date, I can both show him that I, at the very least, have feelings for you, and give him an opportunity to act on that information."

"Awfully chauvinistic, don't you think?"

"No."

"No? Then how come the woman is getting kidnapped?"

"He already knows Max is my partner, so if he wanted to attack through Max, he would have, and, you know, just because the plan leverages the rampant chauvinism of society does not mean the plan itself is chauvinistic."

"So I've got to put myself in a dress, with makeup, deal with my mother about this—and you know how my mother is like about shit like this—so I can get kidnapped, which will tip my dad off that something is weird, don't forget—"

"Never do."

Lola sped up.

She continued, "All so you can get a message from Joyce, a message that may or may not be of any use whatsoever. And that's before we think about the other risks in getting myself kidnapped."

"This isn't half as crazy as the stuff Max did at the Bureau. This is private detecting. Fuckin' A, Lola, half the point of being a PI is getting to play dress-up."

"Yeah, but you don't have to wear heels when you do."

"I don't have to," Trike barely got out.

"How is Joyce going to find out you're taking me to the Ball?"

"The Mayor sees all the RSVPs. He'll pass it on. Even if that bald bitch doesn't pass it on directly, it'll make the gossip rounds. I could even ask you in the office. We know that's being watched. We'll do a planning session. Even if you don't actually get kidnapped, we still learn something."

They jogged in silence for a minute. As much silence as Trike's lungs allowed.

"Take me to Paris."

"What?" Trike said, stumbling.

"When you solve the case, use some of your money to take me to Paris. For a month."

"Paris? Why Paris?" Trike gasped. "Given the unstable nature of our finances, are you sure that's a prudent use of the money?"

Lola sped up again. "Do you really have enough oxygen to negotiate?"

"Jesus. Faster. You. Go. Okay. Okay. Paris from my portion of the reward money."

Lola slowed down to a pace distantly related to reasonable.

"You know what the worst part of the situation is," she said.

"What?"

"Wednesday is my long day."

"Wednesday is your long day?"

"And if you want to preserve the illusion of this jog . . ."

Trike did not have enough air for an appropriate curse.

"You're going to have to jog the whole route."

"This is revenge, isn't it?"

"Figured I'd join the club."

"I thought revenge was a dish best served. Cold."

"Sometimes it's best served sweaty and cramped," Lola snickered. "You picked a helluva week to quit smoking."

AWKWARD, ANXIOUS, AND OUT-OF-PLACE

"After I drop you off," Lola said to Janice, "I'm going to pick them up and we're going to go through all the specifics."

"That's all well and good," Janice said, "but is there anything is this plan to help you with your electricity bill?"

"No."

"And you have, what, two weeks to pay your bill?"

"Not quite. I have two weeks to make a minimum payment and if I don't make that, they're going to shut off my power."

"Can you make the minimum payment?" Janice asked.

Lola shrugged. "Maybe. It'll just depend on what my other expenses are two weeks from now. But I do have the bike set up, so if the power goes out for a little while, it won't be a disaster."

"How can having your power turned off not be a disaster?" Janice demanded.

"My landlord said to just get him whatever I could, whenever I could, and my gas bill wasn't nearly as bad—"

"Because you're willing to live in a fucking icebox," Janice said.

"Because I'm willing to wear the sweaters I've made, but yeah. So, I'll have a roof over my head, a stove, hot water, my phone, and my laptop—"

"I know this is where you remind me and yourself that most of the humans in the world live quite nicely on even less than that, but, still, Lola, I mean, you're going to be without electricity. In America. I mean, how're you going to dry your hair?"

Lola sighed. "Well, you're not wrong, and my mom would lose

her shit if she found out, but, well, this is the life I've chosen."

"The glamorous life of the research assistant to a supercomputer surrounded by a fleshy casing of barely functioning human being."

"I like how you put 'glamorous' in there and almost kept your sarcasm on the inside."

"We all have our talents. And I wasn't being completely sarcastic. I still think you could solve your money problem by just selling your memoir."

"I'm not writing a memoir."

"Well, you're writing something about your life with Trike. I've seen the journal in your apartment."

"Yeah, well, I am writing something about my life with Trike, but it's not a memoir."

"What is it?"

"I don't know yet. That's one of the reasons I haven't tried to sell it."

"Oh, speaking of money you don't have," Janice transitioned, "what are you going to do about a dress?"

Lola shrugged. "I'm going to hit Vicki's Vintage first. She usually has funky stuff. And she lets me pay over time. If there's nothing there, then it's Second Time Around and Goodwill."

"Did you explain how long it can take to find a dress for one of these things?"

"Trike doesn't care what I wear. And it's not like we have any scheduling flexibility."

"You're sure this isn't just some convoluted way to get you to go to the Ball with him?" Janice asked.

"Yes, I'm sure," Lola replied. "He might be a genius with everything else, but when it comes to anything involving me, he has the sophistication and imagination of a twelve-year-old."

"I'm sure his imaginative capabilities reach well into the mid-teens," Janice said, wagging her eyebrows and phantom elbowing Lola in the ribs.

"What was that? Was that supposed to be dirty?"

"With that crazy-boss-friend-not-your-boyfriend thing you've got with Trike, I don't even know. And why doesn't he kick in for your electricity? I mean, I know he's not made of money, and the police stipend isn't much, but at least he's not paying rent."

"I didn't tell him my power was getting turned off."

"I thought he caught you with the bike generator."

"He did."

"So you lied to him?"

"Sure. By omission."

Janice scrunched up her eyes and glared at Lola until Lola reacted.

"What?" Lola said.

"I thought Trike could always tell when someone was lying, even by omission," Janice said.

"Well, yeah, he can, but I've been watching him sniff out lies for years, so I know his techniques."

"So how do you do it?" Janice asked.

"Well, first of all, it's a lot easier over the phone because he can't observe your body language. I don't think I'd bother trying in person."

"Okay."

"And then it's all about how natural your tone is. I've read stuff and seen stuff that talks about how you really need to believe the lie in order to make it work, but really, all you have to do is keep your tone within a natural range for the situation, which is really hard to do on purpose. Which means, it helps to be in a situation where your tone is naturally not going to be natural."

"Like if you've been pedaling a bike generator for, like, an hour, or whatever."

"Exactly," Lola agreed. "And then it helps to load a bunch of empty phrases into it, you know, conversational spaces and that kind of thing, especially in the intro, and then I try to change the subject as soon as possible."

"Right."

"And honestly," Lola continued, "he's inclined to believe me. I could tell him my great uncle was a purple elephant and if he thought it was important to me to believe me, he'd believe me."

"Which makes things easier."

"It does," Lola said. "Want a coffee before I drop you off?"

"No, I'm good. Why are you taking your car, by the way? You avoid driving like the plague with an infection."

"Three reasons. My car is the least likely to be under surveillance. It has, by far, the best gas mileage. And, most important, it's not Trike's car."

"Oh, that's right. Jesus Christ, Trike's car. I think I blacked it out."

"I know what you mean."

Lola pulled up in front of Janice's apartment building.

"Let me know if you can't find a dress," Janice said. "I've got a couple of things. They'd be short on you, but showing a little leg never hurt anybody."

"Thanks, but I should be able to find something, even if I have to fix it up. Besides, I need to conceal a weapon."

"I'll conceal your weapon. Nudge, nudge. Anyway, if you need to, you can totally stay at my place for a bit. I think The Wretched Roommate would get annoyed if you moved into the living room, but a few days should be fine."

"Thanks, but I should be able to work things out. Maybe I'll throw a blackout party. That might be fun."

"Well, I'm good for a box of wine if you do," Janice said.

"Thanks."

They exchanged a quick goodbye hug over the stick shift, a few final words, and Janice was on her way.

Lola drove to the office and picked up Trike and Max.

They had the basics figured out after a few blocks of trying to appear like they were just driving around. Max would arrive first and alone. He would do a sweep of the area and text a code to them if anything looked dangerous. He would also send coded texts if he believed he'd identified the kidnappers. Trike and Lola would show up an hour later.

"So, then it's wait around to see if someone makes a move for me?" Lola asked.

"Pretty much. We should act exactly like we would normally act at such an event," Trike confirmed.

"Awkward, anxious, and out-of-place?"

"Like the kid who forgot to do his sit-ups at the summer's first pool party," Trike confirmed.

"What do I do ... once you're there?" Max asked.

"Surveillance routes around the Ball. Send us a coded text if anything concerns you. The armory has a balcony, so it might behoove you to grab a bird's-eye every now and then."

They spent the next forty minutes working through their contingency plans, all of them imagining possible occurrences and their responses to those occurrences. What to do, where to meet, who to call. Next they established their text-message code. Then they finalized their inventory for the night: phones, cash on hand, weapons, first aid.

"Anybody I know going to be there?" Lola asked after they finalized the necessities.

Trike remembered the guest list. "People you know of, but no one you'd greet."

"Fantastic," Lola said dryly.

"And ... the crisis moment?" Max asked.

"Evidence suggests they will eschew violence. The only time they tried anything the henchman maced himself, so we can expect a low level of competency. At best, they'll point a gun at you and instruct you to come along quietly. Most likely you'll practically have to kidnap yourself. As long as that is the case, you go with them. If things look dangerous in any way, dispatch with your attackers in whatever manner you see fit. Whatever happens, we learn something."

"What about after I'm kidnapped?" Lola asked, taking a turn

she's sure she would have taken if she weren't thinking about what turns to take.

Trike sighed. He looked out the window.

"Just sit around like Dupin in the daytime. Joyce will send a message, and I don't want to have any expectations. I need to be perfectly open. If it gets dangerous, get out."

"Then I guess that's the plan," Lola said.

They drove in silence. After two minutes, Lola began taking turns with purpose. Another minute later, they pulled into a grocery store parking lot.

"What are we doing here?" Trike asked.

Lola parked the car and turned it off.

"My grocery shopping," she said, unbuckling her seat belt.

"That I deduced. But why are you doing it now?"

"Since I was going to be driving anyway, I figured I'd get this chore out of the way. Multitask on gas and all that."

"It must be exhausting," Trike said.

Lola sighed. She knew what was coming. "What must be exhausting, Trike?"

"Being that righteously conscientious. How do you have any energy left over to be smugly self-satisfied?"

"They're part of my emotional triathlon."

Trike sighed. Walking into it, he asked, "What's the third part?"

"Dealing with arrogant pricks who think their unique talent absolves them from any responsibility to interpersonal decency. It's more of an art than a craft."

"Well, throw me a kickback from whatever prize money you win from those things."

"Will do."

"Before we go in," Max said, "an executive summary. I arrive early ... case the joint. You two arrive an hour later. Act as normally as you two ... loonies can. Lola assesses the danger level of the attempted kidnapping and concedes or does not. We return to the office ... wait for the message."

"Sounds like a plan," Lola said.

"Then that's it until the Ball," Trike said, "so I guess we can relax for a few days, if any of us knows how to relax."

"Fantastic," Lola said, while she opened the door. "I can sit around watching a hundred fifty thousand dollars vanish. You guys coming in?"

"Ah-ha," Trike shouted while unbuckling his seat belt. "An additional ulterior motive. Not only are you doing your groceries, you are dragooning our assistance in completing said groceries. Ulteriority compounding. I must protest this flagrant misuse of the agency's precious time on your domestic errands."

"Or, you could sit in the car alone. We'll crack the window for you."

As if Trike were ever going to willingly shorten his time with Lola. He didn't even demand to push the cart.

TOTAL ECLIPSE OF THE HEART

"This is the third-worst bar I've ever been in," Lola said under her breath as she sat down across from Trike later that night.

"You keep your bar lists that far?"

"No. But using absolutes like 'worst' and 'best' with you leads to boring conversations."

"Words have definitions for a reason."

"Yeah, the same reason platypodes have poison spikes on their elbows."

Hazlitt's had a horseshoe bar with the texture of an old skateboard ramp. The bartender was shaped like a curtain draped over a train track. The chairs were mismatched. The tables uneven. Tears in the red patent leather of every booth. A miasma of stale sweat, old beer, and wet newspaper. The waitress was the anthropomorphization of a couch left in the rain overnight. The drinkers drank because bodies demanded a certain level of activity for a certain length of time. The floor was mopped six months ago. To get rid of the evidence.

"Trike, the table is sticky."

"It's a bar."

"And the floor is sticky," Lola said, picking a foot up.

"It's a cheap dive bar."

"The outside of the front door was sticky."

"It's the cheapest, divest, grossest, filthiest aborted approximation of a public house, which was created in the second God stopped to tie his shoes, and I get tested for everything from AIDS to zoster when I drive by on the way to the supermarket, but it's the only place in the area that does karaoke every night of the week."

The waitress grumbled at them. They ordered beers.

"Wait," Lola said, "what did you say?"

"It's the cheapest, divest, gro—"

"The important fact. In what you said."

Trike signed. Did not make eye contact. "They have karaoke every night."

On the stage, a tall thin figure of indeterminate gender with junkie arms leaking from a ratty commemorative March of Dimes event T-shirt, greasy brown hair hanging in tentacles to the clavicle, a nose stuck on its face like a poorly jointed dresser drawer, swayed to the train-track rhythm of and sang "Folsom Prison Blues." Soprano.

"A very special part of me just died, Trike," Lola said, trying to cover her ears with her shoulders.

"Yeah, that'll happen here."

"Then let's just finish our beers and go. I know you're weird about bars and stuff, but this place just makes me want to take a shower."

"We can't."

"Why not? Did a quarantine just drop?"

"I haven't done my song yet."

Lola stared at Trike. And stared at Trike. "I'm sorry. I think I just had a stroke. Did you say we can't leave because you haven't done your song?"

"Lola," Trike said. Took a sip of beer. Looked up at the ceiling. "Let me come clean. Depending on my emotional state, I come here and sing a karaoke song every month or so. There. It's out. I've said it. I come to this place because it has karaoke every night of the week, so I never have to worry about changing my schedule. As an added bonus, there's no chance anybody who knows me, or has read about me in the paper, or is literate, will ever be here. There. Is that so shocking?"

"You know, I guess, now that I think about it, not really."

"I'm not sure how I feel about that."

"Yeah. I mean, I never pictured you as a singer, but still, why not?"

"Well, it is karaoke."

"But why wouldn't the great Trike Augustine also be a singer? Probably just another thing for you," Lola said, gently throwing a hand in the air.

The host called out, "Horn-Rims."

Lola jumped at the name and looked frantically around the room until she noticed Trike getting up. He took another sip of beer, raised his eyebrows, and headed for the stage.

"Unbelievable," Lola thought as Trike took his position in front of the lyrics screen. "Bringing me here, as if I'd be all like, 'Oh, Trike, you can sing? Well, then, ring me, Justice of the Peace me, and get me to the church on time.'"

"Total Eclipse of the Heart" started. Lola smirked.

Trike started to sing. Lola's eyes widened. Her mouth dropped in shock. Trike's performance was the unquestionable, unequivocal, absolute worst song Lola had ever heard.

It invaded moments of conception and turned impending musicians into impending accountants.

Lola downed her beer.

It dimmed pigments in the world's great paintings.

Lola downed Trike's beer.

Jim Steinman woke with a sharp pain in his abdomen.

Lola ordered two shots of whiskey.

In courtrooms, barrooms, and living rooms, confident judges forgot how to operate the idea of right and wrong.

Lola took the two shots of whiskey.

After four and a half minutes, "Total Eclipse of the Heart," as interpreted by Trike Augustine, ended.

Birds returned to calling what they did singing.

Trike sat down. He didn't complain about his missing beer or mention the two empty shot glasses.

"Trike," Lola said with a hint of exhaustion, "why do you do that?"

Trike shrugged. "A man can't enjoy karaoke?"

"No. Well. Yes. But. I mean. You enjoy that?"

Trike shrugged again. "*Enjoy* is not the right word."

"What is the right word?"

Trike sighed. His face went slack for three minutes and forty-three seconds. "Occasionally, aspects of my being challenge the mechanism of metaphor," he said.

"Fucking hell," Lola said.

"Think about why you're supposed to reboot your computer every now and then. There's nothing wrong with it. There are no malfunctions. There are no viruses. There are no errors. All the programs and systems are functioning as they should, but as they have functioned as they should, data has broken away, sifted through gaps, and fragmented. Turbulence has emerged. Drag has developed. Friction has arrived. A tipping point in the inherent accumulation of entropy has been reached and performance suffers. What happens in my brain sometimes is absolutely nothing like that, yet that phenomenon is the closest I have come to describing what sometimes happens in my brain."

"Fucking hell," Lola said.

"Obviously, no matter how much booze you throw into it, you can't just reboot your brain. Trust me. But somehow, being a terrible karaoke singer, of that terrible karaoke song, in this terrible, just terrible bar, is the closest method I've found to 'rebooting' my brain. And yes, I performed many experiments before discovering this successful technique. No, I will not tell you the contents of those experiments. That list would be long, boring, and wrenching of organs that should only be wrenched by EMTs in triage."

Trike flagged down the waitress and handed her a twenty for the drinks. Then he stood up.

"Come on," he said, "I want to pick up a six-pack on the way home. At least I know that beer will have passed some kind of federal or state regulations to get from the brewer to my gullet."

"Want me to go in for you, so you don't have to stare at the wall of cigarette temptation while you pay?"

"Lola, that would be perfect."

THE ONE WORD KNOWN TO ALL MEN AND IT'S NOT "BACON"

"The only reason you're not dead is because you're Lola," Trike said from his bed in his dark bedroom, as Lola walked through the hallway.

"You're not a kill-first kind of guy. You would have subdued me," Lola said, pushing open the bedroom door against a pile of dirty clothes on the floor.

"In my rage at being woken at such an offensive hour, you could have been maimed in the subduing process."

"Ah yes, the eternal injustice of every now and again getting up only five hours later than just about everybody else in the world gets up five days a week."

"Through a long and thorough process of trial and error, I have established that I achieve the most restful sleep between eleven on the clock ante-meridian and two on the clock post-meridian. What everybody else does is their problem."

Lola pushed her way in far enough to reach the light switch. She flipped it. No light.

"Ha!" Trike shouted from the bed. "Foiled again. That light-bulb burned out three days ago. You are powerless now. Powerless, I say!"

Trike covered himself completely with his blanket.

"I finished *Ulysses* this morning," Lola said.

Trike lifted a corner of the blanket. Just enough to expose one eye.

"Prove it," he said.

"How am I going to prove it?"

"Quote something."

"Trike, I just finished it, for the first time, this morning. I don't remember quotes like you do. No one does."

"Okay. A different verification strategy. Did it flow?"

"Yes. And there's this whole big description of the Dublin water system with the name of the reservoir and the pressure and the gallons pumped and all that."

"Okay. Verification acquired. What did you think?"

"I think I'm not going to have a conversation with a one-eyed blanket."

"Is that a euphemism?"

"Yes. It's Ukrainian for quit being a dipshit."

"Lovely language, Ukrainian. If you really got *Ulysses* you could have a conversation about it in any context, be it mundane or spectacular."

"You're just being a dick."

"So it's a mundane context."

Lola breathed in and out deeply and slowly through her nose. She'd had many similar conversations with Trike over the years, and most of the time there was nothing she could do about it. He knew more about more than just about anybody on the planet and didn't give a fuck about the shit that most people gave a substantial fuck about. But this time, Lola was prepared.

"I know the word," she said.

"What word?"

"The one word known to all men."

"Get the fuck out."

"It couldn't be more obvious," Lola said, turning to address the next clause to the door frame, hand on her hip, presenting an eviscerating profile. "Joyce practically tells you what it is. Often, in fact."

"Mother."

"No."

"Sex."

"No."

"Metempyschosis . . . inelectable . . . word . . . home . . . God . . . drink."

Lola shook her head at each guess.

"No, what are we talking about, Rabelais?" Lola turned to consider the other side of the doorjamb, presenting the other eviscerating profile. "We could have a great discussion about this . . . if you would get the fuck out of bed."

Trike glared as much as one could with one eye through an upturned blanket corner.

"A contest of wills, is it? Well, there are few clear-cut rules in this vague yet compelling world, Lola, and one of them is don't get into a contest of wills with a high-functioning sociopath."

"I'll keep that in mind." Lola sighed, and turned so she was halfway out the door. "Anyway, it's free bacon day at the diner."

Trike threw the blanket off so hard it draped over the desk on the opposite wall. He shouted while he scampered around the room looking for acceptable clothing.

"Goddammit, Lola, that deal ends at one-thirty. Why didn't you fucking say something sooner? Fucking goddammit Jesus fucking Christ. You saw the sign jogging this morning, didn't you? You fucking joggers."

Trike stuffed himself into a pair of pants. He did not bother giving the nearest shirt to hand a thorough smell test.

"Morning people, spending their mornings figuring out ways to fuck the rest of us. Holy fucking Christ in a Harold Ramis movie. Fucking let's go," he shouted as he grabbed a stick of deodorant from his dresser and stormed past her into the hallway.

He threw his coat on and opened the door. He looked back at Lola. She was still standing in his bedroom door, wearing a crooked smile.

"Well?"

"Oh, nothing. It's just nice to see you so chipper and energetic after losing all that sleep."

"I swear on Watson's bum knee, Lola, you are the interior decorator of my own personal hell."

THE OLD-TIMER HAS HIS SECOND SAY

It rained again. Empty streets. The cardboard on the northern window in 3E had come loose from the frame. The spider plant in the window pot in 5A, after a noble struggle, had died. There was a new oily stain on the floor just inside the front door. The "OUT OF ORDR" sign had fallen off the elevator. Never let someone point a gun at you without pointing one back. Paint had flaked off the railing. There was a dead rat on The Old-Timer's landing.

Trike brought a few movies he'd picked up at the pawnshop. He knocked on the door.

"Fucking Christ, two visits in one case. Is Moriarty fucking your mom? You better have some whiskey in your pocket, making me think about the same case twice. I'm too old to think about the same case twice. Fucking kids these days. Think I've got nothing better to do than take what they give me and shit out my mouth for half an hour. Well, if you want in, pick the l—" Trike walked in.

"Next time I'm going to set something up for you. See how well you dance when you don't know the tune. Whatchoo got there?"

"Some movies."

"Anything good?"

Trike shrugged. "Couple of kung fu movies. One of them is a Lau Kar-leung so that might be good."

Trike put the movies on the floor by the TV and walked toward the kitchen.

"Don't bother with glasses," The Old-Timer said. "If I'm too

234

old to think about the same case twice, I'm sure as fuck too old to bother with glasses. You brought swiggin' whiskey anyway. Kind that lets you know you're sinning. Always bring swiggin' whiskey when you're a few months from reward money."

Trike took a fifth of swiggin' whiskey out of his trench-coat pocket, opened it, threw the cap on the floor, and handed the bottle to The Old-Timer. The Old-Timer took a swig and handed it back. Trike took a swig and leaned back in his chair. The Old-Timer motioned frantically with his hand. Trike passed the bottle back.

"Fuckin' kid. You brought it here for me, might as well let me hold it. Jesus, no grasp of economics, this one." The Old-Timer shook his head and bolted another portion of whiskey. "Okay, you've tossed your nickel. I'll dance. And I'm a fucking fantastic dancer. What woulda happened if Fred Astaire had fucked Ginger Rogers like we all wanted him to and the thunked-out cunt sprog signed a deal with the devil to dance better than St. Paul at a stoning party. I'm so good I even know when to keep my shirt on, and you know what, I know you want a beware story, because you're afraid some shit is happening to you right the fuck now. So here's my soft-shoe routine. Beware the cases that don't make sense after you've solved them. Some bastard rotting in jail because you put him there and he ain't never getting out and you still wake up in the middle of the night because even the truth doesn't make sense. The one time I hit a wife, I came to from a blackout with this case through my brain like a railroad spike.

"The wife of a wealthy banker was assassinated in her home. Not murdered, assassinated. No signs of forced entry. No struggle. Commando style. Knife in the liver. She was making fresh pasta. Never heard the attacker. Maid was in the next room sweeping. Didn't hear a thing either. Husband was plenty rich, so there were all kinds of motives to track down. Stuff at the bank of course, but he also sat on the boards of a half-dozen other firms and companies. Had himself a fat investment portfolio. Friends in politics. In the law. Basic rich-prick stuff. Which accumulates enemies, known and unknown. When a murder's done that well, there are two paths of investigation. Dig around the motives for people who have the money to buy a pro and wait for the next shoe. Someone gets a knife in the liver and goes down like she fainted, you expect a note that says, 'You're next.' Note never came. Nothing ever came. Cops had the guy under twenty-four-hour surveillance. Phones tapped. Watched everybody with a curly's worth of motive. Nothing. They call me in. I get the background. Looked like a mob hit to me, warning to the rest of the world. So the Feds got into it and started putting the squeeze on their mob connections. Which meant they squeezed the banker himself, which is just how the shit works. Found some tax shit, because, well, fucker was a rich asshole. Rich assholes always have tax shit. Once you get there you're not looking for the guy holding the knife or cutting the check. Those guys are fucking shadows. You're looking for anybody to stick in jail so the world can go on knowing somebody goes to jail when an innocent housewife gets a knife in the liver. Couldn't even find a patsy. Figuring I didn't have anything better to do and needed the money they paid me to dig around in his past and I didn't have anything better to do and I needed the money. And I did it without a computer and without a brilliant fuck hot piece of assistant and without a fucking computer in my head. I discovered that back in Nam this rich fuck's rich-fuck father paid some money and pulled some strings and got the guy's draft number switched so, lo and behold, he didn't go. But somebody did. And that somebody ended up pretty good with a commando knife. So thanks to me and my three sleepless weeks, which worked out to one percent of fuckall per hour, they got this guy. But this shit stuck with me. Why the wife? What the fuck did she ever do? And why not the guy's father? That old bastard was still alive. Or why not all of them? Lash out at the whole fucking world where rich assholes start wars and poor kids die in them. Just the wife. And this guy would have known she was raised by a single mother and worked her ass off her whole fucking life and just happened to marry this rich fuck. The killer was a pro. It didn't make sense. Yeah, I caught him, I got shit for it like I always do, but it sits with me. I know what happened, but I don't know what the fuck happened."

"That was Reggie Birchall, right?" Trike asked.

"If you know, you fucking know."

Trike's face went slack. His hand froze in the process of receiving the bottle from The Old-Timer.

"Fuck's gonna come out of you now?"

"His wife was murdered while he was in Nam," came out of Trike. "House was broken into while she was there. Never found the killers. It's in the cold-case files. I read through them every now and again."

The Old-Timer snatched the bottle back. Chugged the remains and threw the bottle against the wall. It smashed. Its broken glass showered down on a pile of broken glass.

"Fuck," he slurred and gagged. "Once they pegged him, there was no point in digging deeper and he kept his trap shut. They never would have told me anyway. You don't explain shit to the sniffer dog. You are fucked, fucker. Yours will be a hellacious maelstrom of self-disintegration that will take two weeks from your conscious life and who the fuck knows what will be in your hand when you come out of it. You got enough cash for pizza and another whiskey?"

"Yeah. No toppings, though."

"On your fucking way, then. Tell you about the cops I hated when you get back. Even listen to you bitch about that nostalgic asshole you fuck around with."

THE ANNUAL MUNICIPAL FANCY-DRESS BALL

The front doors were the least-used doors at the John Wilson Murray Memorial Armory. They were fifteen feet high and four feet wide apiece and opened out from the middle. The almost-black green of ponderous architecture, they were preceded by fifteen deep weather-dulled granite steps. There was a decorative arch with an inscription of thanks to John Wilson Murray in the decorative keystone. There was a coat of arms above that. A discrepancy in the official records left the sigil unidentified.

The parking lot was in the back, so the back doors were the most used. If there were a big event, like a high school basketball game, or the monthly flea market, the side doors would be used too.

But, because it was The Annual Municipal Fancy-Dress Ball, they used the front doors. And rented tuxes for the two volunteer doormen to wear while they checked invitations. They said the doors added gravitas. Gravitas is a hard element to add on purpose. The junior high was next door and, somewhere, for some reason, a power-driven machine vibrated dully.

Trike and Lola showed up an hour late as planned. Trike wore a navy modern-cut two-button jacket with gray pinstripes, matching vest and slacks, a maroon shirt, and a gray tie. A watch-chain parabolaed beneath his vest pocket.

Lola wore a sparkling blue satin-and-tulle strapless evening dress. Before they'd gotten to the volunteer doormen, Trike concluded it was a Goodwill job done up real nice for the occasion.

Trike handed over their invitation like he'd spent his life going to invitation-only parties. The doorman inspected the card. He nodded to his partner and they opened the doors with all the almost-gravitas three minutes' practice could produce.

The armory was packed everywhere but the dance floor. Crowds around the stand-up tables and in the gaps between them. The buffet line folded back on itself several times, blending into the general mass of people standing where they happened to be. Some of the more rebellious attendees climbed over ropes at the bases of stairs to find seated repose in the minimally restricted balconies. The only place you could feel lonely was the dance floor, but there was no one there to feel lonely.

Trike and Lola stood in the doorway. And stood there. Awkward. Anxious. Out of place.

"Why is it so crowded?" Lola asked, to say something.

"More people decided to attend."

"I figured that, asshole. Why did more people decide to attend?"

Trike shrugged. "Ask them. I've got nothing better to do for a while." His face was so still and reflective that it seemed stupid.

Two minutes of time and four hours of feeling later, Janice shrugged her way through the crowd. Lola would've hugged anybody she knew. The fact of Janice was a sweet bonus.

Janice wore a satin gown with chalcedony straps and a matching pendant. A tall man, thick enough around the chest and shoulders to daydream about lumberjacking and mean it, followed Janice. He wore a gray suit with a white shirt and a salmon tie.

"Lola, Trike, this is Dave. We work together," Janice introduced.

Dave shook hands with Trike and Lola. They both decided he wasn't as tough as he could have been. Unless he was one of those big guys with a bomb buried deep inside him.

"Wait—Trike?" Dave said. "Trike Augustine?"

"If you feel like believing my driver's license."

"Wow. I am just. So honored to meet you," Dave fawned. "My dad teaches criminology at the university and he's told me about your work. It's really. Amazing."

"I just keep my eyes open. Isn't that right, Angel?" Trike said, nodding over at Lola.

Lola rolled her yellow-gray eyes.

"How have you been keeping in shape since the knee surgery, by the way?" Trike asked Dave.

"Mostly water calisthe—" Dave cut himself off and stared at Trike with an intenseness that suggested myopia. "How did you?"

"Your father teaches criminology at the university. Not a huge department, and only one of them teaches me. That makes you Dave Lacassagne, which makes you the All-State tight end whose senior season was cut short by a patellar subluxation which, as we all know, is easily reinjured, especially if you play pickup football on the weekend, which, unless you spend your afternoons punching the ground for fun, it's obvious from the range of small cuts, nicks, and little scars on your hands that you've been doing just that. Since they've almost healed, I can see you haven't played in a little while, and, if you're anything like your mother, and I'm just going to go ahead and assume you are, you'll only stop when they cart you off on a stretcher. Which would certainly mean surgery on that knee. And since you're still in shape, the only thing I couldn't conclude was how you were staying that way. Water calisthenics would've been my guess, but I didn't feel like showing off."

"Wow. That is just amazing."

"That's kid's stuff. What's amazing is that I also know you are not getting laid tonight."

Dave laughed like Trike had told a joke. "You think ... with Janice? Come on, we work. Together. That's ridiculous."

Trike shrugged. "Say what you want, but nobody buys cologne

for the first time in a decade to just hang out with a friend from work. Even if he has to put on a suit to do it."

"Trike!" Lola interceded. "Turn it off for a bit."

Trike shrugged again. "Can't."

"No. No. Don't worry about it," Dave said. "Wow. It's something you can't really believe until you've seen it." Dave shook his head again and his face was twisted with pain and chagrin. He cleared his throat and looked at Janice. "I'm sorry. I know when you asked me to come with you, it was because it was so last-minute and you kind of needed a date, and you just wanted somebody you could hang out with, but, you know," Dave shrugged and held his hands out, his pinkened face slowly returning to its natural color, "I'm really attracted to you and I think you're really cool, and you know, well, that's kind of it, and you know, I totally understand."

Trike let out a low whistle. "No. That is amazing. You meant every word of that. Even the commas. Let me know if you run for office, because I am voting for you. Whatever the race. Bastards in politics will eat you alive, though. Sad. Really. This world we live in."

They all stood there for a minute. Nobody saying anything. Just standing there. Happened often around Trike.

But that awkward silence was preferable to the conversation threatened by The Mayor's approach.

The Mayor wore a square-cut ruby, its sides paralleled by four baguette diamonds that gleamed against the deep green of his cravat. His black coat, cut tight to narrow shoulders, flared a little over slightly plump hips. His trousers fitted round his legs more snugly than was the current fashion. The uppers of his patent-leather shoes were hidden by fawn spats. He wore chamois gloves and a black derby under which the edges of the hair left by his pattern baldness poked. A fragrance of *chypre* came with him. Altogether, he looked like someone who had dressed according to strict instructions.

Trike hoped for a moment that The Mayor could be avoided. To The Mayor, subtlety was a word that knocked him out of spelling bees, and the plan required subtlety. But the crowd was too dense for any quick movements and The Mayor was on them like a sniffer dog.

"Well, if it isn't the great Trike Augustine and his LOVELY DATE Lola Lenore. How do you both do?"

"What is he doing?" Lola hissed in Trike's ear.

"Ruining everything. He'll practically tell Joyce there's a plan," Trike hissed back.

"You BOTH look DIVINE." The Mayor hoisted the phrase over the crowd like he was handing a sweater to someone in a boat.

"Why does he know about the plan?"

"It was the only way to get Janice invited."

The Mayor reached them.

"Wonderful to see you, Mr. Mayor," Lola said before anybody else could speak. "We'll have to catch up again soon. Trike and I figured we'd break the ice on the dance floor, so if you'll excuse us, and do have a lovely evening. Nice spats. Fawn?"

Lola grabbed Trike's hand and his hand in her hand spun his brain around like a man in a crowded lobby who just noticed that his wallet was missing. He didn't recover in time to warn Lola about the DJ. Or his dancing. It's not always easy to know what to do.

Trike shuddered and trembled to the abominable pop music as though knitting needles were poking parts of his brain. He made angry gestures with mouth, eyebrows, hands, and shoulders. A demon was being exorcised sideways. As much as it helped, which wasn't much, Lola restrained her natural grace.

The DJ faded the song out, and if you guessed it was a mercy killing, you guessed before all the facts were in. The inquisitor was just putting on clean gloves. Inquisitors love clean gloves. The pause was long enough for people to think the first syllable of "awkward." The audience groaned when it recognized the song. "Wonderful Tonight." Lola couldn't stop her eyes from rolling. The upper part of her face frowned, while the lower part smiled.

Clumps of the crowd snickered. Max thought about popping the DJ between the eyes just to make it all stop. And Trike, well, Trike had a soft spot for Clapton.

Everybody watched Trike and Lola circling to that stupid song for a full minute before anyone joined them on the dance floor. Janice dragged Dave out first. Others followed their lead. It was maybe ten couples, but it released some of the congestion of the crowd.

The song limped to a close. Rather than putting on something that encouraged people to stay on the floor, the DJ put on instrumental smooth jazz. The Clapton survivors milled around on the dance floor. They were joined by their less demonstrably sympathetic friends and relations.

"Wait here a moment," Dave said to Trike and Lola. "I want to introduce you to someone."

"This makes me nervous," Trike said when Dave left.

"This makes you nervous? You are the nervous one? You, the one with no sense of social decorum and limited-access politeness? I'm the one who always has to clean up things when you're a dick. So, no, you don't get to be nervous. I'm going to be nervous," Lola responded.

"I thought Dave handled himself very well. Came out looking better than if I hadn't said anything. They'll probably ask me to give the toast at their wedding. And I don't have no sense of social decorum. Sometimes I'm just using too much of the rest of my brain to access that part."

"Well, access that part. Dave's coming back."

"No promises."

Dave pushed his way through the crowd talking to someone they couldn't see. Dave and his companion broke through the crowd. Dave's companion was a thin man as far into his fifties as Trike was into his twenties, wearing a no-nonsense brown suit over a plain white shirt with a spouse-selected maroon tie, horn-rimmed glasses, and a haircut that matched it all.

"Mr. Augustine, this is Horn-Rims, the other person my dad teaches at the university."

"This is who you dragged me away from the buffet to meet," Horn-Rims said with disgust.

"It's a long while since I burst out crying because a policeman didn't like me," Trike said.

Horn-Rims's cobalt-blue eyes looked tired right to the void of his pupils. He was one of those old cops who always took more than he dished out but was too tough to either fall or drop the falcon.

His wife Claire stood next to him, wearing a belted crêpe silk dress and holding a matching purse. Her mouth was firmly pressed into a polite smile. Her hazel eyes practically shouted, "Oh, Dave, you foolish boy."

"We've met, Dave," Horn-Rims said. "And keep off that knee. It's gonna kill when you're forty."

He turned on his heel and pulled Claire with him.

Trike opened his mouth to say something, but Lola stopped him with a hand on his elbow. Lola's hand on Trike's elbow.

Then Trike told a story. He talked in a steady matter-of-fact tone devoid of emphasis or pauses. At first, they were more surprised by his telling the story than interested in it and their curiosity more engaged with his purpose in telling than with the story he told.

"About fifteen years ago, in the parlance of those without perfect recall and internal calendars, San Francisco was hit with a rash of burglaries that lasted most of the decade. Hundreds, perhaps even thousands of places were hit, some several times over the years. But the burglar only took little things: reading glasses, spare car keys, junk mail, that kind of stuff. Cans of diced tomatoes. Bookmarks. Lightbulbs. Things most people wouldn't notice were missing right away and when they did, they would assume were lost, or perhaps even that they never had them to begin with. Wine keys and bottle openers. Magazines. Coupons. Chinese takeout menus. Who knows how many spouses fought over vanished remotes or how many kids were grounded because a favorite coffee mug was missing?"

Trike paused to liberate and eat a mini-quiche from an inattentively held plate.

"Throughout this period, the police were called in fifteen times in response to these crimes. Two of the times were because objects that appeared meaningless were actually quite valuable to the rightful owners. One was a souvenir keychain of the Eiffel Tower, a commemoration of where the owners' decision to be married was formalized. The other was a pen, nice gold-plated Cross number, that was just like every other pen of its type, but happened to be passed down by a mentor to a protégé and so was as important to its owner as anything locked in a deposit box or fireproof safe.

"The other thirteen were all calls made by individuals suffering from obsessive-compulsive disorder, people psychologically incapable of losing things. You can just imagine how those investigations went. Just because someone is obsessive-compulsive doesn't mean they're totally disconnected from the more generally agreed upon value of things. So when they reported a stolen cat toy, most did their best to emphasize that they didn't want the police to find their stolen cat toy, but to find whoever broke into their home.

"It was just enough to send a couple of PIs on the case, and let's just say it didn't turn out well for them."

A young man walked by with a handful of cups of punch. "Let me help you with that, kid," Trike said, grabbing one of the cups.

"Thanks, mister," the kid said.

Trike drank it in a gulp. Lola whispered an explanation and apology to the kid. He found it satisfying enough to go on his way.

"So for over a decade in San Francisco, things in people's homes could just disappear, like a fist when you open your hand. Most of the time, people didn't even notice, and when they did, they assumed something typical had happened. Who could blame them? Something becomes typical by happening all the time, and, in the absence of definitive data to the contrary, typical is typically a safe bet. The police did their best when they were called in, but the break-ins were clean. It's not like you could keep an eye out on the hot market for an unopened box of tissues.

"The whole thing reached its conclusion when a mail-carrier called the police because the man who lived in a particular house hadn't picked up his mail for a week. The mail-carrier didn't know the guy who lived there, just that there was a single male name attached to whatever was delivered. A little preliminary investigating turned up that Charles Pierce was a retiree living off Social Security and his pension from the insurance agency he'd worked at for decades. No relations or friends could be found to confirm a vacation or some other reason for the pileup of mail.

"The cops let themselves in two days later and found Mr. Pierce dead of a heart attack in his kitchen. And a house filled with all those missing objects. At first, they assumed the guy was a hoarder, but one of them recognized the Eiffel Tower keychain from when he had to respond to that call. It clicked. For years, Charles Pierce broke into people's houses all over San Francisco with the perfection of a master art thief and stole negligible items.

"Now, this digression is going to come with a lesson in detecting. Obviously, this story raises a lot of questions. If you think about it, everything does. The key to detecting is asking the right question, finding the one question out of all the possible questions that leads to the important truth of the matter. I'll give you a moment to see if you can spot it."

Trike's fingers and hands twitched in the moment. You could watch a cigarette being taken from a pack and twirled around.

"Why hasn't Dave heard of this story?" Lola said.

"Bingo, Angel."

"Oh yeah," Dave said. "This is exactly the kind of thing my father would teach. Actually, this is exactly the kind of thing he would write a book about."

"Exactly. So the natural follow-up question is . . . ?"

"Why didn't Dave's father hear about this?" Janice finished.

"Well done, class," Trike said. "Dave's professor-of-criminology father did not hear about this because the police at the scene never told anybody. The official report was that Charles Pierce was a lonely old hoarder who died of a heart attack in his kitchen. Nothing was ever told to the press, and if it wasn't for the coincidence of the officer and the Eiffel Tower keychain, all those objects over all those years would have just disappeared. The lie about Charles Pierce being a negligible hoarder would have been the truth. I heard about this because the story made its way around law enforcement agencies the way these stories do, conferences, parties, that kind of thing, but always with an understood level of discretion. No matter how many times it's been told around poker tables, it's never been told to someone who would get it in their head to blab about it to the press, and even if they did, it would be impossible to substantiate now."

"But why didn't they tell people about this?" Dave asked. "I mean, it's a fascinating story. You know, who is Charles Pierce really? And it would have answered a lot of questions people had over the decades."

Trike bent his mouth and nodded. "Remember this story the next time you lock your door. You'll think of Charles Pierce and you'll know why it's far better that most of the world can't."

Another smooth-jazz-soaked awkward moment.

Then Trike said, "That mini-quiche was a tease. Anybody else care to join me at the buffet?"

"Now that you mention it, I'm starving," Lola said.

Dave shrugged.

"We ate earlier, but we'll go over with you," Janice said.

"Then it's settled," Trike concluded.

They turned around to face the table. Then The Mayor started talking into a microphone set up onstage.

"Excuse me, everyone, your attention, please," he said.

Whether or not the group cared about the announcement, a surge in the crowd pushed them toward the stage.

The Mayor paused in front of the microphone while the crowd adjusted itself into an acceptable version of attention.

"Good evening, ladies and gentlemen, and welcome to the city's Annual Municipal Fancy-Dress Ball. Every year for over forty years, the city council, in conjunction with The Mayor's office, has organized this celebration, to, uh, celebrate another year in our fair city and to honor those who have contributed to the success of the city and the well-being of all of its citizens. Before we continue with our honors, I'd like to acknowledge some of those who have made this event possible."

The Mayor thanked the volunteers, sponsors, and businesses involved, finding ways to mention campaign contributors whether they'd done anything noticeable for the Ball or not. The next half hour was filled with awards, citations, and other honors. The high school essay-contest winner. The food drive organizer. The teacher of the year. The investment banker who put his name on the city's recreational fields by paying to have them reseeded (tax-deductible donation, of course). The high school football coach who'd retired after twenty-five years. A representative in Congress who'd tacked a rider on a bill about imported food that funneled $275,000 in infrastructure maintenance funds to the city. Applause was perfunctorily given to all.

When those were done, The Mayor transitioned, "I'd like to conclude this evening's presentations with what has been for decades the most reported presentation at the Annual Municipal Fancy-Dress Ball, which is, of course, I'm speaking of the presentation of the King and Queen of the Ball."

In the choreographed pause, a bolt of terror shot through Lola's brain. The color drained from her face. She whispered to Trike, "Did you and The Mayor plan anything else for this?"

"Lola, I already told you—" Trike whispered back until that bolt hit him too. He cursed The Mayor under his breath, cursed him obscenely, blasphemously, repetitiously, while The Mayor continued speechifying.

"Along with these other honors and recognitions," The Mayor looked up when his notes told him to, "every year, the city council, in conjunction with The Mayor's office, selects two individuals who we believe not only contribute to the success of the city and to the well-being of its citizens, but who also embody the nobility of spirit, the energy of enterprise, and the core of kindness and decency that make this city such a great place to live."

The notes said, "Look up for APPLAUSE," so he did. Then, as if anyone ever added further ado, he continued, "And so, without further ado, this year's King and Queen of the Annual Municipal Fancy-Dress Ball are ... Trident Augustine and Lola Lenore."

The crowd applauded. During his handshake with The Mayor, Trike leaned in and said through a smile, "I don't know if this is your idea of helping or your idea of revenge, but I'm going to find out. Either way, the results of my investigation will be very unpleasant."

The Mayor looked like he didn't know it was test day. He regained enough of himself to smile blankly.

Trike and Lola were crowned and sashed and led offstage by gowned attendants rented from an in-state modeling agency. Then The Mayor stepped back to the microphone and said, "And now for the traditional first dance of the King and Queen."

Trike and Lola took their awkward position on the dance floor. And stood there. The silence stretched until nervous laughter made its way through the crowd like a yawn. Eventually, music struggled to the surface, but it was the opening bars to "Wonderful Tonight." There wasn't a single person on the planet who liked Clapton that much. The music stopped like it hit a wall. Then "Lady in Red" whined into the air. Trike and Lola had no choice but to dance to it.

The plan had been simple enough. Show up at the Ball together. Be a little careless. See if someone tried to kidnap Lola while no one else was looking. The King and Queen thing threw it off. They needed to reassess. Without verbal communication, they decided to "get some air" so they'd have a chance to hash out their next step without anyone involved eavesdropping.

Getting some air turned out to be more difficult than getting through "Lady in Red" without grimacing. Everybody had to shake their hands and say congratulations and don't you look beautiful and great work for the city and a dozen other phrases and gestures. They finally got outside a half hour after the end of the dance.

They sat down at the bottom of the front steps, far enough out of earshot that no one could understand what they were saying, but not so far as to arouse suspicion.

Lola started the strategy session. "What the fuck was that with the King and Queen shit?"

"How do I know? I was out in the kitchen mixing an omelet when it all happened, wasn't I?"

"What?"

"Never mind. Never mind." Trike rubbed his hands together. "This makes the whole grab-you-when-no-one-else-is-paying-attention scenario quite a bit less likely. From now to the end of this thing we'll be kicked around like a football in the gutters of Paris."

A moment later, Lola said, "How would you know it wasn't an ordinary piece of detective work?"

The line made Trike jump.

Lola continued, "So it's the women's bathroom back by the stage. Down the little hallway. Around the corner. With the nearby fire exit."

"Guess so. Just have to keep an eye on it. Go when nobody else has in a while. Easy enough for someone else to walk in on the proceedings, though."

"Which is why it wasn't the original plan."

"Indeed."

"But the original plan is fucked now anyway."

"Indeed."

"So that's it."

"That's it." Trike gave a swift nod. "Let's see if these pocket-edition desperadoes do what they're supposed to."

They reentered the Ball arm-in-arm like a Queen and King are supposed to. Trike texted Max the amendment as they strolled through the foyer.

The crowd had thinned considerably. Gone were those who needed to relieve babysitters. Gone were the cops and firefighters whose shifts were imminent or imminently imminent. Gone were the people who had a drive. Gone were the people who always left early for reasons never specified.

All that remained of the buffet was the punch bowl of sugary red fluid abomination. They found Dave and Janice there. Re-greetings and informal congratulations. Dave saw his father across the room and decided that, despite previous events, it would be a good idea to introduce him to Trike.

On another day, Trike might have told Dave that his father had been having an affair for fifteen years, just to get out of the introduction, but he noticed that no one had been to the women's bathroom for a few minutes. Lola noticed that too. It was the opportunity. Lola excused herself and Trike let himself be walked into an awkward moment. Sure, Dave's father taught his work at the university, but he didn't understand a damn thing about it.

One woman left the bathroom as Lola entered. A brief congratulation was offered and accepted. It occurred to Lola this might be the last opportunity she had to actually use the bathroom. She didn't waste it.

On her way out, she shoulder-threw a swart greasy man in notable clothes before her conscious brain caught up to her instinct and told her to cool it. There were two other thugs involved: a tall thin one with a bowler too small for his head and a plump one with an ascot. The thin man looked stupid. The plump man looked more doubtful.

Having never been kidnapped before, and not familiar with kidnapping as a category of crime, Lola would not say for certain that she was involved in humanity's worst kidnapping, but she would have laid even odds on it.

It took long enough that Lola began to worry someone would accidentally come to her rescue. Eventually, the man she'd shoulder-thrown, who was shaped like a spoiled pear, shoved a handkerchief in her face. It took her an instant to realize he was trying to anesthetize her.

She let her body relax and crumpled to the floor like marble dust brushed off David. The thugs gathered her up and carried her out the fire exit into the alley. They put her, with no small amount of difficulty, into the backseat of a large black sedan.

The man in the passenger seat said, "You forgot to pull the fire alarm."

Spoiled Pear shook his head with healthy helping of "Awww, shucks." He trotted back to the door, but it was locked. The man in the passenger seat got out. On long legs he strode to the door, unlocked it, and opened it in the same economical motion. Spoiled Pear walked back in.

Trike whistled two lines from "En Cuba" softly as he strolled back to the punch bowl, ostensibly to meet Lola. The introduction went better than could have been hoped, but what Dave interpreted as an effort to make amends for earlier transgressions was just the result of Trike's brain spending a good chunk of itself worrying about Lola.

Whenever he tried to divert the effort with a calculus problem or topical conundrum it returned to that crushing line from *The Maltese Falcon*: "If they hang you, I'll always remember you."

He poured himself a cup of that red excuse for a beverage. Looked over at the bathroom with two minds, one hoping to see Lola, the other hoping to not. He swept his attention across the rest of the Ball not looking for anything, just open and active. He observed the strangest phenomenon he'd observed in six years, ten months, one week, five days, and eighteen hours.

People were dancing.

The dance floor was full. While Trike half-suffered through an introduction only Dave wanted made, the Ball was infused with the reckless joy of a wedding reception. Trike's attempt to smile was not successful, but he kept the resultant grimace on his mottled face for a moment before letting it fall back to standard. A primal being deep in the recesses of Trike's brain mouthed the words "I'll be gone in a day or two." A vague emotion wafted out of the massive affront to human movement, some mixture of relief and release. It was like hearing that the brake job on your car would cost half as much as you feared.

Trike knew exactly when Spade knew who killed Archer. His life was defined by knowing those things. And knowing things only he could know. And then bringing those things out in a way that society found actionable. Sometimes he was thanked. Sometimes he wasn't. Sometimes he knew more about Charles Pierce than he knew about anybody or anything.

Then the fire alarm went off.

Trike didn't know a damn thing about the dancing.

Most of the dancers threw up their hands. A collective, "Wouldn't you know it, just when we started having a good time." But they'd all gone to school. They filed out in a reasonable approximation of the order that teachers and principals had instructed them to aspire to. Trike stood at the punch bowl while they flowed by, looking for distinctive faces. All faces are distinctive, but in this case, they didn't distinguish themselves the way Trike had hoped. Even spotting Spoiled Pear didn't tell him anything he didn't already know.

Max appeared at Trike's side. He put his hand on Trike's shoulder. "Come on, boss," he said, "time to go."

Trike didn't look at him. "Sure thing, Max. Let's pick up some wings and soda on the way to the office. I'm starving."

"You got it, boss."

"Strange thing, Max."

"Unassailable truth . . . any thoughts?"

"You could offer me three billion dollars for a purple elephant, but what in the hell would that mean?"

Max shook his head. "Ask myself that . . . all the time."

They merged with the end of the crowd and rilled out of the Ball.

INTERLUDE
THE MYSTERIOUS SPARK: A HORN-RIMS CASE

The Proces-Verbal was a hip nightclub on Woodstock between Nero and Fox with a narrow alley between it and an old apartment building that had a drinking hole called The Yard on the ground floor and nothing else.

Rain again. Washed away the DNA evidence. If there was any.

Horn-Rims sipped from a Styrofoam cup of cold convenience-store coffee. Sitting in his squad car. Staring into the alley.

The ambulance drove away over an hour ago. Could've been a mail truck for all it mattered. Renee Faralizq was dead hours before anybody showed up.

Beaten to death. Savagely beaten to death. Head trauma. Four broken ribs. Two broken arms. One leg broken in three places. Twenty-two broken bones in all. Horn-Rims wasn't a coroner, but he'd seen enough internal bleeding and massive organ damage to know Renee had a dose of those too.

It was the kind of beating that required a tool. Two-by-four. Metal pipe. Baseball bat. Cricket bat, if the appropriate nationalities were around. Anything long and heavy. Any of a dozen or so objects in the surrounding Dumpsters. And evidence of sexual assault, if you trust the way dresses rip and wrists bruise.

Short black dress, matching high heels, and an array of bracelets, necklaces, and rings. Renee was done up for the evening, and why not, she was a pretty girl at a nightclub on a Saturday night.

They found the purse next to the body. A ticket stub told them she'd been to Proces-Verbal. Eighty-seven dollars in cash told them it wasn't a robbery. The stats, the cash, and the hickey told Horn-Rims she most likely knew her attacker. Probably even liked him.

But something had gone wrong. You wouldn't think something could go wrong in a sexual assault/murder, but something went wrong here. Horribly, horribly wrong.

The Man with the Facts sat in the passenger seat, also looking straight ahead into the alley. He had an earpiece plugged into the radio. He was transcribing the statements from Renee's friends without looking down at his notebook. There was a break in the relay.

The Man with the Facts took out his earpiece and, without turning, said, "All testimony from friends congeals into this single narrative: Renee was with her cadre of female friends for the entire evening, enjoying what three of her friends identified as 'girls' night out,' until she went to the bathroom alone and then was not seen again until her body was recovered. After a span of time, delineated by her friends in the range of thirty to forty-five minutes, they went looking for her. When she was not found in the bathroom or anywhere else in the club, they concluded that Renee had gone home. None of her companions was worried, as Renee had a strict curfew and was, as one of them explained, 'weird about getting in trouble with her parents.' No further insight was provided, although, through their testimony, a list of male classmates known or suspected to be attracted to and have some kind of relationship with Renee has been generated. Pictures of said male classmates are being acquired and will be shown to employees at the club as soon as possible."

A long pause.

A cleaning crew of Hispanic workers filed into the front door of the nightclub. Time to undo what the white people did all night so they can do it again tonight.

The Man with the Facts said, "There is nothing to do here."

A long pause.

Street debris collected over a storm drain creating a small, swirling, filthy pond.

The Man with the Facts said, "There was no reason for us to come back after talking to her parents."

Streetlight at the corner flickered and went out. Then came back on.

"There's something dark here," Horn-Rims said, bringing the coffee up to his mouth but setting it down without taking a sip. "Something strange. It takes more than strength and anger to beat someone to death like that. It takes dedication. It takes commitment. A pro beating somebody to death looks one way. If a pro has to do it and a two-by-four is the only tool around, then a pro is going to use a two-by-four and stick with it until the job is done. But this wasn't done by a pro. The blows are too haphazard, too ineffective. It takes work, it's ugly, but a pro would've killed her in half the strikes.

"But this isn't how an amateur does it either. Most of the time, if someone gets beaten to death by an amateur it's a couple of lucky blows. No one is supposed to get killed, but then the bat or the two-by-four or whatever it is catches the skull just right. Even when someone loses their shit it doesn't look like this. They focus all their blows on the face and head because they're not attacking a body, they're attacking an emotional trigger, an idea, a memory, an insult. It can't be a pro and it don't look like an amateur."

"Soundly reasoned, HR, but why does it lead us back to the scene?"

"We're missing something."

Horn-Rims started the car. Pulled into the street. The city still unaware it had a body to mourn. If this were a mourning city.

As they drove away, Horn-Rims repeated, "We're missing something."

•

Horn-Rims sat at his desk. A half cup of lukewarm coffee precariously close to a precarious pile of paperwork. He was trying to figure out what the fuck was up with this Joyce case, why The Chief called that rabid jackoff Augustine in on the first day, and why they were keeping the city's top homicide detective on a kidnapping case. And the fucking FBI.

He was trying to find what they missed in the alley.

You could say all of it was giving him a headache, but everything always made his head pound. He saw Renee's mangled body every other time he blinked his eyes.

One of the detectives investigating Renee's murder rushed up to Horn-Rims's desk.

"We've got a lead," he said.

"What?"

"Frank Geyer."

"One of the guys the girls mentioned?" Horn-Rims pursued.

"Yep. A waitress at the club said she saw him talking to Renee by the bathrooms."

"Match with the timeline?"

"As much as it could."

"Where'd they go after that?"

"Waitress didn't see. She just happened to notice them, because she thought they looked cute together. It was a busy night. She said she was practically on roller skates."

"Were they affectionate?"

"Not that she saw."

"Anybody else see the kid?"

"No one would say for sure they didn't see him."

"Right."

"I guess the underage kids pretty much just go dancing at this place. Once they get past the bouncers, they go right to the dance floor, never interact with the staff, and the dance floor is just a bunch of kids all dressed the same, dancing the same."

"Any other leads?" Horn-Rims asked.

"He's the only one anybody's even suspected of being there."

"Nothing on the other pictures?"

The detective shrugged. "More of the same. All of them could've been there or none of them could've been there."

"Right. All right. Well, I'll pay a visit. See if you can track down some of this kid's friends and see if they'll place him there. Might as well talk to the other guys on the list anyway. Kid got a record?"

"Not even a parking ticket."

"Well, maybe he can at least tell us where she went after he saw her."

"And he didn't come forward with the info already?" the detective asked.

"Don't you remember when you were a teenager? You thought hanging out with your friends was the most important thing God gave humans to do, and that's when you can get your hormone-fucked-up brain to do any thinking at all. If he saw her with a buddy of his, there's no way he'd come forward on his own. He'd keep it to himself and hope the shit just worked out. Then some guy with a badge shows up, his parents give him the 'What did you do?' look, and he spills about the buddy and the one time he cheated on a math quiz. There's no point in taking a tone with a fucking kid, you got that? You feed some obstructing justice line at the kid and his mom, mom is around, right?"

"Yeah. Both parents."

"His mom will eat your lower colon while dad punches your face through the floor if you make their kid feel like a criminal. You got that?"

"Yes, sir."

"Good. Got your coat handy?"

"At my desk."

"Grab it, get the other guys on this kid's friends and come with me to see him. Consider it training."

"There's one more thing you should know."

"Yeah."

"Both his parents are lawyers."

Horn-Rims's shoulders collapsed. His lips twisted around hundreds of contained curses.

"Civil or criminal?" he asked.

"One of each."

Horn-Rims leaned back in his chair and looked up at the ceiling. Nope. Still nothing useful up there. He took a deep breath.

"Ever had a prostate exam, detective?"

"Can't say I've had the pleasure."

"Well, you'll be ready when the time comes. Get your coat and meet me back here."

"Yes, sir."

Frank Geyer's house was a nice two-story number at 191 Benwell Ave, on the border between the suburbs and the city, painted an inoffensive but not entirely characterless blue. Nice lawn. Two-car garage. Winding walkway. What you'd expect from a couple of lawyers in this town. Probably had a summer house somewhere.

Horn-Rims knocked on the door. A middle-aged man, slightly above average height, with narrow shoulders, a fit physique, and a long nose, still in his tie, with most of his brown hair, answered. Horn-Rims didn't recognize him. That meant Mom was the criminal lawyer, confirmed when she met them at the door. Horn-Rims knew her, but he couldn't pull the first name out of his brain. She was the same height as her husband with a stockier build but long delicate-looking fingers, lush auburn-colored hair, and chocolate-brown eyes.

After the formal introductions, Horn-Rims and the detective were shown into the living room and gestured into matching plush chairs. Mr. and Mrs. Geyer sat down on the sofa.

When everyone was settled, Horn-Rims said, "We'd like to speak with your son Frank, if he's around."

"Frank? Why?" Mrs. Geyer asked.

"We hope he might have some information for us."

"Information about what, detective?" she asked.

"The murder of Renee Faralizq—"

"I can't imagine he'd know anything about that," Mr. Geyer offered.

"Well, Mr. Geyer, in these investigations we need to pursue all possible avenues—"

"And the lead detective would examine all avenues? I'm assuming you are the lead detective on this case," Mrs. Geyer said in a tone Horn-Rims was prepared for.

"I am the lead detective in the case, ma'am, but I want to be very clear. We are here because there is a chance your son has information about the night in question. There are about ten other detectives, sitting in ten other living rooms asking parents and kids these questions as well," Horn-Rims explained.

"As his parents, I think we have a right to know what led you to believe Frank has any information at all," Mr. Geyer said.

"Of course, of course. We were given a list of Renee's other acquaintances by her friends, people she might have seen on the night in question. Your son's name was on that list. We showed pictures of the kids on the list to the staff at the nightclub and one waitress said she saw Frank talking to Renee."

"There must be some mistake," Mrs. Geyer said. "Frank wasn't at the club that night."

"Well, ma'am, in a murder investigation we must pursue every avenue, and there is a chance that even if he wasn't there, he might still have something useful, so I would like to speak with Frank myself, if you don't mind."

"His mother just told you he was not at the club that night. I'm not sure why you still need to talk to him."

Horn-Rims noticed that Mr. Geyer had willfully ignored the already offered explanation. Nothing that happened on the inside of Horn-Rims in reaction to the statement made it to the outside. Sometimes, cops can't let others notice what they notice.

"Was he here that night?" Horn-Rims asked.

"He was at a friend's house," Mrs. Geyer answered.

Horn-Rims leaned forward and put his elbows on his knees. "Here's what I expect Frank to tell me. I'm going to ask him about Renee, he's going to say he chatted with her at the club, sorry Mom and Dad but it's all-ages Friday and all the cool kids go, and then she went to the bathroom and I went somewhere else. But if there is anything he could add to that, anything at all, it would be extremely valuable. What time he saw her, how long they talked, if he saw her talk to anybody else or with anybody else. And if the waitress made a mistake, I just want Frank to tell me where he was—"

"So you can verify his alibi," Mrs. Geyer interjected.

Horn-Rims leaned back off his knees and raised his hands. "You both know we have to be thorough. A girl was brutally murdered. I'll ask Frank what he saw. If he says he wasn't there, I'll ask him where he was. And if he doesn't want to say where he was in front of you, I'll let him tell me in another room, or outside or something, and then we'll be on our way."

"I still don't see why the lead detective on a homicide case would come here," Mrs. Geyer looked derisively at the other detective, "with an assistant, for such a slim lead."

Horn-Rims made himself look abashed. "To be honest, we don't have much else. We are grasping at straws."

"And Frank is one of those straws," Mr. Geyer said.

"Frank is one of those straws," Horn-Rims confirmed.

Mr. and Mrs. Geyer looked at each other for a moment. Communicated with expressions. Made a decision.

Mrs. Geyer stood up. "He's upstairs. I'll call him down."

She left the room. Horn-Rims heard her walk to the stairs and gently call to "Frankie." There was an exchange that Horn-Rims couldn't hear. The exchange was followed by the unmistakable tromping of an exasperated teenager abandoning a video game. Horn-Rims and the other detective stood up for semiformal introductions. Frank looked just like his dad, but an inch taller and with the musculature of an athletic teenager.

Frank's parents sat him down on the couch between them. He didn't look happy about that either. Horn-Rims and the other detective returned to their chairs.

Horn-Rims said, "How are you doin', Frank? Were you close to Renee?"

Frank shrugged. Didn't make eye contact. "Not really. I mean, I knew her, and all, but we weren't, like, friends or anything."

"It's still hard though," Horn-Rims said.

Frank shrugged. "Yeah, I guess."

There were a lot of different ways to ask questions, but not many of them produced answers. Even fewer if you were a middle-aged white man with a badge and a gun. No matter what needed answering, people got defensive when a cop was asking.

So Horn-Rims usually took the long way around. Asking about everything around the case, except whatever it was. Sometimes it established a rapport. Sometimes the meander revealed more than the goal. Sometimes, the interviewee got thinking that maybe Horn-Rims wasn't even asking about the big thing and so their guard was down when he asked about the big thing. Sometimes they forgot for a second that anything they said could and would be used against them in a court of law.

But whatever else happened, the long way around made them talk, and the more they said, the more information Horn-Rims got, no matter how clever they thought they were.

But with the Geyers sitting there and Frank just a kid, Horn-Rims decided to just get it over with.

"A waitress at the club said she saw you talking to Renee. Did you see where Renee went after that, or if she talked to anybody else after you saw her?"

"I wasn't at the club that night."

"Okay. I'm sure the waitress just made a mistake, but, well, I'm a cop, so I've got to ask: Where were you? Your parents said you were at a friend's house. Could you tell me which one?"

Frank looked nervously back and forth at his parents.

"You know, Frank, if you don't want your parents to hear what

263

you've got to say, we can go in the other room, or outside, but you're on your own when they ask about it afterward," Horn-Rims said with a slight smile.

Frank looked down at his hands. After a minute, he realized that Horn-Rims was waiting for an answer. Frank just shook his head.

"How about this, then? You just tell me the name of the friend you were with that night, and if I need to talk to you again, I'll come talk to you at school," Horn-Rims essayed.

"Detective, as I understand it, there is one *waitress* at the nightclub that *says* she saw him there. Someone who's never met him and who sees hundreds of people every night, and even more on these all-ages Fridays. At this point, I see no reason to invest her statement with the weight you seem to be investing in it. Just because a *waitress thinks* she saw him does not mean you have the right, or even a good reason, to track down his every movement, especially when you yourself have admitted that you don't expect the information you *might* get to be particularly valuable."

"Well, ma'am, any information would be useful. Frank, here's my card."

Frank took the proffered card.

"You feel free to call me if you can think of anything that might help, even though you weren't at the club that night. Anything somebody might have said or done at school. Anything at all. And if I'm not there, you can leave a message. I'll get back to you."

Horn-Rims stood up. Everyone else but Frank stood up in response. Then Frank stood up. Hands were coldly shaken. Please-calls and if-we-hear-anythings and these-things-are-hards were exchanged. A minute later the two detectives were outside in the car.

Horn-Rims pulled out into the street.

"That was weird, right?" the other detective said, exploding with everything he'd kept pent up during the interview. "I mean, that was really fucking weird, right?"

"Yeah. It was weird," Horn-Rims calmly responded.

"Why didn't you press him for the name of the friend?"

"Because we weren't going to get it. I get the sense we're not going to get much else without a warrant."

After a few minutes of silence, Horn-Rims asked, "So, what's your take on it?"

"My take? You mean besides that it was weird?"

"Yeah, besides that."

"I don't know. He's definitely hiding something. And his parents are helping him. But it could be anything, you know. Maybe he was at a party that got busted. Or took a joyride or something. Maybe he's been selling a little weed on the side. There's all kinds of trouble a good kid could get into."

"Yeah. Yeah. You're probably right," Horn-Rims said, more to the world than to the detective.

Horn-Rims gunned it through a yellow light.

"You don't think it's something like that?" the detective asked.

Horn-Rims was quiet for a moment. They passed the station.

"No. I don't think it's something like that."

"You think he did it?"

Horn-Rims didn't answer right away. Took the next left. "Yeah. I think he did it. Something about the way he looked at us. About the way his parents looked at us. And talked to us. You could hear something."

"Yeah. I could. But why would they stonewall us like that? I mean a party or a little weed is one thing, but this is murder."

"They're telling themselves there's no point in destroying two lives. They're telling themselves he's a good kid who made one big mistake. Or they're not telling themselves anything and they just don't want their son to go to jail."

"Beating her to death with a two-by-four, or whatever, is a big mistake?"

Horn-Rims shrugged. "I don't know."

He swung the car around the block, back toward the station.

"It's just a hunch anyway. Got no proof. We'll stick with the other leads for now. No use banging our heads against this wall."

"You got it, HR."

"And keep my hunch to yourself."

"You got it."

"You know how the public gets when a pretty girl is killed, and there is no way we're going to get anywhere with the Geyers if a hint of an implication gets out."

"You got it."

"So if the D.A. comes sniffing around—"

"Send him to you and flip him the bird behind his back."

"Good man."

Horn-Rims had three piles on his desk. One was hundreds of statements all saying they didn't see a damn thing, that it was a damn shame what happened to that girl, but it was a night-club and they didn't see a damn thing. Another was a hand-ful of very detailed, practically cross-referenced and footnoted statements all saying they didn't see a damn thing, that it was a damn shame what happened to that girl, but it was a nightclub and they didn't see a damn thing. The third was much taller than the other two with twice the testimonies and five times the de-tail. Those statements all said they didn't see a damn thing, didn't know a damn thing, and didn't particularly give a damn about this Joyce guy.

Three big piles of shit Horn-Rims had to stick his nose in.

A detective dropped another pile on his desk.

"Transcript of the girl's diary," he said.

"Anybody take a look at it?" Horn-Rims asked.

"Yeah. Didn't find anything. Figured you'd want to look any-way."

"Right. Thanks."

The detective left.

Horn-Rims made reading space in front of him on the desk. He got over reading diaries years ago, not just because he was a cop and sometimes cops needed to know your secrets, but also because most diaries were boring as shit and completely useless in investigations. But you had to read 'em all.

Renee's was no different. Who she liked. What she wore. How she felt. It jibed with what her friends said. No secret older boyfriend. No serious drugs. No second life. Nothing to imply who sexually assaulted her and then savagely beat her to death.

He could get profiles of the nightclub staff. Maybe one of them had a history. He could get the names of the boys who presented psychological concern to the school.

A predator could have coincidentally been there. Coincidence was deduction dynamite, but that didn't make it impossible. A predator would lie low, keep an eye on things, then strike at a vulnerable moment. Horn-Rims could ask the staff if they saw somebody lurking. Or maybe there was someone there they'd thrown out a few times for creeping on the teenagers. Sometimes you had to ask specific questions to get general answers.

He had to swing his pickaxe in those caves, even though he knew those mines were empty. He had the answer. He just couldn't render it in the form required by our justice system.

He looked up from the diary. The Mayor stood in front of him. The Chief of Police stood a step behind him. Horn-Rims looked back and forth at them for a moment.

"What the fuck do you want?" Horn-Rims asked.

The Mayor ran his fingers through his obvious hair plugs.

"Horn-Rims, you're a good cop. Everybody knows you're a good cop. Hell, you're one of the best. Who knows what the city would be like if we didn't have you out there? It'd be a shit buffet and we'd all have to go back for seconds, is what it would be."

Horn-Rims leaned back in his chair. Gave The Mayor a look that would crack Plexiglass.

"But some issues have come up," The Mayor continued, "and,

as I'm sure you know better than anybody, there are some problems that good cops just aren't good for. Situations where there are too many gray areas, you know, where the right and wrong, criminal and citizen of the good cop's world just get in the way of solving big problems. Of taking care of bigger issues."

Horn-Rims just kept looking.

"And The Joyce Case is one of them. It's just kind of tangled up in some complicated stuff. You know how it is with guys with money. They have connections. They have friends. It's never easy with a guy like this, and sometimes the best cops, the cops we all need, the most important cops, sometimes with guys like this Joyce character, the best cops aren't the right cops for the job. So, you've been removed from The Joyce Case."

Horn-Rims leaned forward. Put his elbows on his desk. Interdigitated.

"Since I'm the lead detective on the case, you can't remove me from it," Horn-Rims said.

The Mayor nervously cleared his throat. "You are no longer the lead detective on The Joyce Case."

Horn-Rims unlaced his fingers. Folded his arms on the desk in front of him. "As the highest-ranking homicide detective, I'm the one who decides who is the lead detective on homicide cases."

The Mayor rubbed his hands together. "I'm-I'm s-s-sorry, HR, you are no longer the, ummm, highest ranking homicide detective."

Horn-Rims slammed his fist on his desk. He stood up so fast his chair fell over. The Mayor winced. The Chief of Police took a half step forward.

"Why didn't you ask? Why didn't you just ask me to give up The Joyce Case? I would've shoveled that pile of bullshit off my desk in a heartbeat. I've got more important shit to do than chase after some billionaire who probably isn't even dead. The only reason I haven't is because nobody else has really pissed me off lately. Shit. All we'd have to do is change it to a missing-persons case.

Probably gonna do that anyway. Let that side of the office deal with it."

"I'm sorry, HR."

"Why didn't you ask?"

"Well—"

"It doesn't matter. You didn't ask because you're a couple of assholes. Fucking Christ, heaven is just a place where assholes aren't always in charge. Just stop the demotion. I'll take myself off The Joyce Case, or reclassify it, or whatever the fuck you want."

The Mayor and The Chief exchanged a nervous look.

"The demotion has already gone through," The Mayor said.

"Then fucking promote me back."

Another nervous glance.

"I'm sorry, HR, but the union contract stipulates that no changes can be made to an officer's rank after a demotion for six months, unless the officer commits an actionable violation of policy."

"Demotion," Horn-Rims said. "You can't demote a guy again until after six months."

"The language in the contract is ambiguous and we would prefer to avoid litigation."

Horn-Rims swallowed. He slammed his fist on the desk. Again. A third time.

He should've resigned right then and walked out. No one would blame him. He'd be hired just about wherever he wanted to go. But wherever he went, it would take longer than six months to get back to the top. Plus, he didn't want to move the kids. And even if something was available in the next town, even if they'd put him right back on top. There was Renee.

"Two things," he said in a tone that eats bullets and craps handcuffs. "If I'm not promoted back to my current rank in six months to the day, I walk. If I look at my desk that morning and I don't see the promotion paperwork, I don't even take my coat off. And two, not one single fucking cop is voting for you next election."

The Mayor started to say something. The Chief quieted him with a hand on his shoulder.

"Again," The Mayor said, "we greatly appreciate your service."

"Yeah, I'll bet."

The Mayor and The Chief left. Horn-Rims picked up his chair and sat down. Picked up where he left off in the diary transcript. He felt the other officers not looking at him. Not knowing what to say. Not knowing what to think. Wanting to punch The Mayor right in his fucking mouth. Turning back to their own problem piles.

Horn-Rims was the last person in the office. He was looking at profiles of the nightclub employees working that night. Only one had a history, and that was nonviolent drug stuff. And he was a bouncer, standing in the same spot, checking IDs all night. Not worth the time.

He picked up the report of the boys the school guidance counselors were concerned about. He was shocked that he got it, but there was no better grease for the wheels of law than a dead white girl. Every one of the boys had an alibi. Another report said no known predators were known to be in the area at the time, and if a sicko had sneaked in, he'd sneaked right back out.

Horn-Rims's phone rang. He looked at his watch. It was late. He cursed under his breath. He answered.

"Hi, Claire. Well, I know what time it is now. Yeah, I know. I'm sorry but you know how it is when it's a kid. It just stays with me. Yeah, it's about the boys, but, it's also about being a kid once too, you know. Knowing what she missed. Yeah, that's true, love, but I'm cynical enough already without thinking about it that way. Yeah. Well, I could leave right now or stay all night. No, nothing new. Just trying to see and think about things in a different way. I don't know, Claire. Dark, crowded club. And you know how loud they play the music. And the way these kids dance, anything could be going on and nobody would think twice about it. I know. To think, our parents were upset about "I Want to Hold Your Hand." And "Satisfaction," that's right. My mom hated "Satisfaction." I remember getting into a big fight with her over it. Or was that *Sticky Fingers*? Was that on *Sticky Fingers*? I know. Well, I don't plan on telling her what the boys listen to. Yeah. No. I should probably just call it a night here. I can think about this stuff anywhere. Oh yeah, no problem. Sure. Eggs. Milk. Cheese. Yep. Really? What's that for? Baked mac 'n' cheese? He wants to make baked macaroni and cheese for dinner tomorrow night? Since when did he want to cook? Oh yeah? Well, maybe the cable will start paying for itself. I know. Better not give him a reason to change his mind. Yeah, okay. Do you want me to get anything for dinner? Oh, okay. You know what, why don't you just call in the pizza and I'll get some chips and soda at the pizza place and then go out again. No, it won't be a problem. The extra drive will be some nice quiet time. I know, Claire, I know. Okay, I've got a few things to put my signature on and then I'll go. Five, ten minutes, tops. Okay. I know, Claire, I know. See you soon. Love you."

. Horn-Rims hung up. He put his signature on a few things and went.

Elsewhere and everywhere, summiting boulders rolled back down the mountains. We watched and the bravest of us rappelled back to ground to take up the toil they had turned into not toil. To some, it was a refilling in-box. To others, murder victims and the murderers who ran.

A cop that didn't get pain like an angry rat in the gut while working on a case was a shitty cop. Or a psychopath. The rat pain had a range; sometimes sharper, sometimes duller. Sometimes relaxing after a few hours away from the desk, sometimes not. Working on Renee's case, Horn-Rims's rat didn't relax.

Cases have a natural trajectory. You show up at the scene and don't know what the fuck happened or who the fuck did it. Then you bust your ass for days, weeks, months, years and you figure out what the fuck happened and who the fuck did it. But the truth is one thing, admissible evidence, quite often another. So when you find the truth, you turn all the clues into evidence. Sometimes that ain't no thing and sometimes it's impossible.

But Renee's case wasn't on that trajectory. It didn't have any trajectory. It was just sitting there rotting away, the who squared away after the first interview with Frank Geyer and the what-the-fuck locked behind a wall Horn-Rims didn't have the evidence to bust down. He couldn't even get a warrant. A conviction was unthinkable.

Horn-Rims wasn't hungry, but he had to put something in his stomach. The diner was one of his places. Five-minute drive from the station, on Meunier Street in a part of town some affectionately and derisively called Little SoHo. Always open. Passable and bottomless coffee. They didn't give him any crap when he nursed a couple of rounds of rye toast. Didn't ask him how his day was going.

He sat at the bar and nodded to Matilda for a cup of coffee. There were a couple of newspapers in a messy pile at the other end of the bar. He didn't have to look at them to know what was on their front pages. The department projected its basic confidence that the killer would be brought to justice soon, but anybody who really knew how to read the newspaper saw through that front. He picked up a menu.

Someone sat next to him. He jumped a little when he saw who it was.

"What the fuck do you want?" he asked.

"Information exchange."

"I don't have time to mess around with your little game of tiddlywinks."

"I can put him at the scene of the crime."

Horn-Rims grunted.

"Since it's a kid at the high school," Trike continued, "I can put him at the scene of the crime on the night in question."

The coffee arrived.

"All right, hotshot, you can shit in my ear if it makes you feel better. But then buzz off. I've got lives on the line."

"That club is exclusive. Even on the all-ages dance nights, it's hard to get in. Low capacity. Dress code. Guest lists. That kind of thing. Kids at the high school keep their ticket stubs in their wallets as a status symbol. Whoever this kid is, he's not a professional. That ticket stub went right in his wallet the second he got it back from the doorman and it's still there. And it's dated. And if his parents or their lawyers or someone are stonewalling you, you can place him at the club on the night in question."

Horn-Rims took a deep breath. A long sip of coffee. A longer sip of coffee. He nodded for a refill. When Matilda came over, he ordered a Reuben.

"Someone has been systematically removing every honest cop from The Joyce Case," he said. "One demotion and a bunch of re-assignments. A lot of paperwork just isn't getting done. The case is getting pushed around and pushed around with nobody doing anything about it and without being closed. As of yesterday, pretty much all work on it has stopped."

"Why?"

Horn-Rims shrugged. "Don't know what the point is, but the result seems to be that you're the only one with any chance to solve the case."

Trike slunk back to his booth. He left the diner a few minutes later.

Disaster. Top to bottom. The whole case was shit. Pure and utter shit. And it wouldn't get better when they found the stub in the kid's wallet. It was there all right. Being right had nothing to do with what kind of person you were.

But he had to get the wallet in a constitutionally allowed manner. Anything remotely questionable and the kid would walk. The case would go cold. Frank wouldn't get the help he needed. And then, some night in college, he'd get drunk or he'd just get mad and he'd beat another girl to death. And then he'd go to a real bad prison and stay there a real long time.

Matilda cleared the dishes from Trike's booth. Collected the newspapers that were piled there. She stood by the booth for a moment, looking out the window. "Raining again," she muttered. She put the papers on the pile on the bar and took the dirty dishes to the kitchen.

She brought Horn-Rims's Reuben with her on her way out.

The pickle was floppy.

The fries were soggy.

The slaw was runny.

The Reuben tasted like Justice.

Horn-Rims ate it without stopping.

Horn-Rims had a long talk with the DA about Frank Geyer's wallet. There were a million ways to get a teenager's wallet, but not many led to admissible evidence. They could pull him over while he was driving and ask for his wallet instead of just his license. They could contrive something at school; a survey or a study or something, and go through everyone's wallet. They could tail him and nab him for jaywalking or bust him on some blue law nobody'd enforced in a century. But the worst lawyer in the world would slap those right out of court.

Each time they ruled out an option, the DA said something like, "Don't you have anything else on this guy that I could get a warrant for?" and each time Horn-Rims responded that the stub was the only thing they might have that might lead to a warrant.

After the tenth time around that track, Horn-Rims dropped his head into his hands.

Exasperated, he asked, "Can we just ask him if we can look in his wallet?"

"What do you mean?" the DA asked.

"I mean, can a cop just walk up to him, in some public place, and say, 'Hey, kid, can I look in your wallet?'"

"What happens if the kid says no or asks why the cop wants to look in his wallet?"

"Then the cop squints at him and says, 'Wait, are you . . .' and then says some other name and Frank says no and the cop apologizes up and down."

"Don't you think that'll make him suspicious, so maybe he goes home and throws out the stub?"

"If we can't get it, it's as good as thrown out anyway. Will it hold up in court?"

The DA was quiet for a minute. He took a deep breath.

"Give me an hour to come up with something better. If I can't, go with it, but the cop has got to stick to the script. He can't argue with the kid, he just asks, and if the kid says or does anything but hand over the wallet, the cop gives him the line about looking for somebody else. No convincing the kid. No nothing. Just ask and if the kid says any remote version of no, the cop bails."

An hour later, the DA gave Horn-Rims the go-ahead.

Horn-Rims prepped a uniformed officer with the script. Set the cop up with a wire. They drove in separate cars to the high school. Horn-Rims and The Man with the Facts parked around the corner. Fifteen minutes later the uniformed cop radioed them.

"He's got the ticket stub for the night in question."

"All right, give him a ride to his house," Horn-Rims responded. "We'll meet you there."

The two police cars arrived at the Geyers'. Horn-Rims saw profound fear in Frank's eyes. Only his mother was home. Horn-Rims and The Man with the Facts arranged themselves with Frank and his mother in the living room. The uniformed cop left. It took half a look for Horn-Rims to know she wasn't going to break. Not for an instant. And she'd tear his throat out if he got tough.

"Mrs. Geyer, we're here because we found a ticket stub in your son's wallet from the nightclub for the night in question. Now, Frank is not an official suspect. We just want to know what he saw and don't particularly care why he didn't feel comfortable talking to us in the first place. The important thing is figuring out who murdered Renee. We're not going to worry if a teenager or two is squeamish about talking to us."

"And how did you come to find the ticket stub in his wallet?" Mrs. Geyer asked.

"A uniformed officer asked Frank if he could look through Frank's wallet and Frank said yes. This was outside the high school just now."

"Is that how it went, Frank?"

Frank nodded. Radiating terror.

"The question was recorded, Mrs. Geyer, if you have any concerns about the exchange."

"You seem to be spending an awful lot of time on a boy who isn't an official suspect in the case, detective. If I didn't have the utmost respect for you, I would assume you were looking to throw someone, anyone, to the clamoring public, whose confidence, by now, has been much diminished by the department's inability to produce even a primary suspect, let alone make an arrest. Though I can sympathize with your plight, let me be quite clear: you are wasting your time with my son. In fact, let me make this even easier for you: unless you have a warrant, do not bother speaking with my son or any other member of this family. I assure you, you will not be shown in on your next visit."

Horn-Rims was ready for this. Horn-Rims expected this. If there were incriminating clothes to be burned, they'd been burned early last Sunday morning.

He talked as he stood up and put on his hat.

"Right now, a judge would most likely sentence Frank to some time in juvie followed by a regimen of therapy and counseling and house arrest, and with good behavior and demonstration that he is emotionally and mentally healthy after what had to be an extremely traumatic ordeal, he would most likely be able to start college in about five years. But in three months, he turns eighteen. Sure, the crime was committed when he was a minor, but you know how the public gets when ugly things are done to a pretty girl. Renee was a very pretty girl and very ugly things were done to her. There's no telling what time he'd get then, especially if he fights it, but there is a good chance it would be a long time, all of it in prison."

"Get out of my house."

Horn-Rims tipped his hat as he left.

Horn-Rims was the last person in the office. He'd talked to a few of Frank's friends. Once he'd told them about the ticket stub, they confirmed that Frank was at the club, but none of them saw him with Renee. They got separated at some point. None of them knew for sure when he left. They didn't look for him. When he didn't answer his phone they figured he just went home. He often bailed on them.

Horn-Rims needed more. A lot more.

No witness. No motive. No murder weapon. No forensic evidence in the alley or on the body.

Nothing.

Something clicked.

The mysterious spark.

Something about the alley. Something caught. Something snagged. Something about the alley. Something that wasn't a weapon.

What was a weapon? Why the word *weapon*? How does an object become a "weapon"?

Horn-Rims wanted to pound on his desk. He wanted to pound on his head. He wanted to pound his head on his desk until whatever was rattling around caught the hook in the language center of his brain.

? . . . !

"The emergency stairs!"

Horn-Rims leaped from his desk. He grabbed his coat and rushed to his car muttering about how much of a fucking idiot he'd been.

There were two exits into the alley from the club. They assumed Renee and her killer had come out through the door on the first floor. The other exit was just a fire exit. But it was at the bottom of a long flight of concrete stairs. The stairs led to a back hallway, where the club's offices were. If Frank was just being a stupid, bullheaded teenager and got into a tussle with Renee near the stairs, and somehow she fell, the fall would have accounted for all the trauma. No need for a two-by-four or a baseball bat. Just concrete and gravity. And if Frank were just a kid being hormonal and stupid, he could have panicked and started dragging the body out of the club toward the Dumpsters.

And that's manslaughter, not murder. Of course, it was also trying to destroy evidence and lying to a police officer, but at this point, with so little evidence, best just to forget the second act of the tragedy. Manslaughter was an entirely different negotiation with the parents. All he needed was to place Frank and Renee in that back hallway.

Horn-Rims called The Man with the Facts at home and picked him up on the way to the club. A badge flash at the door and they were in. It was early for the club scene, so it was just the staff inside. The music was already on. And loud.

Horn-Rims went right through the door to the hallway and the offices. Horn-Rims nodded at The Man with the Facts to check out the stairs, and then knocked on the manager's door.

"Come in, detective," the manager said.

Horn-Rims walked in, leaving the door slightly ajar. Sat down in an old plush chair across from the desk. The manager was six-foot-two, at least 220 pounds, wore a sharp suit, and had a shiny bald head and a face well-practiced in the art of looking like it should not be fucked with.

"How can I help you, detective?" the night manager said, not bothering to look up from the work he pretended to do.

"Sorry to bother you again, sir."

"But here you are."

"I've got to ask you again about that night."

"I'm not entirely sure why I need to tell you that I didn't see or hear anything," the manager said. He put his pen down, leaned back in his chair, and looked at Horn-Rims. "Again."

"Right, I remember your first answer, that the music is too loud for you to hear anything when you're working back here," Horn-Rims said.

"That is correct."

"But the music is on right now. It was on when I walked in. And I'm sitting here. With the door open. And I don't really hear it."

"It's a lot louder when there are people in the club."

"That's true. That's true. But I've heard that too. It's louder, but not ten times louder. And frankly, if I owned this place and I wanted the night manager to make the most of his time at the club, I'd probably invest in some soundproofing."

"What are you getting at?"

"This hallway is a fire exit. I'm sure you hear shit going on in this hallway every night. I imagine people are always sneaking back here for a grope or a fuck and you learned a long time ago to just ignore whatever you heard. And nobody is going to expect you to be able to hear the exact moment when a grope goes too far."

The Man with the Facts came in. He sat down in the other chair.

Horn-Rims continued.

"So whatever you heard, ain't gonna be no skin off your nose. You're not up for anything, even though you've kept it to yourself. Now," Horn-Rims made eye contact with The Man with the Facts, who gave him a quick nod, "that all changes if forensics finds some of Renee's blood at the bottom of the stairs and you continue to keep your trap shut."

Horn-Rims paused. Let the manager give him a hard stare for just a second.

"We prove they were back there, and you didn't tell us about it, because of some kind of hope that this murder wasn't really connected to the club, well," Horn-Rims started a casual gesture with his hand, but ended it with a look that could've stopped a train. "But that isn't even the point. I don't want to threaten you. We have a dead girl and a traumatized boy. Now, the boy is connected to a lawyer who has advised him to keep his mouth shut, but that was about murder. I think we might be able to get this kid the help he needs if we're talking about manslaughter. If he and Renee were in this hallway before she died, then we're talking manslaughter."

The manager leaned back in his chair and folded his hands together across his stomach. He took a deep breath.

"And there isn't going to be anything about withholding evidence?" the manager asked, looking down at his hands and then over at the corner of his desk.

"Does it have to be about that?"

The manager's head dropped.

"I heard a couple of couples back here that night," he said. "Always do. It's bad enough that we're thinking about renovating to put the offices on the first floor, or at least not right in this fucking hallway with the fire exit. One of the couples was definitely older. Way older. One of them could have been the girl and the guy."

"What time did you hear the younger couple?"

"Around eleven-thirty, I guess. Coulda been ten minutes in either direction around then."

Horn-Rims looked at The Man with the Facts. A nod.

"That fits with previous testimony."

Horn-Rims stood up and extended his hand. The manager shook it.

"Thank you very much," Horn-Rims said. "You'll hear from us

if you're called upon to testify. And don't be shocked if a forensic team shows up in the next hour."

"Sure, sure," the manager said.

Back in the car, Horn-Rims asked, "Is it worth it to sic forensics on the stairs?"

The Man with the Facts was quiet for a moment. "Yes. Though it is unlikely they will be able to extract DNA evidence, I saw some stains on the mat at the foot of the stairs and on the door that could be blood or other bodily fluid or residue of bodily tissue. They could prove somebody fell down the stairs, even if they could not prove who."

"Call 'em. Maybe Frank's prints are on the inside of the door. That could get us the warrant."

The Man with the Facts called 'em in. Horn-Rims started driving.

"I'll swing you by your place on the way back to the station."

"Thank you, HR."

"And if you end up with a sleepless night tonight, spend it figuring out what to do if we don't find his fingerprints on the door."

"I'll add it to the schedule."

"Because if we don't get those prints, we might not get the warrant, and we might not get any further."

"Will also add a block of time for irrationally hoping for the best," The Man with the Facts said.

Horn-Rims gunned it to get through a yellow light.

"Yeah, let me know how that feels."

Horn-Rims sat at his desk, going through the eyewitness testimony of a shooting murder. For the most part, it looked like your basic domestic abuse gone wrong, but there were a few things about the scene that didn't jibe. The victim was all the way on the other side of the room facing the shooter. These kinds of shootings almost always take place at close range and when they were at a greater distance the victim was always shot in the back as he or she was running away from the confrontation. Horn-Rims picked up a cup of cold coffee off the corner of his desk. Wondered if there was money hiding somewhere. Before he could take a sip, another detective rushed up to his desk.

"Frank Geyer's fingerprints were on the inside of the door," she said.

Horn-Rims gave the detective a curt nod. In eight minutes, he was at the Geyers'.

He knocked on their door. Mrs. Geyer answered.

"I believe the last time we spoke, you were told that we would not speak to you again without a warrant."

"That is true, Mrs. Geyer, but we were talking about a murder case then. That's not what we're talking about now."

"Oh? Are you recruiting for a book club, detective?" she said with vicious sarcasm. "Or perhaps some kind of debate society where we discuss the nature of facts? Or why not just talk about the weather? That's what strangers do, after all."

"Manslaughter, Mrs. Geyer. New evidence has changed this from homicide to manslaughter."

Horn-Rims saw Frank walk by inside.

"We know Renee fell down the stairs, Frank," he shouted.

Frank stopped. Wide-eyed. Looked at his mother.

"We know it was an accident, Frank," Horn-Rims said much quieter.

"Frankie, go to your room. Now."

Frank dashed upstairs. Mrs. Geyer stepped out onto the stoop. Horn-Rims stepped back to accommodate her. She closed the door behind her.

"Now what the hell are you talking about?" she demanded.

"I don't know what your son told you, but this is what we've figured out. Frank was at the club that night. He bumped into Renee after she went to the bathroom. That was when the waitress saw them together. They decided to go make out in the hallway where the offices are. The night manager heard them, but people are always making out back there, so he didn't do or say anything about it. Your son went a little too far. You know how teenage boys, even good teenage boys, can be. Whatever happened next resulted in a struggle. Who knows, maybe Renee flipped out and Frank had to defend himself. Maybe he didn't know his own strength, or just lost track of where they were in the hallway. Maybe she wasn't used to the heels she was wearing. Whatever it was, Renee fell down a two-story flight of concrete stairs. Frank panicked. He tried to hide the body by dragging it out to the Dumpster. Something made him drop it before he got there. Maybe a car drove by or his arms got tired. It doesn't matter. Now, maybe the clothes he wore that night have been cleaned or burned and maybe they haven't. Maybe there's something on his shoes or his belt. Maybe this whole thing would've been over if it hadn't rained that night."

Mrs. Geyer opened her mouth to respond but Horn-Rims continued before she could.

"Mrs. Geyer, I don't want Frank to go to prison. Everything points to a good kid who made a mistake that just happened to be next to a big-ass set of stairs. He'd done the same stupid thing five feet in the other direction and I'm not here talking to you. But he suffered a major emotional trauma and needs help. Bringing him in will be the best way to get him that help."

"What proof do you have that any of this nonsense is true?"

"Frank's fingerprints were found on the inside of the emergency exit door. Blood was found in the stairwell. Mrs. Geyer, I want to help Frank. But I am a police officer. I need to bring the criminal to justice first. I could certainly just arrest him and bring him to the station for questioning. And he would talk. You know he would talk. He would talk in the car on the way to the station.

"However, if you, your husband, and Frank come down to the station and Frank confesses, I will ensure that his sentence consists of mandated therapy, probation, and house arrest. I'll even forget about your obstruction of justice."

"Cops make those promises all the time, detective. Those are not promises cops can keep."

"Well, Mrs. Geyer, I can keep those promises."

"Oh, really? And why is that, detective?"

"Mrs. Geyer, I am the one and only Horn-Rims. I keep my promises."

THE LIFE AND TIMES OF BARRY ROCHECHOUART

Forty-seven fucking minutes. Max sat in his car and Trike sat in Lola's car. In the parking lot of the John Wilson Murray Memorial Armory for forty-seven minutes. The fire trucks blocked three of the four exits. Once they moved, it was gasoline-powered *Lord of the Flies*.

There was a line at the wings joint too, just to top it off.

Fucking finally at the office, they took off their coats and Trike made a quick call on his cell while Max checked the agency's phone and e-mail for new messages. Trike unlocked all his desk drawers. He unpacked the takeout on it, putting an order of fries under it. Max sat down in a client chair. They ate without speaking for seven minutes.

Abruptly, Trike stood up and walked to the window. He stood there, hands in his pockets, looking out. While looking out he said, "What if something happens, Max?"

"Something always happens, boss," Max said through a wing.

"What if she gets hurt?"

"Jogging. Riding the bus. Driving. Life is constant . . . risk of harm."

"This is different, Max."

"This is, boss."

Trike returned to his desk.

"Give me a cold case, Max," he said.

"A cold case, boss?"

"A cold case, Max. Something unsolved from that American Old Bailey you carry around above your shoulders."

"Preferred . . . genre, boss?" Max asked.

Trike shrugged his shoulders and shook his head. "I need to keep my mind completely clear of assumptions and preemptive conclusions to be perfectly open to whatever message Joyce tells us, however he tells us, and, given the situation, The Joyce Case neurons won't stop assuming and preemptively concluding. Anything that'll occupy some neurons would be crackerjack."

Max finished a wing. Used two napkins to wipe his fingers clean. Adjusted himself in his chair. Took a moment to find an effective unsolved case.

Everything Trike did not say to Lola, every gift he did not give her, every time he did not see her, was preserved, perfectly, with everything else in his brain. Nearly all of those nots were correct, and Lola was somewhere, in some state.

"All right, boss. I'll give you the basics and we'll go from there. If you don't like the basics, I'll find . . . an alternative."

"Basics away, Maximize."

Max cracked his fingers, cleared his throat, and gave Trike the basics. "In the late seventies, a struggling art gallery owner named Barry Rochechouart got together with a highly technical but visionless painter and two other friends in the art world to create the artist Cashel Fitzmaurice, a self-taught son of a dock worker—"

"An Irish dockworker, no less," Trike said.

"Rochechouart designed the paintings, the highly technical painter painted them, and then Rochechouart and the other two touched up the paintings with errors someone self-taught might make. Throw in a year and a half of hype, a backstory involving a physically abusive alcoholic father—"

"They made the Irish dockworker an abusive alcoholic?" Trike asked.

Max shrugged. "Times were . . . different. When the fraud was exposed, that fact became a . . . sticking point."

"Good."

"But before the fraud was exposed, everyone in the art world was talking about the troubled, talented, and mysterious Cashel Fitzmaurice. But people want mysteries solved, and Fitzmaurice's was. But the cold case comes after the fraud was exposed."

"And here begins the part of the story Max believes will be of particular interest to one Trike Augustine."

"That's the plan, boss. Now, after the exposure of the ... creative identity, the Cashel Fitzmaurice paintings ... drifted. Some original owners kept them, others gave them away, some were confiscated for evidence, and others were just ... lost. And then, after anger over the deception had cooled for a decade, the paintings were seen not just as public extensions of a particular identity, but as works of art. Even though they knew each painting was a dishonest collaboration, or because they knew that, collectors, critics, and other appraisers decided that the paintings, as collaborations, were actually pretty darn good. Then pretty darn valuable."

"And with value comes crime," Trike color-commented.

"Three different new collectors found themselves with a painting called 'Intractable and Irresistible.' Only one was listed in the original catalog."

"Fuck yeah!" Trike exclaimed.

Max held up a wait-there's-more finger. "The copies are identical except for one detail. The painting includes an incorrect proof of a famous unsolved math problem, and each painting has a different error."

"Oh, fuck the duck truck, yes. That is delicious. You, Max, are a fucking champion."

"I do my best, boss."

"Load me up with whatever you can print off the Internet, especially about the life and times of Barry Rochechouart and the unsolved math problem."

"What about ... wings?" Max asked.

"I'll wings while you print, you wings while I brain."

"But—"

"It is the only way, Max. My intriguer is erect. It pulsates with impatience," Trike demanded.

"Your sense of punishment is ... swift and precise, boss," Max said with grudging admiration, heading to his computer to produce the printouts.

It took him twenty-three minutes of searching and printing to get Trike started, including color printouts, which they absolutely could not afford, of the painting's three iterations.

Trike spent thirty-two minutes reading the printouts and processing the data, after which he leaped to standing behind his desk and began talking through his reasoning.

"I am tantalized by the possibility that all three paintings, the original and the two fraudulent copies, were physically painted by the same person, but, though that fact may become relevant, it will not help identify the original. The first question, and what might be the most difficult of the cascade of questions this cold case represents, is: Who made the authentic fabricated error? It could be the painter, Rochechouart, in his design of the painting, or either of the other two tasked with adding calculated imperfections."

Trike gestured as though about to escape from behind his desk, but froze in that posture. "And so we must begin by forgetting completely the existing errors and reconstruct, as much as possible, the errors each potential error-inserter would make. Given that the error, in and of itself, has nothing to do with the artistic technique of the painting, I believe it is safest to assume, at this point in the process, that Rochechouart is its source. We have to assume Rochechouart understood that whatever was offered in the painting as a solution to the Riemann Hypothesis would be incorrect, and so, once enough of the intractable problem was included to make it identifiable, he had the freedom to be intentional and the freedom to be random."

Again, Trike jolted as though beginning to pace his office, and again, he froze in the preemptive posture. "So, while we wait, Max,

I'm going to need a lot more about the Riemann Hypothesis and even more about Rochechouart, especially the nature of his mathematical education, both formal and informal. After that, I'll need to examine as many of the Cashel Fitzmaurice paintings as—"

Trike stopped when he heard the door to the outer office open. Someone walked lightly across the room.

AND THE LADY DREW A GUN

The kidnappers propped Lola up in the middle backseat of the car and blindfolded her. Poorly. Two thugs scrunched in beside her. One bound her wrists. Poorly. The car drove out the back alley and turned away from the armory to avoid notice by those evacuating the building. At least the kidnappers did that right.

Lola realized she'd acted herself into a puzzle. She knew the ether or chloroform on the rag bit didn't really work, but in the moment, Hollywood's images reached her brain before reality's facts. Chloroform was just as likely to kill you as it was to knock you out, and the point of ether was docility, not unconsciousness.

Since they weren't driving at emergency-room pace, they either meant ether or didn't know a damn thing about chloroform. And if they meant ether they either knew she was faking or didn't know a damn thing about ether.

The evidence indicated that they made the same mistake in planning that Lola had made in haste; they kidnapped her the way it happened in movies. The movie meant she should struggle to groggy consciousness.

Lola made waking-up noises.

"Now just relax, Lola," a reedy tenor voice said from the front passenger seat. "We're going for a little drive. If you're a good girl and don't try anything funny, no one will get hurt. If, however, you decide to misbehave, I cannot in good conscience assure you blood will not be spilled. We just need to get a message to that insensitive, sociopathic, over-intelligent, autodidactic, lovesick little puppy nipping at your heels. So behave. And relax."

Lola did not react. It was the plan.

The car seemed to take every offered turn, meaning, though the ride lasted a least an hour, they could not be far from the armory. They were still downtown somewhere. But that only narrowed the location field slightly. There were plenty of places a group their size could enter and remain unnoticed.

When the car stopped, the reedy-voiced man said, "Take her out, pick her up, and spin her around. We don't want to take any chances."

The backseat doors opened. One of the thugs grabbed Lola under her arms and dragged her out. She put up as much of a struggle as she imagined someone nauseated and light-headed from ether would put up, as the other thug ran around the car and grabbed her feet.

They spun her around. Way too fast.

"Slow down. You're not a fucking carnival ride," the reedy voice commanded.

The thugs kept their footing despite their initial velocity. Barely.

"Now take her inside. Do not say a single word."

"You got it, James."

Lola heard a flat fleshy thwap. A palm striking a forehead.

They took her up a short flight of stairs into a building and down a hallway, spinning her every twenty feet or so. They took at least one left turn, but spun her enough to confuse her mental map of the building. After five spins, another door was opened and Lola was brought into a room and set down on what felt like linoleum tile.

"Tie up her feet, as well," James directed.

The binding on her wrists was adjusted. Rope was wound round her ankles, but she was tied up only in the loosest sense of the word.

"Good. That's perfect. You stay here and keep an eye on her. Do. Not. Say. Anything. You two, come with me."

Lola heard the door open and close. She assumed she'd been left with her guard. Lola shifted into a more comfortable position and found she leaned against what was likely a sturdy table leg not far from the door. The blindfold was loose enough that she could see over its top edge and beneath its bottom edge. She saw a twenty-minute portion of the clock on the wall.

She assessed her security situation.

One confirmed exit of the room. First floor of a building. Schematic of the building unclear. No apparent imminent threat of bodily harm. One guard who might or might not be armed. With the basics established, Lola wondered more about her situation.

"Not everybody knows how to tie a decent knot," she thought, "so maybe that's just poor preparation. But why leave me with just one guard? Even if they don't know my training, they were there when I threw my first attacker. Even if they assume the knots are enough, they know how physically incapable they are. Unless they needed every other member for whatever message is being sent to Trike." Lola's train of thought was interrupted by a rumble in her stomach. "Fucking Ball," she thought.

The twenty minutes passed. The thug shuffled nervously about. Hummed short portions of old show tunes.

If a message was being sent, it was being sent now. Things were happening separately from Lola about Lola.

After what she guessed was another twenty minutes, the door opened. Someone whispered back and forth with the guard, but no one came in or left. After a minute, the door closed. She deduced her guard was given additional instructions.

The pace of his pacing increased. He was nervous. Agitated. Unsure about his instructions.

He started mumbling. Eventually, he settled into a steady rhythm, repeating words and phrases. Lola listened to the loop. After a few dozen iterations, she discerned what he was saying.

"Safety. Chamber. Squeeze, don't pull."

Someone had hastily told him how to use a handgun.

A professional kidnapper had a specific goal for the kidnapping. As long as that goal was being pursued, the hostage was safe. A gun might be waved. A face might be slapped. But no trigger would be pulled or throat slit. A professional with a handgun was not going to shoot you by accident.

But an amateur with a gun could shoot anything and anybody at any time. Lola was not about to hang around an armed idiot.

And she was fucking starving. Trike and Max probably got wings on their way back to the office. The bastards.

Lola shifted around as if trying to prevent her legs from falling asleep. She positioned herself to see the thug's feet as he made his nervous circuit. When they faced away, she struck. The blindfold fell off with the velocity of her forward somersault. On the upswing of the somersault, Lola shrugged off the poorly tied rope around her wrists, catching the gun hand as she rolled to her feet. The thug swung around in a wild panic, providing more than enough momentum for Lola to guide into a dramatic throw. The thug was on his back. The gun was in her hand.

When his lungs regained the required air, he leaped up as much as he could, threw the door open, and ran down the hallway wailing, "Sheeeeeeeeeeeeeeeeee's freeeeeeeeeeeeeeeeeeee!"

The gun wasn't loaded. At least the kidnappers got that right. Lola wiped her fingerprints off and left the gun in the room. She finished untying the rope around her ankles. Took a deep breath. Cautiously entered the dark hallway.

She slid against the wall, away from whatever reinforcements the thug might rally. She encountered a number of doors, but all were locked. At one point, she bent around a water fountain. The architecture was distantly familiar.

A hallway presented itself. Lola took it, sliding down its left wall. This hallway ended at a set of large double doors. She heard voices approaching. The doors were unlocked. She silently pushed one open and slid through, holding it ajar a crack to listen to the voices. A flashlight circle stopped at the intersection.

"Sir, she's gone already," James said.

"I'm not surprised," a new voice said.

"What should we do?"

A pause suggested a gesture. "Let her go. Someone trying to catch her will get hurt. We've got what we needed out of her."

"Yes, sir," James said.

The two walked away. Lola let the door close without a click. She felt herself in a large open space. She took a deep quiet breath. Directly across from her, about one hundred feet away, she saw a thin film of light about the width of a door along the floor. She walked toward it, sliding her feet along the slick floor, her hands out in front of her.

Her father's first advanced lesson was about the two brains; one did the thinking and one did the sensing. Most of the time, the thinking brain talked without stop, which was how it should be. People are supposed to do a lot of thinking. But sometimes the situation moved too fast for thought. Reaction was vital. Conclusion secondary.

The air was cool and felt recently but not currently conditioned. It smelled clean, perhaps mildly disinfected. There was the loud quiet of open spaces and distant machinery. The texture of the floor made things click.

She was in a school gymnasium.

The light's source was a door, an unlocked door. Lola slowly pushed it open. She was in an alley behind the building, lit by streetlights.

"Lola," a woman's voice said behind her.

Lola spun around, knife drawn. She saw a compact woman, shaped like Hollywood tells us indomitable Eastern European woman were shaped. She wore a ragged buttonless sweater over a stained and deteriorating housedress, a pair of teal stretch pants, and at least three pairs of socks. She drew as Lola drew.

And the lady drew a gun.

"What a lovely dress you're wearing," she said. "You can put the knife away."

"Who are you?" Lola said, not about to put her knife away. "And how do you know my name?"

"My apologies. I know so much about you, I forget we've never met. It is one of the constant situations of my life. Your partner may have spoken of me as The Lady on the Corner. People come to me because I know things. For example, I know the training you received from your father, and exactly what Lola Lenore is capable of with the knife in her hand. Note my absence of fear.

"Now, put it away, so I can put my gun away, and we can talk."

Lola could tell from the grip that The Lady knew how to use the gun, and she slowly put her knife away. The Lady on the Corner as slowly put her gun away.

"What brings you to this part of town in such a lovely dress?"

"Information isn't free," Lola said.

The Lady on the Corner raised an eyebrow and nodded slightly. "An exchange then. Question for question. Answer for answer."

Lola knew what Trike went through and how much he paid for information from The Lady on the Corner. This was an opportunity. If she asked and answered the right way, she might find the information they were missing. But she also needed to get home.

"Agreed. I was kidnapped and brought here by the kidnappers."

"Interesting. Very interesting. And well played. It begs followups. You may ask me a question."

Lola went with the immediately actionable. "Where am I?"

"A very good question. Practical. Actionable. You are in an alley behind the H. H. Holmes Elementary School. Vidocq Street is behind you."

Lola thought, "Eighty-six bus. Take me to the office." She wanted to turn and run to make sure she got the last bus. But there was another question in The Lady's eyes, and if The Lady had another question, Lola could get another answer.

"How did someone of your abilities come to be kidnapped?" The Lady on the Corner asked.

"I allowed it to happen."

The Lady on the Corner laughed a deep, echoing, diaphramic laugh. "My, my, my. You might have to settle for the detecting machine so enraptured with you. Very few other humans on the planet have the inherent confidence to be your partner. If you want one, of course. I owe you an answer."

"Why can't we find Joyce?"

The Lady on the Corner smiled. Gave a congratulatory nod. "Trike will solve the case. But he will never understand it. As an artist, though you might not be able to solve the case, you will easily understand it. Don't explain it to him. Everything, absolutely everything, has its limit, and this is beyond Trike's."

"What do you mean?"

The Lady on the Corner shook her head. "You do not have another question. Information isn't free and there's not enough tucked into your bra for both that information and bus fare. You'd better go now. The Eighty-six will be at the corner soon. It's the last one for the night."

The Lady on the Corner turned and walked out her end of the alley. Lola jogged to the street and just caught the bus as it was pulling up to the stop.

ON THE RAG

"Hey, guys," Lola said as she entered Trike's office. "Did either of you pick up my purse? I dropped it when I was kidnapped. There wasn't anything really in it, but I've only got, like, two purses total."

"Huh," was all Trike initially managed. He checked his cell phone for missed calls. He dashed to the hallway. Looked for a note on the door or the floor. And then on every reasonable surface the office and environs offered. He double-checked the phone messages. He checked the agency's e-mail, his e-mail, Max's e-mail. Nothing.

While Trike searched, Max said to Lola, "Only gone . . . two-plus hours?"

Lola flopped into the available client chair. "Yeah, well, eventually they gave one of those inept thugs a gun and there was no way I was going to spend much time near an armed idiot. And anyway, I overheard them say they'd already gotten what they wanted from me. Didn't they call or something?"

Trike sat down, on his face the stoic expression of a warlock whose spell worked too well. "I called the janitor. Let him know to look for your purse. Fire alarm went off before anyone else went to the bathroom. Purse is still where you dropped it. We can pick it up tomorrow."

Trike's eyes narrowed. He pressed his palms together in front of his face. "No, they did not call. They did not leave a note any-where in space where we would find a note. They did not drive up in an imposing black sedan to proclaim threats on your life at us. They did not hire thespians to depict potential horrors as a way to induce particular actions on our parts. They did not throw a note-wrapped brick. We have heard nothing from them."

"Easy escape?" Max asked.

Lola rolled her eyes. "They did the whole cover-my-face-with-a-rag thing, but they didn't put on the rag whatever they meant to put on the rag. I was only tied up in the loosest sense of the phrase. They left me with just one guard. The only thing they did right was make sure the gun they gave the thug wasn't loaded."

"Tell me everything," Trike said, unmoving, "from beginning to end, leaving nothing out, no matter how trivial it might appear to you."

Lola noticed the remains of takeout. "Are there any fries left? I'm fucking starving."

Trike reached under his desk, retrieved the full order of fries, and handed it to Lola.

"Now, in between bites," he said, "tell me everything."

Trike sat monolith-still while Lola told her story, until she reached the name of the school.

"Stop—H. H. Holmes Elementary School?" Trike confirmed.

"Yep," Lola said, stuffing fries into her mouth.

"You are certain it was H. H. Holmes Elementary School?"

" 'Cause I'd just make that shit up to fuck with you."

Trike nodded.

"Max?" he said.

"Boss."

"Lola?"

Lola muttered a vague affirmative through a face full of fries.

"Though the world's languages are rich with words, terms, phrases, and idioms of hatred, though there is a wealth of curses, profanities, and blasphemies, though humans have joined word and fury as long as both have coexisted in consciousness, though poets and scholars, popes and pundits, geniuses and savants, have committed rage to language for eons, there are no curses, profanities, blasphemies, or idioms of hatred in the lexicon of expression capable of capturing the satanic anger boiling my soul."

Lola and Max knew to just wait these speeches out.

"As you both recall, we wanted Joyce to use Lola as a means of communicating directly with me, and in that sense, our plan succeeded beyond our wildest booze-soaked fantasies, for Joyce, though he did not call us to explain the kidnapping, nor send a message by post, analog or electronic, nor do anything more than bring you, Lola, to a specific location, has made a direct statement. At least, he assumes so."

Trike stood and began pacing around his office.

"There are many in both the detecting world and the emerging world of neurophysics who spend much time and spill much ink on the subject of my memory, many seeing it as a particularly dramatic demonstration of the limitless potential of the human brain and the truly paltry understanding we have of its abilities, with two postdocs currently working on a postulation that the brain is a quantum computer, a theory they believe will explain how the bioelectricity of its actions become thoughts and why so much of our experience is mysterious to us.

"In the interest of these investigations, I told the story of my memory many times, a condensed version of which I will share with you now because without this context you cannot begin to comprehend the satanic anger boiling my blood.

"Sometime in seventh grade I realized that my memory was capable of information acts beyond those delineated by typical experience. I discovered I could train it to automatically and semiconsciously record specific sets of information, storing them in an organized and accessible manner. From that unremembered moment forward, the process was much like a slowly developing photograph, as I improved the techniques, structures, and images to the point where they reached their current level of sophistication and utility four years, two months, four days, and three hours ago.

"That is the level the public is familiar with, through my exploits in this agency, but before that moment, my memory was not uniquely distinctive. It was different by degrees rather than in nature. And so this brings us to this moment in which Joyce, making a rational assumption, did no more than bring Lola to H. H. Holmes Elementary School, because I attended H. H. Holmes for only one year, sixth grade."

"What happened in sixth grade?" Lola asked.

Trike continued as if Lola hadn't spoken. "One might guess Joyce is making a statement about my father's murder, which happened the summer after sixth grade, but if he knows me well enough to steal only my radio when he breaks into my office, he must know that nothing occurred at H. H. Holmes that could in any way reference the following summer's tragedy."

Trike sat down in his chair.

"There can be only one conclusion. Joyce used Lola to tell me he is getting revenge for something I did in sixth grade."

He put his head in his hands.

"And I have no ideas what it is," he concluded.

"So this whole thing," Lola said with a gesture encompassing the beautiful world, "all these millions and millions of dollars are to get revenge on you for something that happened in sixth grade?"

Trike put his feet up on his desk. "As indicated by the evidence."

"It's not absurd," Max explained. "Sixth grade . . . beginning of social life. An insult, slight, prank . . . could retard someone's social development . . . dramatically."

"But that would only be memorable to the victim," Trike said, "and to me after seventh grade."

Max shrugged. "I gave an explanation . . . not an answer."

Trike sighed again. His gaze drifted around the room as if following a gnat. After a minute, Trike snapped his eyes back to his companions.

"Okay. The plan. Max, you drive Lola home, assuming Lola wants to go home and does not insist on jogging home in her formal wear. My sixth-grade class picture is in the box of pictures in the closet I never use. I will go home, drink something caustic and alcoholic, and stare at that picture until I figure this out. I will contact both of you when I do and both of you will contact me immediately if you come up with anything. Plan approved?"

"Plan approved," Max said.

"Plan approved, but only if Max is willing to swing by Store24. The fries were nice, but I need something else."

"Amendment approved . . . and on me."

"Max, you don't have to—"

"You were kidnapped. This is . . . combat pay."

"Thanks, Max. See you tomorrow, Trike."

"See you, boss. Good luck."

Trike did not respond. His drifting gaze returned.

Max and Lola left. Both tossed an additional goodbye wave over their shoulders as they went through the door.

It took Trike fifty-eight minutes to get himself out of the office. He sat in all the chairs. He drank all the tallboys. He looked out the window. He rifled through the filing cabinets. He turned off the computers. He tapped on his desk with the eraser end of his favorite pencil. He sighed. He sulked. He muttered, "At this point, one could be forgiven for being skeptical of my conclusion, but as the evidence mounts, the darkened room becomes more suspicious," as he left the office.

Much of detecting is unpleasant. Which is part of the point. You sign up for the job because it engenders emotions of substance. Not the junk one felt at the office. But unpleasant is still unpleasant, no matter what ancillary psychological benefits are conferred. And whatever was in that class picture was sure to be unpleasant. Unpleasant in an unpleasant way.

STANDING IN THE WAY OF THOSE WHO HAVE ALREADY REJECTED THE LAW

A bottle will hold vodka as well as a glass. And you don't have to wash a vodka bottle when you're done drinking. And then there's all that extra effort glasses pose.

Bring bottle to glass.

Unscrew cap.

Pick up and pour.

Determine portion.

Set down and cap.

Return bottle to place.

Trike decided to drink out of his favorite fuck-my-life vodka cup, so all that effort would slow down his pace. It was a plastic tumbler with a handle of almost the same height as the cup itself and with enough width that he could interlace his fingers within it. Its original color was a reasonable blue that had since faded into an approximation of mid-nineties teal. In the middle, facing into the world when held by the handle by the right hand, was an equally faded Disney World logo, encircled by the archaeological traces of the catchphrase "WHEN YOU WISH UPON A STAR." He was still drinking pretty damn fast.

He added pacing to his pacing.

Holding the class picture, Trike walked past the table through the living room, around the couch, to his bedroom desk, to the front door, and back. He emptied the cup on each circuit. Trying to figure this out.

Trike had four basic mental analysis techniques: data-frame, matrices, annotated images, and narrative columns.

With data-frames, he framed an argument with scrolls of facts, like TV news tickers, allowing him to fact-check his reasoning as he reasoned. With matrices, he set known facts at four corners and positioned possible explanations in the space between them based on how strongly they correlated with particular facts. With annotated images, Trike held a single image in his mind, such as a picture from the crime scene, and surrounded it with conclusions, observations, and relevant data. With the narrative columns, he told up to four concurrent stories about the case, instantly replacing those deemed impossible with new stories, allowing him to churn through hundreds and, occasionally, thousands of possible explanations, because sometimes the key to the case was the least insane possibility Trike could imagine.

He ran narrative columns starring his sixth-grade classmates.

John Ottney.

William Pinkerton.

Trevor Bingham.

Emily Gourbin.

Alice Burnham.

Harry Villers.

None of them looked like Joyce of the portrait, so he had to be a proxy. Joyce in the portrait was decades too old to have been a classmate of Trike's. But his proxiness was not necessarily meaningful in the ultimate meaning of the case. Or maybe Joyce was a disguise, which was not necessarily meaningful in the ultimate meaning of the case.

Walter Drew.

Julian Gault.

Bernard Spillsbury.

William Melville.

Trike had to lengthen his route. He was getting back to the vodka bottle too often. He added the almost-empty second floor. There was a point to boozing. It made permeable barriers between intelligences that are typically impermeable. For whatever that is worth.

John Wilson Murray. John Wilson Murray was Trike's accountant. If it actually was Trike's accountant, the case would not end up in a court of law.

Bill Wilcox.

Joseph Holle.

Winny Moore.

Trike found himself in one of the empty second-floor bedrooms. When that drunk on vodka, as good a place as any to speechify.

"I have thrown criminal kingpins in jail. I have outdueled mafia hit squads. Toppled international syndicates. Bested brilliant psychopaths. Tapped on the shoulder those who thought they had gotten away. By definition, perhaps by design, my career collects revenge-seekers like loan consolidation offers. I get more death threats than thank-you notes, more curses than congratulations, more bricks than bouquets. And in that sense, I know dozens, perhaps hundreds of people in rooms and cells plotting or imagining revenge against me.

"So I will not be surprised if someone, someday, sneaks into my house and shoots me while I sleep. I will be prepared if someone endeavors to track down all my friends and family to subject them to an amplified version of whatever it is they believe I subjected them to. I expect specters of my youth to appear before me in my crippled and broken old age to avenge actions decades ancient. Such is the lot of standing in the way of those who have already rejected the law.

"The amount of money involved in this case greatly expands the possible explanations. With enough money, what is impossible becomes easy. But the extremity of the money itself highlights how this case is distinguished from the normal course of revenge.

Revenge is supposed to be extreme. But what do we have here? Childish taunts, duplicitous paperwork, bloodless frustration, a diminishing reward; these are not the techniques of revenge. They are something else. Something different. Something troubling. I. Am thirsty. A problem with a solution."

Trike went where the vodka was.

Marie Latalle.

Edward Drew.

William Gilette.

All rejected.

Other students.

Teachers.

Janitors.

Parents.

Who the fuck.

Trike grabbed the vodka bottle, took a desperate gulp, and cut-marionette can-canned himself to sitting in a chair at the kitchen table.

Trike said out loud, to the table, to the bottle, to the picture, to the night, to the idea, to the image of Lola always just there, "God-damn it. Sixth grade. Dad. Fuck it. For tonight. New plan. Before I fucking kill myself. New plan. Step one. Pass the fuck out right here at this fine kitchen table. Step two. Wake up and hate myself for awhile. Step three. Get my shit together for the conference. Step four. Call Max and Lola and have them start searching the quote-unquote surrounding area of my sixth-grade year. Maybe have Lola chat with The Butler. Yeah. Knitters are weird. Step five. The conference. Shit. Wanting to do this for years. Perfect state of mind for the microphone, though. Step four-A. Get some nicotine patches for the conference. Amendment approved. Plan accepted. Now, step one."

Trike capped the vodka bottle, pushed it to the middle of the table, folded his arms in front of him, put his head on them, and passed the fuck out.

THE COLUMNS

JOHN OTTNEY:
Ottney was a negligible kid until the trauma, with enough friends to not be noticeably unpopular while never coming up in conversation for any other reason. His first flash of brilliance was remaining negligible while developing his plan. The second flash was in realizing that he did not have the resources to seek revenge on someone of my caliber. He applied himself to private study, and by the time he left for college had had become an expert in a range of fields useful in the pursuit of revenge. He applied himself with the obsession of revenge openly in college, finishing undergrad in two and a half years, after which he went into law school. In

this time I established myself as a private detective, and knowing my abilities, Ottney needed a way to approach me without being detected. He condensed law school into two years, all the while searching for someone who could act as proxy for his revenge. As sometimes happens, the solution came to him. His academic excellence, coupled with his perseverance, drew the attention of the FBI, who needed someone to administer a complex marijuana-growing operation, one that already had a figurehead acting as the public face of something entirely different. Because of the relative size of the operation, Ottney had a level of independence in the project that allowed him to [. . .] ["New Hardware Store Opens," article from two years ago in *St. Lawrence County Gazette* naming John Ottney, matching age and birthplace, as the proprietor of said new hardware store.]

WILLIAM PINKERTON: Bill started big and stayed big. There are few paths available to big, dumb sons of big, dumb fathers, and Big Bill rolled right into one. He started taking lunch money from the weaker of the flock. The closest thing he ever had to a brilliant idea was figuring out it was much more profitable and much less risky to shake kids for their drug money because authorities were never told. One of his friends had an older brother who carried a knife and drove a car he'd paid for with his own money and knew some people willing to give a tough kid with big bones a chance to make good money in this heartless world. Though Big Bill didn't know it, he was lucky. Most older brothers who carry knives and drive cars are full of shit. This brother ran with real pros, the kind who know that the best way to have loyal operatives is to grow them. Bill was a loyal soldier for a

TREVOR BINGHAM: [Bingham is a chillingly average lieutenant in the force, whose documented whereabouts would have made it virtually impossible for him to direct the observed operations.]

EMILY GOURBIN: Most likely due to an undiagnosed learning disability, Emily struggled through school, and in the end she made an extremely prudent decision: she dropped out to get her GED. Her academic challenges were somewhat balanced by a practical resourcefulness and an easy rapport with people. A pretty smile, a nice body, and a rock-solid sense of propriety made her practically pressed out of a mold into a receptionist job at the largest insurance company in the city. After she'd worked three years for the firm, they decided to trust her with managing a particularly complex client. The client presented her with a company, a person, a house, and an opportunity ["High

few years before a SNAFU, weapons in a trunk maybe, landed him in a cold room with an austere desk and a two-way mirror. The federal agent sitting across from him had a very interesting proposition: go back to his hometown and help them move some marijuana into the market. Once he got his head around at least a bit of the Joyce House, Bill realized he finally had his chance. ["Local Man Convicted in Armed Robbery," from *The Daily Register* four years, two months, three weeks ago, reported that one William Pinkerton, matching age, place of birth, and high school, was convicted of armed robbery and sentenced to fifteen years. No confirmation of subsequent release.]

ALICE BURNHAM: A penchant for the scientific coupled with a critical level of inherent empathy led her to major in environmental sciences with a focus on sustainable horticulture and green-plant-based

HARRY VILLERS: His military father kept Villers moving around the world, only landing in town for that one year. The inherent emotional instability of this lifestyle eventually found a base in the desire for revenge against me. Focusing his general intelligence around the need for revenge led to academic excellence in his many schools, which he parlayed into admission to and success at West Point. Through this and his father's connections, he was able to secure a position of some influence in Military Intelligence ["Former Elementary Schooler Uses Overseas Deployment for Good Cause," article in *The Daily Register* describing a Major Harold Villers, appropriate age, stationed in Germany, who organized German pen pals for fifth-graders at a local elementary school, with the article stating that he was permanently stationed in Germany and had been there for three years.]

308

School Dropout Makes Good," from *The Daily Register* six months, three weeks ago, describing an "Emily Gourbin," picture corresponds with class picture, who got an entry-level job at the national bank call center and worked her way up to manager. Face time necessary to hold such a position renders it nearly impossible for her to orchestrate this range. Random Chance, bless these slow news days.]

WALTER DREW: [Current beat reporter for "Channel Four News." The public nature of his profession makes it nearly impossible for him to be involved. All evidence suggests he is still a dick.]

JULIAN GAULT: Julian went to high school the next town over, because the local high school still had not been retrofitted with wheelchair ramps. [No ramps, lifts, or elevators, excluding the dumbwaiters in the Joyce House, greatly complicating the

carbon capture. After graduation, she secured an internship at an international crop development nonprofit. ["Alice Burnham to wed Dr. Edward Locard," marriage announcement in *The Daily Register* from three years, nine months, two weeks ago. Article asserted that they were in the Horn of Africa studying indigenous agriculture in the hopes of developing carbon-negative techniques. Random Chance, bless the marriage announcements and obituaries.]

BERNARD SPILLS-BURY: [Owner of five McDonald's franchises in the area and so in love with that identity that there is simply no way he would risk it in any kind of crime.]

WILLIAM MEL-VILLE: Will's inherent linguistic talents greatly aided his performance through high school, as virtually all courses utilize, at some level, verbal expression. A skill set such as

JOSEPH HOLLE: [Shift supervisor at a telemarketer's local office, discovered one year, eight months, three days ago when I asked to speak to a supervisor who said, "This is Joseph Holle, shift supervisor. How can I help you, sir?" Been generous with ability so far, but if Joseph Holle is any more than a nice guy once you get to know him, I'll fly a hang glider full of explosives into the Grand Canyon.]

WINNY MOORE: Moore's commitment to overachieving was not diminished by "the Traumatic Event," as whatever it is that drives people to absolutely fucking need to be the best fucking everything there ever was can only be intensified and focused by the need for revenge. In most ways, her need for revenge continued through high school, meaning that she committed herself to being the best human being on the planet: cheerleading, student council, Odyssey of the Mind,

JOHN WILSON MURRAY: [My accountant. He knows he'd never make it to a court of law. Well, bits and pieces of him might.]

BILL WILCOX: "The Traumatic Event" produced a hardened core of hatred buried in the gooshy-fleshy wishy-washiness that seemed to define his sixth-grade character. Throughout high school, this core did no more than whisper in the quiet moments when the brain continued its endeavors despite having nothing important to do. However, after enrolling in ROTC in college [Bill Wilcox is a high school science teacher, another profession demanding face time that would make it nearly impossible for him to run the operation. "High School Science Club Makes Regional Finals," appeared in *The Daily Register* one month and two days ago, and the club named "Local Man Bill Wilcox" as its adviser.]

possibility of Gault's involvement.]

MARIE LATALLE: [Marie is married to Marty on the city council and is dumb the way Golden Retrievers are dumb.]

EDWARD DREW: [Died in a car accident in eighth grade. Good kid.]

WILLIAM GILETTE: Will, along with his deep hatred for me, moved to Tucson in tenth grade. There he was radicalized by anti-immigrationists. He attended nearby Pima Community College to get his bachelor's in business management and worked as a teller at a local bank. On the weekends he trained with a militia. Unfortunately for Will, the militia was involved with illegal arms sales and he was caught in a raid by the FBI. They could tell he was as innocent as someone who spent weekends practicing how to shoot Mexicans could be and, seeing where he'd been born, offered him a deal: go to jail for five years, or go home

this poised him for an entire realm of economic success, from speechwriting, to law, to marketing and advertising, but, as inexplicably still happens, he wanted to write. In this endeavor, his desire for revenge was a boon, as it taught him the obsessive attention to a project required for literary success. In addition, Will had a roiling emotiveness with a kernel of violence. He excelled enough in school to get into Columbia, an environment that nurtured and developed his creative being. Of course, driven by his need for revenge, there was a violent vein running through his work, a layer of malice condensed around the core of his pulsating hatred for me, but those who read his work, both peers and professors, interpreted the violence as a dark humor particularly relevant in modern times. The occasional myopia of his work was understood as a radical response to the fractured American consciousness. There was an

mock trial, volunteering at the soup kitchen, AP classes, the school newspaper, and despite all of that, I still didn't give a shit about her. Some people can work that hard and not end up at an Ivy League school, but Winny Moore was not one of them. One of the key skills of the super-wealthy and -powerful is the cultivation of relationships with far more talented and motivated others, incorporating those others into whatever projects they use to become and remain super-wealthy and -powerful, and Winny was cultivated by such a person. This cultivation led Winny to a job in a major lobbying firm that would argue anything for anybody as long as that anybody paid, and it was as an assistant project manager working on tax loopholes on income made through currency speculation that the FBI took notice of her. They had a project that would greatly benefit from someone of her

Could it be none of them?

But why use Lola to point to an elementary school I went to for one year if you didn't go to school with me?

Revenge doesn't count if I don't know who is getting revenge.

310

and manage the Joyce House. Even without the debilitating need for revenge, it was an easy choice. ["Hey, Trike, it's been like, a decade since I saw you." "Yeah." "You remember me, Bill Gilette? We went to elementary school—" "Yeah. Photographic memory. Listen, can I get this all in twenties with the last twenty in ones?" Conversation four years ago at a bank in Santa Fe, New Mexico.]

additional convergence in his desires, as Will's only career ambition was to make enough money to support his writing and his revenge. As graduation approached, he had to develop a strategy for just that: should he go to grad school and pay for an official legitimization that could lead to making money from his writing, should he try to get a job in the city that paid well, should he pursue a career that would leave him time and energy to write and to get his revenge, or should he just go into finance so at least he would have a shit-ton of money to let him do whatever he wanted? In his wildest dreams, he never imagined that the answer to this question would also offer him an opportunity to get revenge. Several weeks before graduation, a drug dealer friend of his approached him with a unique opportunity: manage a weed-growing operation overseen by the Feds, in a house with an older, fatter man

intelligence and work ethic: growing weed of a very particular strain and working it into the drug market to study how weed moves through its economy by seeing where it ends up being confiscated, and since it returned her to her hometown in a clandestine manner, Winny saw a chance for revenge in the position. She would work behind the scenes while an actor played the public face of the endeavor. Once she was installed in the position, it was only a matter of waiting for an opportunity. ["Yeah, you might have known her, grew up in your hometown, about your age. She's now in Denmark or something working for the U.S. embassy," said Detective-Inspector Haigh, a British friend of Max's in a humorous story about a dinner party that tangentially involved a woman named "Winny."]

Teachers? Janitors? The principal? Who else would have been there?

Another whole realm of possible research. Of course.

311

who would portray
the steward of the
house; a house that
just happened to be
in his hometown,
where the grand
offense of his life
had been commit-   *It's like the goal is*
ted. Once installed   *to make me hate*
at the Joyce House,   *my job, as if it's the*
directly after gradu- *work about my job*
ation, Will began to   *that I hate.*
formulate his plan
for revenge, and he
decided to utilize
some of the existing
circumstances, such
as the insane nature
of the house. His
first step was es-
tablishing a level of
trust with his em-
ployer that would
allow him to lever-
age its resources in
manipulation of law
enforcement. [Wed-
ding Announce-
ment in *The Daily
Register* two years,
two months ago,   *Who the fuck is*
"William Melville   *this?*
to wed Mathilde
Dosd of Belgium,"
stating that the
couple would be
living in Dosd's na-
tive country"]

Fuck my life.

THE MARY TUDOR AND WHAT HE DISCOVERED ABOUT GEORGE MULLINS

Detecting could be real shit, but there were consolations. Running from thugs was great cardio. Tracing the financial malfeasance of a professional embezzler made it easy to keep tabs on your accountant. And if you weren't a fan of surprise parties, no one could throw one for you.

Lola consoled herself with how depressing The Butler's radiating loneliness was by focusing on the work she would finally get done on the sweater she promised Janice for her birthday.

And as much as she didn't want Trike to be right about knitters.

Lola had The Butler go over all the old details again, just to get him talking. She threw in quick questions about his work. Enough to make the conversation go, but not so much that he felt manipulated. She asked about his past. She asked about his family. She asked about his job. She asked about his great-aunt.

Then she got names out of him. Any names. Accountant. Real-estate agent. Relatives: Joyce's and his own. The gardener. The cable-repair technician. The mail carrier. All to make him think about names. A composition just like everything else.

With the conversation flowing the way conversations were supposed to, she diverted it from the case to the Mary Tudor sweater in a frame on the wall. That thing was just killing her.

"The Mary Tudor," The Butler said with a tone that hoped to

convince her he'd almost forgotten it was there. "Just finished it last year, no, two years ago. And before you ask, let me make this perfectly clear. It was not worth it. At all. You try to tell yourself that something like this is an accomplishment and all the other stuff about hard work and all that, but let me tell you, it just sits on that wall, only a handful of people know it's the most impressive thing in the whole house, and it's not like you can put it on a résumé."

"So why did you finish it, then? One of those you-started-it-so-you-might-as-well-finish-it projects?"

"Ha. No. I've never had a problem letting those projects go. Even projects as impressive as that. You probably won't believe this, but—well, I suppose you're going to pass all of this along to that detective."

Lola shrugged. "My job is to find out everything I can. Wouldn't mean much if I didn't pass it on."

"And what if you don't believe what I tell you?"

"I give him the data. He sorts it out."

The Butler sighed. He focused on his work for a moment. It was a hat with felt-lined earflaps. Which meant he finished the socks. In time to felt lining. Which meant either he didn't really work or he didn't really sleep. Lola noticed a receipt on the coffee table for $376 worth of yarn, dated the day before. It looked like The Butler was still getting paid.

The Butler stopped knitting and looked up. "My aunt—"

"The one who got you the job with Joyce?"

"No, that was my great-aunt. My aunt, my father's sister. She was also a knitter, and she was, well, a bit slow. Charming woman. Lovely. Kind. Raised three kids and all that, but, well, a little slow, if you know what I mean. She wasn't mentally disabled, but she wasn't mentally abled either. I don't know what got it into her head but she decided that she was going to knit a Mary Tudor. Her work was fine. I think I still have a scarf of hers somewhere around here, but, well, a Mary Tudor was just way out of her league. Way out.

"So, being the good nephew that I was, I offered to help, which

ultimately meant undoing everything she'd done and doing it myself. God, there was nothing worse than getting home from work
and seeing her there showing off another forty rows. I don't know
if she noticed or not that I had to fix everything, but she always
said how proud she was and how much fun she was having with
her knitter nephew.

"Well, it's not hard to see the breast cancer at the end of this
tunnel. She got it. She was a lovely human being, proud of a sweater
she ultimately had nothing to do with, and then she died. What
could I do? Not finish it. I considered it. I certainly did. But, then,
whatever else you think about these things, it meant I'd have a
Mary Tudor on my wall. And that is not nothing."

"You're right about that. I don't have one on my wall."

They turned back to their projects for a few minutes. Lola got
to a casting-off point and restarted the conversation.

Lola had a choice. A rapport had been developed, but there
was still distance. Distance Lola would not be able to bridge as long
as the conversation occurred in the context of the case. She didn't
think The Butler had been scared into silence. He was lonely. And
proud. And not about to pretend to himself that Lola would ever
be his friend.

She had no legal way to compel him to share information, but
she could convince him in ways that did not feel like convincing.
He was also in crippling need of respect. She decided on a technique that demonstrated respect.

Lola cleared her throat. "Now, you're intelligent, so I'm not
going to bother trying to hide what I'm doing. You'd see through
any techniques. So I'm just going to proceed directly to the next
phase of the interview. I'm going to give you names. I'm not going
to tell you what I want to hear about these names. I'm not going to
tell you where the names came from. I'm not going to give you any
context for these names. I just want you to tell me whatever you
can about them. I will be noting your answers and observing your
nonverbal reactions. You are welcome to lie to me in whatever way

you believe necessary, but, if you haven't realized it by now, I am very good at my job, and the truth will come out."

As expected, the moment went cold. Lola waited.

"Well, if that's the way it's going to be, well, I am the sacrificial butler, but, before, I was just, do you have a knitting group? It's just. It would be nice. I had one, for years, but, well, you know how these things are. It kinda petered out."

"Counting Sheep runs a couple."

"Do they?"

"I'm pretty sure there's at least one on Thursdays. And I think there might even be a men-only one on Sundays. Ball-Busters or something. You have to ask Lucy about it. She handles that stuff. Margaret, I don't think really likes, well, people."

"Ah, yes. Margaret's the only one who ever seems to be there when I am, but I'll do that. Well, thanks. I guess that's it."

Lola gave a sharp professional nod and quickly started down the names of Trike's sixth-grade classmates. The first two names registered no recognition. The third he knew, for unrelated reasons. There was a hint of potential in the fourth name. Lola followed it through five follow-up questions. In the end, inconclusive.

Lola posed a fifth name. Then received a text from Trike.

"Huh," she said. She read it twice to be sure it said what it said.

She looked at The Butler. She squinted at The Butler. The text said what it said.

"Well, I guess that's it then," she said to The Butler. "Thank you for your time."

She stood up with no more explanation and left The Butler to his project.

Max got the same text.

He was at the office researching the quote-unquote surrounding area. His shirtsleeves were rolled up. The text was the best news he'd heard in months. It meant he wouldn't have to tell Trike what he'd discovered about George Mullins.

THE E. P. ALLEN O'PINE CONFERENCE ON DETECTING

Trike was in the registration line for the E. P. Allen O'Pine Conference on Detecting at 8:57 a.m., pipe jaw-clenched, jaw unshaven, hat on, presentation suit in a suit bag slung over his shoulder. A sleeping bag hung by its straps from his right index and middle fingers. He wore a dirty T-shirt proclaiming the 1986 Red Sox "WORLD CHAMPINS" and his thoroughly spritzed jogging sweatpants under an open, belt ends hanging like the arms of a knocked-out propped-up boxer, teal bathrobe, and Max's large mirrored sunglasses. As he waited and shuffled in line, he periodically reached with his left hand across his body into the bathrobe pocket that fell almost to his knees on his right side to extract and sip from a flask of coffee. He wore state-issued identification around his neck on a lanyard made of duct tape. His hangover could be seen from space.

When he reached the registration table, at a brisk and efficient 9:37 a.m., he held the sunglasses up off his

We are all familiar—at least on some level—with Edgar Allan Poe's masterpiece of detective fiction, "The Purloined Letter." Whether we have read the work or not, the ideas central to its stated themes—that an object can be hidden in plain sight, that the solution to a crime can be too obvious to be discerned, and that typical methods of search and detection are ill-fitted for some crimes—follow us throughout our careers, whether through the ill-formed comments of armchair detectives flailing about the chaos of existence for convincing illusions of order or the string of abductions perpetrated by the man living next to the playground. One cannot complain about the persistence of the idea, as it is fueled by a vein of truth: the reading glasses on the forehead, the bottle of ketchup behind the milk, the car keys on the counter right where they belong, like Dupin's game of finding words on maps—one of the few reasonable statements he makes in the entire story—there is an eyes and leaned forward to display his ID at eye level to the attendant. He'd been hungover when the ID picture was taken, so no confirmation problem there. Then he waited. The attendant stammered a few attempts at interaction against Trike's bloodshot eyes, unflinching stare, and boozy breath. After forty-two seconds, "Charles" got the message and handed Trike his conference ID badge, schedule of events, and complimentary presenters' gift bag containing an assortment of healthy energy- and focus-enhancing snacks and beverages, to ensure that all presenters were at their best during their presentations and throughout the conference's engaging and enlightening programs. Trike let go of the sunglasses and took the proffered materials.

Still standing at the registration desk, Trike fished a nicotine patch out of his left bathrobe pocket and slapped it onto his upper arm. "The alternative delay would be much longer," he grumbled to those waiting behind him as he fumbled away.

He sloughed to a stop at the nearest bench, rolled out his sleeping bag, and lay down on it with his suit bag as a blanket. Over the next hour, several concerned onlookers and one hotel security guard were shooed away, for their own safety, by conference officials. Visual evidence suggested that he slept, but Trike watched, identifying all of the conference attendees and officials that passed through his field of vision. It was probably too much

observed, observational mechanism or observational system that can prevent us from finding what we seek precisely because it is so easy to see.

In "The Purloined Letter," a certain "Minister D___" happens upon a royal personage—who we can assume is the Queen of France—as she opens a letter that would dramatically compromise her relationship with the King; the letter, we assume, was written by her lover and confirmed the individual's status as such. In a moment of distraction, caused by the arrival of the King himself, Minister D___ is able to trade a letter of no importance that he happened to have with him for the compromising letter, which has been left on the dresser. With that letter as leverage, he blackmails the Queen for political advantages not described in the text. In her efforts to recover the letter, the Queen personally contracts the Prefect of the Parisian police.

Unable to find the letter on the person of the Minister, or in the Minister's hotel, despite dramatically meticulous searches, the Prefect comes to Dupin for advice. Dupin suggests that the Prefect, "G," thoroughly research the hotel room. Several months later—eighteen in total since the letter was purloined—the Prefect visits Dupin again, at a loss as to how to proceed with the investigation. Dupin extracts a promise of fifty thousand francs for the production of the letter, the Prefect makes out the check, and Dupin hands him the letter. Actually to hope that the profoundly fucking weird aspect of the conference would just saunter by while he pretended to sleep, but three previous cases had been solved when their answers just happened to saunter by while he pretended to sleep.

At 11:09 a.m., Trike sprang to sudden sitting on the bench, inducing a few shouts of surprise from the latercomers in the registration line. He liked to keep folks on their toes. He methodically ate and drank everything in his complimentary gift bag, throwing the wrappers and containers back in the bag itself. When he finished consuming, he picked his legs back up onto the bench, lay down, and continued to watch the lobby through Max's sunglasses. He discovered one interesting fact: the conference actually attracted some of the best minds in detecting and criminology and not just charlatans, magicians, and résumé padders.

At 11:31 a.m., Trike got up from the bench at a less-shocking speed. He rolled his bathrobe into the sleeping bag and left it on the bench with a note that said, "Trike Augustine's (Yes, THAT Trike Augustine) stuff. If you touch it, I will destroy you by the end of the decade, especially you, Alfred Gordon, you nosy motherfucker." Trike slapped a nicotine patch onto his other arm while he walked to the bathroom. Once there, he changed into his presentation suit, put his morning outfit in the suit bag, and dropped the bag off with the

dumbfounded, the Prefect staggers out, letter in hand. Dupin then explains to the narrator that the letter was changed in outward appearance and placed in a shabby card rack, and thus went undetected by the police, and he describes how he came to acquire the letter. The story concludes with Dupin explaining how he used the letter to get revenge on the Minister D___ for some un-narrated wrong suffered in Vienna, the European capital of un-narrated wrongs.

We have many reasons to accept Dupin's story. He alone was able to sort through the tangle of languages, to see the hair that could not have been human, to differentiate between an unbroken nail and a broken nail, to reconstruct the escaped Ourang-Outang fleeing up a water pipe and through a window, who panicked in a moment of shaving pantomime and killed two women, and to act on that deduction in such a way as to bring the sailor responsible for the Ourang-Outang to justice without additional violence. Furthermore, Dupin was able to take the distortions reported in newspapers, unpack the preconceived notions that led to their mistakes in order to extract useful facts, and solve a case that had also baffled the Parisian police. At this point in English literature, there is no more authoritative voice on logic and deduction. But, perhaps most definitively, we are inclined to accept Dupin's version of events because it is the only one we have.

sleeping bag and the note. Then he investigated the conference and the hotel. Starting with the conference's complimentary coffee station. It was complimentary coffee at a quality implied by the dignity of the conference but still pleasantly surprising once confirmed. To strengthen the verification of his conclusion, Trike investigated a second cup. And took a third with him.

Next, he entered the conference's locked offices and printed a full list of attendees, presenters, officials, and volunteers, as well as a title page for his presentation. "Borrowed your printer," he said, waving the stack of paper at the official who showed up as Trike left. "Couldn't find a public printer anywhere. You should complain to the hotel," he offered as he left the room far too quickly for the official to ask any questions.

Trike memorized the list while he walked, cross-referencing it with the observations he'd made in the lobby, the publicized list of presenters and workshops, and everything he remembered about the names he saw. Next, Trike finagled his way behind the hotel's front desk and secured a printout of its guests. He recycled the memorized conference list and covered the hotel guest list with his title page. When he bumped into a hotel employee on his way out he said, "Sorry, had to use your printer. The one in the business center was totally tied up. Henri said it was cool." Halfway through the door he added,

But there are actually two versions of "The Purloined Letter"; Dupin's version and what we can extract from the manner and substance of his telling. A critical—in the literary sense of criticism—examination of Dupin's version reveals inconsistencies, inaccuracies, and absurdities. Questions are raised and receive tenuous answers. Structures are constructed of flimsy materials. Atypical phenomena are left unjustified. In short, upon closer inspection, Dupin's explanation for the police's inability to find the letter while he could is downright absurd. But if Dupin's version is not true, what is? Why were the police unable to find the letter? If the letter was not in Minister D___'s hotel, where was it? And if Dupin's version is not true, how did he come to possess the letter? To borrow another oft-quoted detecting principle, if you remove the impossible, you are left with the answer. Where was the purloined letter? Dupin had it the whole time.

It might be a comfort to know that this answer is not hiding in plain sight, but only becomes apparent when Dupin's testimony is examined with the intellectual equivalents of microscopes and long needles. We must explore for what is not written. We must interrogate every assertion. We must move fact by fact through the story as if an archaeological grid has been placed over it and every square must be the focus of obsessive inspection. What arises through this

"You know, the conference itself has made almost no resources available to presenters. I would complain to their organizers if I were you."

As he lurked around the lobby elevators waiting for a member of the hotel staff to use the one that went to the basement, Trike called Max. Max was working on The Joyce Case, but Trike had him keep the police scanner on, in case he'd been lured to the conference to keep him, and perhaps three other area detectives and cops, out of the way of something for the day. But since he wasn't usually a while-the-body-is-warm-or-the-bank-vault-smells-of-C4 kind of detective, few crimes, with the exception of stealing his shitty shit from his shitty house, would be facilitated by tying him up for the day. Given his relationship with local authorities, someone pulling an intensely intricate plot would be doing him a favor by giving him an electron-tight alibi.

"Maxeration, what's the chatter," Trike asked.

Without preamble, Max read a list of times, police codes, and officer names. Trike kept an eye on the service elevator while absorbing Max's stream of unremarkable data. A porter with a cart full of dirty dishes got into the elevator. Trike darted through the closing doors as though absentmindedly trying to catch an elevator, waited until the elevator started moving down, punched the lobby button, and stood cluelessly in front of the buttons to make sure the porter could

critical inspection is a range of implausibilities and absurdities that we are—in the course of a typical reading—manipulated into accepting as truth; a range that includes Dupin's description of his acquisition, his parable of the "even and odd" master, and other assertions and arguments. But ultimately, under rigorous examination, there can be only one explanation for the observed phenomena: Dupin had the letter the whole time.

To demonstrate this, I will work chronologically through the story until we reach Dupin's explanation, at which point I will divide my examination into a scrutinization of what Dupin intended to say and then what Dupin revealed without intending to.

The story opens with a setting of the scene, in which Dupin and the narrator sit in the dark—as is their wont, as was established in "The Murders in the Rue Morgue." The Prefect of Parisian police, "G," enters and after a pleasant greeting admits that he is actually there on business and at this point the first question is raised. Poe writes, "We had been sitting in the dark, and Dupin now rose for the purpose of lighting a lamp but sat down again without doing so, upon G's saying that he had called to consult us, or rather, to ask the opinion of my friend, about some official business which had occasioned a great deal of trouble." Dupin then says, "If it is any point requiring reflection... we shall examine it to better purpose in the dark." One could be forgiven not stop the elevator or see that he'd chosen the floor he'd just left. When he finally let himself be interrupted by the porter, Trike assured him that he'd head right back up, that he was sorry for the confusion, you know how business is, gotta get everything done yesterday at 10 percent under budget with a free upgrade for the boss's sister-in-law's college-age nephew, and they should really make the signs for these service elevators a lot more obvious, anyway, sorry, thank you, have a good day.

Trike rode the elevator back to the lobby, held the door closed, and took it right back down. On the short trip to the basement, Trike told Max to keep up with the scanner and the surrounding area of sixth grade. He reminded Max to send three blank texts in a row if something came up, as if that wasn't the emergency-when-you-can't-have-a-conversation procedure that Max himself had suggested for their first split-location stakeout way back in The Case of the Cemetery Cognac.

"Anything weird, boss?"

"Not yet, Max," Trike said, "I'm tempted to say it's quite too quiet, but instead of talking like a paid-by-the-word ghostwriter, I'm going to say the chance my original assessment is inaccurate has increased slightly."

"What?"

"Ear to the scanner, eye to the surrounding area, Max. Will be in touch," Trike said, hanging up.

Trike thumbed vigorously on his

for assuming that thinking in the dark was merely one of Dupin's "odd notions," as G describes them, but there is a more direct, possible explanation. Dupin would have deduced from the circumstances that G was there to consult on the purloined letter. With that deduction, Dupin would have left the light off because the letter was in the apartment and he did not want to give G the slightest chance of spotting it, whether it was directly visible or in some desk drawer that could be bumped open should social graces in lighted rooms call for movement. At this point, one could be skeptical of my conclusion, but as the evidence mounts, the darkened room becomes more suspicious.

Then G begins to tell Dupin about the mystery at hand, but he doesn't get far before Dupin inserts his theory of an item being too obvious to be seen. Latching on to G's statement, "the affair is so simple, and yet baffles us all together"—a statement that has more to do with the case in general than the solution to it—Dupin responds, "Perhaps it is the very simplicity of the thing which puts you at fault." Given G's statement, and the fact that such phenomena exist, it is an expected, even prudent bit of detecting advice—for we often must be reminded of what we know—but the statement is followed by two needling rehashes of itself. "Perhaps the mystery is a little *too* plain" and "A little *too* self-evident," dickish emphasis in the original. Why belabor the point?

phone, so if a hotel employee saw him when the elevator door opened, he would look like one of those assholes who spends more time in his cell than in his head. Trike stepped aggressively out of the elevator as the doors opened. The hallway was empty. Accessing the floor plan from The Case of the Oval Portrait, he went to the temp employees' locker room. The room was empty, as expected for the time of day. Trike went to a locker set up by one of his irregulars and extracted and put on the temporary caterer's uniform, "HENRI" name tag, and thin, fake mustache. "Henri" made a thorough investigation of the service level, including the employees' parking lot, the HVAC center, the server room, and the laundry room, asking the seven employees he encountered innocent and rational questions for a totally lost, kinda douchey temp caterer. After twenty-two minutes, two longer than Trike had delineated but within the margin of error, Trike de-Henried in the locker room and returned to the elevator. The same porter that initially let him down to the service level stared at him after the elevator doors opened.

To the porter's incredulous face, Trike said, "Goddamn, Neo-Futurist architecture. And this fuckin' Henri asshole didn't know shit about where anything was. I might send a complaint."

The porter just shook his head and wheeled another dishes-laden cart out of the elevator. It was definitely

It is important to note that Dupin insists upon this point before hearing what the matter at hand actually is. I contend that the purpose of this insistence is to establish the logic system from which, ultimately, the mystery is analyzed. G laughs the idea off and continues his description of events.

Dupin knows two things about the case at this point: the Parisian police are extremely thorough in their searches, and they did not find the letter in D's hotel. Therefore, he needs an explanation for how he found the letter when the police could not, and it is in a system in which the obvious can go unseen where such an unlikely event is possible. As we shall see in his account of acquiring the letter, Dupin hedges his bets on this point, but he has planted the seed that G could be perfectly thorough without finding the letter.

The Prefect then describes the theft of the letter. Though we are unable to deduce anything conclusively—as there is not enough evidence—I still think it is important to consider the odd level of coincidence present in the theft; first Minister D___ arrives in the "royal boudoir"— this is most vital—right after the King himself has entered causing the Queen to "place [the letter] open, as it was, upon the table," to avoid drawing attention to it; second, he "recognizes the handwriting of the address," meaning he knows, at least on some level, the letter writer; third, he happened to have "a letter of somewhat not his job to deal with lost and abrasive guests. Trike took the elevator up to the level with the fitness center.

As he put on the workout costume left by another irregular, including a fake Fu Manchu and a custom temporary tattoo of an anthropomorphic bald eagle swinging an anchor over its head by a chain of lightning bolts, he retrieved the names of the current board of trustees for the conference from a fundraising letter and cross-referenced that list against current events; criminal, legitimate, and undetermined. In The Case of the Guy Who Didn't Get *The Maltese Falcon* at All, a grudge-bearing executive assistant set up a fake conference to gather and gain revenge on all who had wronged him in his professional life, but he was only able to pull it off because the executive he assisted was the utterly incompetent son-in-law of the corporation's owner, relegated to that exact high-level position so he would quit his bitching about "getting ahead," but not be able to do anything. The Board of Trustees of the conference was one of the four boards Trike had encountered in which every single member was competent, so if the shenanigans were conference-wide, they had to come from the top and they had to involve the entire board. Which would be some serious shit to get those twelve personality-rich, law-enforcement professionals together for a crime.

The fitness center was clean. Trike changed out of that costume

similar appearance" and "of no importance" that he can exchange for the one of value. These coincidences are all possible, but it would be a poor investigator who did not, at the very least, consider them.

Next the authorities logically deduce that, in order for the letter to be useful as blackmail, Minister D___ must have easy access to it, so that it can either be presented to the King or destroyed. Though their logic is sound, the logic itself creates a problem for their efforts to recover the letter; their reasoning creates the truth they deduce, for the deduction carries the same consequences as the truth itself. It does not matter whether Minister D___ has the letter at hand or whether the Queen concludes that he does, because the subsequent actions are identical. The consequences of the truth and of the conclusion are the same, which collapses both possibilities into a singular, paradoxical phenomenon. I introduce this paradox to establish the logical possibility—despite the previous sound reasoning—that the letter is not in the Minister's apartment.

Next we see our first stated connection between Dupin and the Minister, and though it seems incidental at this point, it is worth noting. They establish that the Minister is "not altogether a fool," though the Prefect goes on to say, "but then he's a poet, which I take to be only one remove from a fool," to which Dupin responds, "I have been guilty of certain doggerel and remembered all the news reports of major criminals escaping, either through legitimate or illegitimate means, from prison, and cross-referenced that with the capacity to blow up a filled-to-the-brim-with-detectives hotel. But if blowing up the hotel was the plan, the villain had access to explosives with techniques of concealment neither the conference's security service nor Trike had ever encountered or could sniff out, and the only criminals Trike knew with that theoretical capacity, Sir William Gentle and the security director of the Gustav Mace family, knew that such an assault on law enforcement would, ultimately, be suicide.

As Trike took the elevator to the pool level and changed into his own swimsuit, he considered the odds that someone had conspired to put him on that presentation stage at that exact moment in order to shoot him right between the eyes. Such a plot would demand either being a confirmed law-enforcement professional, which, given how Trike interacted with confirmed law-enforcement professionals, was not absurd, if, at the moment, rendered unlikely by the evidence; impersonating an existing confirmed law-enforcement professional; or fabricating a fictional confirmed law-enforcement professional, both of which were difficult feats and would have left evidence of their achievement all over the fucking place; or being a hotel staff member with security clearance for this particular

myself." One might argue the fact that both write poetry is hardly a connection, but if one does so, one knows nothing of poetry and poets.

Then the Prefect details for Dupin and the narrator the search of the Minister's apartment, and here we have, perhaps, the most erotic passage of inspection porn committed to paper. "Fine long needles." "From the tables [they] removed the tops." They "examined the rungs of every chair in the hotel, and, indeed, the joinings of every description of furniture, by the aid of a powerful microscope." They even "examined the moss between the bricks." The most accurate rulers in Paris. Turning over every page in every book. Measuring their covers. G says, "We divided its entire surface into compartments, which we numbered, so that none might be missed, then we scrutinized each individual square inch on the premises..." Oh! To search for a letter that does not decompose in an apartment that does not change. In short, G describes what might be the most thorough search in the history of searches—even the adjoining apartments are searched— and the letter is not found.

Perhaps what is most important is what is not directly mentioned in the description of the search. G mentions tables, chairs, mirrors, and books, but not a card rack. This is significant. When Dupin produces the letter he will need an explanation for finding it. Given G's description, any explanation like, "It was in a copy of conference, which, in some ways, was the most difficult of the three possibilities. However, if the goal was to kill him, it'd be vastly more practical to just wait until he drank himself unconscious and shoot him where he fell. Middle of the night. Silencer. Gloves. Shoes at the door. They'd never catch you. Of course, the proposed assassin could intend to make a statement. Putting a bullet between Trike Augustine's eyes in front of an audience of crime-fighters would be a hell of a statement, but that would add the extra difficulty of getting a gun into the conference, on top of the already outlined challenges. The only remaining possibility: poison in Trike's specific complimentary bag of healthy energy- and focus-enhancing snacks and drinks would require new poisons beyond Trike's detection. Humanity had put a man on the moon using computers the size of Studebakers, so Trike couldn't categorically rule it out.

As Trike dried himself off from the one lap in the hotel pool it took to confirm that no shenanigans would be pool-based, he realized two things: his hangover was pretty much gone, and this was the longest stretch of time he had been conscious without thinking about The Joyce Case since it had started. At different times, both Lola and Max had advised "looking away" as a technique for finding what you seek. Once independent research confirmed the existence of the phenomenon, Trike pestered Lola, for like

the Bible," or "Behind a portrait of his mother," would raise suspicions. But because he primed the logic system with which the problem is considered and because G did not mention a card rack or any similar object specifically, Dupin's explanation is plausible. He hedges those bets, but we will trim those hedges later.

After the description of the search, we have our first truly suspicious act on Dupin's part. Until this point, only problems of logic and plausibility have caused us to wonder if things are as they seem; a limitation of logic led to the conclusion that the letter was at the apartment, and it is implausible that it was not discovered in G's search. But then the narrator says this: "You have been making a miscalculation, and the letter is *not* upon the premises, as you suppose. 'I fear you are right there,' said the Prefect. 'And now, Dupin, what would you advise me to do?'" Dupin, whose keen observation spotted the difference between a broken nail and a whole nail and whose imagination was vivid enough to see an escaped Ourang-Outang at the core of an inexplicable crime, then advises G "to make a thorough re-search of the premises." As G accurately states, "That is absolutely needless... I am not more sure that I breathe than I am that the letter is not at the Hotel."

Why would Dupin give such bad advice? Even if the letter is in the hotel, in the too-obvious place that Dupin suggests, a re-search using the three goddamn days, for an explanation, until she physically threw up her hands in frustration and said, "Okay. All right. Fucking okay. Just let me think about it for a few days. I'll send you an e-mail. Fuck. Sometimes it's okay to not understand something." The e-mail said: "Here's the image I came up with. Imagine you're looking for a note on your desk (and you weren't a freak of nature that would remember exactly where you put it).

You keep picking stuff up and putting it down and every time you look in a new spot, you move the note somewhere else. So you look where the note just was and now it's gone and it's like your desk has an extra spatial dimension because you've looked everywhere on it without finding the note. So you stop moving shit around and look away from the desk. You look away to forget the pattern of stuff on the desk because when you remember the pattern you see it whether it's there or not. Sometimes it takes a minute and sometimes you've got to get up and leave for a day. Then you just look. Because you're not moving stuff around and because you are seeing the actual things on your desk and not the pattern of things you remember, you find the note."

Arthur Gordon nearly fell over backward. As dignified as possible, he walked to the complimentary-coffee station.

Trike looked away from The Joyce Case and focused entirely on same method is guaranteed to return the same results. It would be one thing if Dupin said, "Search the apartment again, but this time, forget all the microscopes and long needles and just look around. Remember that sometimes the words that are hardest to find on the map are those in the biggest letters." That would have been useful advice. Instead he says, "a thorough research," which can only mean those luxurious needles. Unless there is some ulterior motive, this advice is incomprehensible. And if the ulterior motive is that Dupin has the letter, a whole world of explanation is born. First, it would give him more time to come up with a way to possess the letter without implicating himself in its theft; second, it would allow for more blackmailing; third, it would give Dupin and the Minister an opportunity to confer; fourth—to cut the list off at four—it would increase the likelihood that G will offer Dupin a cut of the substantial reward for the letter's retrieval. After the terrible advice, G reads a description of the letter—not shared with us—to Dupin and the narrator, and takes his leave of them, only to return a month later, having conducted the research, without finding the letter.

Upon G's return, Dupin questions him, first and foremost about the reward for the letter. Without further prompting—and though he does not name the original figure—G says, "I wouldn't mind giving my individual check for fifty thousand francs to the conference. Still hadn't solved that either.

Trike was in the hotel kitchen, after clearing the security command center, the penthouse, and the business center, in a Lola-knit argyle sweater-vest and fake dad-stache, posing as Neil Lofty, the organizer of the following week's conference on textile arts, when the preponderance of evidence shifted to suggest that some unlucky motherfucker just up and died right before his or her decades of thankless toil were going to pay off.

Maybe Trike's really was the last presentation rejected. Maybe the conference always gave last-minute spots to detectives local to that year's conference location. Sometimes shit just happened; it was his least favorite truth in the world. Just to be sure, Trike still investigated the roof. He had an HVAC technician costume, but his top lip stung and no one would be surprised to find the eccentric genius being eccentric on the roof. It took the eccentric genius eleven minutes to clear the roof.

As he headed back to the lobby and the conference rooms, taking the stairs from the top floor, his mind a fertile soil of information stitched by deep and varied roots of ferns, grasses, and other resilient weeds, embroidered by the burrows of woodland mammals, laced by the tunnels of ant colonies, above a roiling, cataclysmic, gelatinous, apocalyptic, relentless plate of tectonic violence, which was, itself, supported by a

anyone who could obtain me that letter." What follows is one of the great moments of inexplicable, inexcusable, inhuman dickishness committed to literature. Dupin taunts G by admonishing him to take advice, even though G has just taken Dupin's specifically, definitively, terrible advice. Perhaps Dupin seeks some intricate legal protection around bribery or entrapment or whatever, but the tangible result of Dupin's malevolent, malodorous, malicious dick-punching of G's ego is that G says, "I am *perfectly* willing to take advice, and pay for it. I would *really* give fifty thousand francs to anyone who would aid me in the matter," at which point Dupin has G make out a check and hands over the letter. The astute reader might wonder why this particular consultation took place in a room lit well enough for checks to be written and letters to be read, but that question is negligible. G is so thunderstruck, that—without uttering another word—he leaves, letter in hand.

However, had he asked Dupin how Dupin came to possess the letter, Dupin would have had a response ready, which he gives the narrator.

But not before he again establishes the logical context in which his acquisition of the letter is to be considered. First, he argues that one of the Prefect's fundamental problems is his inability to accurately assess the acumen of the person under investigation; in short, believing the Minister is a fool, because he is a poet, the Prefect only looked in places where dense, impenetrable, unforgiving foundation of dread, which was, itself, merely an eroding barrier between the perceived stability of the surface world and the core of nuclear destruction at the center of all things, Trike decided to try something different. Both Max and Lola had, independently, suggested creating a quiet mind as a problem-solving technique, arguing, in their own way, that the silence allowed for processes of the unconscious to bubble to the surface.

"Might as well," Trike thought. "If nothing else, might shut up that fucking voice in the back of my fucking head reminding me how fucking awesome a cigarette would be."

After four failed attempts, and with a mere twenty-three floors between him and the lobby, Trike imagined his brain as a main street full of shops. He saw himself standing in the middle of a two-lane street lined with shoulder-to-shoulder shops, unpunctuated by benches, parking meters, trees, or fire hydrants. No parked cars. No walked dogs. A bright autumn evening. Shop-filled street to the horizon.

Trike walked down the street pulling metal grates over storefronts and locking them to steel rings in the sidewalk with padlocks.

He did not look into the shops. He did not observe window displays. He did not record visible wares. He did not deduce the financial viability of the business model. He did not conclude the emotional state of the

a fool would hide a letter. Dupin illustrates this point with a story about a boy who was exceptionally good at a game called "even and odd." In this charming schoolyard game, one boy holds a certain number of marbles behind his back, and marbles being rational integers, that number must be even or odd. (Though one has to wonder what would happen if a bold little bastard held zero marbles behind his back.) His companion in the game then guesses which it is; if he guesses right, he wins the held marbles. In this parable, one boy was alarmingly proficient in his ability to deduce whether the number was even or odd, by reasoning in relation to the intelligence of the opponent, assuming that person of intelligence X will naturally choose action X. Still intellectually skullfucked by the presentation of the letter, G—had he stayed—would have been emotionally unable to see how absurd this parable is; no matter how many kinds of intelligences there are in the world, there are only two possibilities allowed by the game: "even" and "odd." This means that entire ranges of divergent intelligences—the most brilliant to the most imbecilic—would share the same action, rendering the entire exercise of establishing the opponent's intelligence, as a technique in discerning action, utterly pointless. The technique is pointless even before Dupin describes how the boy determined the intelligence of his opponent. Dupin quotes the boy, "When I wish to find out how wise, proprietor from the placement of the cash register and the selection of impulse items. He pulled metal grates over storefronts and locked them to steel rings in the sidewalks with padlocks.

Thousands of stores. One at a time. Each grate locked a thought process behind it. A conjecture. A deduction. A memory. Behind metal grates, locked to steel rings with padlocks, whatever spoke was no longer heard.

Thousands of stores.

Until the only open business was a street vendor selling cigarettes, trailing a few blocks behind, shouting his wares. It was as quiet as Trike's brain would ever get.

"Trike, hey, Trike. I got something for ya," PI Mike Canler shouted from across the lobby.

Canler was a dick based a couple of towns away. He got his start in bail bonds and marital disputes and was successful enough to land a gig as a loss-prevention consultant for a number of big retail chains. He flossed the woodwork enough to keep out of the nasty side of the PI business, but he shined enough shoes in the shade to buy a new Cadillac every two years.

Trike left the quiet street with surprising reluctance and figured out what Canler had for him before Canler reached out to shake hands. A talking Canler might spill something about the conference, and Trike still had seven minutes before his presentation started.

or how stupid, or how good, or how wicked is any one or what are his thoughts at the moment, I fashion the expression of my face, as accurately as possible, in accordance with the expression of his, and then wait to see what thoughts or sentiments arise in my mind or heart, as if to match or correspond with the expression." If you do not instantly apprehend the inherently absurdity of that statement, get the fucking fuck out of my fucking lecture, you intellectually impotent weeping shit-stain on the profession. A sense of suspicion should be raised in the astute reader's mind at this parable, even if, at the moment, the astute reader is unsure what to be suspicious of.

Dupin, though, is a masterful manipulator of logic systems, and he quickly transitions from issues of assessing intelligence to the limitations of mathematical reasoning. In essence, Dupin argues, mathematical logic—at least as it stood in the early 1800s—was a limited system of ratiocination, applying only to entities with fixed properties, like numbers as understood at the time. Algebra, arithmetic, and other mathematical systems of reasoning are only accurate when every "2" has the exact same properties as every other "2." Though such a system allows you to aim a cannon, it will not allow you to solve a crime, for all people do not share all of the same properties all of the time. No matter how similar two people are, there are no grounds for

"Saw you on the presenters list," Canler said, giving Trike an enthusiastic but dignified handshake, "figured you might be interested in somethin' that stuck in my radiator last week."

"Stranger things have happened, Canler."

"I know. I saw you on the presenters list. But seriously, Trike, this is Greenstreet."

"This is when you show me the MSRP."

"Listen, Trike, I ain't askin' much. Just want to be able to give you a call sometime. You know, in case someone cottons my chamber. Just a call."

"Sure you don't want to button that belfry, Canler?"

"Just a call. For a wink at the scorecard. Or some advice. I'm giving you a bargain here, with all the shit I could ask."

Trike was a lot of things, but he was not the kind of man who made vague promises. He smirked, "You started nosing around The Joyce Case and a day later got a call suggesting your contract with JC Penney would be jeopardized if you continued your investigation, and, not one to leave a paycheck on the sidewalk, you surveyed the craps game, and learned that three to five of your buddies were CC'd on the smell-o-gram."

"Motherfucker," Canler said with a smiling shake of his head.

Trike gave him a good-natured pat on the shoulder and said, "Specifics next time, Canler. Maybe you'll get

concluding that they will act the same way in the same situation. Math, as generally understood, cannot conclusively calculate when X is really an infinite number of possibilities. Dupin, perhaps—as is central to our problem—says it best himself: "Mathematical axioms are not axioms of the general truth." The truth of this point cannot be denied; the Prefect, essentially, used mathematical reasoning in his search, and since the problem was not one of stable properties, he did not find the letter. We are supposed to conclude, then, that because Dupin knew the Minister's intellect to include the rigor of the mathematician and the creativity of the poet, he was able to discover the method of hiding the letter when G could not. He concludes his establishing of the logic system with the analogy of a game played with maps, in which the players try to stump their opponents by challenging them to find words on the map. Very often, the hardest word to find is written in the largest letters. Thus, had the Prefect bothered to ask Dupin how the fuck he got the fucking letter, G would have been primed to examine Dupin's answer through a certain logic system.

Now we come to Dupin's explanation of finding the letter. Here I will divide my investigation into two trajectories: first, I'm going to discuss what he told us that he intended to tell us, and second, I'm going to discuss what he told us that he did not intend to tell us.

to slice the sandwich," as he walked toward his presentation room.

There were only seven seats still free in Trike's room as he strode to the platform. From the limited amount of information he could glean, a solid 20 percent, perhaps even 27 percent of attendees were actually interested in the topic matter. The rest seemed evenly split between those uninterested in the other offerings at the time and those hoping the circus freak swallowed flaming chickens.

Trike reached the microphone and stood silently, staring at the back wall. His silence osmoted throughout the crowd until only a few murmurs and cell-phone vibrations were audible. "Finally, the world gets to hear the real motherfucking Purloined Letter. Goddamn right," Trike thought with an internal fist bump. At exactly 3:30 p.m., without clearing his throat, Trike began to speak.

"Evidence within Evidence: An Exploration and Demonstration of the Data Contained within the Presentation of Data and the Importance of Logic Systems with which the Problems are Considered Through a Reinterpretation of Edgar Allan Poe's 'The Purloined Letter': How Dupin Confesses to Concealing the Letter Himself. The full text of this presentation, available tomorrow on the conference's website, includes this epigraph from the story itself: 'It would imperatively lead him to despise all ordinary nooks of concealment.'

"We are all familiar—at least on

A lie is transformed reality. There is a truth: "X stole the painting," and X transforms that into "X did not steal the painting." No matter how thorough the lie is, no matter how well sculpted, no matter how convincing, or subtle, or intelligent, or artistic the lie is, the transformation leaves traces of itself on the lie. The potent investigator can see the dust, the faint marks of the machine, the effort, and even if upon initial examination the truth is invisible, the process is not, and from that process, much if not all of the truth can be rediscovered. But, first, that which Dupin intends to tell us.

Dupin calls on the Minister while wearing spectacles that allow him to scan the room with his eyes, without the Minister noticing the investigation. He engages the Minister in conversation about a topic that the Minister cannot help but be engaged in. Then he discovers the letter, a moment I shall quote in entirety:

"At length my eyes, in going the circuit of the room, fell upon a trumpery filigree card-rack of pasteboard, that hung dangling by a dirty blue ribbon, from a little brass knob just beneath the middle of the mantelpiece. In this rack, which had three or four compartments, were five or six visiting cards and a solitary letter. This last was much soiled and crumpled. It was torn nearly in two, across the middle—as if a design, in the first instance, to tear it entirely up as worthless, had been altered, or stayed, in the second. It had a large black seal bearing the some level—with Edgar Allan Poe's masterpiece of detective fiction, 'The Purloined Letter.' Whether we have read the work or not, the ideas central to its stated themes—that an object can be hidden in plain sight, that the solution to a crime can be too obvious to be discerned, and that typical methods of search and detection are ill-fitted for some crimes—follow us throughout our careers, whether through the ill-formed comments of armchair detectives flailing about the chaos of existence for convincing illusions of order or the string of abductions perpetrated by the man living next to the playground . . ."

Trike's mind drifted from his presentation. He had gone over it so many times, a person with above-average recall would have been able to recite it. He thought of The Joyce Case, and, almost carelessly, began wandering through the evidence. The columns of classmates and explanation matrices. The police reports. The incorporation. Lola's folders. Everything Max had been able to turn up with the lawyers and everything he had been unable to turn up with the FBI. The slapstick kidnapping. Horn-Rims's demotion. The purchase of the house. Figuring out *Chinatown* with Lola, because Trike's mind could only wander for so long before Lola appeared, in the dress she wore to the Ball, in the sloppy T-shirt and ratty jeans she wore painting, under a blanket hands encircled by lamplight knitting insomnia away, in running gear

D___ cipher *very* conspicuously, and was addressed, in a diminutive female hand to D___, the minister himself. It was thrust carelessly, and even, as it seemed, contemptuously, into one of the upper divisions of the rack.

"No sooner had I glanced at this letter, than I concluded it to be that of which I was in search. To be sure, it was, to all appearances, radically different from the one of which the Prefect had read us so minute a description."

Once discovered, Dupin must extract the letter. Knowing the violent capabilities of the Minister, it would have been imprudent, if not suicidal, to take the letter and run. Instead, he memorizes the appearance of the letter (through green spectacles), plants his snuff-box for an excuse to return, and leaves. That night, he creates an exact duplicate of the letter. The next day, he brings it back to the apartment, creates a distraction, and then, while the Minister is looking out the window, switches his duplicate (Dupinlicate) for the original.

Dupin's explanation is a nation of absurdities. First, we are asked to believe that somehow the Prefect's numbered squares did not include the card-rack, and if they did, that the officer tasked with the square did not go through its contents, and if said officer did go through the contents he did not look at both sides of the letter, even though they turned over every page in every book in the apartment. Given the Prefect's willingness to looking like a runner ... always the thought in his mind that life would be better ... every aspect of life would be better ... needed things would no longer be needed because what drove him to need them would be removed or if an absence drove him it would be filled because there would be no time alone in the labyrinth of his brain where he is the walls and Theseus and the Minotaur and the thread and the walls because a connection can be made where even if no one could ever really get into the consciousness of another, another could be in the fields or nets or oceans or quantum computers or galaxies or labyrinths of his consciousness... and she did not have to be his spouse, did not have to be his lover, did not have to spend much time with him, just somehow... give him permission to believe that connection even if it were only in his mind, and even if he only used it as a trick to help him sleep on nights when he was sick of drinking until he passed out, or sick of thinking until he passed out, and just to live in that empty floor in his house, to not even see him much at all, just to be there, and that she has committed to sharing something permanent with him even if she does not share her body or her love or any of the other things people ask for in relationships because his trains move so fast so fast the rails always almost about to disintegrate so just a step back from that speed of near disintegration... the smallest of perfect steps back... Lola. To his

search the two adjoining apartments, to search for two entire months, and to completely repeat the search, it is ridiculous to assume that the letter would have gone unnoticed. Second, the way Dupin pushed the "too obvious to notice" theme, one would assume that he found the letter lying open on the desk, or perhaps hung in a frame on the wall, but that is not the case. The letter is technically in the open, but its appearance—by Dupin's own admission—is radically different from what the police were hired to look for. The issue, then, is not the obscurity of the obvious, but techniques of misdirection. The Minister has done what magicians do: drawn attention to particular visuals so that others go unnoticed. And yet, the final logic system image is of the game on the map.

Here we see the intent of Dupin's entire manipulation, and how he hedged his bets. Had G asked, he would have been primed to believe that his officers skipped the card-rack, and if the officer responsible for said square insisted he had not, Dupin would argue that because they were not inclined to believe a purloined letter would be hidden in a card-rack, they would not have looked past outward changes.

Finally, we are expected to believe that he was able to exactly duplicate the letter from memory—which, given me, we have to allow the possibility for—even though he had only seen one side of it, as he did not take missing radio. The pig dropped on the kitchen floor. The empty threats from The Mayor's car. The seppuku-inducingly beautiful woman with the student loans. Horn-Rims at the diner. The three bottles of vodka, bottle of whiskey, four bottles of wine, and fifty-three tallboys. Max's rolled sleeves. Lydia Kennedy's apartment. Misbehaving cases. Lola. To the other lingering mystery of where Stephen Dedalus went after he left the Blooms. Back to his first examination of the Joyce House, with the bloodstain, the hidden door, the referential rooms, the concealed dumbwaiter, the artistically empty attic with the one latticed window—

¶

Trike stopped mid-presentation.

He knocked over the podium as he rushed offstage to a chorus of surprised shouts and grunts. Without breaking stride, he grabbed his bags off the bench by the conference registration table. He dashed through the busy lobby, hurdling luggage, swim-dodging mouth-agape hotel guests, and tuck-jumping through a porter's cart, so he could time his departure with the revolving door still revolving from the preceding exit.

He smashed his face against the glass because the manual revolving door had been replaced by an automatic revolving door that revolved at a slow steady pace sometime after The Case of the Oval Portrait. His life was

the letter out of the card-rack until he had constructed the simulation. Dupin's story raises more questions than answers, but there are three things we know for certain that point to our ultimate conclusion: Dupin had the letter at the end, the letter could not be found in the Minister's apartment, and Dupin made fifty thousand francs.

Before moving on to what Dupin tells us without intending to, one more question must be raised. Given how radically different the letter is supposed to be, the Prefect's dumbfounded reaction is strange at the minimum, but grotesquely unprofessional when fully considered. Shouldn't he have asked why the letter was different? Shouldn't he have paused to confirm that, despite outward appearances, the letter was the purloined one in question? Even if he could tell by the handwriting and content of the letter, shouldn't he have prepared himself with an explanation should the Queen request one? And, for those of you who have not had the pleasure, the Queen always requests an explanation. The Prefect does none of these things. In a fit of joy, shock, and embarrassment, he accepts the letter without question. The simplest answer to this question is that whatever changes were made—which Dupin himelf could have made—were just enough to fit into the prepared logic system, but not drastic enough to draw a question from the Prefect.

However, the appearance of the

a hangover. He recovered from the collision before the inexorable march of the door ran him over.

There were no cabs in front of the hotel. His car was in the hotel lot, but it would actually be faster to run from hotel to hotel to find a cab than to cast the spell that usually got that fucking monstrosity started.

At the third hotel, he caught a cab, and sent a text to Max and Lola letting them know they could quit whatever they were doing and that he would touch base with them at the office in two hours. There was nothing to indicate that Joyce wanted to meet Trike alone, but Trike sure as fuck wanted to meet Joyce alone. There would be no bodily danger, but the setup was bad enough without his best friend and the woman he loved witnessing his humiliation.

"I'm not going to ask him why," Trike thought. "Just deliver a crushing one-liner, tell him to send the check to the office c/o Max, and give him a goodbye wave with the back of my trench—shit, didn't wear the trench coat."

Trike worked on that crushing one-liner. The portrait of Joyce really did look like Sidney Greenstreet from *The Maltese Falcon* so maybe Trike could riff on something Spade said. And *Ulysses* had a couple of really killer insults. There was dignity in being told one could vomit a better face if one knew the source material. And Joyce knew the source material.

For the first time since he quit

letter is more another problem of logic than it is evidence. It is more important to consider what Dupin has told us without intending to.

From his story, we learn that he is on close enough terms with the Minister to just drop in on him some random morning "quite by accident." Dupin also knows how to see through the Minister's pantomime of ennui. Dupin says, "He is, perhaps, really the most energetic human being now alive—but that is only when nobody sees him." Dupin then also says, "I protracted my visit as long as possible, and, while I maintained a most animated discussion with the Minister on a topic which I knew well had never failed to interest and excite him." Dropping by unannounced on a random morning. Knowing what the Minister likes to talk about. Seeing through the Minister's public performance to the true man. Without intending to, Dupin has told us that he and the Minister are, in fact, friends. Who else knows what you hide from the world? Who else knows what you cannot stop prattling about? Who else can call upon you, unannounced, in the morning, without getting maimed? One could argue that the true point of "The Purloined Letter" has nothing to do with detecting, but rather, is to provide a succinct and complete definition of . . . friendship.

Given the evidence, as presented, the most logical explanation, the explanation that leaves the fewest smoking, Trike was truly, meaningfully grateful that he did not have a lit cigarette in hand, because if he had, he would have shoved it into his eye. Octavian never smoked anything until The Case of the Roget Runaway, which forced him to share a hookah while investigating a suspect. But Octavian loved the enforced silence, the pacing of the conversation, the rhythm of breathing of the hookah, not enough to pick up a serious habit, but enough that, after the case, he bought his own hookah and every month or so would set up on the porch and enjoy a sit and a smoke. For Octavian, it never progressed beyond those occasional moments of quiet, paced breathing. A few times, Trike sat down next to him while he smoked. It was the only time he could be near Octavian without feeling the pulsing intensity that Octavian inherently radiated. Most of the time they were silent while sitting. One time, Octavian turned to Trike and said, "The rocks and the swimmer confirm the current," and nothing else for the rest of the week.

The cab pulled up in front of the Joyce House. "We fall prey to the manipulation of logic systems that Dupin employs, and thus constantly describe the story on his terms, and through systems of logic that benefit him," he muttered to himself. He paid the driver and threw his bags onto the sidewalk in front of him.

The cab drove off.

Trike stood for a moment at the

unanswered questions and unexplained atypical actions, is this: The Minister stole the letter as described. Before he was put under investigation—for there had to be a delay—he transferred the letter to his friend Dupin for safekeeping. Because it is assumed that the Minister has the letter in hand, he blackmails the Queen as though he does. When the Prefect comes to Dupin for advice and a reward is mentioned—as well as immunity, given that the Prefect cannot tell anyone he consulted Dupin—Dupin sees an opportunity to squeeze even more out of the letter. He sends G on a fruitless search, consults with the Minister, and then prepares the letter for the moment when the Prefect will make out a check. (It should be noted here, as well, that one should ask why Dupin waited for G to return of his own accord, rather than contacting G once the letter was secured, but already the case is damning.) We can only assume that Dupin then notified the Minister that the letter has been returned.

"The Purloined Letter" is a masterpiece of fiction, because the reader is as manipulated by the story as the characters are. We fall prey to the manipulation of logic systems that Dupin employs, and thus constantly describe the story on his terms, and through systems of logic that benefit him.

The logic system from which a case is investigated will determine the conclusion drawn from the base of the walkway just looking up at the Joyce House. It was the first time he'd observed the house from that angle. Absent were the usual gate accoutrements of wealth. No fence. No hedges. No security-guard station. The gate itself was decorative. There were no cameras installed in the house to monitor the garage, the walkway, the gate, the road, or the lawn.

Trike added one more conclusion to his assessment of the house; it was too damn big for one man to live in alone.

Trike turned around and faced the little white house across the street.

A figure in the window vigorously waved at Trike; a flabbily fat figure with bulbous pink cheeks and lips and chin and neck, and a great soft egg of a belly. Joyce had gained weight since he sat for the portrait. He smiled a wicked smile at Trike and let his waving subside.

"You wouldn't think he had it in him... yet you would," he thought.

Trike crossed the street to finally meet Joyce.

He cursed under his breath, "Motherfucking Purloined Letter," and thought to himself, "and damn near perfect too."

investigation. The most successful criminals in the world are successful through manipulating the logic systems from which their actions are assessed, creating logic systems that determine no crime was committed. But that manipulation is data itself. Data within data. Evidence within evidence. The process of manipulating the logic system leaves traces on the presented data in the same way that the process of transforming the truth into a lie leaves traces on the lie.

SUNDAY MORNING COMING DOWN

You give up the big stuff. That's in the contract. True love. Nice house. Kids. Enough money for decent vegetables. Vacations. You're ready for that.

They steal the little shit. The second halves of close games. Catching a movie. Going on a date. Having a sit on your porch.

The sleepless nights, the boozing, getting your face rearranged; we're ready for all that. Shit, those aren't consequences, they're fringe benefits. We've got some sick little thing inside us that don't feel right unless it's being damaged. And roller coasters, horror movies, and video games don't count. We got something that needs our noses to be in it. That's what we lined up for.

The little shit ain't even in the fine print. Sitting down for your favorite meal at your favorite restaurant and getting told to hit the bricks because the guy you busted for running hookers is the owner's brother. Getting told you can get your muffler fixed somewhere else and good luck finding somebody in this town you snitching bastard. Getting a speeding ticket once a month for three years because you were the one that sent a crooked cop up the river. Your best friend never talking to you again because you figured out, by accident, out loud, without meaning to say anything, his girl was banging a bartender, because that's what your brain does, bring things out. A hundred more at least.

Telling yourself you're just going to stay out of the fucking marital bedroom because that ain't justice and that ain't what it's about and being loud about it because you're proud and you're young and you're brilliant and you've got your ribs broke a couple times and kept swinging and then it's a year since a paycheck and the bank that really owns your house tells you exactly what it thinks about the sanctity of the marital bed and it doesn't hit until the first camera shutter clicks.

Thinking, you know, enough of this fucking shit, I've had enough of this fucking shit, I'm fucking done, and starting to pull together your fucking résumé so you can get a job without the bullets and the bullshit and you don't have a single reference because you've worked for yourself for thirty years, and getting told a half-dozen times that it doesn't matter how many criminals you caught, how many cases you solved, how brave the articles in the paper said you were ten years ago, if you don't have prior retail experience.

It's finally getting some fucker you've been chasing for six months, a sick bastard who's been running whores and then carving them up and you're not getting paid anymore because the cops gave up, because he's just carving up whores, but you haven't given up, because you can't give up, because this bastard cannot be allowed to continue, because everything worth it in the world evaporates if you spy on wives while this bastard continues, and you're standing in the rain outside his building and it looks lucky to be erect with most of its windows cracked, shutting the door to the worst car on the planet that you have to drive because you'd never take a real car to this neighborhood and you're finally kicking that fucking door down with your gun out and no fucking backup and pretty sure most of your vital insides were going to take a bullet-sponsored trip outside and that shit-stain on humanity is slapping his wife while three kids, two boys and one girl, ages five, seven, and eight, are crying quietly in the corner by the rusted-out heater because they've learned what happens when they cry out loud and you can see the roaches and the grime in the gaps in the floorboards and the water damage on the ceiling and the cracks in the window and the rusted sink faucets in the bathroom you can see from the front fucking door and the first thing that goes through your head isn't knowing you're taking this bastard down, it's knowing no one is going to make things right for the wife and kids and that even though they'll finally be free of that crazy bastard, they won't be free of his debts, they won't be free of the back rent, they won't be free of the bills, they won't be free of the damage, and when the blood in my ears calmed down enough for me to hear what else was going on, my favorite Johnny Cash song was playing on the radio.

You know you're going to get shot.

But never being able to listen to "Sunday Morning Coming Down" ever again. They steal that.

WHO THE FUCK IS THE QUEEN'S LOVER?

They finished the first bottle of champagne. When the reward money comes through, you can use adjectives like "first" to describe bottles of champagne. Trike took the bottle to the recycling bin and returned to the living room with beers for Lola, Max, and himself. He passed out the beers, cracked open his own, and sat down on the couch.

He sighed like the lush fields of wheat were a week from harvest. Max and Lola stared at him. He sighed again.

"I promised you not one half of one hour ago," Trike said, "that upon completion of the first bottle of champagne, I would explain, with as much precision as possible, the events of Joyce's disappearance. However, having reached the delineated point in our celebration, an honest appraisal of my state of mind, and abilities implied therein, reveals I am incapable of performing the task with the necessary gravitas. But fear not, friends, companions, fellow travelers, for I will not be idle while developing the required gravitas, but will begin the process of fulfilling my promise by laying an intellectual foundation through an informal and increasingly intoxicated corollary theory to my now world-famous, yes, in part, because of the manner of its conclusion, Purloined Letter Presentation."

"Corollary theory?" Max asked.

"Indeed, an addendum, or perhaps an entirely new, though related, theory, if you will, that, though not necessarily extending the reach of the method of detection I previously explored, will add an intellectually satisfying and somewhat salacious level to our understanding of that foundational work of detective fiction, 'The Purloined Letter.'"

Lola looked at Max. "Does this count?" she asked.

Max gave a terse nod.

"Good thing I have a full beer," Lola said.

Trike did not miss the exchange. "Though a full beer is always preferable to an empty one, why, Lola the Lethal Leotard, is it a good thing, in this particular instance, to have a full beer?"

"Well, Trike the Terrifying Tutu, it's best to start a drinking game with a full beer."

Trike breathed deeply through his nose just to let everyone know he knew he was about to ask a terrible question. "What drinking game are we playing?"

Lola cleared her throat and boomed in her best game-show-announcer voice, "Trike Has a Theory."

"Fantastic," Trike said. "What are the rules?"

"Can't tell you," Max replied. "Now, please," Max took a deep breath and shook the walls with his game-show-announcer voice, "Tell Us Your Theory."

"Jesus, Max, you get a degree in that?" Lola asked.

"MBA," Max responded.

What could Trike do? Not tell them his theory? If you believe that for a second you are dead inside. Dead. Inside.

Trike took a sip of his beer and started his theory. "The common understanding of 'The Purloined Letter' is that its central concern is observation, what people see and can't see and why they can or can't see what they can or can't see. But when you consider why everything happens, you see that it is about something else entirely."

Max and Lola took a sip.

"What was that for?" Trike asked.

"The 'everybody is wrong' sip," Lola answered.

"Guaranteed sip," Max added.

"Every drinking game needs a few," Lola concluded.

What could Trike do? The logic was sound. He took the "everybody is wrong" sip and continued. "At its core, 'The Purloined Letter' has very little to do with observation and everything to do with relationships."

Max leaned heavily forward, putting his elbows on his knees.

"Ha!" Lola shouted, and pointed. "Max has to drink."

"Why does Max have to drink?"

"For expressing skepticism in the first movement of the theory," Lola answered

"Without saying anything?" Trike asked.

"It's Max," Lola explained. "You have to calibrate for his preferred method of communication."

"Tough game," Max concluded, and then drank.

"Interesting," Trike said, before continuing his theory. "Once you stop looking at looking at looking, you see a structure of relationships." Sip. "Dupin and the Minister I discussed in the aforementioned presentation, but there's also the Minister and the Queen, Dupin and the Prefect of Police, the Queen and the Prefect of Police, the King and the Queen, and, of course, the relationship without which the events do not happen, the Queen and her lover, the unidentified source of the conflict and focus of my corollary theory."

Max and Lola took a sip. "Transition sip," Lola explained.

Trike took his transition sip and continued, "I'll spare the quotes, so if you have any quote-based sips, best to get them in now." Max and Lola took three sips. Trike mirrored them. "It all comes down to one question: How did the Minister know the letter was from the Queen's lover?"

Sip.

"Ah, the 'key question' sip. I think I'm beginning to pick up the rules. When the Minister enters the Queen's boudoir, the dangerous letter has been set on her dresser is such a way that only the address is visible. From the handwriting on the address alone the Minister immediately knows the identity of the sender. The address presents two possibilities: either it is the seducer's real name or it is a pseudonym. In a way, that answers the key question, but raises others at the same time. How could the Minister recognize the handwriting from such a small sample? And how did the Minister know that the owner of the handwriting is, in fact, the Queen's lover?" Sip. "Both questions have the same answer: the Minister has some kind of relationship with the Queen's lover.

"And there is enough evidence to make, at the very least, a tenuous conclusion about the nature of that relationship. Affairs were, and still are, a commonplace occurrence in all concentrations of power, so much so that many powerful institutions have developed systems and mores to manage extramarital affairs. Remember the story is set in France, which certainly had those systems and mores. But, given the level of power the Minister is able to exert through this letter, we know that this particular affair does not fall within the confines of the existing system. For some reason, it is destructively different, it is not generally known throughout the court, and it could, perhaps, imply there is something extraordinary about this particular lover. This means that not only did the Minister know the identity of the lover, but that the evidence suggests he had unique knowledge of the identity of the lover, which means, given that a minister would not be privy to the social states of the court itself, said knowledge would have to come from the lover himself.

"Furthermore, we should wonder whether the Minister arriving in the boudoir at roughly the same time as the letter, with a letter of no importance in hand, was really just a coincidence. Coincidence exists, but accepting it transforms one from a detective to a cleric."

Platitude sip all around.

"Though we can allow some coincidence in the timing,

perhaps, for example, assuming the arrival of the King while the letter was being read is coincidental, it is far more likely that, in order to time his arrival with that of the letter, and to know the letter was, in fact, from the Queen's extraordinary lover—"

"The Minister was actually the Queen's lover!" Lola shouted.

"What? No. Of course not."

"Lola takes a shot!" Max shouted.

"Goddamn it!" Lola cursed. She got the whiskey and three shot glasses from the kitchen. She poured and took her shot.

Trike continued, "—the Minister has a relationship with the Queen's lover."

Max and Lola twitched as if to speak, but, after making competitive eye contact, relaxed and leaned back into their seats. Trike looked back and forth between them.

"Ah, I get it," he said, "you have to take a shot if you ask me a question. I must say, this is a vicious game. A vicious drinking game indeed. Almost punishes, or at least intoxicates, the pursuit of truth. I am a fan of vicious drinking games and intoxicating the pursuit of truth. And look, our dear friend Lola brought whiskey and shot glasses . . ." Trike trailed off, put his hands behind his head, and leaned back. Smirked.

"Oh no," Lola said.

"Oh yes," Trike said.

"Max, he's not really going to do this to us," Lola said.

Max observed Trike for a hot second. "He . . . is."

"But I just did a shot. Wait. No. Fuck this. I can read this fucking story," Lola started.

"You haven't read it?" Trike asked, but Lola continued without responding.

"I can read it. I can figure this out. Knowing you, you've probably already fucking told us if we knew what to listen for. So, yeah, fuck it. I got this. Just. Later. Sober," Lola concluded.

"You cool with this, Max?" Trike asked.

Max answered with a shrug. Undercover work taught comfort

in uncertainty. And, all told, with the requisite effort, he'd get it too.

Trike stood up and poured three shots of whiskey.

"You're pouring shots anyway," Lola managed to say without forming a question in case the game was still active.

"A toast," Trike said. "This is a celebration and we haven't done a toast and since the glasses and the whiskey are here, I decided now is the best time for a toast. A toast to Edgar Allen Poe, for inventing and destroying the detective story."

What could Max and Lola do? The shots were poured, and, after all, they were celebrating detection. They raised, toasted, clinked, drank, and slammed.

Trike had an extra shot, grabbed the second bottle of champagne from the kitchen, then settled into a relaxed posture on the couch. "Now, speaking of detecting brilliance, I would love to hear all about your adventure in the sewer."

When the reward money comes through, you can tell stories about being completely wrong. Lola did the narrating with occasional interjections from Max, while the second bottle of champagne was finished.

Trike set the empty bottle on the floor and rolled it into the kitchen so it curled around the table and bumped into the recycling bin. When he looked up from his feat, Max and Lola were staring at him.

He steepled his fingers in front of his face and hummed a tune of concentration. "No. Not yet. We finish the champagne first. Then the profound revelation."

He observed their faces. Neither desired additional champagne.

"Amendment. I will finish the final bottle of champagne, but would prefer to do so while playing my favorite drinking game."

"What's that?" Max asked.

Trike held up a one-moment finger. Went to the kitchen and returned with an open bottle of champagne. Sat back down on the couch.

He game-show-announcer boomed, "We shall play, Max Tells Us Some Crazy-Ass Shit that Happened in His Life."

Lola clapped her hands. "This is my other favorite drinking game."

Max held up questioning hands.

"The rules of the game are thus," Trike explained, "you tell us some crazy-ass shit that happened in your life. We drink. The crazier the shit is, the more we drink."

"The beauty of the game is its simplicity," Lola said, getting up to get a beer. "You want one while I'm up, Max?"

Max nodded. What could he do? Not tell them some crazy-ass shit that happened in his life. Telling people is the consolation prize for crazy-ass shit happening in your life.

"Okay," he said after Lola returned with beers. He shook his head and clapped his hands once. "I'll tell you something crazy from my life."

He leaned forward. Elbows on knees. Looked down at the coffee table in front of him.

"I was married once."

Lola dropped her beer. Her reflexes, normally sharp enough to catch it, were hindered by Trike spraying an entire mouthful of champagne all over her.

"Really?" Max said as they recovered themselves. "Deep cover. Drug cartels. Organized crime. Rookie mistakes. Agent antics. Nothing. Being married. Spit-take."

"The facts cannot be denied," Trike said, wiping champagne off his lips.

Lola grabbed a towel and a new beer from the kitchen. She said as she wiped off, "Well, that was all FBI stuff and we always understood you as 'Max the Former FBI Agent.'"

"Former FBI agents can't get married?"

"Of course they can, but, I don't know, I just. I never pictured you as a divorcé."

"That's it," Trike said between gulps of champagne. "Lola

nailed it. It's not that I can't imagine you getting married. I can't imagine you getting divorced."

Max sighed and leaned back in his chair. He cleared his throat and rolled his shoulders, getting into storyteller voice. "Okay, well, here's the story.

"It was after a long undercover assignment, Operation Maelstrom, that I've already told you guys so much about, and I had a month off. The bureau will give undercover agents a sabbatical after a long assignment just to give them a chance to get their heads out of whatever world they were in. Because you become part of that world. You become the person you are pretending to be. And that person is usually a criminal.

"So I was on one of those sabbaticals, I had my salary, and really, nothing to do for a month, so I figured that was the best time to go to Vegas for a week. Not to do anything crazy, but just because a month off with some money is the best time to visit Vegas. So I did some gambling. Went to strip clubs. Camped out in the desert. Drove around in a rented convertible. You know, Vegas stuff, mixed with some general getting-your-head-together stuff.

"So it was my second-to-last night there and I was just about done with the whole Vegas thing. I had some drinks. I'd eaten good food. I'd only lost a couple hundred bucks gambling. I was gonna do one more light night at the blackjack table, drink some complimentary booze, and then have a relaxed day of walking around and then head out. I had some coins in my pocket when I got back to the hotel from the table and figured I should use them. Seemed wrong to go to my room with them in my pockets, so I sat down at a slot machine in the hotel lobby.

"And there just happened to be an attractive woman at the machine next to me. I don't know how we got to talking, but we did. Someone came around with drinks, as they do in Vegas, and well, we chatted and flirted and drank and occasionally played the slots. What struck me was how natural it felt. How obvious. It was obvious I would be talking to her. I should be talking to her. It's like we'd been friends since high school or something. So I got to my last coin and said, 'This was fun. If I hit the jackpot, I'll marry you tonight,' and she said, 'I would have settled for "I'll bring my own condom," but "I'll marry you" is nice, too.'"

Max sipped and continued. "Well, you know what happened. I hit the jackpot and we were married by an Elvis impersonator named Steve that night. Jackpot paid for the ceremony and the celebration dinner. We were together for two years."

Max took a long sip and settled back in his chair.

Lola asked, "How did it end?"

Max shrugged his shoulders. "She was perfect for the Max who wasn't an FBI agent."

"And for the Max who was?" Lola asked.

Max shrugged again. "A tour of an alternative."

They sat there for a moment, quietly sipping through vague visions of alternatives.

Then Lola took a big swig of beer. "Almost makes me feel kinda left out," she said.

"Of what?" Max asked.

"You two have you-themed drinking games. Another boys' club."

While Lola took a sulking sip, Max and Trike exchanged a smirk.

Trike said, "Hey, Lola, whatcha been up to in the toolshed?"

"Well, I've got a few things, but the one in my head now is a project I started when I found this old little black-and-white TV on the curb"—sip—"and then this whole image came together from a bunch of the other stuff I have in the shed, like that broken old typewriter I've been dying to use. So it's a piece that's going to be about the tension, both physical tension"—sip—"and philosophical tension"—sip—"between our abstract relationship with the digital information world and the physical infrastructure that powers the digital world." Sip. "So it's going to be that old typewriter, that old TV, and the old camera and radio that are also in the shed"—sip—"all connected into a single object by antennae that will rest on a platform. Below that platform, and I'm still sketching this out, will be either a whimsical"—sip—"or a sardonic"—sip—"representation of a coal..."

Lola noticed the two quick sips. She narrowed her eyes and glared at them.

She said, "Reappropriated content."

Sip.

She said, "Cultural hegemony."

Sip.

She said, "Banana split."

"Does that count as a Warhol reference?" Trike asked Max.

"No," Max replied.

Trike took a sip anyway.

Lola decided to make them take a shot. She scrolled through the key ideas guiding her art. Terms and phrases simultaneously reduced and elevated. She remembered the last few times she told them about her projects and realized that she fell into a myopia and didn't notice much else while she was seeing and describing a project. It had to be one of three terms. Of those, one was the kind of idea where Trike and Max would feel obligated to castigate themselves.

She said, "Manifestations of patriarchy."

Trike and Max both threw up their hands. What could they do? They had to take the shot. While they poured and drank, Lola thought about her art—all the money, all the hours and hours, all the effort—and briefly, drunkenly, timidly, nervously, wondered what she had to show for it. And then just as briefly, just as drunkenly, just as timidly, just as nervously, she wondered what anybody ever had to show for it.

Lola leaned forward and poured three more shots. Before Max or Trike could protest, she stood up with shot glass in hand and said, "To art." Sure, they'd just taken a shot of whiskey, but what could Trike and Max do? Not toast art? "To art," they toasted, taking their shots, and slamming their glasses down on the coffee table.

Arthur Conan Doyle was a man from the future who gambled on Super Bowls.

Trike observed the impatience radiating from Max and Lola and considered the drinking-game-diminished contents of the champagne bottle. He stood up, holding the bottle by the neck in one hand, made a sweeping gesture with the other like a magician whipping a cloth off the now-empty box, brought the bottle to his mouth, and guzzled what champagne remained. He took a deep, sigh-sharp breath, as if there were a thirst that guzzling champagne could slake. He set the empty bottle on its side on the coffee table, spun it, and said, "Lola and Max. Hold in your respective minds an image of Paris and an image of the cabin, respectively. Are you holding your image?"

They nodded.

Then, bottle still spinning, Trike sat down and explained, with as much precision as possible, the events of Joyce's disappearance. "On the night in question, long after The Butler left for the day, most likely around three or four a.m., Joyce poured between one-point-nine and two-point-three pints of blood on the carpet in the study, walked out the front door of his mansion in clean shoes, and, making sure he had not been seen and would not be seen, crossed the empty street and walked into the little white house."

Torn with mediocre vehemence and discarded with a dash of contemptuous frustration, seventeen letters and their envelopes filled the trash can in Trike's office. Torn and discarded after Trike had read each with his unique species of meticulousness and discovered that they correlated to every day the case went unsolved after the announcement of the anonymous eroding reward. Each letter, replete with sophisticated *Ulysses* references, artfully composed insults to Trike's skills as a detective and a man (including the—likely accurate—assertion that no woman or man would ever love him) and formulaic assertions of Joyce's own villainous brilliance, was a mocking reminder of just how much money Trike's inability to see the little white house cost him. Earlier, leaving the office for the last time before the month in Paris, Trike had bumped into his mailman, who handed Trike the stack of letters, while explaining that he (the mailman) had been on a cruise with his wife for three weeks—including the relevant seventeen days of the case—that he felt bad for those staying in neighboring cabins if Trike knew what he meant (Trike did), and that the replacement mail carrier could not compensate for the reasonable error made at the post office when the "3" in the street address number written, along with the rest of the text, in a baroque calligraphy, was mistaken for a "5," and that he apologized for any inconvenience caused by the mixup. Staring at the torn and discarded letters in the trash, one of the greatest brains ever born in a human skull did not know whether to laugh or cry.

"Contingency divides our lives from the events of literature and storytelling. The division is not caused by the hero never getting shot. It's caused by the hero never having hay fever."

COSMOPOLITANISM AND JUSTICE

Two elderly men in white jackets and gray chinos sat in one of the red vinyl booths doing crossword puzzles. A nuclear family sat in another booth, the parents fretting over how the menu options interacted with their new diets, the kids racing and crashing, complete with a cappella sound effects, toy cars across the Formica table. A pile of old newspapers cluttered the other end of the bar.

Max put his coffee down. Poured a quarter-cup of ketchup on his hamburger. Ketchup dripped over the sides onto his hands when he picked it up and took a bite.

"You want some burger with that ketchup?"

"Just pass me a napkin."

The napkin was passed.

"You know, Max, I'd expect more from a guy who usually displays such cosmopolitan taste."

Max chuckled.

"Ketchup is the world's most cosmopolitan condiment . . . scientifically proven." Max gestured with his elbow at his companion's order. "Like you can talk. You ever order anything else here?"

"Nope."

"No . . . curiosity?"

"Max, the Reubens here taste like Justice."

"Justice?"

"Capital 'J' blindfold, skirts, and scales Justice."

Max shook his head.

The parents shushed the kids as the waitress came over to take their order. One of the old men set his crossword puzzle on the table and vigorously solved a clue. Matilda started organizing the mess of papers.

"So Trike's gonna be gone a whole month, huh?" Horn-Rims asked.

"Yep."

"Sure he can't make it two?"

"In a week, he'll be solving crimes in the paper. In two, calling me to see if there's anything urgent. In three, turning art forgers over to the Parisian police."

"How does it suck us in, Max? How does it take over our lives?"

"Your question . . . is in the wrong direction."

"How's that?"

Max set his hamburger down and wiped his hands clean. Cleared his throat. "The job doesn't suck us in; we seek out all-consuming jobs. We gravitate toward them. We need them. Police, Bureau, PI, none of it can be done successfully any other way. If you don't give everything to it, you fail. So the only people who end up doing it are those looking to give their entire selves to something."

"And Trike's got whatever it is?" Horn-Rims asked.

"Maybe more than even we could understand."

"Well, he's still a fucking asshole," Horn-Rims said.

"He does not show police much respect, but, respect might . . . work differently for him."

"How convenient."

"He takes a lot more than he gives."

"I guess I'll accept that as a consolation prize."

One of the race cars slipped from the driver's grasp and plastically clattered to the floor.

"Motherfucker solves cases, though," Horn-Rims concluded.

"He does, HR. He does."

They took a couple of bites from their sandwiches, a couple of sips of coffee, ate a couple of fries.

Horn-Rims said, "I always wanted to ask you something, and I never remember until it's too late. Or there's just more important shit to talk about. When his face goes slack, you know, and all the muscles relax, you know what I'm talking about."

"I do."

"What the fuck is going on there? I know it probably has something to do with his memory, and him looking stupid for a few minutes is the least of my gripes, but it drives me fucking nuts. You're talking to this asshole, and then he's just fucking gone."

"So, what's going on there?"

"Exactly. What the fuck is going on there?"

"He described it to me this way," Max put his burger down and wiped his hands clean. Then he cleared his throat. "Imagine you've got a house full of filing cabinets and each drawer of every cabinet is filled with folders and each folder has a particular piece of information in it. Even if you know which folder, in which drawer, in which cabinet the thing you want is, it still takes time to get it."

"So, he's walking around his house of filing cabinets?"

"He's running at the speed of sound through a city of houses of filing cabinets."

Horn-Rims raised his eyebrows in his version of awe. "Jesus. No wonder he looks like he's had a stroke."

"No wonder."

"Does he get what it's like for us?"

"I knew it."

"Knew what?"

"That's your actual question."

"How the fuck would you know?"

" 'Cause I solve motherfucking cases too, you know."

"Yeah, yeah. You got an answer?" Horn-Rims persisted.

"First, I get to ask you . . . a five-year question."

"So this is an exchange?"

"It is now."

"All right, shoot."

"Why don't you join the Bureau?"

"After all the shit you've told me about it, you wonder?"

"You're wasted here, HR. And they're demoting you while wasting you."

"So why don't I move on to bigger and better?"

"Exactly."

"And you thought this was a tough question," Horn-Rims said. "The closest Bureau office is an hour from here, Claire loves this city, I don't want to move the kids, and I sure as fuck don't want to drive two hours a day on boring days, and who knows how the fuck long for an investigation. Nope, I'm staying put despite the shit."

"That's it?"

"Said by a man who's never had a wife and kids."

Max shook his head. Grimaced. "I hate that argument."

"Yeah, well, I don't care. It's the argument. And you owe me an answer."

"You're not going to like it."

"I didn't ask because I knew I'd like the answer. No point in that."

Max cleared his throat. Rolled his neck. Cracked his knuckles. "Imagine what a Zulu warrior in the seventeenth century felt like in his own brain. Or a Victorian housewife. Or a convict deported to Australia. You can't do it. The distance between us and them is too great. Where that distance is created by time and circumstance, the distance between us and Trike is created by biology. His brain is as different from ours as the brain of any Greek politician, Roman centurion, or Japanese samurai. Frankly, it's a miracle he can even carry on a conversation."

Max picked up his burger. Started eating again.

"So that's his excuse," Horn-Rims asked.

"No," Max said through a mouthful, "that's his life."

"I'm not letting him off, Max. Your theory is fine if you've got to share an office with him, but with me, nobody gets a free pass."

Max set his burger down. He'd had a thought off and on since he started working with Trike. This was his first chance to put it into words.

"Think about everything Trike already has going for him. The memory. The intelligence. The observation. The martial arts. I saw a beautiful woman tell him he's cute in an indie-band-drummer kind of way, whatever that means. Think of all that, and imagine if, on top of it all, he was a nice guy. How would you feel about him?"

Horn-Rims glared at nothing in front of him. "Fucking Trike Augustine. Fucking PIs."

UNIFIED THEORY OF ART

Brain like a beaten dog from the jet lag, alone at a cafe, Trike else-where Triking, reeling in unreeling-like ways from her visit to Le Centre Pompidou, sitting outside, watching it all walk by, wondering, with her wet-cat jet-lagged reeling unreeling brain how it could all be expressed, Lola got The Joyce Case, and why it would be impossible to explain to Trike.

THE OLD-TIMER HAS HIS THIRD SAY

"Dumb sentimental shit. Nobody evens these things out," The Old-Timer muttered, standing at his government-subsidized P.O. box holding a bank statement about the account opened in his name.

MAX CATCHES UP

Max stood by the window thinking of new ways to describe the moon; he was that bored. Paperwork'll do bad things to a man. Big moon. Low over the city. Clear sky. First clear sky in weeks. He settled on "bare bulb in a big room strewn with low furniture and battered books." If there were anything to look at, he might've lingered, but the office was in a borderland between the business and residential districts. The view had all the activity of an Amish village after the big old barn had been big old raised.

They had a great plan: divvy up a portion of the reward between the three of them for personal use, set up 401(k)s for Trike and Lola and substantially add to the one he had from the Bureau, and put the rest in a series of checking accounts to use for that stalagmite of back bills that had accumulated between paychecks. He figured it'd take a couple of days to work through it all with an accountant, and it did. Then it was just writing checks until his fingers fell off and he was free and clear for a three-week vacation at the cabin. Maybe call Jessie when he got back.

Max had to admit throwing all those zeroes around was thrilling for a couple of days. Three months back and two years' advance rent on the office. Invoices from the alarm company and Constable Wensley's Law Enforcement and Home Defense supply store, where they got a big credit line because Max knew a guy. A few of the credit-card bills with more digits than was heart-healthy.

But eventually he got to the more lenient licensing agencies.

The utilities you can't pay in advance. The credit cards they used for Chinese takeout and other necessities. And then, what was once just a bluesman cliché became The Thrill Is Gone.

He sat heavily back down at his desk. He had forty to sixty-five minutes left of addressing and signing and then he was done. Just a little more than an hour. Maybe not even that much. Then he could sleep in and head up to the cabin as free as he'd been since—as free as he'd ever been. His mind drifted to the books he'd packed: *The Maltese Falcon*, *The Daughter of Time*, and *Ulysses*. The last one just so he could tell that arrogant bastard he gave it a shot. He thought about the Adirondack chair at his fishing spot. Tried to remember the last time he'd changed his oil. He pictured the fire he would build in the fireplace. The contents of his freezer. He thought about the first long walk. He considered his cases journal and how he would add The Joyce Case to it, because telling people was the consolation prize for crazy-ass shit happening in your life. He wondered if he'd remembered to put a hold on the newspapers. He thought about listening to the game on the radio on the porch with no lights for miles.

He was thinking about listening to the game on the radio on the porch with no lights for miles when it hit him so hard, he had to say it out loud.

"Trike's in Paris . . . I can smoke in the office."

Max grabbed an empty tallboy from the recycling bin. Put his feet up on his desk. Lit a cigarette. The windows were closed, so the smoke loitered in cirrus clouds around the still fan blades.

He figured Trike and Lola were out on their first day in Paris. If the beast ran according to form, they'd be on their way to a lesser-known museum on that day—because Lola was a traveler, not a tourist, goddammit—and Lola would find out that Trike had consumed a book on interpreting brushstrokes while she slept on the flight, when she tried to explain the significance of a painting to him. Reminded again why he was beyond the loving people evolved with.

Max finished his cigarette and dropped the smoldering butt into the tallboy. He'd hoped some vague resource would be renewed, the whatever-it-was that one used to sign checks for hours. But it wasn't. The pile of bills grew in stature while he smoked. It was like the Mongols made camp for the night and woke up next to a wall. Staggered, they could say nothing about their experience. Borders are not built things to nomads. The gap and a different possession and the most demolished of them explained their return by demons and monsters.

"New strategy," Max thought. "Take the rest home ... finish it watching ... my freshly repaired cable. Mail on the way out."

He started to gather the papers together. He almost fell over when the phone rang. Almost hit the ground when he recognized the caller.

One of the guys from the Bureau.

Jesus, one of the guys from the Bureau.

A few of them, and one guy who'd retired two years before Max did, were in town for a conference and wondered about giving him a call. Finding the agency number online made the decision. He noted that Max was working late again. They were getting a beer in about an hour. Max knew where the bar was. No, he didn't have any plans. Yes, he would meet them there. No, he couldn't believe how long it'd been. Yes, it would be great to catch up.

It would be terrifying to catch up.

The only drama missing from Max's last day at the office was him getting shot and using what little blood remained in his heart and air remained in his lungs to tell his partner to get the bastards whatever it took. Painful goodbyes. Crippling guilt. Monuments of regret.

But it was the carpet that struck him.

As he left, it occurred to him for the first time that someone had to pick the carpet. The color. The material. The brand. And since he was walking through a government building, it was a committee decision. Which meant there was a discussion. A long discussion. Factoring regulations and pork-barrel funding streams. Until the committee got so sick of looking at samples, they shoved the catalog at the interns and told them to earn the résumé line.

Once he saw the decision on the carpet, he saw the decisions everywhere. The walls. The ceiling. The desks. His desk. Elevator buttons. Vending machines. Handles on the water fountains. Paint in the parking spots. Papers in the bathrooms. In the photocopiers. In the printers. Decision pyramids balanced apex to apex. There was a committee at the carpet company too.

The enormity of his departure initially wasn't vivid. It was just a thing in his life, like his address. It came to life two weeks later at the copy shop.

Max was waiting to make copies of his passport and credit cards. He overheard two employees at the large format printer, complaining about their boss, calling him Herr Manager. Max and a few of his buddies called one of their bosses Herr Manager. They had their reasons. So did the guys at the copy shop. But they weren't going to get killed spiral-binding an order.

Max heard the bullets and the blades.

The eyes desperate to kill.

The eyes desperate to live. To flee. To be anywhere or anyone else.

Max's desk was next to Jabez Balfour's. They both worked deep cover and went for years without seeing each other.

Lives depended on what they did. And deaths.

The bar was about a half-hour walk from the office. The remaining paperwork looked like fragile vials of infectious disease.

Max stood up. "TV plan . . . after the bar," he said.

He gathered the rest of the bills into a folder, then got his coat and hat.

"Nice night . . . nice stroll."

Max turned on the recently paid-for security alarm, locked the door, and left. He put the folder in the car. He stood still for a moment after he closed the car door.

The city was quiet. Which was just a consequence of attention. "Spiral my way to the bar," he decided.

Something made him think of the special hell that was watching football with Trike, when Trike tried to be polite. Most of the time, Trike just let it all flow out—the stats, the coverages, the reads, the upcoming plays once he cracked the coaches' codes—because it was in his head piling up with everything else that piled up. But every now and again, Max told him to zip it for a minute so he could just watch the game. That was a different worse. Having a guy jabber in your ear is one thing; sitting next to a brain vibrating like a paper shredder is another torture altogether.

Max passed the Hanoi Cafe. Its green-and-white striped awning was tattered. The brick exterior was dingy and covered with long out-of-date concert posters. The inside matched the outside. The drinking water was warm. Talk radio was on so loud in the kitchen, you could hear it in the dining room. No matter the weather, no matter the season, there was always at least one big black fly buzzing around. The utensils were never quite clean. But the Hanoi Cafe served honesttogod whitesofcharlieseyes pho. Max learned about pho the hard way. The best way.

Sixteen years ago, Max woke up in Hanoi in the already sweltering morning after a sweltering night in a sweltering hotel with the *ruou de* hangover he earned cultivating a relationship with a potential contact who might move the joint FBI/CIA/Interpol Snakehead investigation forward by trekking them out to a suspected hideout in the jungle that afternoon. Max felt death and decay from his eyelashes to his toenails. Dragged what was left of himself into the street. Dragged the dragging thing dragging himself along with it to a cart selling pho. He was reborn, vibrant and strong. The primordial clay reformed over the wounds of his soul recreating the whole being he was before the fall.

As long as the Hanoi Cafe was there, Max could get a bowl of pho when he needed it. Maybe for breakfast tomorrow. Especially if it ended up being a long night. Propel him into his vacation.

The surrounding architecture shifted to residential with a

scattering of businesses. Bodega. Check-cashing joint. Hardware store. Consignment clothing store. Hair salon.

Then the row of mill housing spared by the 1974 urban renewal. The Section 8 housing in the brick apartment complex. The Victorian with the landlocked widow's walk. Stairs up to front doors. Porches without yards. Cars parked on the street.

Max suddenly suspected he'd been to this neighborhood before with Trike on one of their early cases. "The Charleston Fraud." "The Case of the Precarious Philatelist." "The Misplaced Malice Murders." "Bad Blood Over the Rainbow Diamonds." As Max tried to remember, he doubted. Maybe it was later. "The Case of the Black Mask." "The Peregrine of the Mediterranean." Doubt unfurled. "The Listener to Distant Music." "The Two Lost Keys." "The Irishman Who Fell Off the Ladder." Max couldn't drag it out of his head.

Maybe he'd never been there on a case.

He turned at the transition to the purely residential. The turn took him past the pawnshop where Trike bought all his office chairs. He looked in the window. Costume jewelry. Obsolete stereos. Tennis rackets. Purses. Bureau. Leather jacket. Evening gown. Multi-function gaming table. Home cappuccino machine. Set of steak knives. Through the gap in the window display, a wall of guitars.

The only thing Max had ever pawned was a guitar. It was his first year at his second undergraduate college. He couldn't remember why he wanted the money. Life changed soon after that.

Max lit another cigarette standing by the window. He took a few puffs, then sauntered on.

His next turn took him into the nice-restaurant district. It was the part of town college kids took their parents to when the parents were buying. You could wear a tie to those places. Get a nice glass of wine. Rustic bread on the table. Cheese plate for dessert.

Max paused at the last one on the block and looked in. A young man wishing he'd worn a tie sat next to a young woman in a dress that made her look way too sexy for the situation and they were both across from an older couple who were clearly the young woman's parents and clearly not impressed with the young man sitting across from them and next to their beautiful, precious, perfect daughter. Straight backs. Mild glares. Conversation like dentistry. Max could say this: he lived a life with very few of those dinners.

Max lit a new cigarette off the ember of the last. Last in his pack. He still had half an hour. He headed to the convenience store on the edge of the downtown. It was the only one that carried his brand. And it would kill some time.

The smoke curled around a lamppost like the ghost of a fatigued constrictor remembering the trunk of a sheared jungle tree above a strange ape stalking, in tentative steps, across the concrete mass of interstitial habitats, a scentless, soundless prey persistently too distant to capture.

Dispersed smoke-ghost of a fatigued constrictor peered through windows at secular ceremonies of static reverence, vague terrains in the contained twilight, and unnaturally illuminated surfaces.

Disintegrated smoke-ghost of a fatigued constrictor rose until it could gaze with enlightened disdain on what qualified as action below:

the slow skitter of the ape
the permanent paths of rigid quadrupeds
the exquisitely eroded mineral structures
the confluence and dissonance of their interaction.

Then it was too separate to any longer be itself, be anything but an integrated and forgotten element of the atmosphere.

Max passed a sports bar slowly, trying to see the scores. There were only a handful of people scattered about the available seating. Mostly alone. Picking at food. Sipping at beer. Killing time. Living lives of time mostly killed. You can see that in someone's eyes. Empty bottles and pint glasses. Remnants of nachos. Coats over the backs of chairs. Sighs. Throat clearings. Jukebox quiet. Max could say this: he lived a life with very few of those evenings.

Max put his cigarette butt in the smokers' station outside the convenience store. A decrepit enclosure of contemporary commerce. Sparse shelves. Snack foods. Instant meals. Soft drinks. Assortments of automobile maintenance supplies. Trash bags. Toilet paper. Magazines. The best cigarette selection in the county.

Max got a pack. It reminded him that he needed to stop for a carton on his way to the cabin. The cashier moved like he'd just woken up. Max paid, thanked him, and left.

He checked his watch. Somehow he still had twenty minutes. And that would be if he showed up right on time. No route presented clear advantages or disadvantages. He decided to go by the old courthouse. There and back to the bar would just about do it. And being five minutes early never killed anybody. Or rather, the five minutes were never really the vital facet of someone's demise.

The old courthouse was built in 1882, when the city was the federal seat for the county, built for grandeur. Columns. Bronze of Justice on the domed roof. Latin carved in foot-high letters above the looming entrance. Granite steps and lion statues. It still managed to be grand—dignified and grand, nostalgic and grand, impressive and grand—despite being a bank for the last fifteen years.

Max walked up a few steps. Only security lights on inside. He heard a vacuum cleaner.

The old courthouse was an argument for the inherent grandeur of justice. Quiet voices. Confident steps across marble. The fading echo of gavels striking decisions into the record of human civilization. Everything asserting masculine certainty. Hats. Mustaches. Stern nods. Terse greetings. Hearty handshakes. And it's not hard to imagine Max in that world: his badge tarnished because he hadn't had a chance to put his boots up for a spell, let alone polish his badge, a draw twice as fast as anybody who drew against him because if you draw fast enough you never have to shoot, the gnarled and toughened face and hands from knowing when to take one punch to throw two, walking up those stairs day in and day out and walking back down in some state of just about to pack it all up and head West no matter what the judge said to bring the gavel down and it all builds up or breaks down with oil or rails in a distant city in a saloon backroom, where he bursts in on a scene gun ready, to discover the outlaw he'd been chasing was seconds away from doing right by the world and making the real villain no longer with us—the glaring gap in Max's personal story of justice. He decided not to think about the courthouse any longer.

He pushed his mind back to The Joyce Case. The big question blinking on the side of the blimp was still "Why?"

"Why did Joyce do all this?" Max almost said out loud.

He lit another cigarette to give his hand something to do while he thought.

"Five years of effort . . . money for the setup, the reward, salaries . . . plus whatever it took to avoid other charges. Managing incompetent thugs. Coordinating lawyers. Erasing data. Sixty-hour work weeks easy. Then Trike knocks on the door . . . Joyce goes home.

"Not like any revenge I've seen. Trike's spending a month in Paris with the woman he loves . . . Bit of revenge there, but none Joyce knew of. So much. For what?

"A hidden reward. Something buried so deep not even the three of us can uncover it. Has to be. Otherwise . . . millions and millions of dollars and hours and hours of time for . . . a prank.

"Trike's been coy about the solution. 'Eliminating the impossible.' 'Greater quotient of explanatory scenarios.' But there's always a . . . thing. Sometimes it must be . . . dragged out, but there's always a . . . Sherlock clue. Kind of bulb in the lamp . . . An ID is required to cash a check . . . another . . . made me want to smash my face through the coffee table . . . Toenail clippers instead of fingernail clippers on the counter. Eyes almost combusted halfway through that explanation.

"Know him better than anybody. Know his brain better than

anybody. Heard hundreds of metaphors. Still no idea what it could feel like. There's a primal separation, but we're all allowed to guess. Not with Trike. Maybe Lola could. Maybe Joyce knows. Maybe Joyce has a brain like Trike's. Maybe this was the only way he could think of to connect with someone . . . who understands.

"Trike would've explained that. Just as baffled as me. And the revenge was against—"

Max was at the bar. Ten minutes early.

"Got thinking. Started walking fast."

Max considered taking a walk around the block. He could just go in, order a beer, and nurse it till they showed up. Pretend he'd just gotten there. Trike would know based on the condensation ring on the coaster, but he wasn't meeting Trike.

Or he could just go in, order a beer, and not care what they thought about suspecting he got there first. Hell, Max could buy the night for them.

Max decided to smoke another cigarette. He lit up and leaned against the wall.

"Maybe for once I shouldn't care why. Nobody died. We're set for money . . . for a while. Lola can paint between cases without worrying about the rent. Wonder if she understands what the trip means to Trike. She must. She knows those things. Got that from her dad, too. He broke a lot of spirits around the poker table. Miss the hell out of him. Miss the hell out of Octavian while I'm at it. Wonder if Trike knew right away or if he . . . detected it. Octavian could do a lot of things . . . best at keeping a secret. His is a crowded grave. Can't imagine what it was like raising those two. Hear it's hard enough with normal kids. Wonder if they'll call."

Max looked up at the bare bulb in a big room strewn with low furniture and battered books. Parts of his brain could be our contemporary American Old Bailey. Others were an anthology of hard-boiled detective fiction. There's a working-class hero in there too. There was less and more left over after those parts were considered than one is inclined to assume. Monuments and monoliths so persistent, Max wasn't aware of them until something drastic happened. Just like everybody.

Max crushed his cigarette out in the smokers' station and blew a last stream of smoke from his mouth. Then it hit him. He leaned against the outside wall. Rested the back of his head against the brick. He had never felt so stupid in his life. Never. Maybe money went to your head faster than he imagined. Unless the guys had become ardent textile artists, their conference happened last week.

The FBI had hundreds of reasons for cryptic meetings with Max. In a way, he was surprised that this hadn't happened years ago. Though coincidence does not imply causation, it'd be one hell of a causeless coincidence for the first surprise meeting and The Joyce Case to be unrelated. "Besides," Max thought with half a smirk, "coincidence is boring."

Max opened the door. "Won't know till they get here. Might as well have a beer while I wait," he thought as he walked in.

Max grabbed a seat at the bar. Figured they'd get a table when the others arrived. Or leave right away in unmarked cars. He ordered a beer. Left a two-dollar tip. Made a visual sweep of the room. No detectable threats. Nice place to grab a quick drink.

Max knew the stranger would be answers and that those answers would be inadequate, but he understood that, even after everyone was at home, behind bars, or in the ground, mystery would persist. He heard the bar door open behind him. Decided to let them approach him. He doubted they'd tase him in public without a "hello" first. He wrapped his hand around his pint glass and an image rose in his mind. Footsteps approached. Glass is really just slow-flowing liquid sand. Someone tapped him on the shoulder. People are really just slow-flowing liquid questions.

ABOUT THE AUTHOR

Josh Cook is a bookseller at Porter Square Books in Cambridge, Massachusetts, and grew up in Lewiston, Maine. His fiction, criticism, and poetry have appeared in numerous magazines and journals. He blogs for Porter Square, at In Order of Importance, and lives in Somerville, Massachusetts. This is his first novel.